REGRESSION

CULLEN BUNN
STORY

DANNY LUCKERT
ART

MARIE ENGER
COLORS/LETTERS

JOEL ENOS
EDITOR

IMAGE COMICS, INC.

ROBERT KIRKMAN — CHIEF OPERATING OFFICER
ERIK LARSEN — CHIEF FINANCIAL OFFICER
TODD McFARLANE — PRESIDENT
MARC SILVESTRI — CHIEF EXECUTIVE OFFICER
JIM VALENTINO — VICE PRESIDENT
ERIC STEPHENSON — PUBLISHER
COREY HART — DIRECTOR OF SALES

JEFF BOISON — DIRECTOR OF PUBLISHING PLANNING & BOOK TRADE SALES
CHRIS ROSS — DIRECTOR OF DIGITAL SALES
JEFF STANG — DIRECTOR OF SPECIALTY SALES
KAT SALAZAR — DIRECTOR OF PR & MARKETING
DREW GILL — ART DIRECTOR
HEATHER DOORNINK — PRODUCTION DIRECTOR
BRANWYN BIGGLESTONE — CONTROLLER

IMAGECOMICS.COM

REGRESSION, VOL. 2: DISCIPLES. FIRST PRINTING. JULY 2018.
PUBLISHED BY IMAGE COMICS, INC. OFFICE OF PUBLICATION: 2701 NW VAUGHN ST., SUITE 780, PORTLAND, OR 97210. COPYRIGHT © 2018 CULLEN BUNN, DANNY LUCKERT, & MARIE ENGER. ALL RIGHTS RESERVED. CONTAINS MATERIAL ORIGINALLY PUBLISHED IN SINGLE MAGAZINE FORM AS REGRESSION #6-10. "REGRESSION," ITS LOGOS, AND THE LIKENESSES OF ALL CHARACTERS HEREIN ARE TRADEMARKS OF CULLEN BUNN, DANNY LUCKERT, & MARIE ENGER, UNLESS OTHERWISE NOTED. "IMAGE" AND THE IMAGE COMICS LOGOS ARE REGISTERED TRADEMARKS OF IMAGE COMICS, INC. NO PART OF THIS PUBLICATION MAY BE REPRODUCED OR TRANSMITTED, IN ANY FORM OR BY ANY MEANS (EXCEPT FOR SHORT EXCERPTS FOR JOURNALISTIC OR REVIEW PURPOSES), WITHOUT THE EXPRESS WRITTEN PERMISSION OF CREATOR NAME & CREATOR NAME, OR IMAGE COMICS, INC. ALL NAMES, CHARACTERS, EVENTS, AND LOCALES IN THIS PUBLICATION ARE ENTIRELY FICTIONAL. ANY RESEMBLANCE TO ACTUAL PERSONS (LIVING OR DEAD), EVENTS, OR PLACES, WITHOUT SATIRIC INTENT, IS COINCIDENTAL. PRINTED IN THE USA. FOR INFORMATION REGARDING THE CPSIA ON THIS PRINTED MATERIAL CALL: 203-595-3636 AND PROVIDE REFERENCE #RICH-801979. FOR INTERNATIONAL RIGHTS, CONTACT: FOREIGNLICENSING@IMAGECOMICS.COM. ISBN: 978-1-5343-0688-2.

SIX

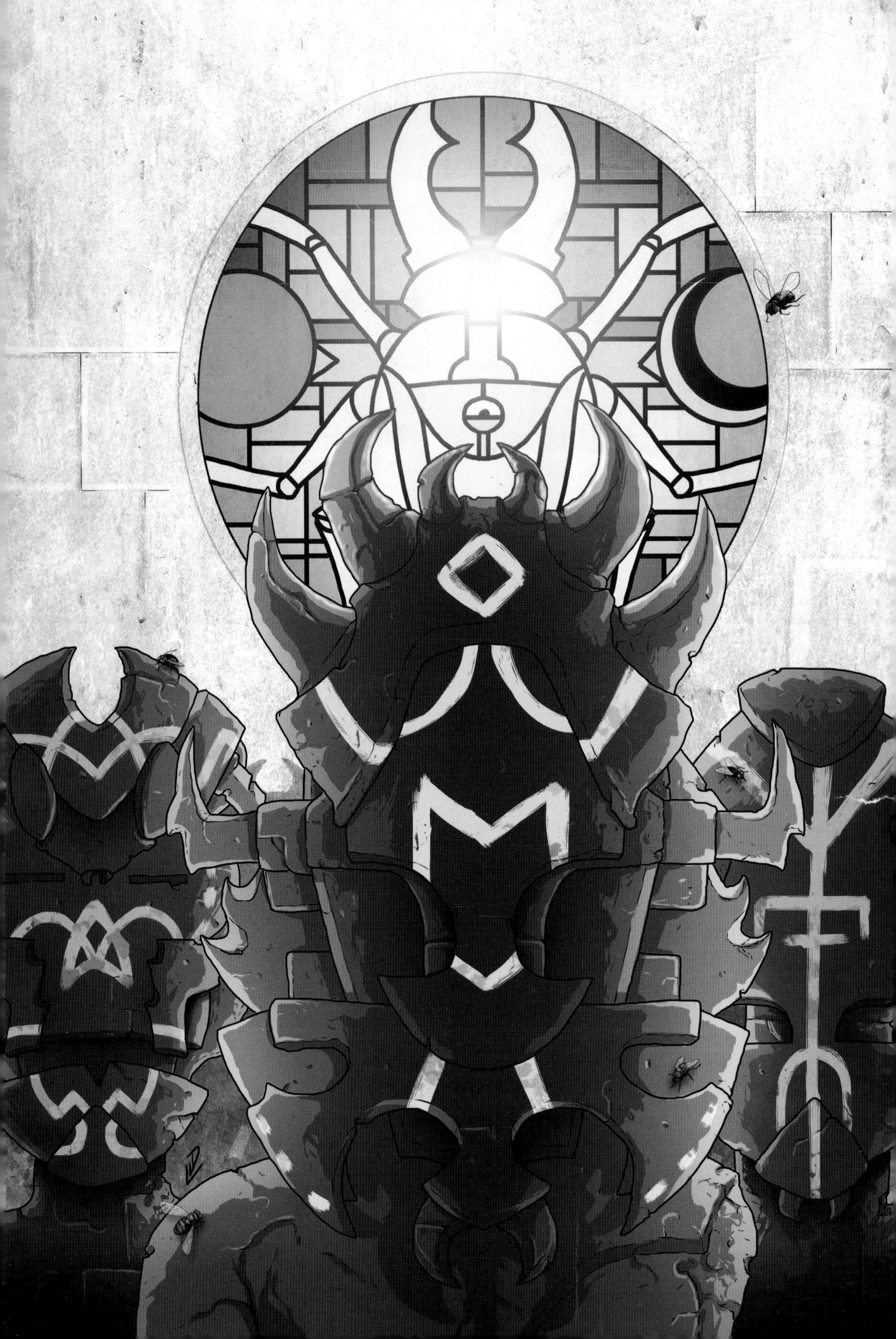

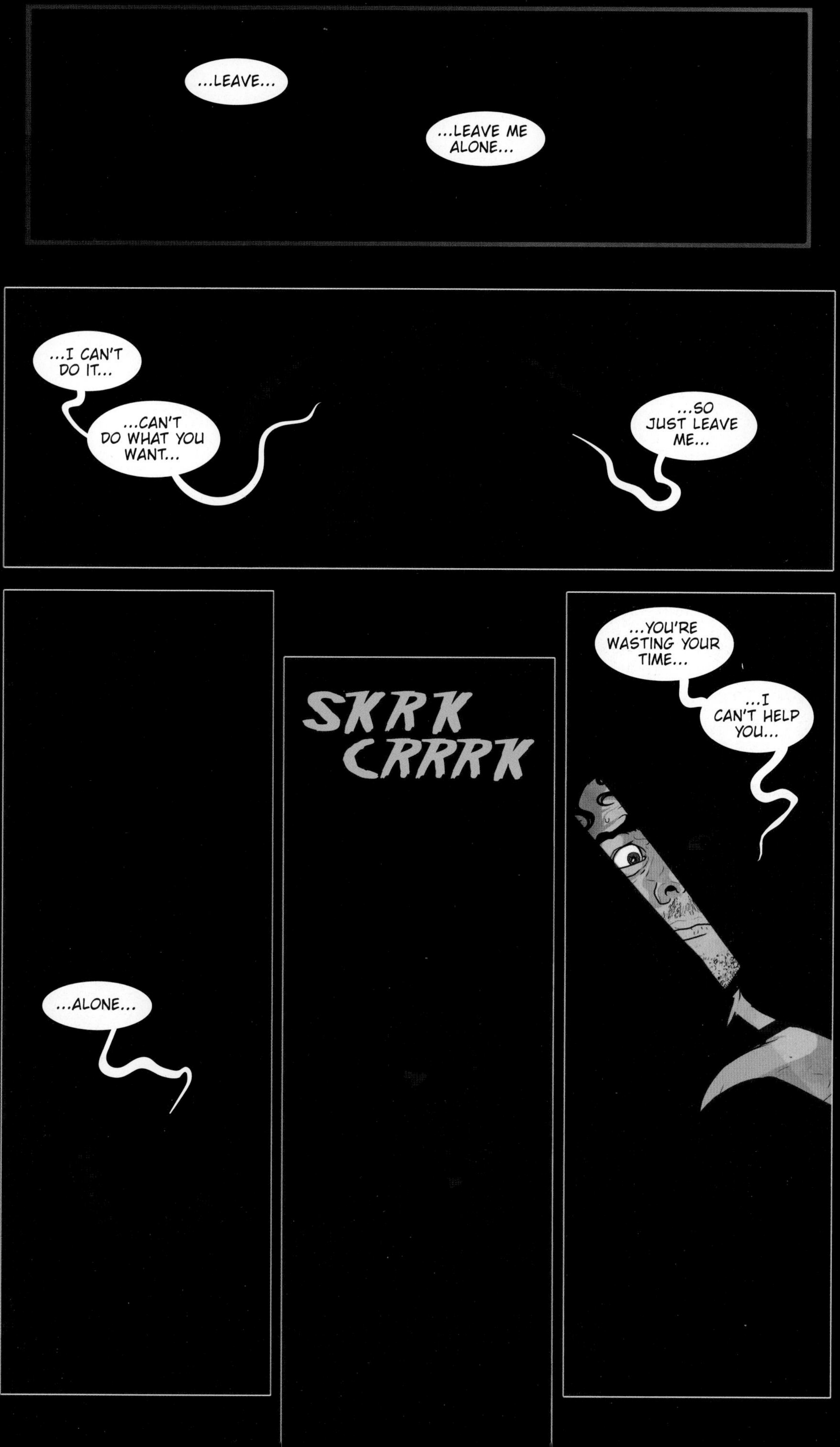

...LEAVE...
...LEAVE ME ALONE...
...I CAN'T DO IT...
...CAN'T DO WHAT YOU WANT...
...SO JUST LEAVE ME...
...ALONE...
SKRK CRRRK
...YOU'RE WASTING YOUR TIME...
...I CAN'T HELP YOU...

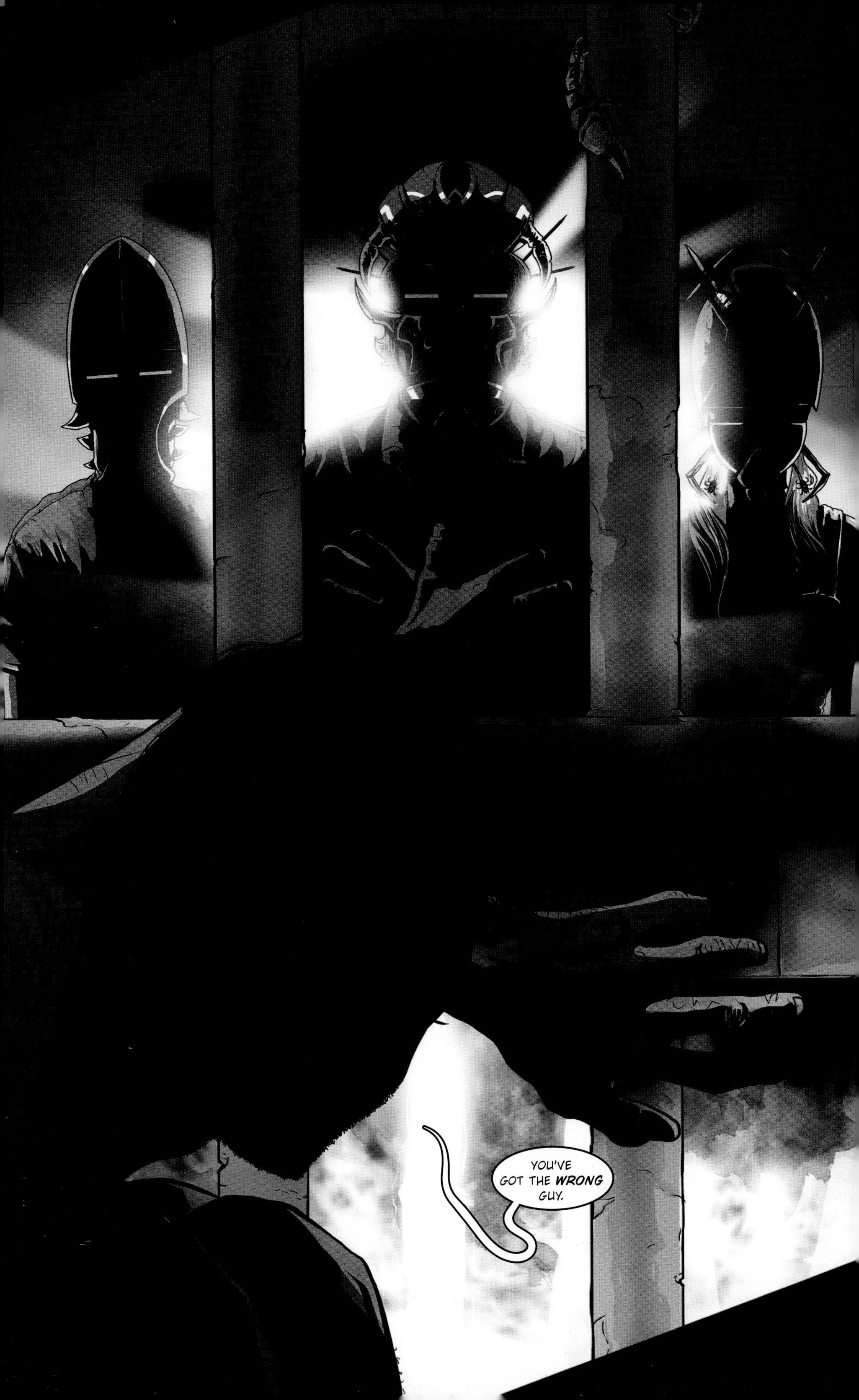
YOU'VE GOT THE WRONG GUY.

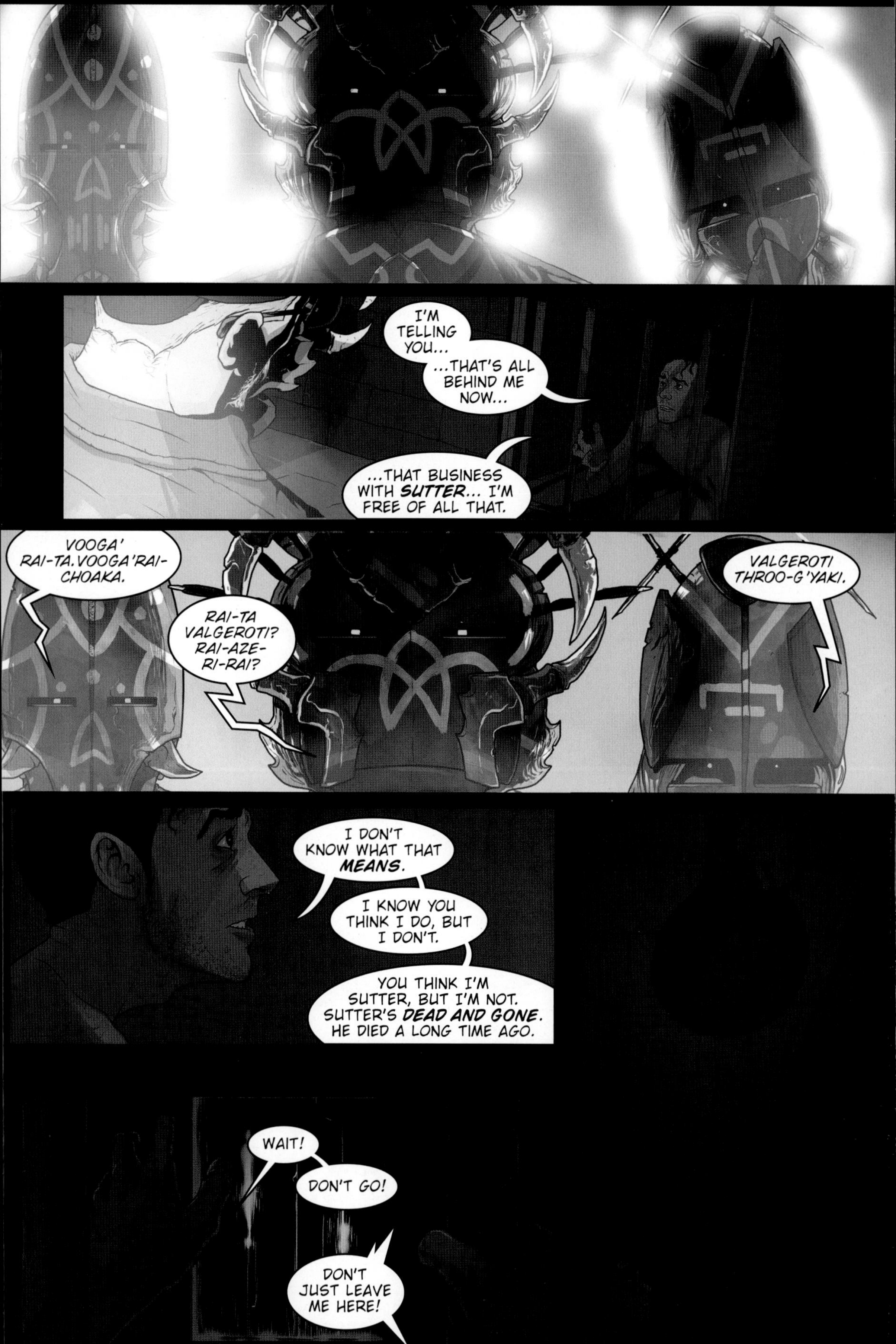
I'M TELLING YOU...
...THAT'S ALL BEHIND ME NOW...
...THAT BUSINESS WITH **SUTTER**... I'M FREE OF ALL THAT.
VOOGA' RAI-TA.VOOGA'RAI-CHOAKA.
RAI-TA VALGEROTI? RAI-AZE-RI-RAI?
VALGEROTI THROO-G'YAKI.
I DON'T KNOW WHAT THAT ***MEANS***.
I KNOW YOU THINK I DO, BUT I DON'T.
YOU THINK I'M SUTTER, BUT I'M NOT. SUTTER'S ***DEAD AND GONE***. HE DIED A LONG TIME AGO.
WAIT!
DON'T GO!
DON'T JUST LEAVE ME HERE!

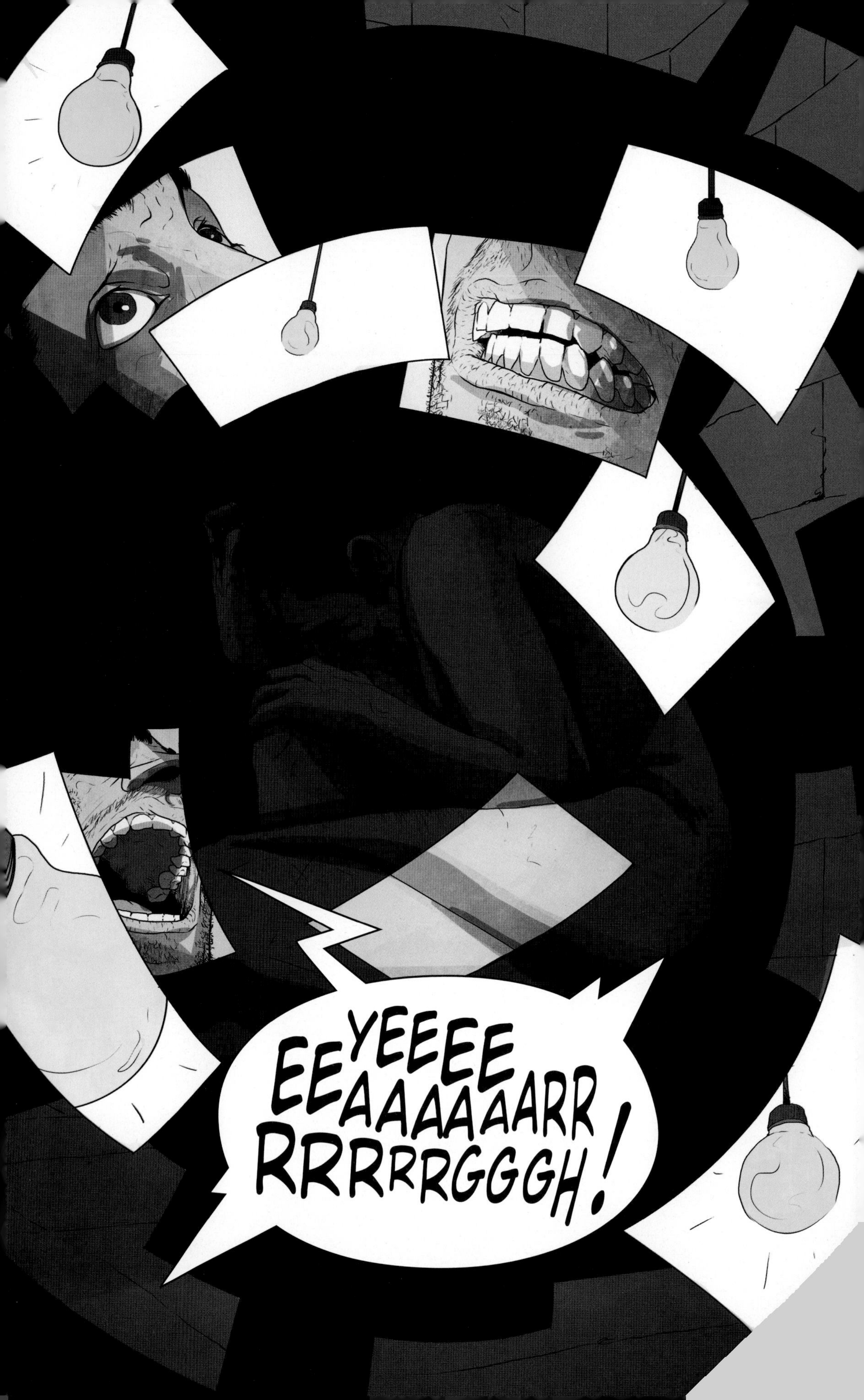
YEEEEE EEAAAAAARR RRRRRGGGH!

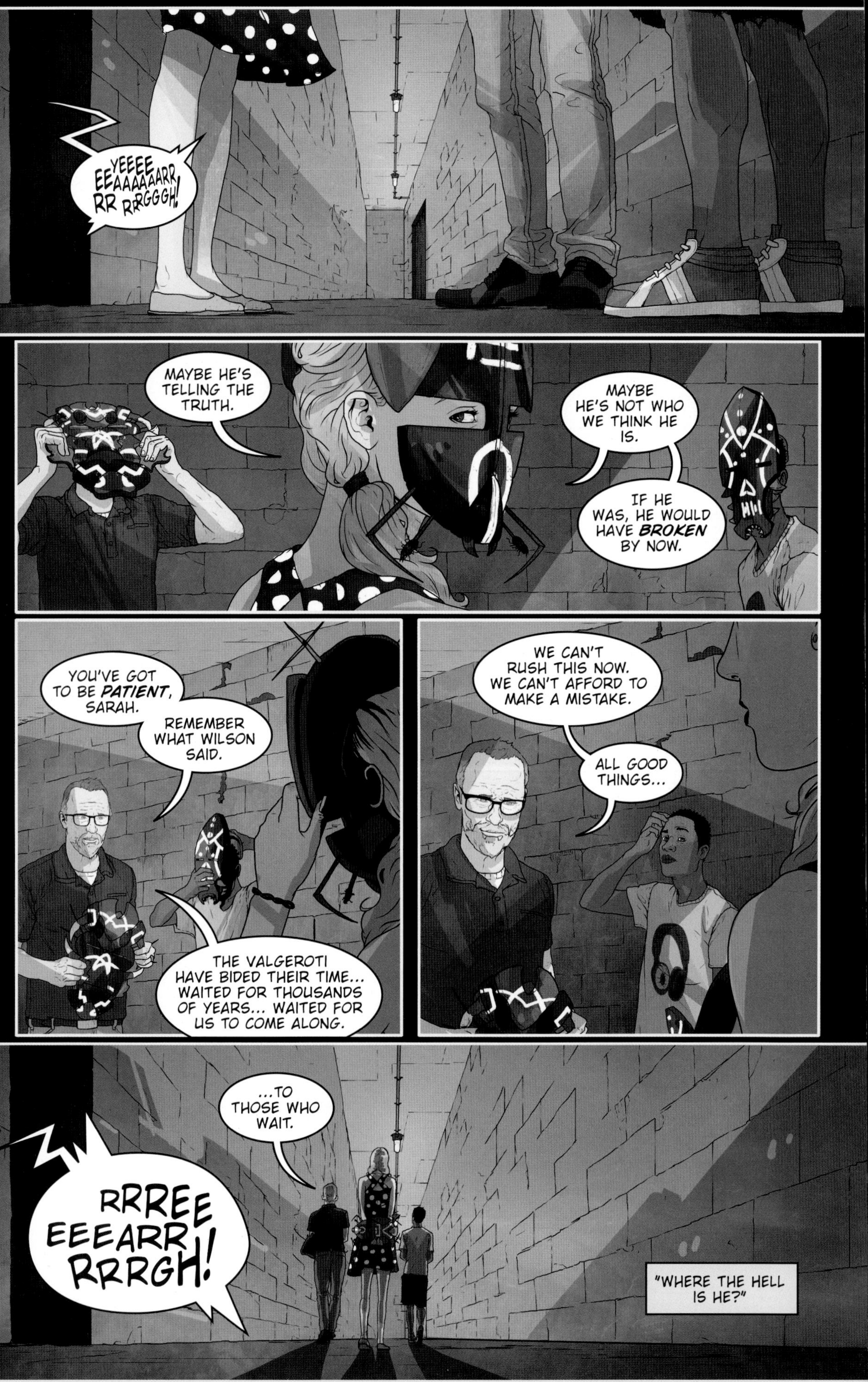

YEEEE EEAAAAAARR RR RRRGGGH!
MAYBE HE'S TELLING THE TRUTH.
MAYBE HE'S NOT WHO WE THINK HE IS.
IF HE WAS, HE WOULD HAVE **BROKEN** BY NOW.
YOU'VE GOT TO BE **PATIENT**, SARAH.
REMEMBER WHAT WILSON SAID.
THE VALGEROTI HAVE BIDED THEIR TIME... WAITED FOR THOUSANDS OF YEARS... WAITED FOR US TO COME ALONG.
WE CAN'T RUSH THIS NOW. WE CAN'T AFFORD TO MAKE A MISTAKE.
ALL GOOD THINGS...
...TO THOSE WHO WAIT.
RRREE EEEARR RRRGH!
"WHERE THE HELL IS HE?"

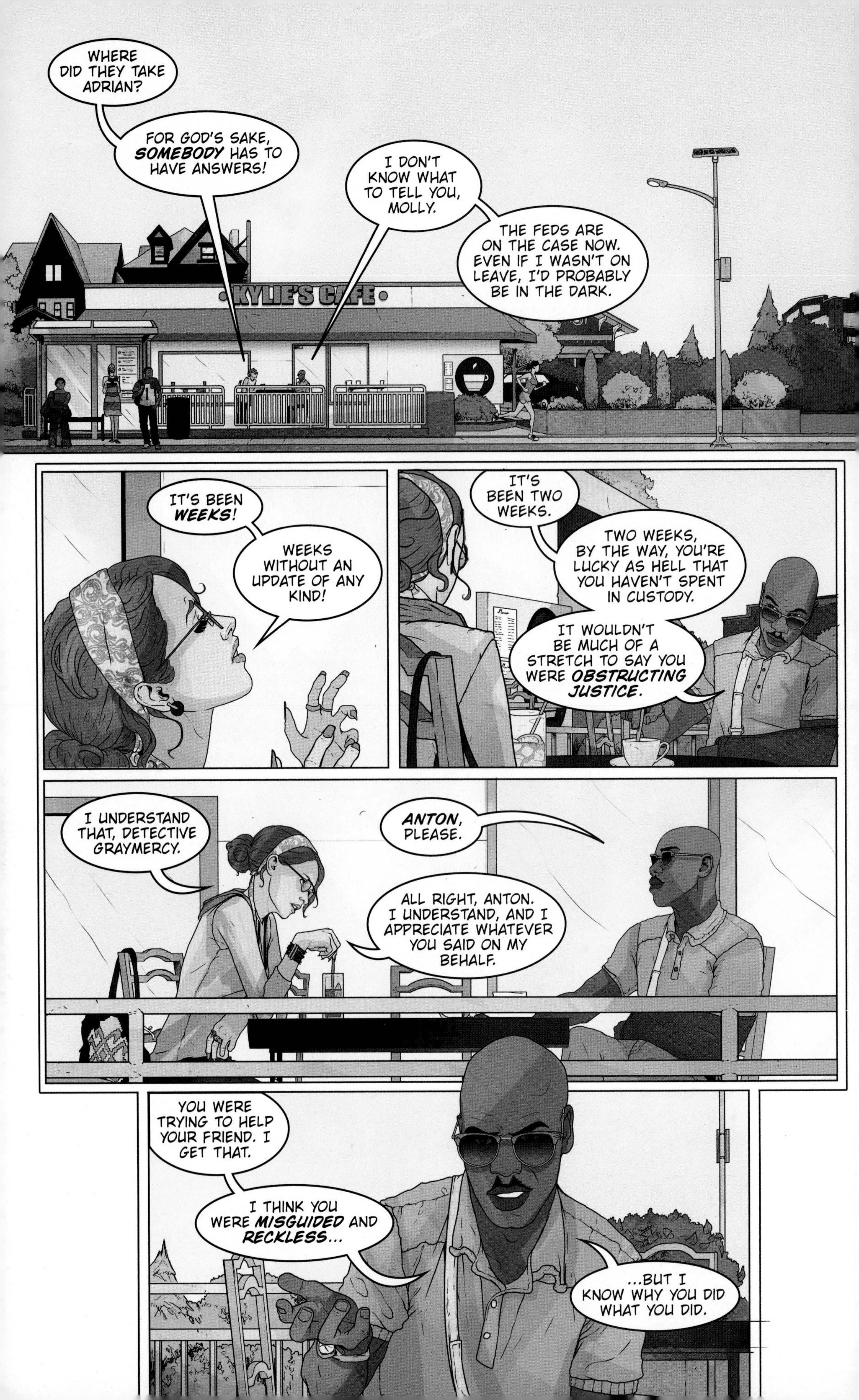
WHERE DID THEY TAKE ADRIAN?
FOR GOD'S SAKE, SOMEBODY HAS TO HAVE ANSWERS!
I DON'T KNOW WHAT TO TELL YOU, MOLLY.
THE FEDS ARE ON THE CASE NOW. EVEN IF I WASN'T ON LEAVE, I'D PROBABLY BE IN THE DARK.
KYLIE'S CAFE
IT'S BEEN WEEKS!
WEEKS WITHOUT AN UPDATE OF ANY KIND!
IT'S BEEN TWO WEEKS.
TWO WEEKS, BY THE WAY, YOU'RE LUCKY AS HELL THAT YOU HAVEN'T SPENT IN CUSTODY.
IT WOULDN'T BE MUCH OF A STRETCH TO SAY YOU WERE OBSTRUCTING JUSTICE.
I UNDERSTAND THAT, DETECTIVE GRAYMERCY.
ANTON, PLEASE.
ALL RIGHT, ANTON. I UNDERSTAND, AND I APPRECIATE WHATEVER YOU SAID ON MY BEHALF.
YOU WERE TRYING TO HELP YOUR FRIEND. I GET THAT.
I THINK YOU WERE MISGUIDED AND RECKLESS...
...BUT I KNOW WHY YOU DID WHAT YOU DID.

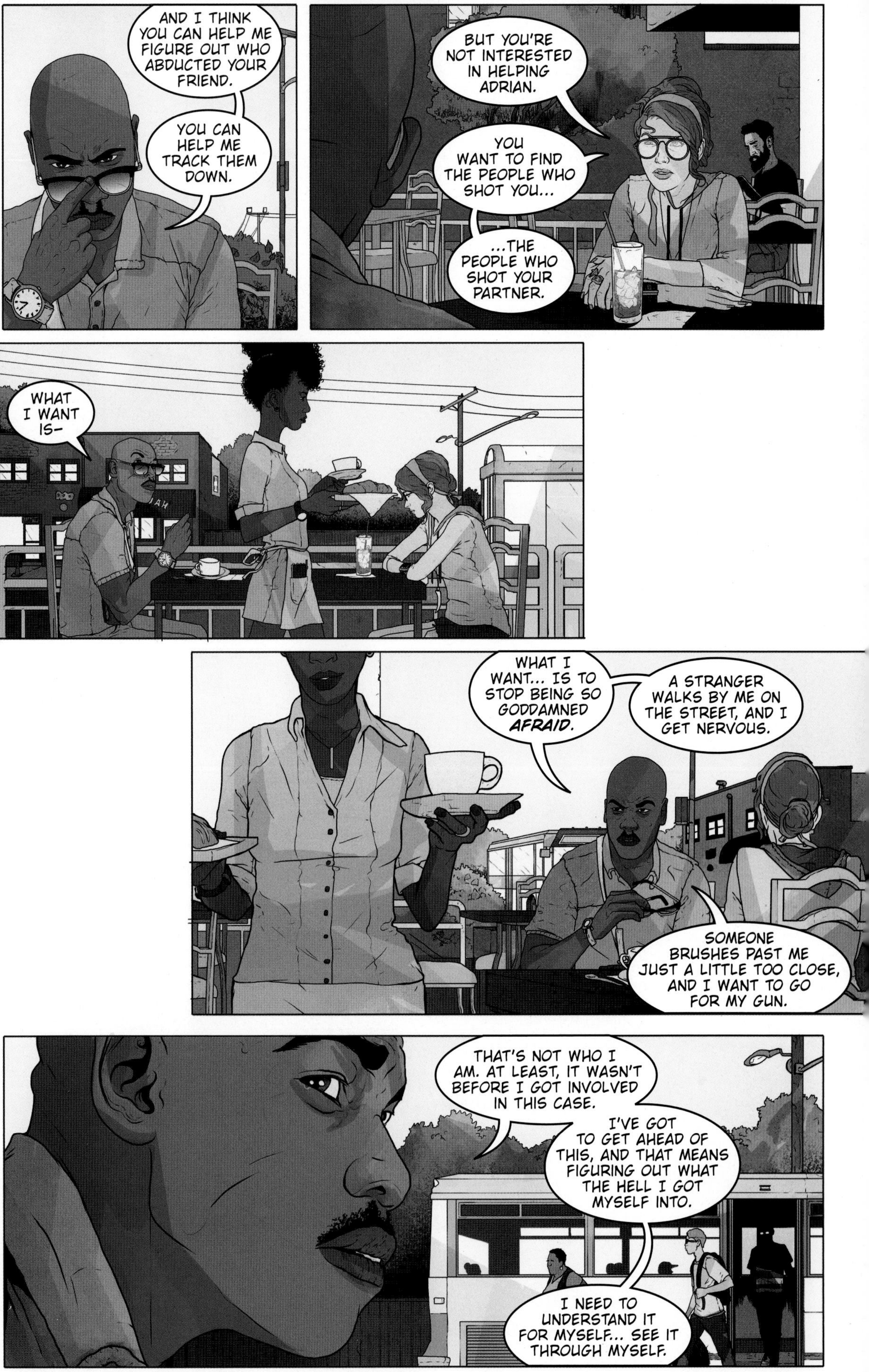
AND I THINK YOU CAN HELP ME FIGURE OUT WHO ABDUCTED YOUR FRIEND.
YOU CAN HELP ME TRACK THEM DOWN.
BUT YOU'RE NOT INTERESTED IN HELPING ADRIAN.
YOU WANT TO FIND THE PEOPLE WHO SHOT YOU...
...THE PEOPLE WHO SHOT YOUR PARTNER.
WHAT I WANT IS-
WHAT I WANT... IS TO STOP BEING SO GODDAMNED AFRAID.
A STRANGER WALKS BY ME ON THE STREET, AND I GET NERVOUS.
SOMEONE BRUSHES PAST ME JUST A LITTLE TOO CLOSE, AND I WANT TO GO FOR MY GUN.
THAT'S NOT WHO I AM. AT LEAST, IT WASN'T BEFORE I GOT INVOLVED IN THIS CASE.
I'VE GOT TO GET AHEAD OF THIS, AND THAT MEANS FIGURING OUT WHAT THE HELL I GOT MYSELF INTO.
I NEED TO UNDERSTAND IT FOR MYSELF... SEE IT THROUGH MYSELF.

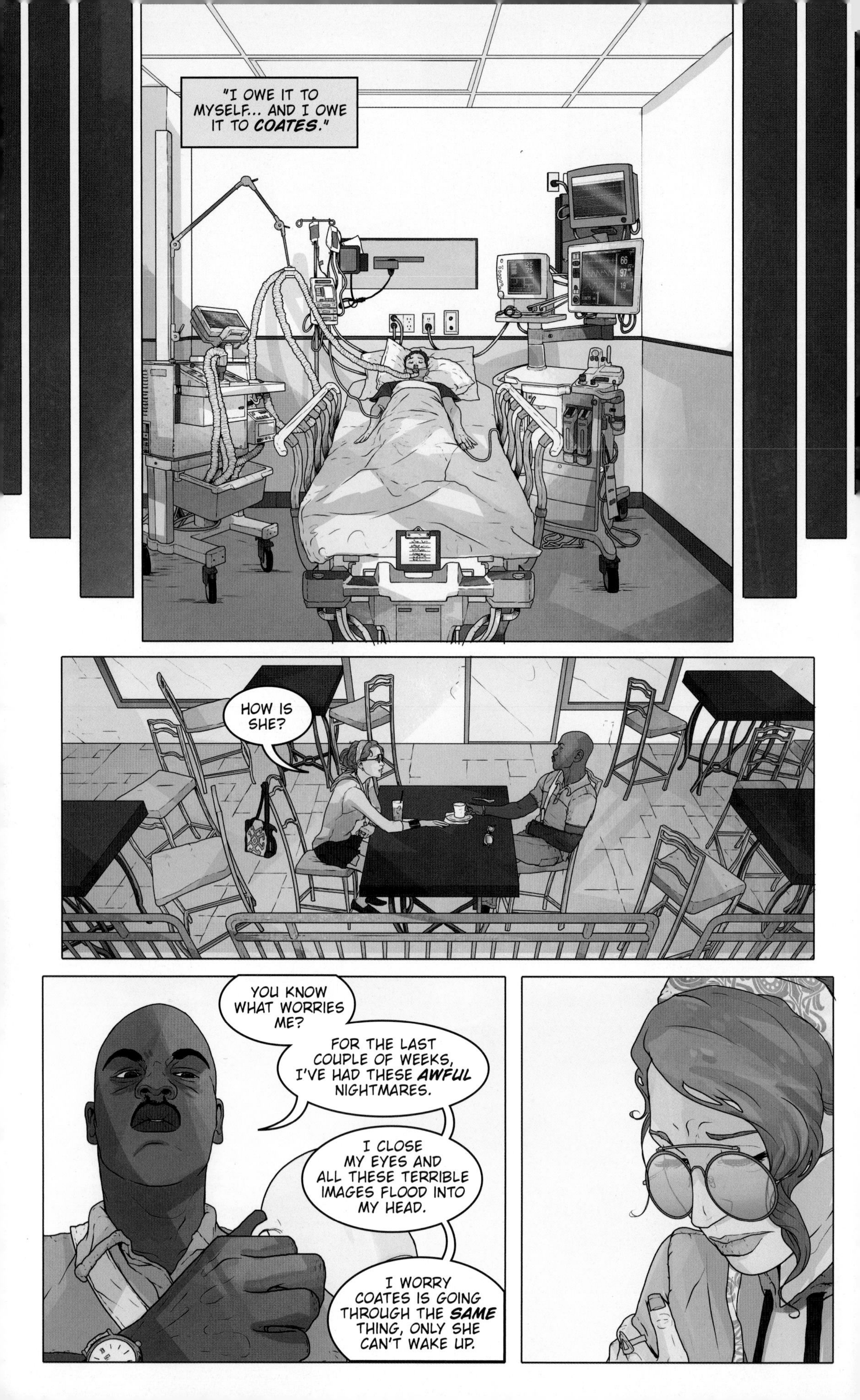
"I OWE IT TO MYSELF... AND I OWE IT TO COATES."
HOW IS SHE?
YOU KNOW WHAT WORRIES ME?
FOR THE LAST COUPLE OF WEEKS, I'VE HAD THESE AWFUL NIGHTMARES.
I CLOSE MY EYES AND ALL THESE TERRIBLE IMAGES FLOOD INTO MY HEAD.
I WORRY COATES IS GOING THROUGH THE SAME THING, ONLY SHE CAN'T WAKE UP.

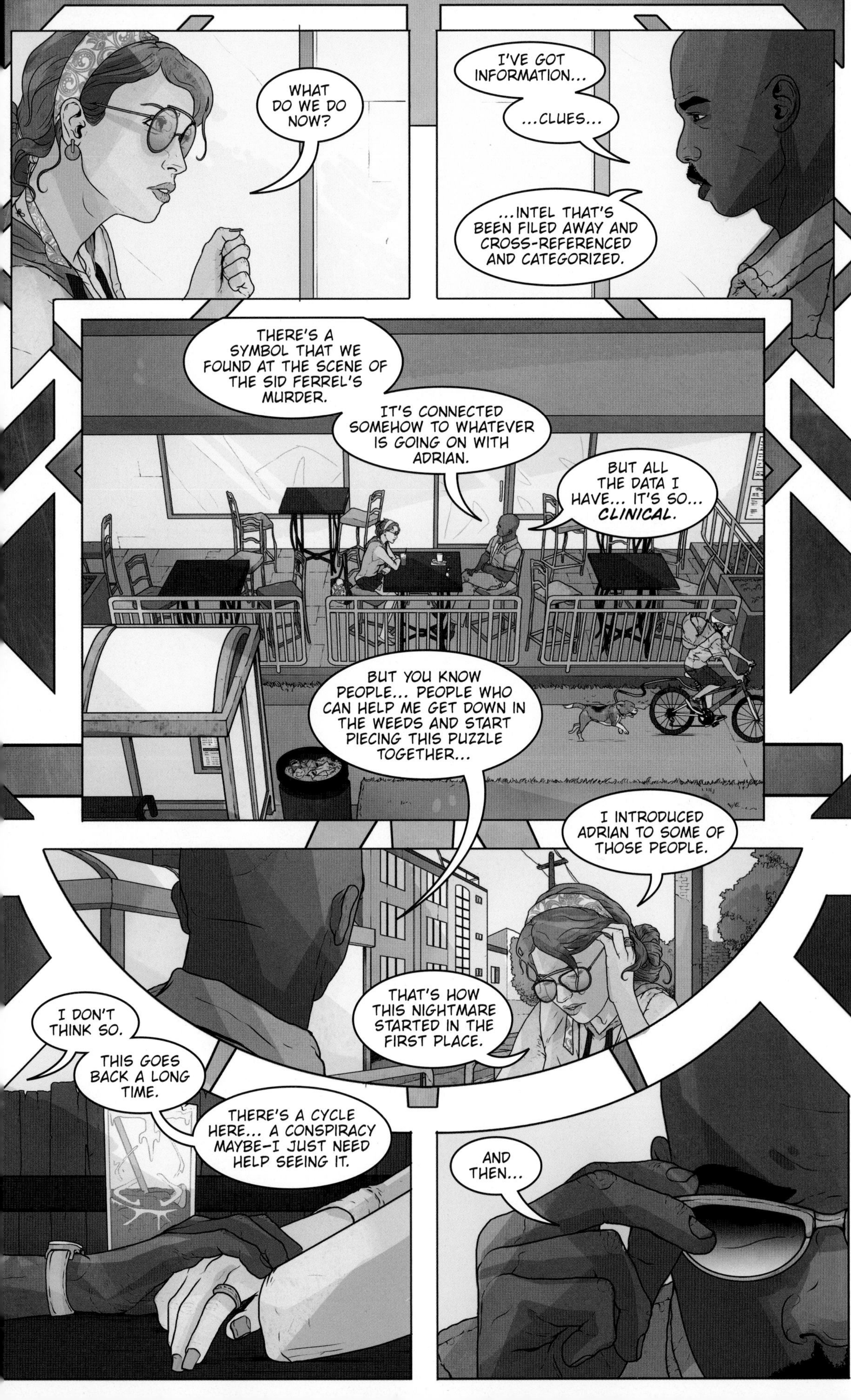

WHAT DO WE DO NOW?
I'VE GOT INFORMATION...
...CLUES...
...INTEL THAT'S BEEN FILED AWAY AND CROSS-REFERENCED AND CATEGORIZED.
THERE'S A SYMBOL THAT WE FOUND AT THE SCENE OF THE SID FERREL'S MURDER.
IT'S CONNECTED SOMEHOW TO WHATEVER IS GOING ON WITH ADRIAN.
BUT ALL THE DATA I HAVE... IT'S SO... *CLINICAL.*
BUT YOU KNOW PEOPLE... PEOPLE WHO CAN HELP ME GET DOWN IN THE WEEDS AND START PIECING THIS PUZZLE TOGETHER...
I INTRODUCED ADRIAN TO SOME OF THOSE PEOPLE.
THAT'S HOW THIS NIGHTMARE STARTED IN THE FIRST PLACE.
I DON'T THINK SO.
THIS GOES BACK A LONG TIME.
THERE'S A CYCLE HERE... A CONSPIRACY MAYBE–I JUST NEED HELP SEEING IT.
AND THEN...

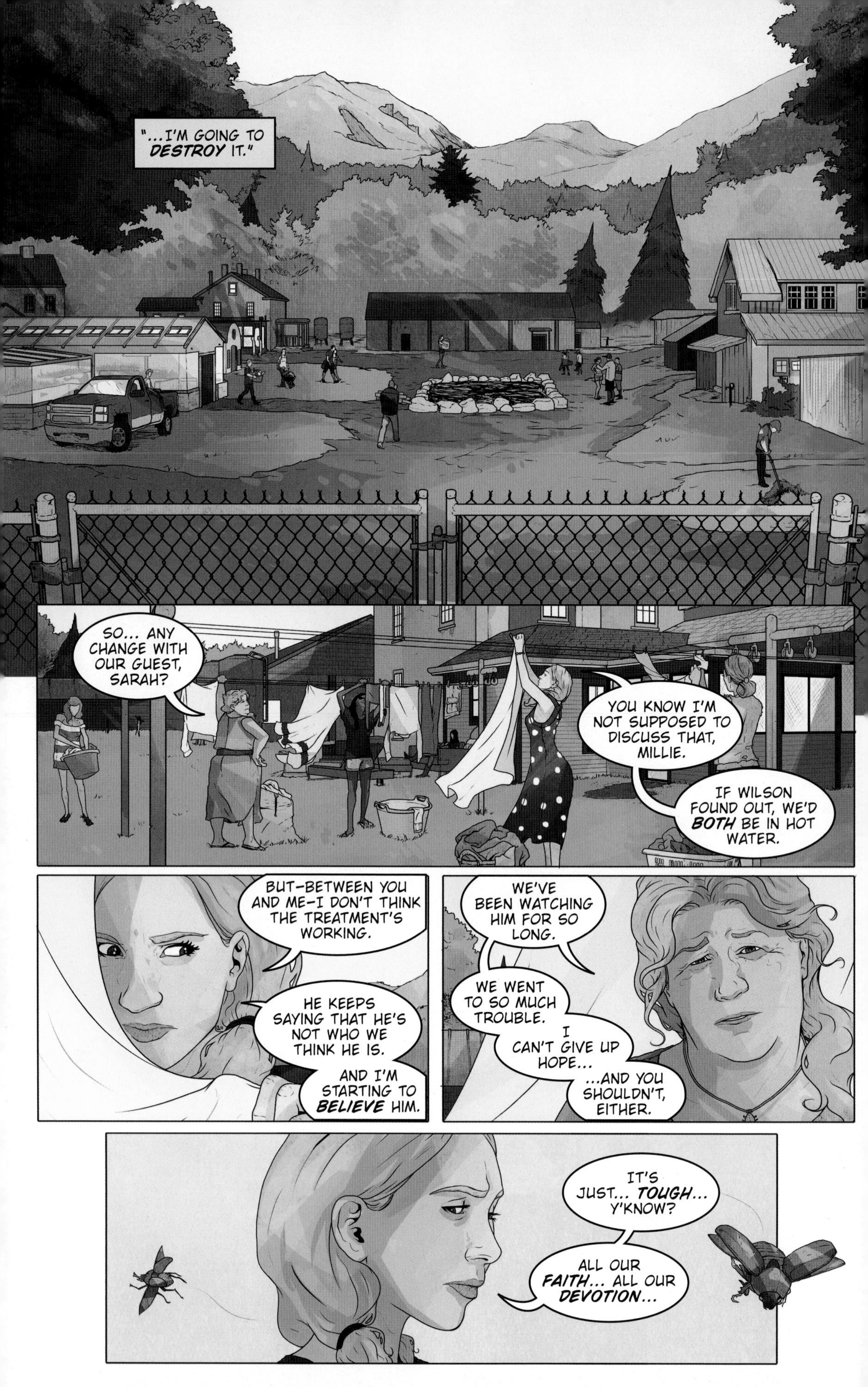
"...I'M GOING TO DESTROY IT."
SO... ANY CHANGE WITH OUR GUEST, SARAH?
YOU KNOW I'M NOT SUPPOSED TO DISCUSS THAT, MILLIE.
IF WILSON FOUND OUT, WE'D BOTH BE IN HOT WATER.
BUT–BETWEEN YOU AND ME–I DON'T THINK THE TREATMENT'S WORKING.
HE KEEPS SAYING THAT HE'S NOT WHO WE THINK HE IS.
AND I'M STARTING TO BELIEVE HIM.
WE'VE BEEN WATCHING HIM FOR SO LONG.
WE WENT TO SO MUCH TROUBLE.
I CAN'T GIVE UP HOPE...
...AND YOU SHOULDN'T, EITHER.
IT'S JUST... TOUGH... Y'KNOW?
ALL OUR FAITH... ALL OUR DEVOTION...

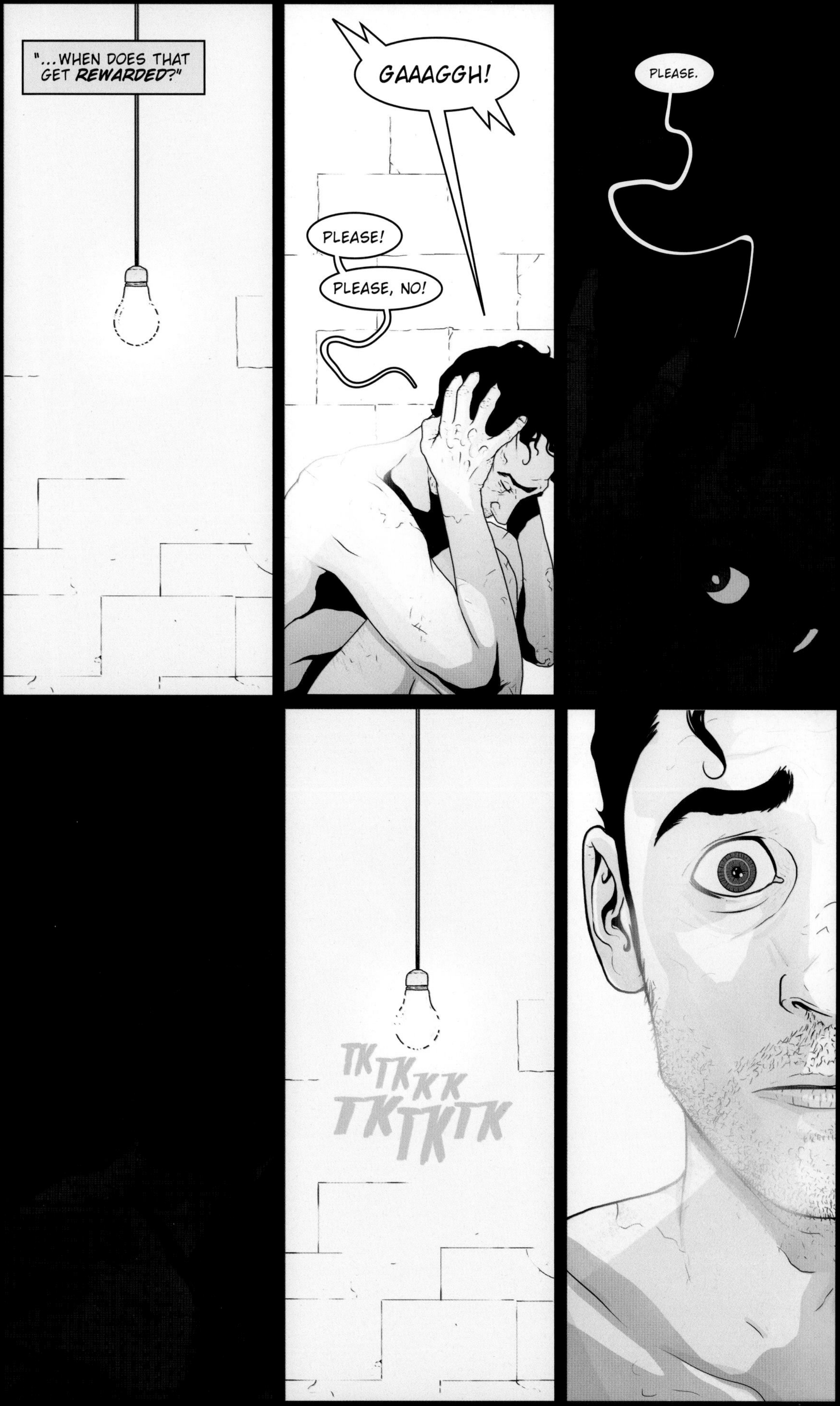
"...WHEN DOES THAT GET REWARDED?"
GAAAGGH!
PLEASE!
PLEASE, NO!
PLEASE.
TKTKKK TKTKTK

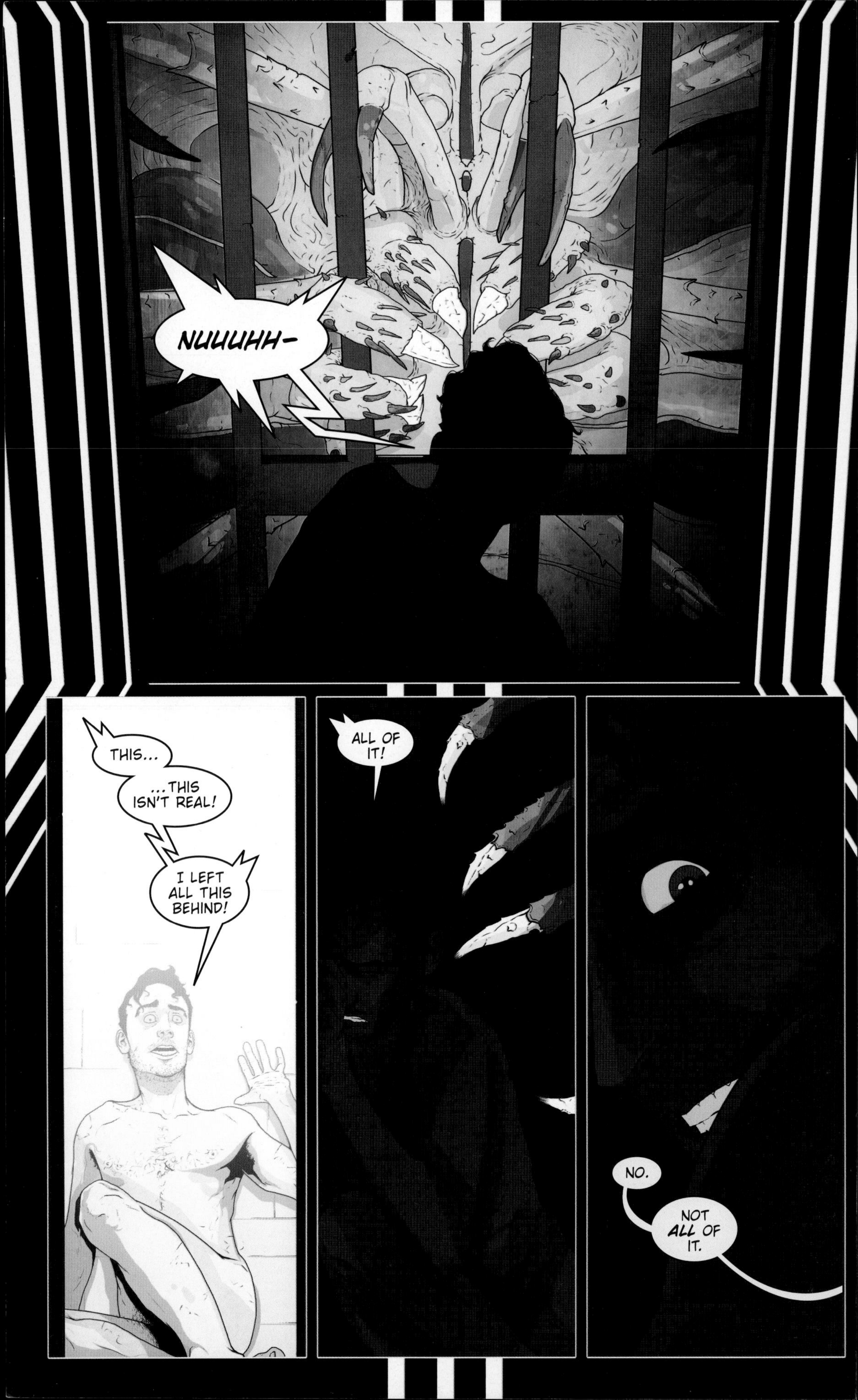
NUUUHH-
THIS...
...THIS ISN'T REAL!
I LEFT ALL THIS BEHIND!
ALL OF IT!
NO.
NOT ALL OF IT.

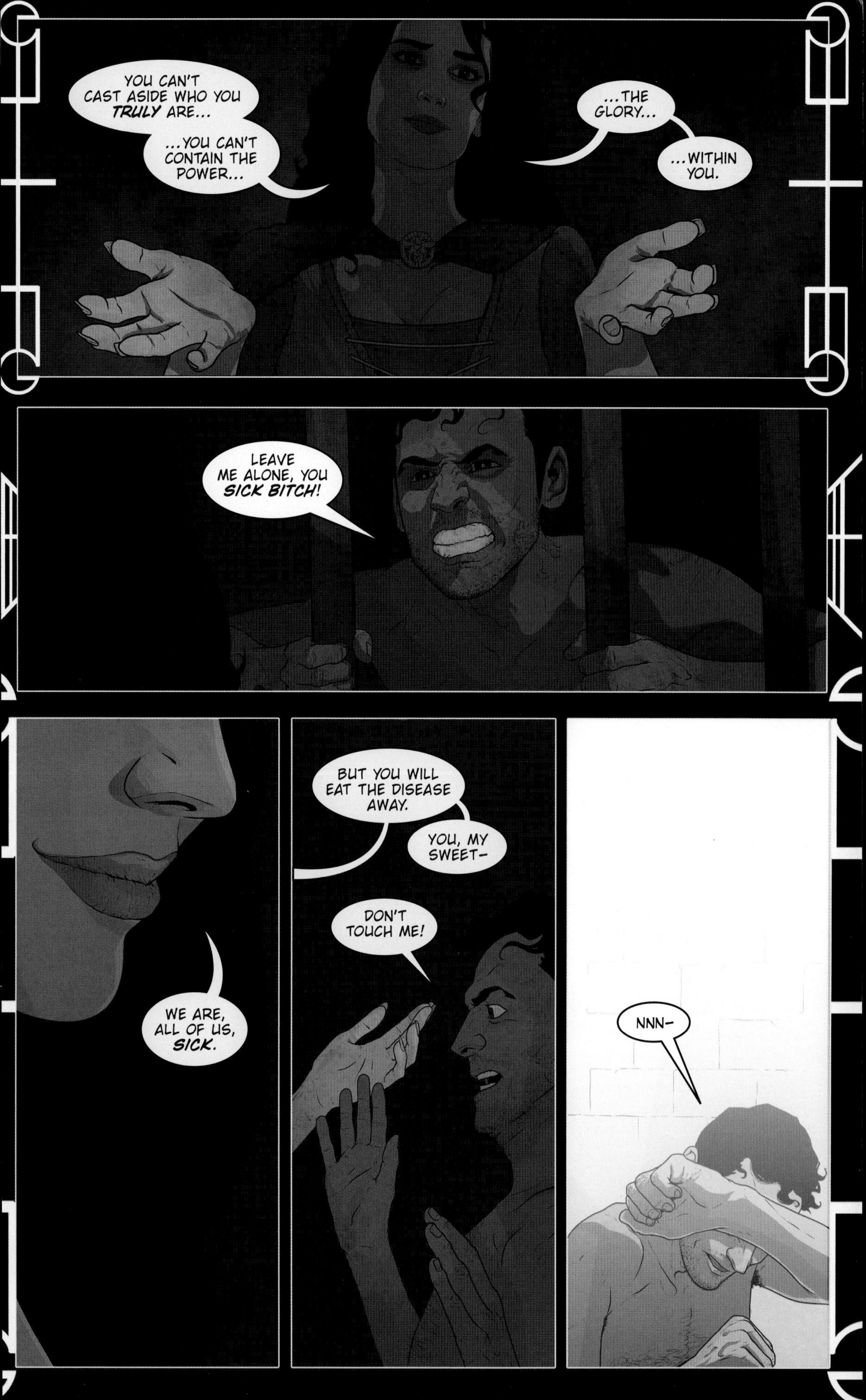
YOU CAN'T CAST ASIDE WHO YOU *TRULY* ARE...
...YOU CAN'T CONTAIN THE POWER...
...THE GLORY...
...WITHIN YOU.
LEAVE ME ALONE, YOU *SICK BITCH*!
WE ARE, ALL OF US, *SICK*.
BUT YOU WILL EAT THE DISEASE AWAY.
YOU, MY SWEET-
DON'T TOUCH ME!
NNN-

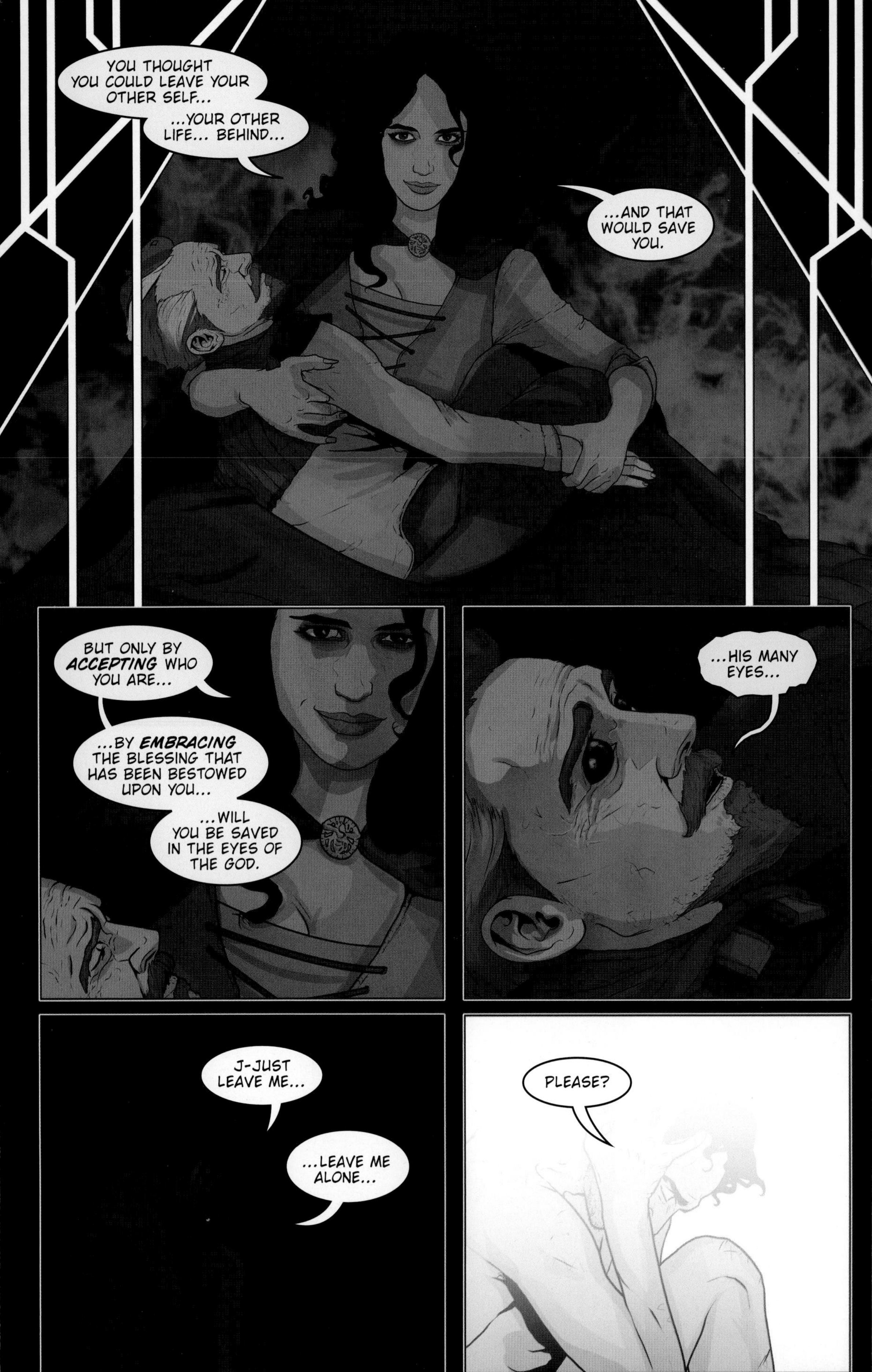

YOU THOUGHT YOU COULD LEAVE YOUR OTHER SELF...
...YOUR OTHER LIFE... BEHIND...
...AND THAT WOULD SAVE YOU.
BUT ONLY BY ACCEPTING WHO YOU ARE...
...BY EMBRACING THE BLESSING THAT HAS BEEN BESTOWED UPON YOU...
...WILL YOU BE SAVED IN THE EYES OF THE GOD.
...HIS MANY EYES...
J-JUST LEAVE ME...
...LEAVE ME ALONE...
PLEASE?

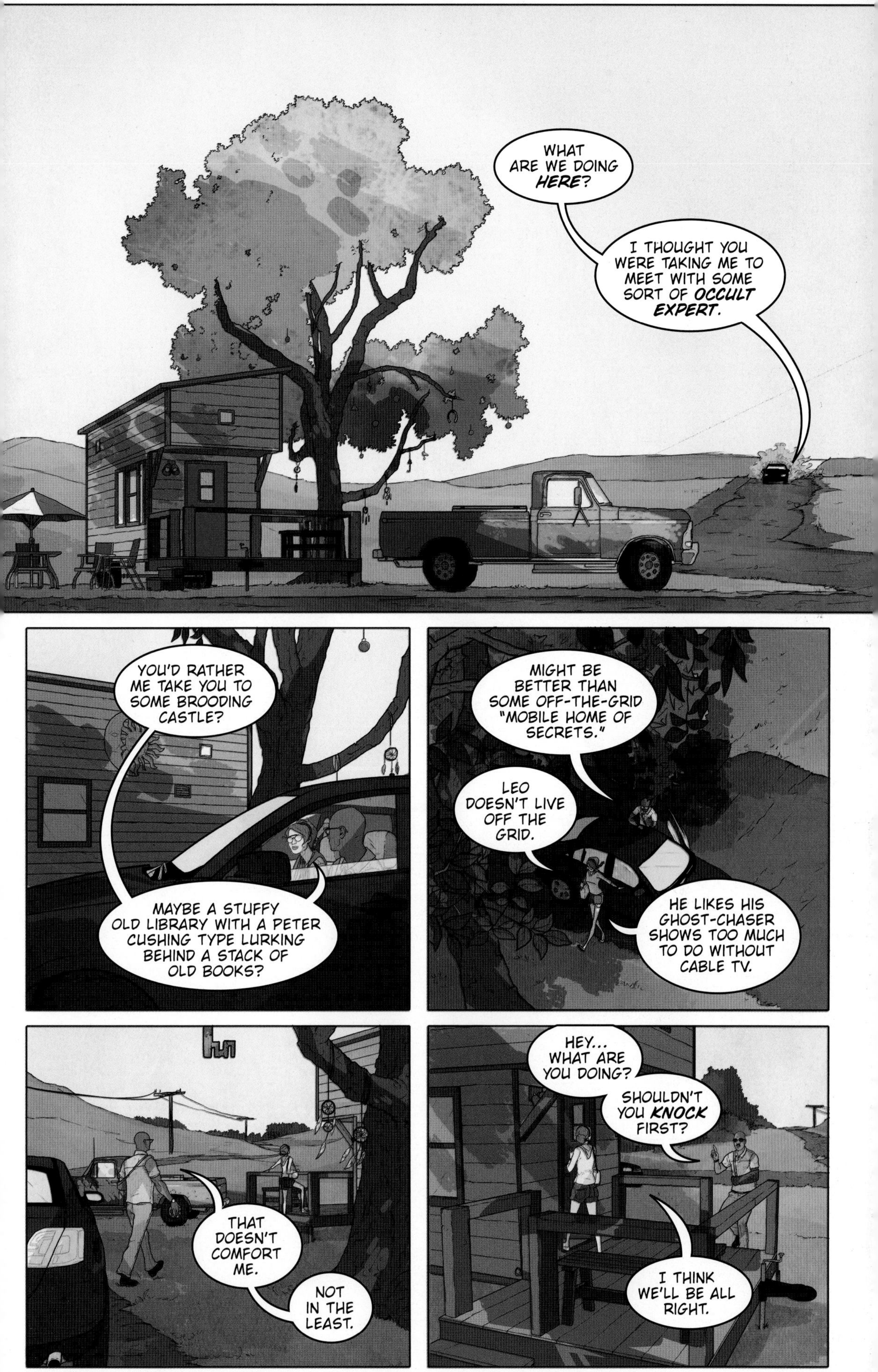
WHAT ARE WE DOING HERE?
I THOUGHT YOU WERE TAKING ME TO MEET WITH SOME SORT OF OCCULT EXPERT.
YOU'D RATHER ME TAKE YOU TO SOME BROODING CASTLE?
MAYBE A STUFFY OLD LIBRARY WITH A PETER CUSHING TYPE LURKING BEHIND A STACK OF OLD BOOKS?
MIGHT BE BETTER THAN SOME OFF-THE-GRID "MOBILE HOME OF SECRETS."
LEO DOESN'T LIVE OFF THE GRID.
HE LIKES HIS GHOST-CHASER SHOWS TOO MUCH TO DO WITHOUT CABLE TV.
THAT DOESN'T COMFORT ME.
NOT IN THE LEAST.
HEY... WHAT ARE YOU DOING?
SHOULDN'T YOU KNOCK FIRST?
I THINK WE'LL BE ALL RIGHT.

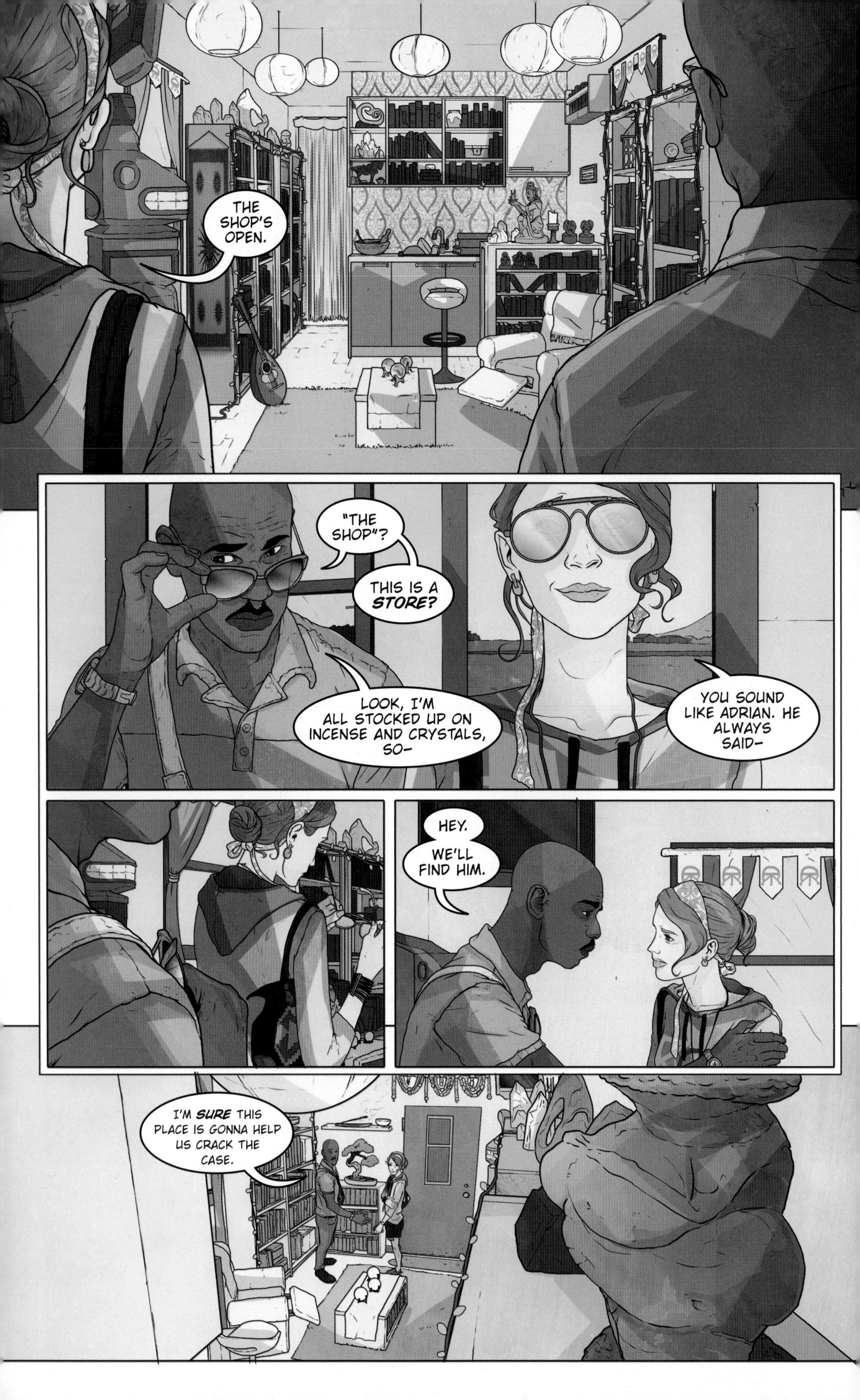
THE SHOP'S OPEN.
"THE SHOP"?
THIS IS A *STORE?*
LOOK, I'M ALL STOCKED UP ON INCENSE AND CRYSTALS, SO-
YOU SOUND LIKE ADRIAN. HE ALWAYS SAID-
HEY.
WE'LL FIND HIM.
I'M *SURE* THIS PLACE IS GONNA HELP US CRACK THE CASE.

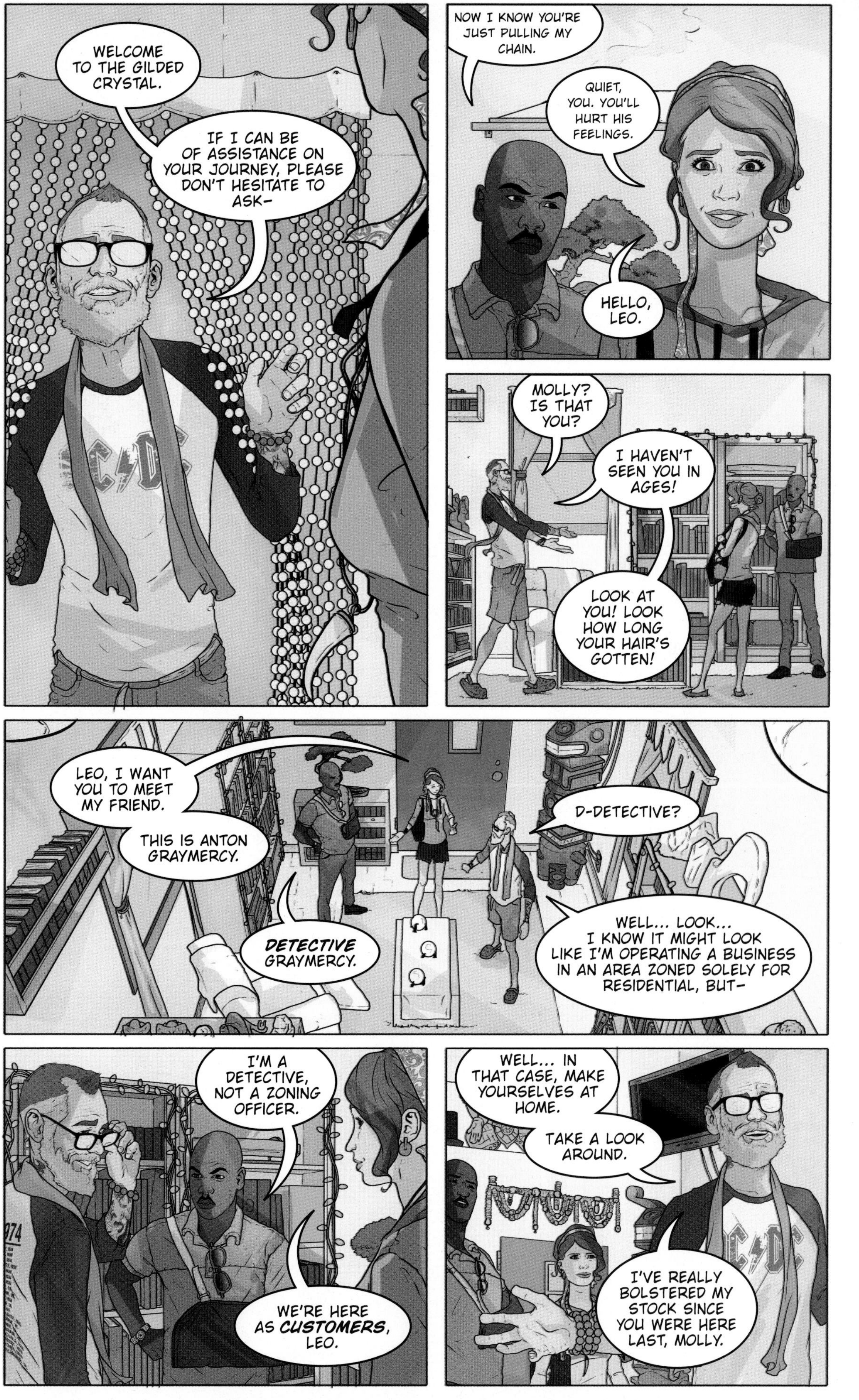
WELCOME TO THE GILDED CRYSTAL.
IF I CAN BE OF ASSISTANCE ON YOUR JOURNEY, PLEASE DON'T HESITATE TO ASK-
NOW I KNOW YOU'RE JUST PULLING MY CHAIN.
QUIET, YOU. YOU'LL HURT HIS FEELINGS.
HELLO, LEO.
MOLLY? IS THAT YOU?
I HAVEN'T SEEN YOU IN AGES!
LOOK AT YOU! LOOK HOW LONG YOUR HAIR'S GOTTEN!
LEO, I WANT YOU TO MEET MY FRIEND.
THIS IS ANTON GRAYMERCY.
DETECTIVE GRAYMERCY.
D-DETECTIVE?
WELL... LOOK... I KNOW IT MIGHT LOOK LIKE I'M OPERATING A BUSINESS IN AN AREA ZONED SOLELY FOR RESIDENTIAL, BUT-
I'M A DETECTIVE, NOT A ZONING OFFICER.
WE'RE HERE AS *CUSTOMERS*, LEO.
WELL... IN THAT CASE, MAKE YOURSELVES AT HOME.
TAKE A LOOK AROUND.
I'VE REALLY BOLSTERED MY STOCK SINCE YOU WERE HERE LAST, MOLLY.

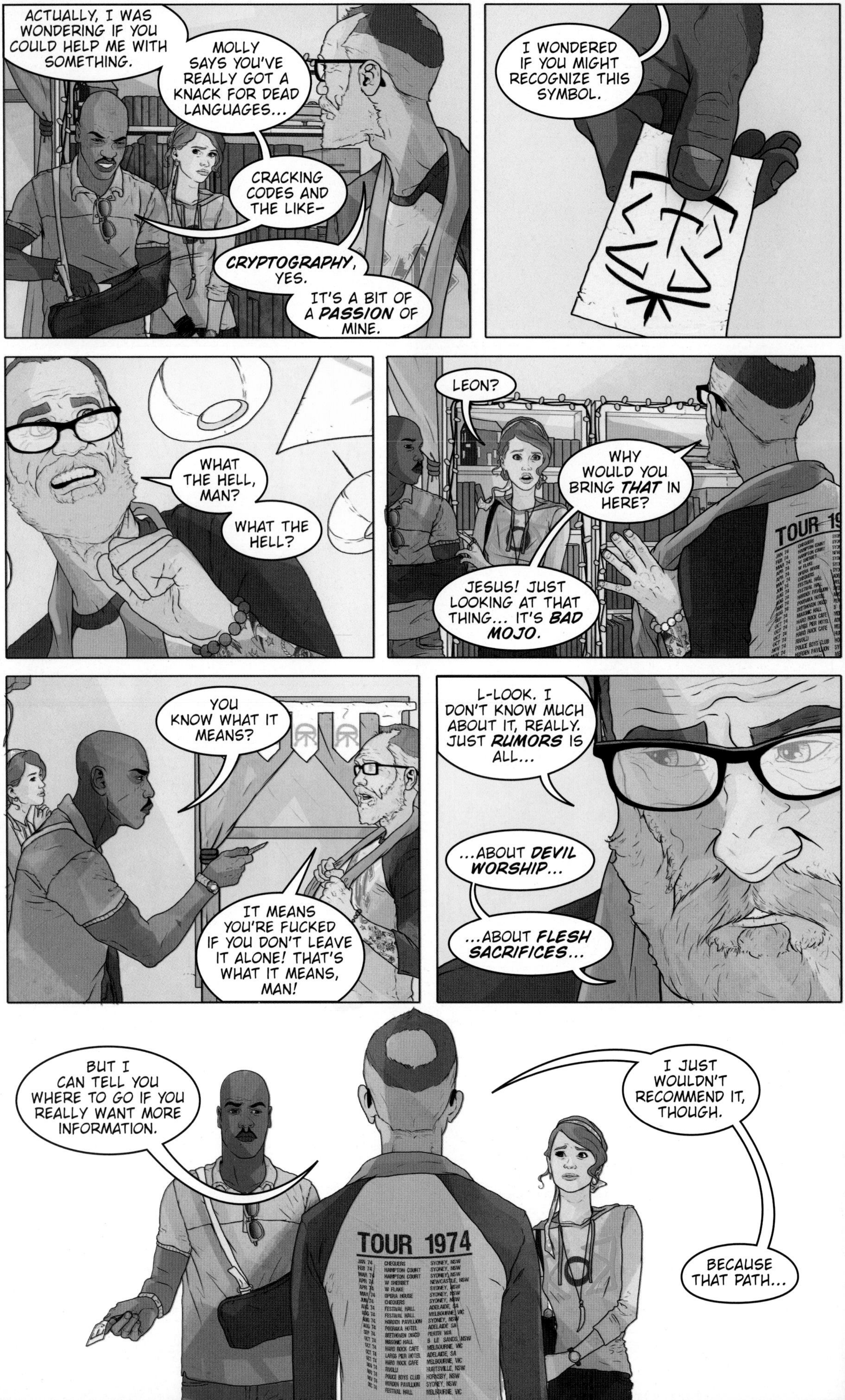
ACTUALLY, I WAS WONDERING IF YOU COULD HELP ME WITH SOMETHING.
MOLLY SAYS YOU'VE REALLY GOT A KNACK FOR DEAD LANGUAGES...
CRACKING CODES AND THE LIKE-
CRYPTOGRAPHY, YES.
IT'S A BIT OF A PASSION OF MINE.
I WONDERED IF YOU MIGHT RECOGNIZE THIS SYMBOL.
WHAT THE HELL, MAN?
WHAT THE HELL?
LEON?
WHY WOULD YOU BRING THAT IN HERE?
JESUS! JUST LOOKING AT THAT THING... IT'S BAD MOJO.
YOU KNOW WHAT IT MEANS?
IT MEANS YOU'RE FUCKED IF YOU DON'T LEAVE IT ALONE! THAT'S WHAT IT MEANS, MAN!
L-LOOK. I DON'T KNOW MUCH ABOUT IT, REALLY. JUST RUMORS IS ALL...
...ABOUT DEVIL WORSHIP...
...ABOUT FLESH SACRIFICES...
BUT I CAN TELL YOU WHERE TO GO IF YOU REALLY WANT MORE INFORMATION.
I JUST WOULDN'T RECOMMEND IT, THOUGH.
BECAUSE THAT PATH...
TOUR 1974

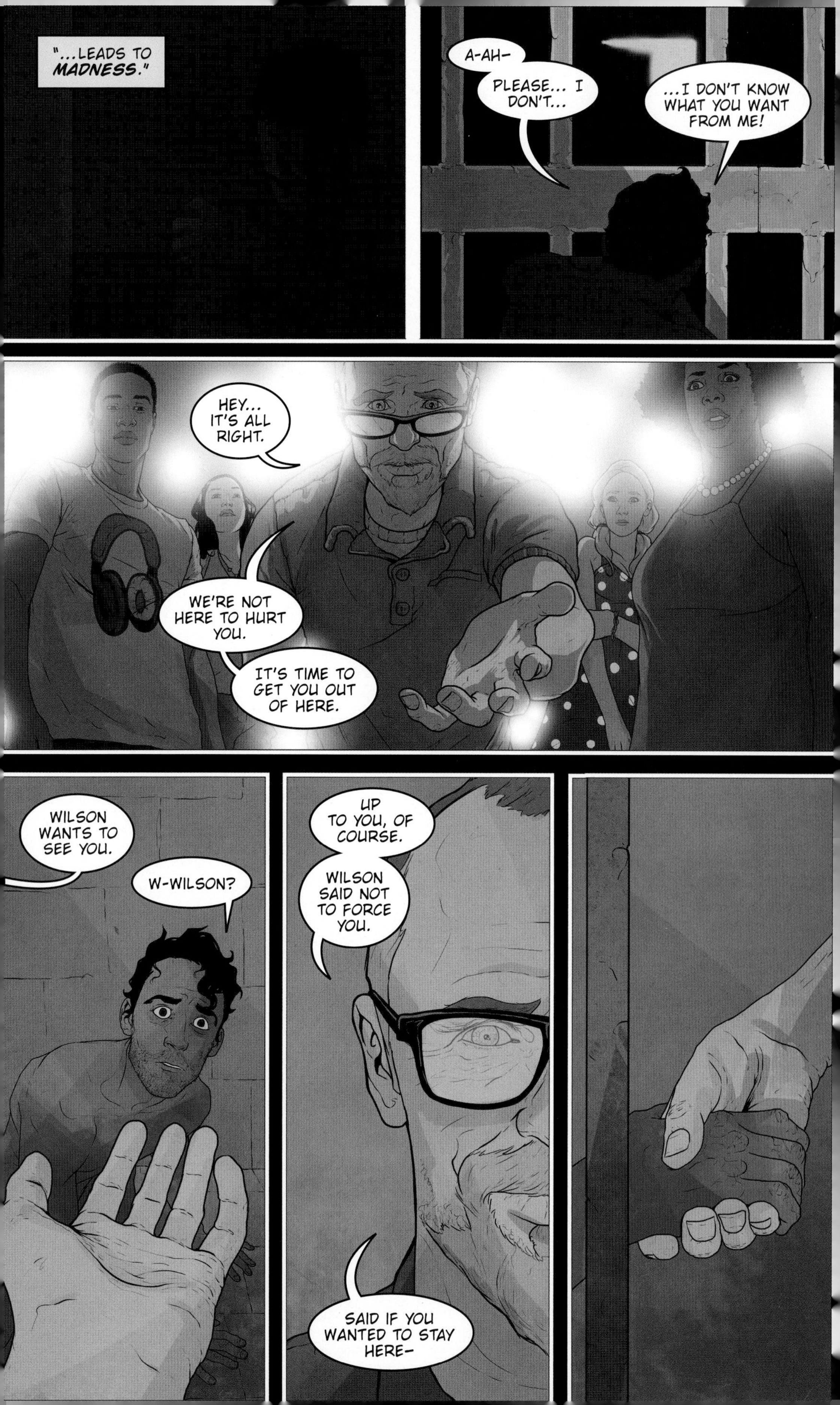
"...LEADS TO MADNESS."
A-AH-
PLEASE... I DON'T...
...I DON'T KNOW WHAT YOU WANT FROM ME!
HEY... IT'S ALL RIGHT.
WE'RE NOT HERE TO HURT YOU.
IT'S TIME TO GET YOU OUT OF HERE.
WILSON WANTS TO SEE YOU.
W-WILSON?
UP TO YOU, OF COURSE.
WILSON SAID NOT TO FORCE YOU.
SAID IF YOU WANTED TO STAY HERE-

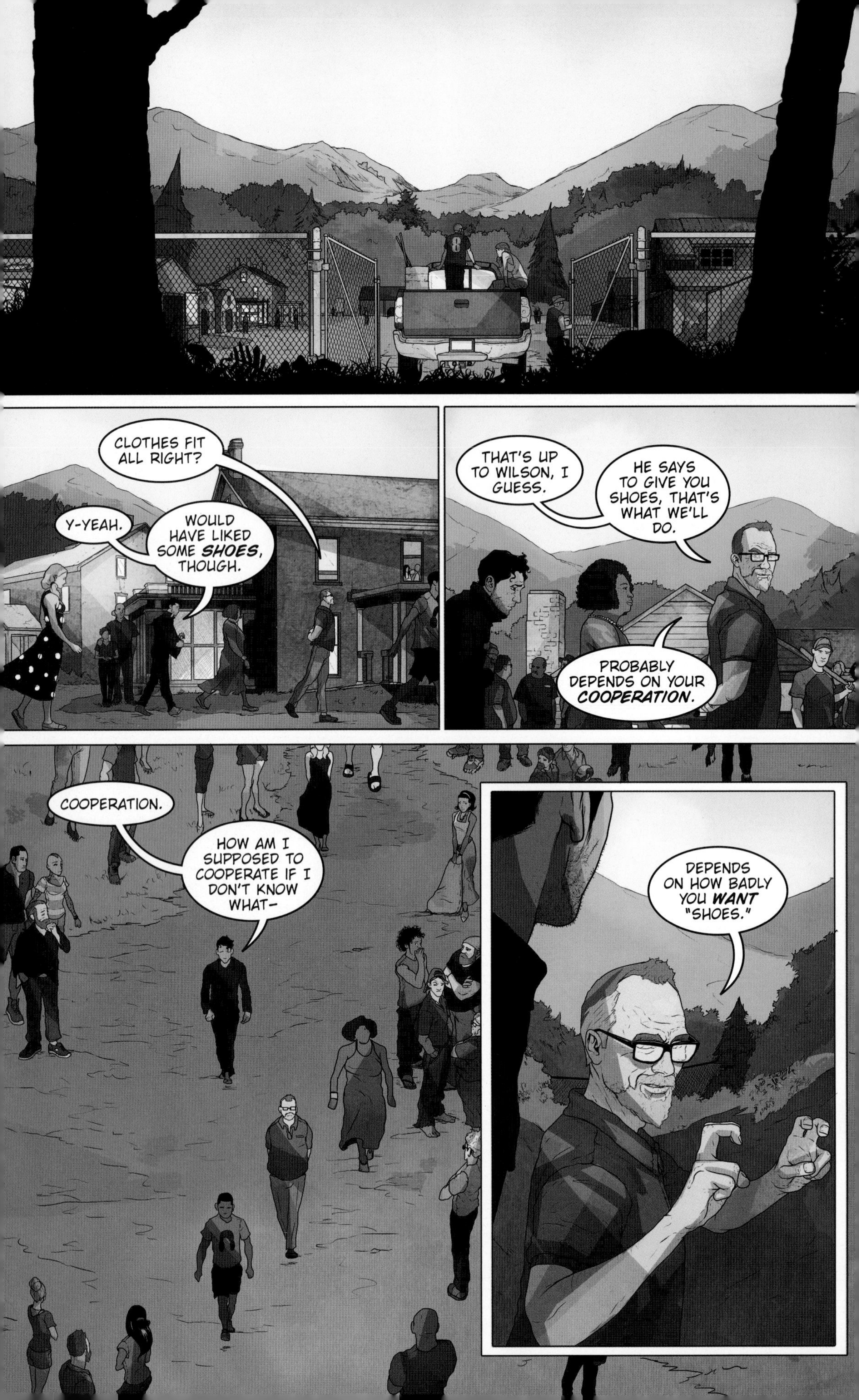
CLOTHES FIT ALL RIGHT?
Y-YEAH.
WOULD HAVE LIKED SOME SHOES, THOUGH.
THAT'S UP TO WILSON, I GUESS.
HE SAYS TO GIVE YOU SHOES, THAT'S WHAT WE'LL DO.
PROBABLY DEPENDS ON YOUR COOPERATION.
COOPERATION.
HOW AM I SUPPOSED TO COOPERATE IF I DON'T KNOW WHAT-
DEPENDS ON HOW BADLY YOU WANT "SHOES."

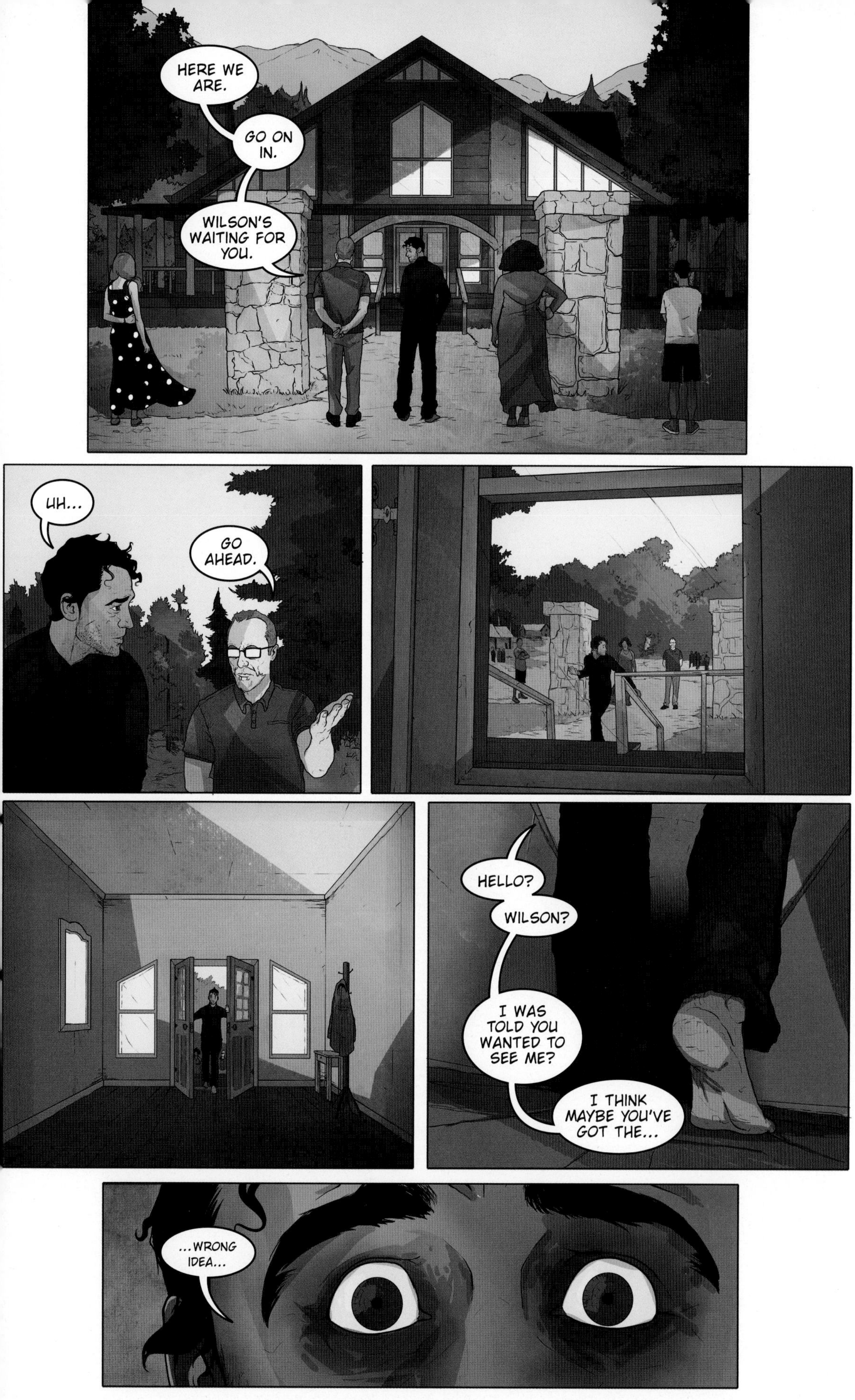
HERE WE ARE.
GO ON IN.
WILSON'S WAITING FOR YOU.
UH...
GO AHEAD.
HELLO?
WILSON?
I WAS TOLD YOU WANTED TO SEE ME?
I THINK MAYBE YOU'VE GOT THE...
...WRONG IDEA...

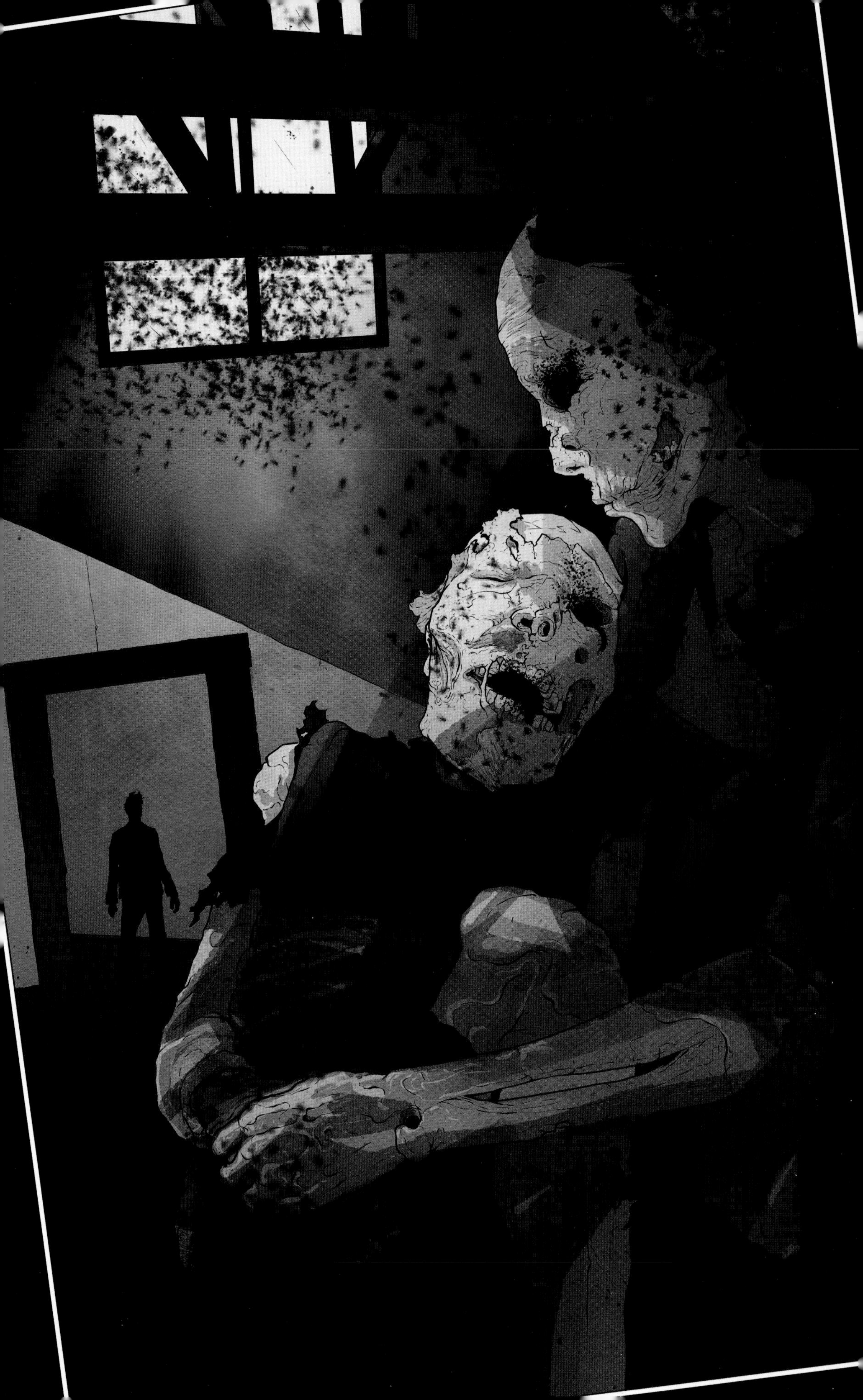

SEVEN

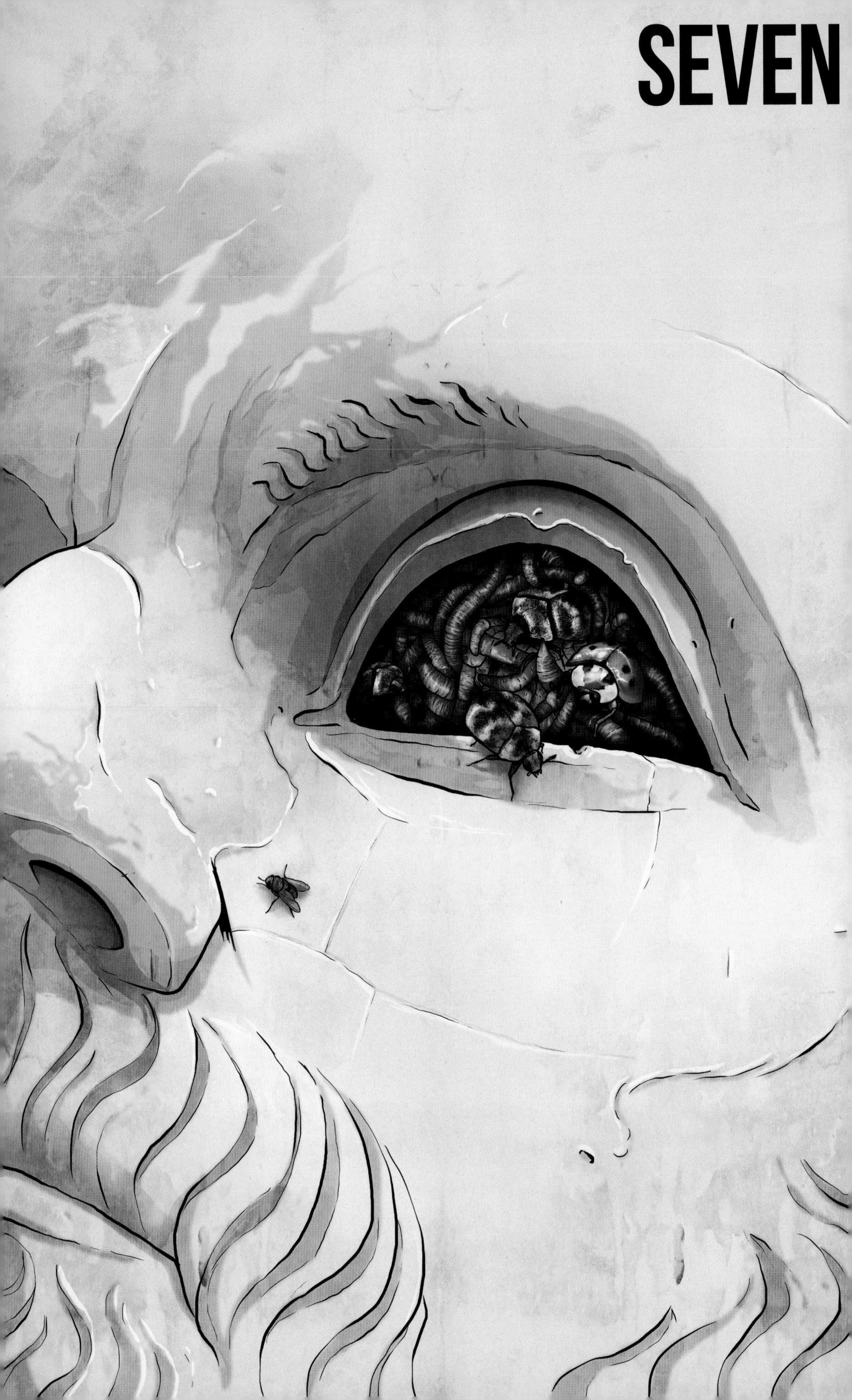

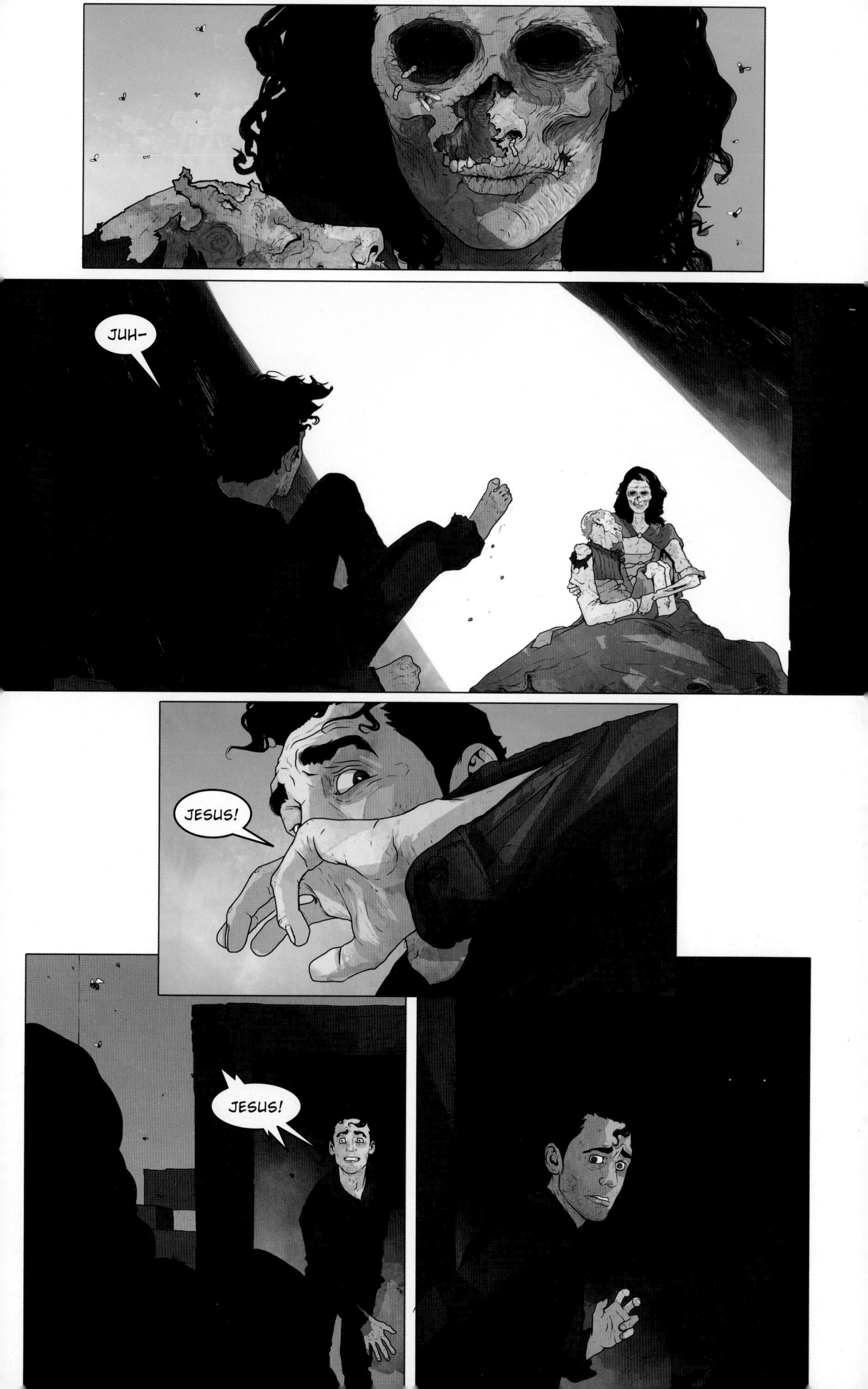
JUH-
JESUS!
JESUS!

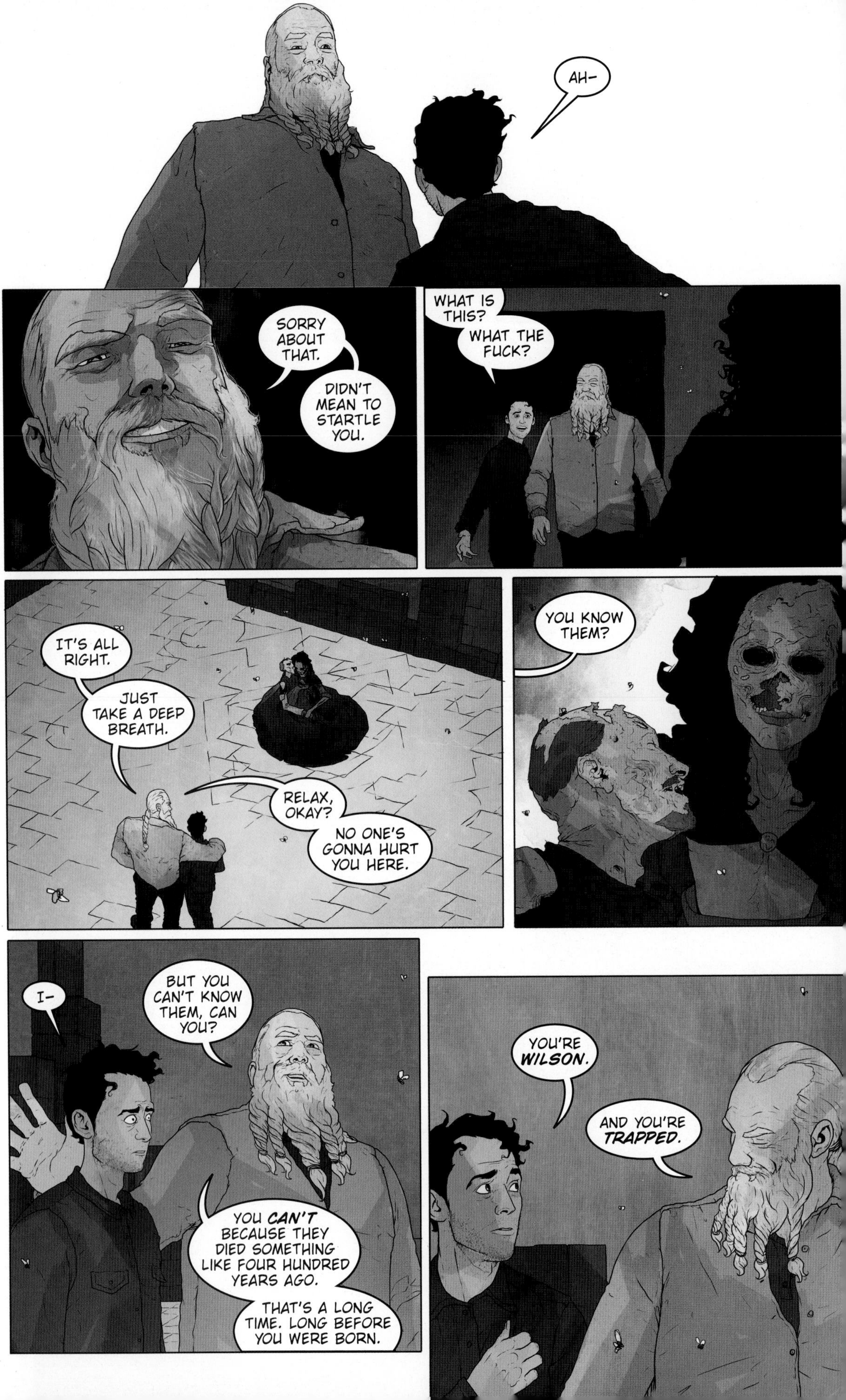
AH-
SORRY ABOUT THAT.
DIDN'T MEAN TO STARTLE YOU.
WHAT IS THIS?
WHAT THE FUCK?
IT'S ALL RIGHT.
JUST TAKE A DEEP BREATH.
RELAX, OKAY?
NO ONE'S GONNA HURT YOU HERE.
YOU KNOW THEM?
I-
BUT YOU CAN'T KNOW THEM, CAN YOU?
YOU CAN'T BECAUSE THEY DIED SOMETHING LIKE FOUR HUNDRED YEARS AGO.
THAT'S A LONG TIME. LONG BEFORE YOU WERE BORN.
YOU'RE WILSON.
AND YOU'RE TRAPPED.

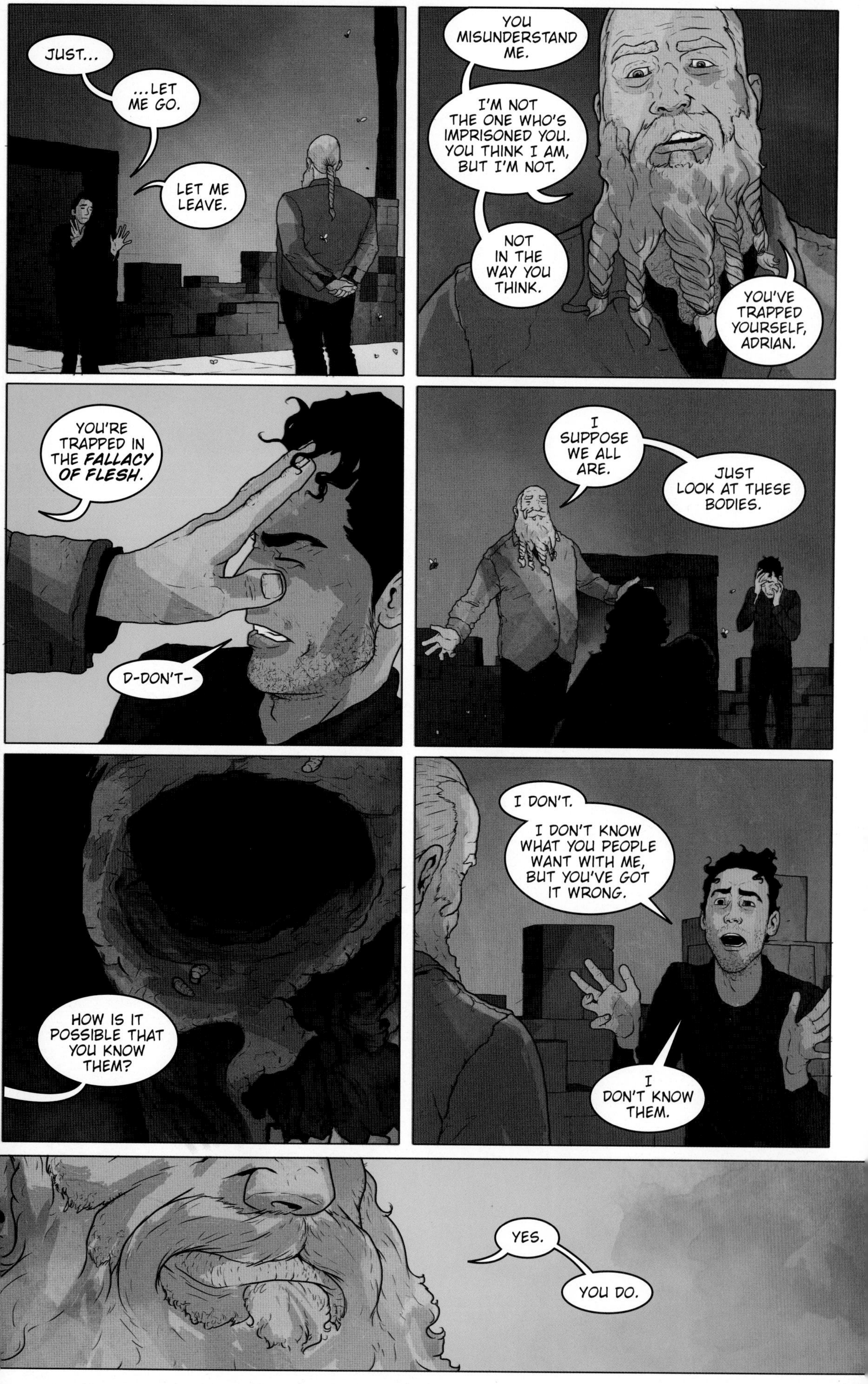
JUST...
...LET ME GO.
LET ME LEAVE.
YOU MISUNDERSTAND ME.
I'M NOT THE ONE WHO'S IMPRISONED YOU. YOU THINK I AM, BUT I'M NOT.
NOT IN THE WAY YOU THINK.
YOU'VE TRAPPED YOURSELF, ADRIAN.
YOU'RE TRAPPED IN THE FALLACY OF FLESH.
D-DON'T-
I SUPPOSE WE ALL ARE.
JUST LOOK AT THESE BODIES.
HOW IS IT POSSIBLE THAT YOU KNOW THEM?
I DON'T.
I DON'T KNOW WHAT YOU PEOPLE WANT WITH ME, BUT YOU'VE GOT IT WRONG.
I DON'T KNOW THEM.
YES.
YOU DO.

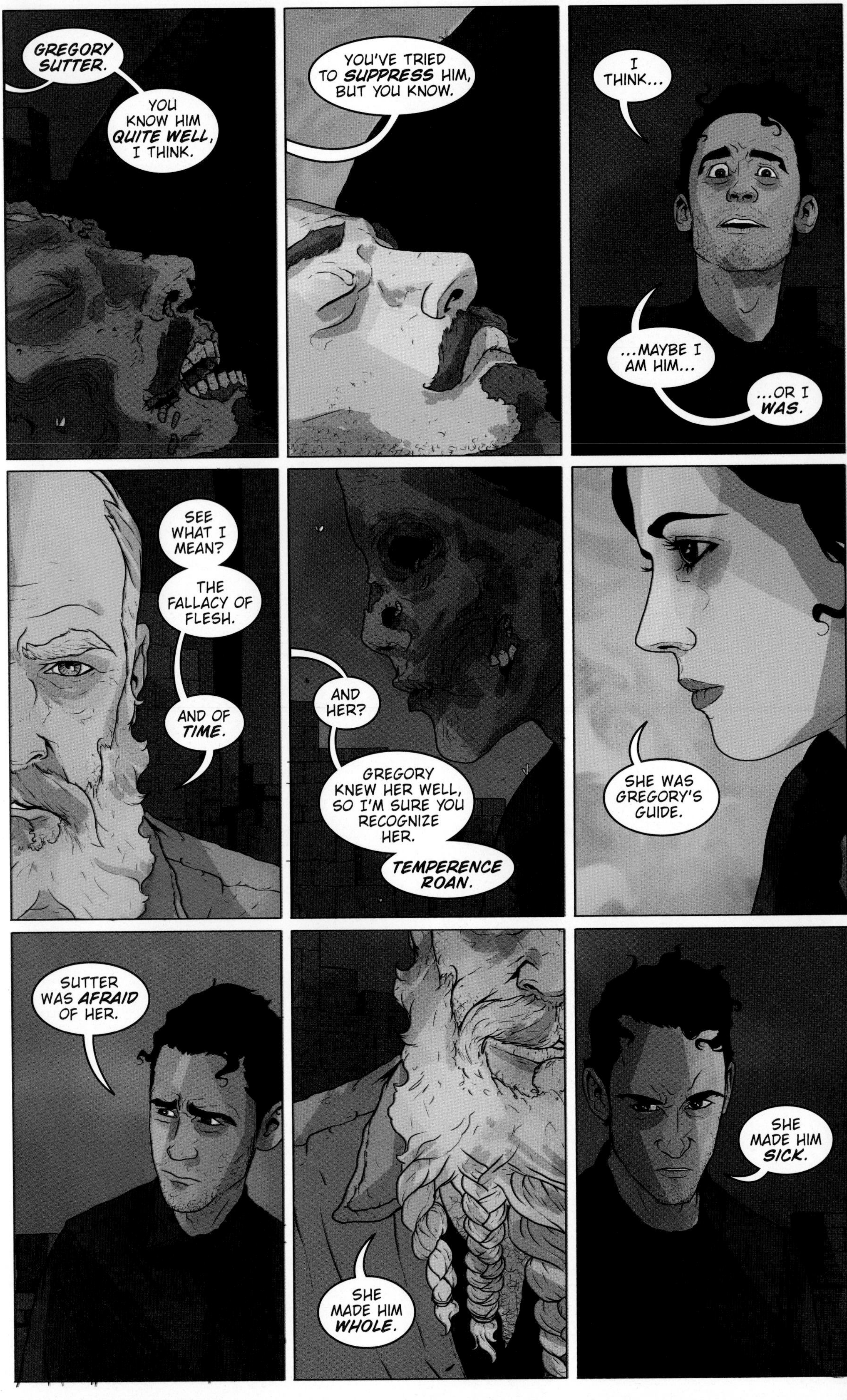
GREGORY SUTTER.
YOU KNOW HIM QUITE WELL, I THINK.
YOU'VE TRIED TO SUPPRESS HIM, BUT YOU KNOW.
I THINK...
...MAYBE I AM HIM...
...OR I WAS.
SEE WHAT I MEAN?
THE FALLACY OF FLESH.
AND OF TIME.
AND HER?
GREGORY KNEW HER WELL, SO I'M SURE YOU RECOGNIZE HER.
TEMPERENCE ROAN.
SHE WAS GREGORY'S GUIDE.
SUTTER WAS AFRAID OF HER.
SHE MADE HIM WHOLE.
SHE MADE HIM SICK.

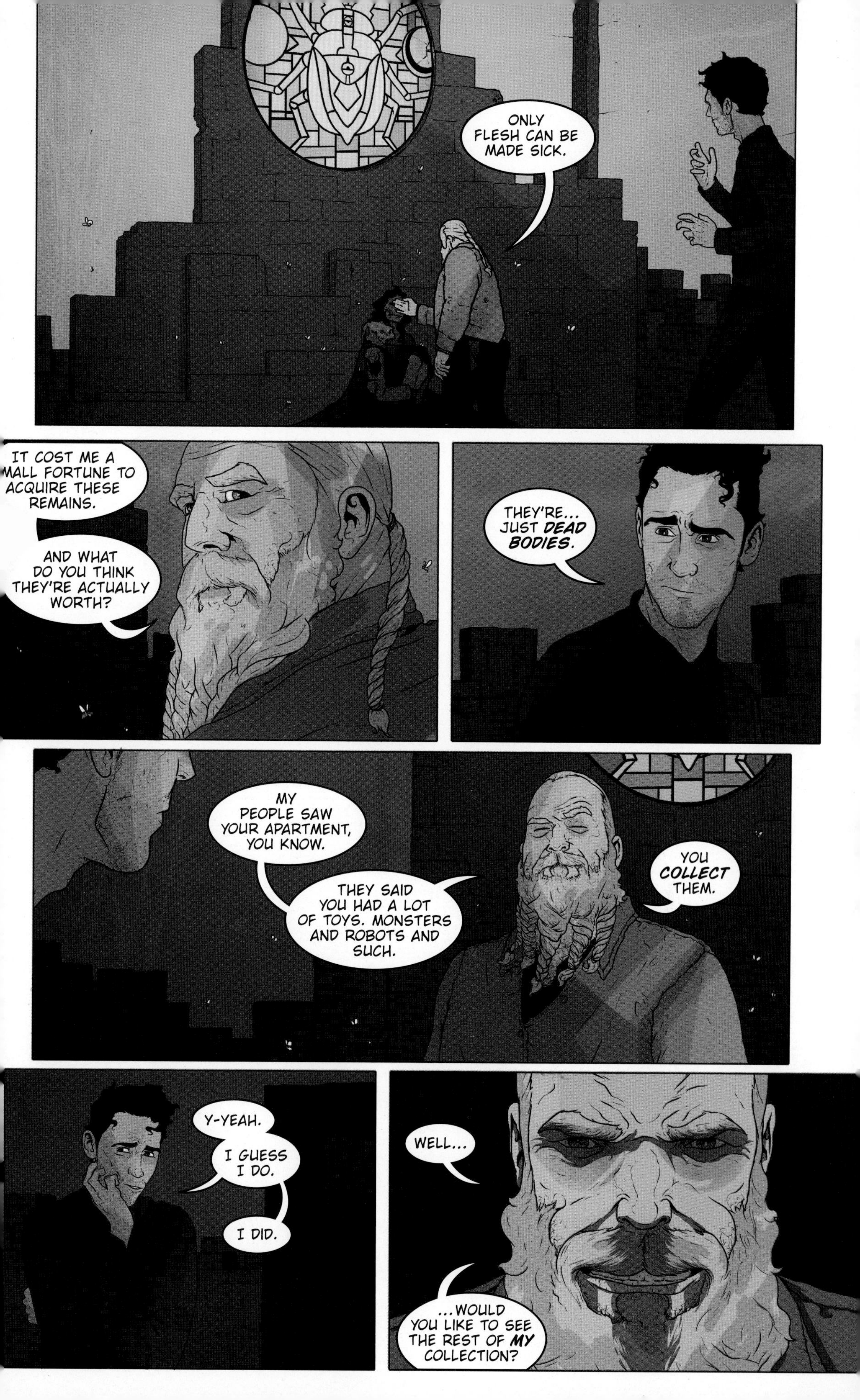
ONLY FLESH CAN BE MADE SICK.
IT COST ME A MALL FORTUNE TO ACQUIRE THESE REMAINS.
AND WHAT DO YOU THINK THEY'RE ACTUALLY WORTH?
THEY'RE... JUST DEAD BODIES.
MY PEOPLE SAW YOUR APARTMENT, YOU KNOW.
THEY SAID YOU HAD A LOT OF TOYS. MONSTERS AND ROBOTS AND SUCH.
YOU COLLECT THEM.
Y-YEAH.
I GUESS I DO.
I DID.
WELL...
...WOULD YOU LIKE TO SEE THE REST OF MY COLLECTION?

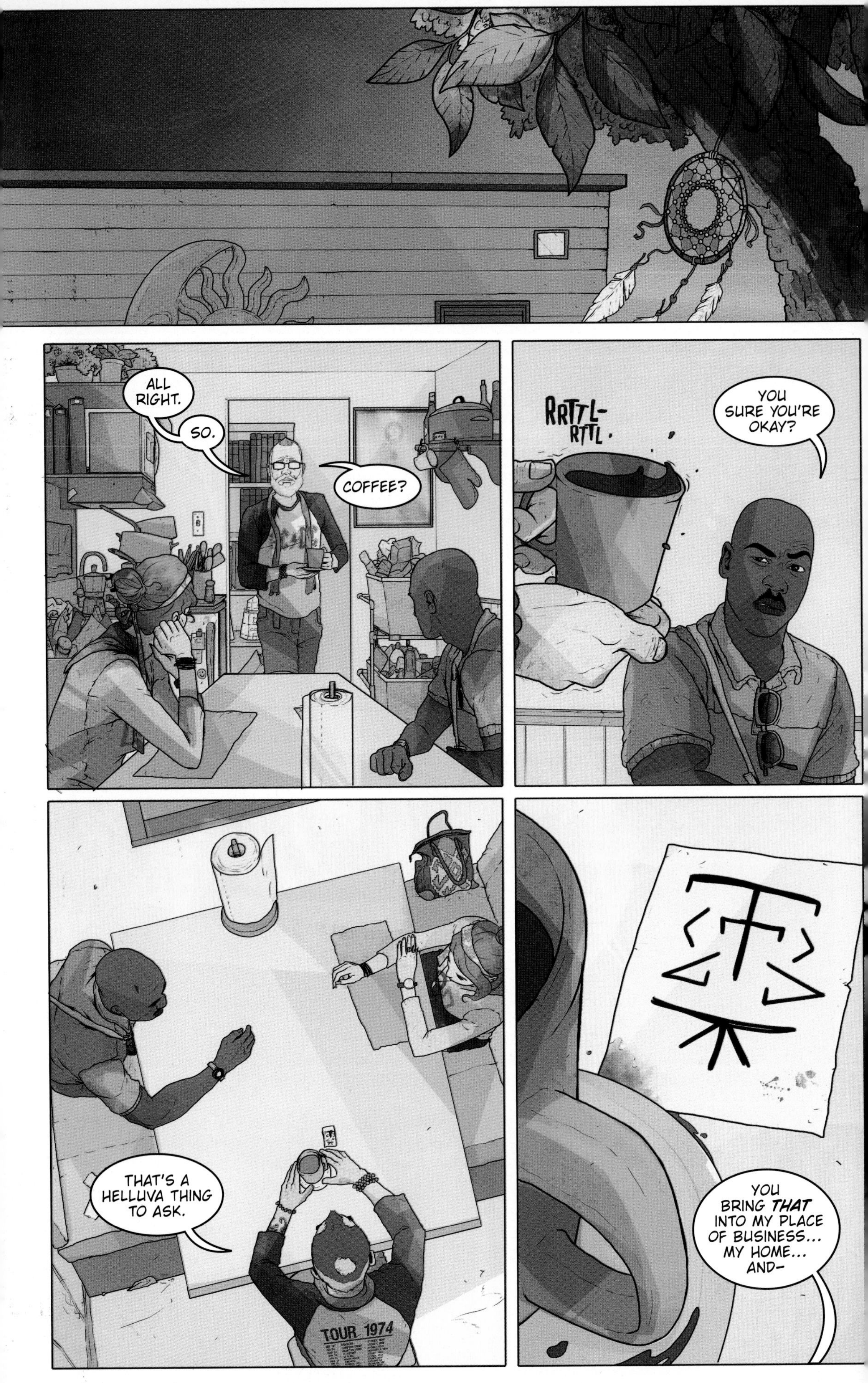
ALL RIGHT.
SO.
COFFEE?
RRTTL-RTTL.
YOU SURE YOU'RE OKAY?
THAT'S A HELLUVA THING TO ASK.
YOU BRING ***THAT*** INTO MY PLACE OF BUSINESS... MY HOME... AND–

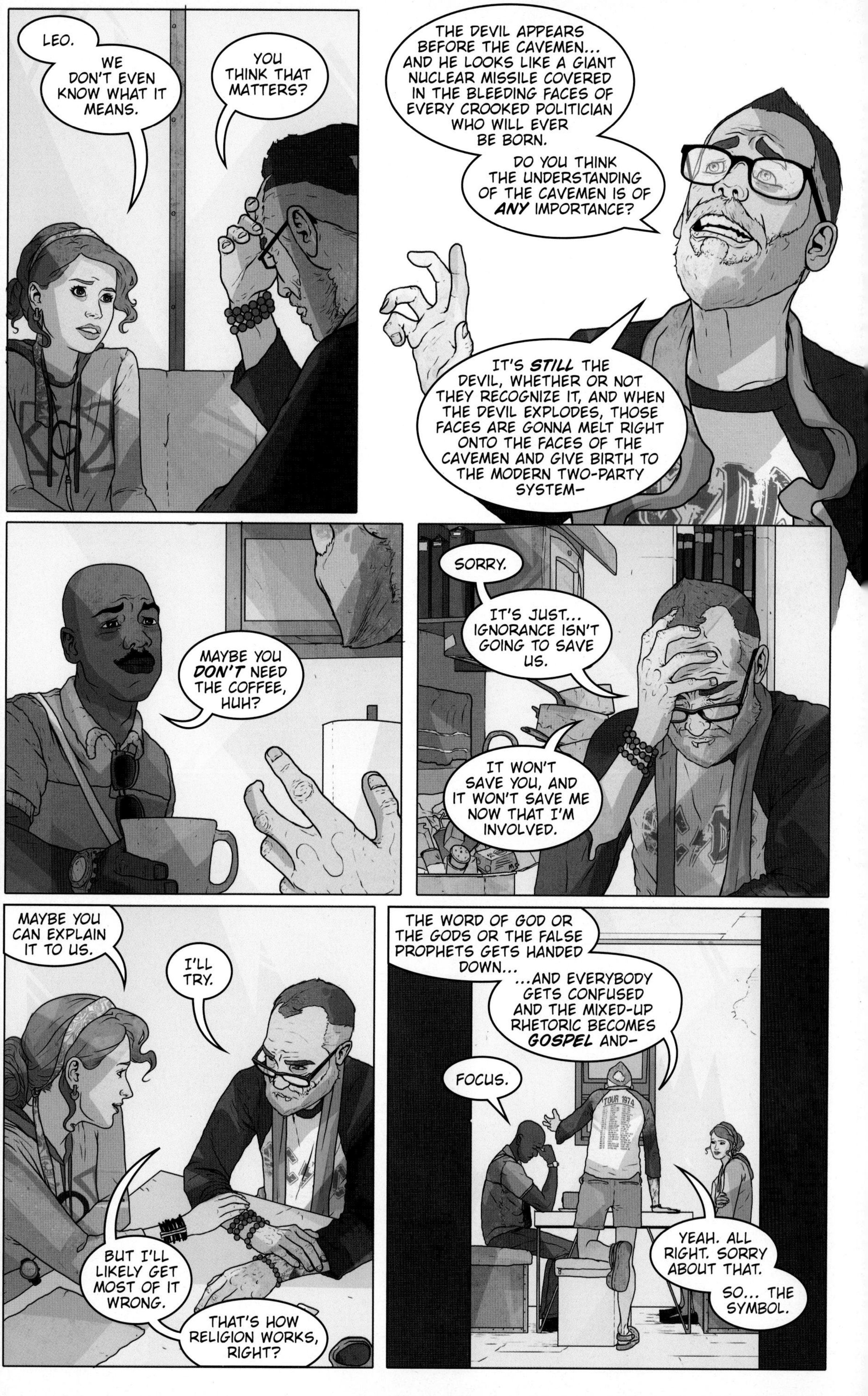
LEO.
WE DON'T EVEN KNOW WHAT IT MEANS.
YOU THINK THAT MATTERS?
THE DEVIL APPEARS BEFORE THE CAVEMEN... AND HE LOOKS LIKE A GIANT NUCLEAR MISSILE COVERED IN THE BLEEDING FACES OF EVERY CROOKED POLITICIAN WHO WILL EVER BE BORN.
DO YOU THINK THE UNDERSTANDING OF THE CAVEMEN IS OF *ANY* IMPORTANCE?
IT'S *STILL* THE DEVIL, WHETHER OR NOT THEY RECOGNIZE IT, AND WHEN THE DEVIL EXPLODES, THOSE FACES ARE GONNA MELT RIGHT ONTO THE FACES OF THE CAVEMEN AND GIVE BIRTH TO THE MODERN TWO-PARTY SYSTEM–
MAYBE YOU *DON'T* NEED THE COFFEE, HUH?
SORRY.
IT'S JUST... IGNORANCE ISN'T GOING TO SAVE US.
IT WON'T SAVE YOU, AND IT WON'T SAVE ME NOW THAT I'M INVOLVED.
MAYBE YOU CAN EXPLAIN IT TO US.
I'LL TRY.
BUT I'LL LIKELY GET MOST OF IT WRONG.
THAT'S HOW RELIGION WORKS, RIGHT?
THE WORD OF GOD OR THE GODS OR THE FALSE PROPHETS GETS HANDED DOWN...
...AND EVERYBODY GETS CONFUSED AND THE MIXED-UP RHETORIC BECOMES *GOSPEL* AND–
FOCUS.
TOUR 1974
YEAH. ALL RIGHT. SORRY ABOUT THAT.
SO... THE SYMBOL.

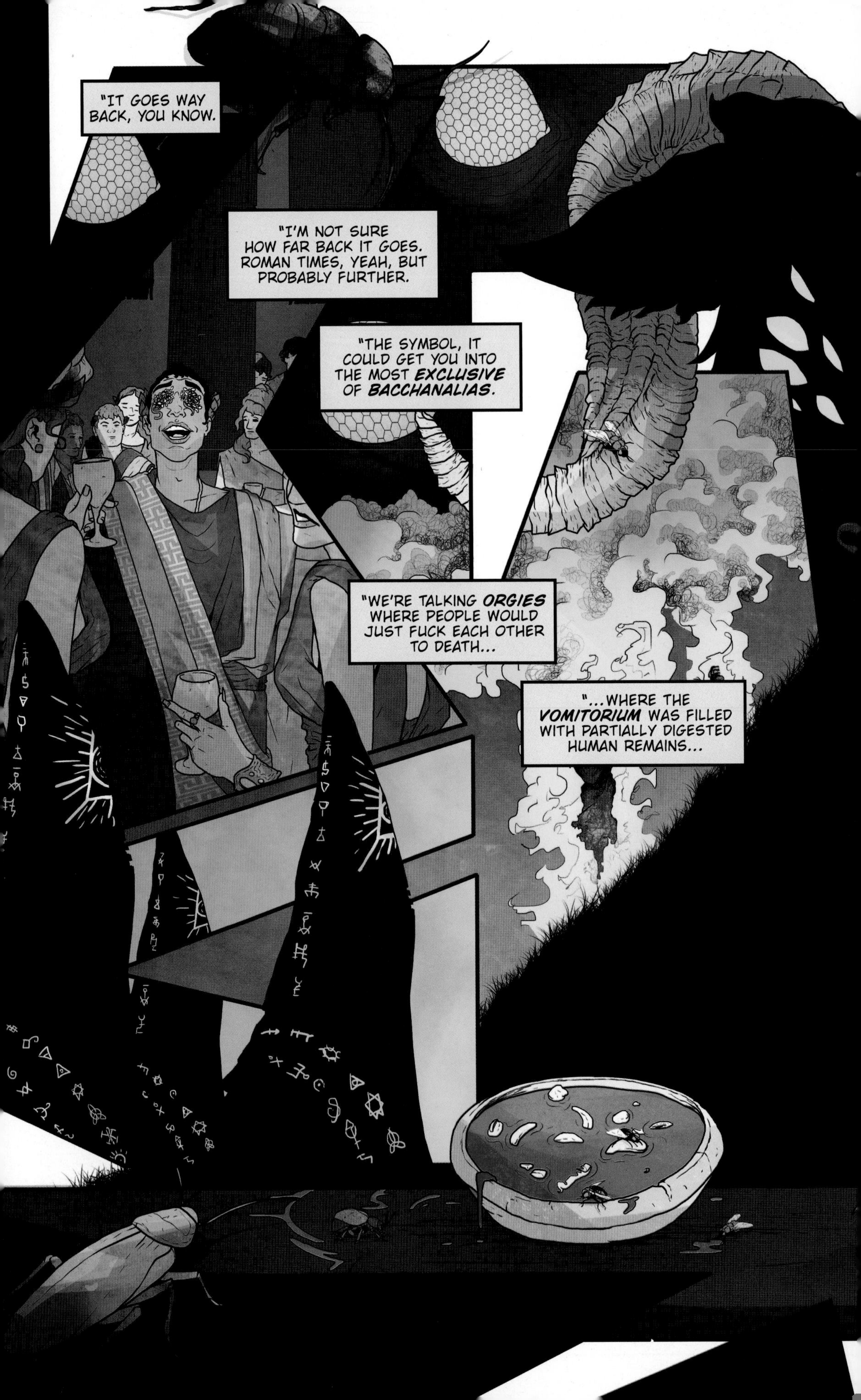
"IT GOES WAY BACK, YOU KNOW.
"I'M NOT SURE HOW FAR BACK IT GOES. ROMAN TIMES, YEAH, BUT PROBABLY FURTHER.
"THE SYMBOL, IT COULD GET YOU INTO THE MOST EXCLUSIVE OF BACCHANALIAS.
"WE'RE TALKING ORGIES WHERE PEOPLE WOULD JUST FUCK EACH OTHER TO DEATH...
"...WHERE THE VOMITORIUM WAS FILLED WITH PARTIALLY DIGESTED HUMAN REMAINS...

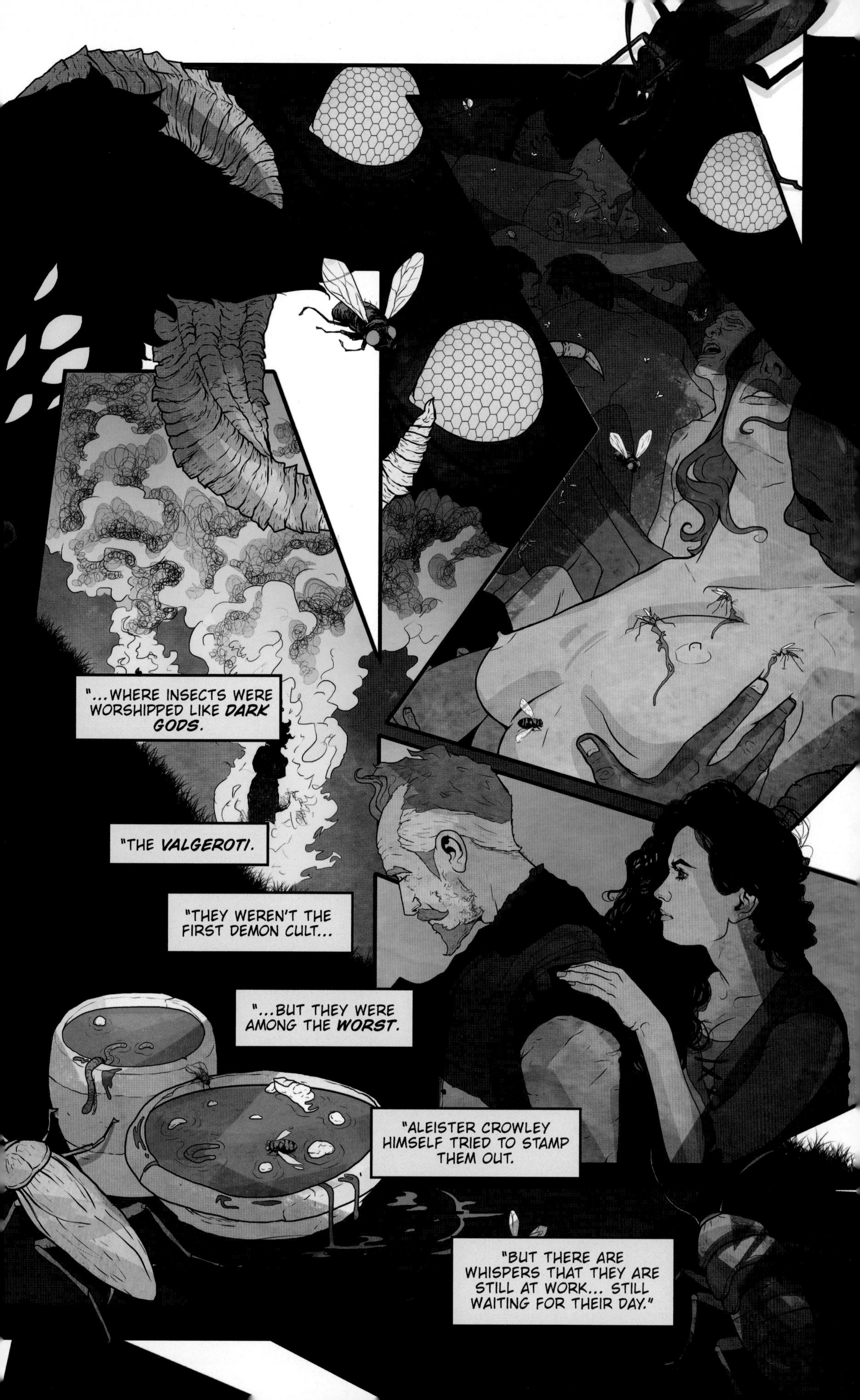
"...WHERE INSECTS WERE WORSHIPPED LIKE *DARK GODS*.
"THE *VALGEROTI*.
"THEY WEREN'T THE FIRST DEMON CULT...
"...BUT THEY WERE AMONG THE *WORST*.
"ALEISTER CROWLEY HIMSELF TRIED TO STAMP THEM OUT.
"BUT THERE ARE WHISPERS THAT THEY ARE STILL AT WORK... STILL WAITING FOR THEIR DAY."

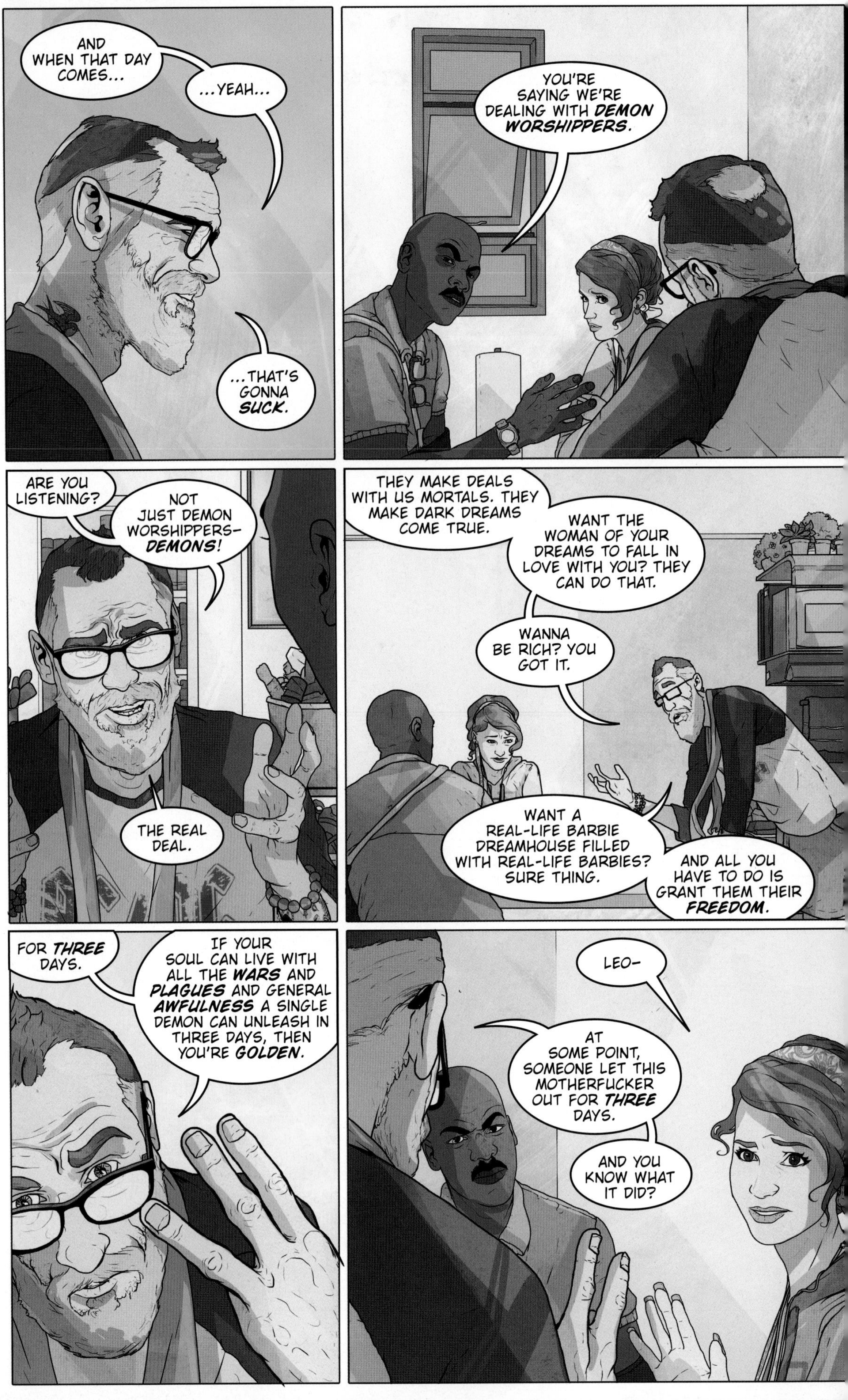
AND WHEN THAT DAY COMES...
...YEAH...
...THAT'S GONNA SUCK.
YOU'RE SAYING WE'RE DEALING WITH DEMON WORSHIPPERS.
ARE YOU LISTENING?
NOT JUST DEMON WORSHIPPERS- DEMONS!
THE REAL DEAL.
THEY MAKE DEALS WITH US MORTALS. THEY MAKE DARK DREAMS COME TRUE.
WANT THE WOMAN OF YOUR DREAMS TO FALL IN LOVE WITH YOU? THEY CAN DO THAT.
WANNA BE RICH? YOU GOT IT.
WANT A REAL-LIFE BARBIE DREAMHOUSE FILLED WITH REAL-LIFE BARBIES? SURE THING.
AND ALL YOU HAVE TO DO IS GRANT THEM THEIR FREEDOM.
FOR THREE DAYS.
IF YOUR SOUL CAN LIVE WITH ALL THE WARS AND PLAGUES AND GENERAL AWFULNESS A SINGLE DEMON CAN UNLEASH IN THREE DAYS, THEN YOU'RE GOLDEN.
LEO-
AT SOME POINT, SOMEONE LET THIS MOTHERFUCKER OUT FOR THREE DAYS.
AND YOU KNOW WHAT IT DID?

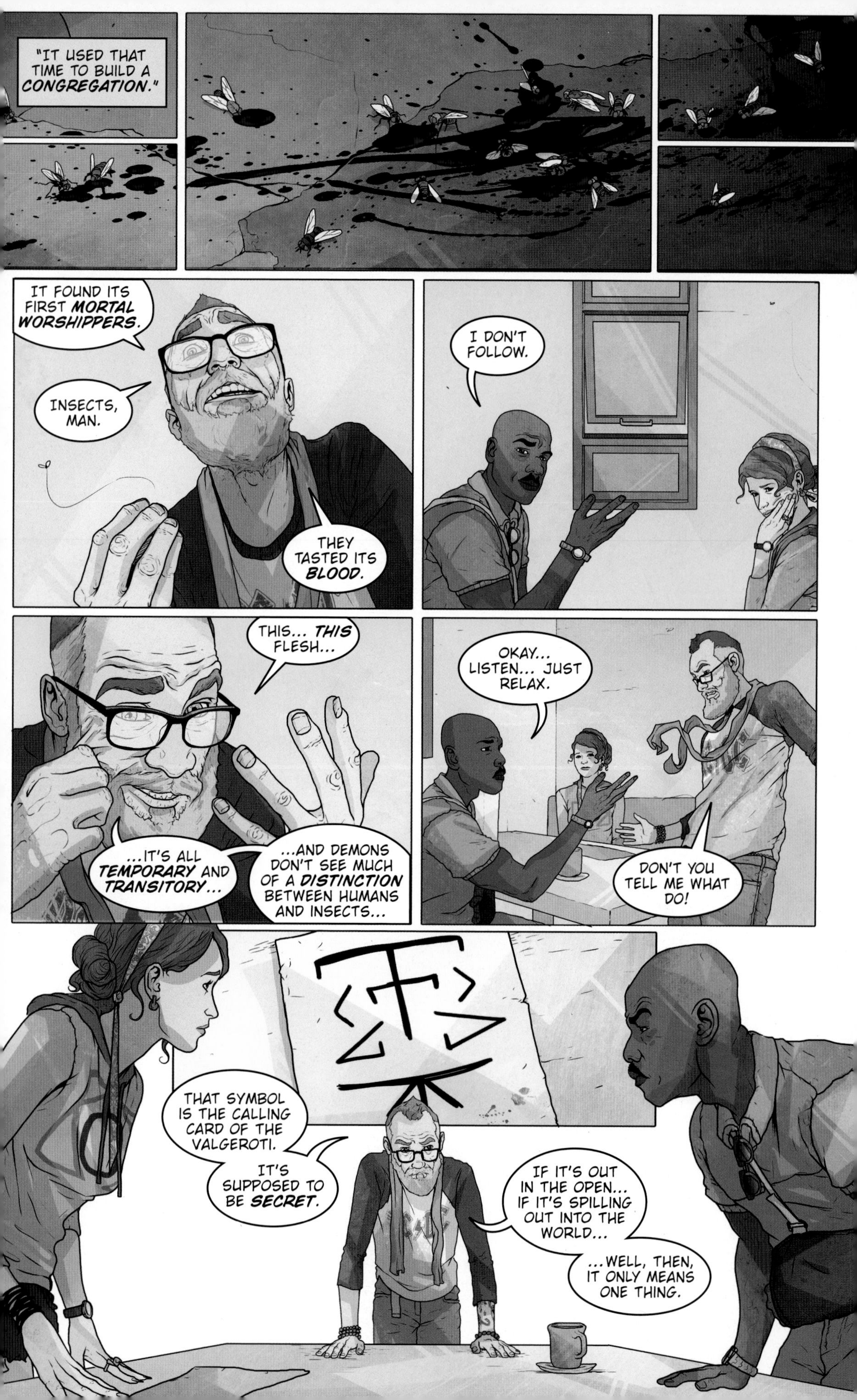
"IT USED THAT TIME TO BUILD A CONGREGATION."
IT FOUND ITS FIRST MORTAL WORSHIPPERS.
INSECTS, MAN.
THEY TASTED ITS BLOOD.
I DON'T FOLLOW.
THIS... THIS FLESH...
...IT'S ALL TEMPORARY AND TRANSITORY...
...AND DEMONS DON'T SEE MUCH OF A DISTINCTION BETWEEN HUMANS AND INSECTS...
OKAY... LISTEN... JUST RELAX.
DON'T YOU TELL ME WHAT DO!
THAT SYMBOL IS THE CALLING CARD OF THE VALGEROTI.
IT'S SUPPOSED TO BE SECRET.
IF IT'S OUT IN THE OPEN... IF IT'S SPILLING OUT INTO THE WORLD...
...WELL, THEN, IT ONLY MEANS ONE THING.

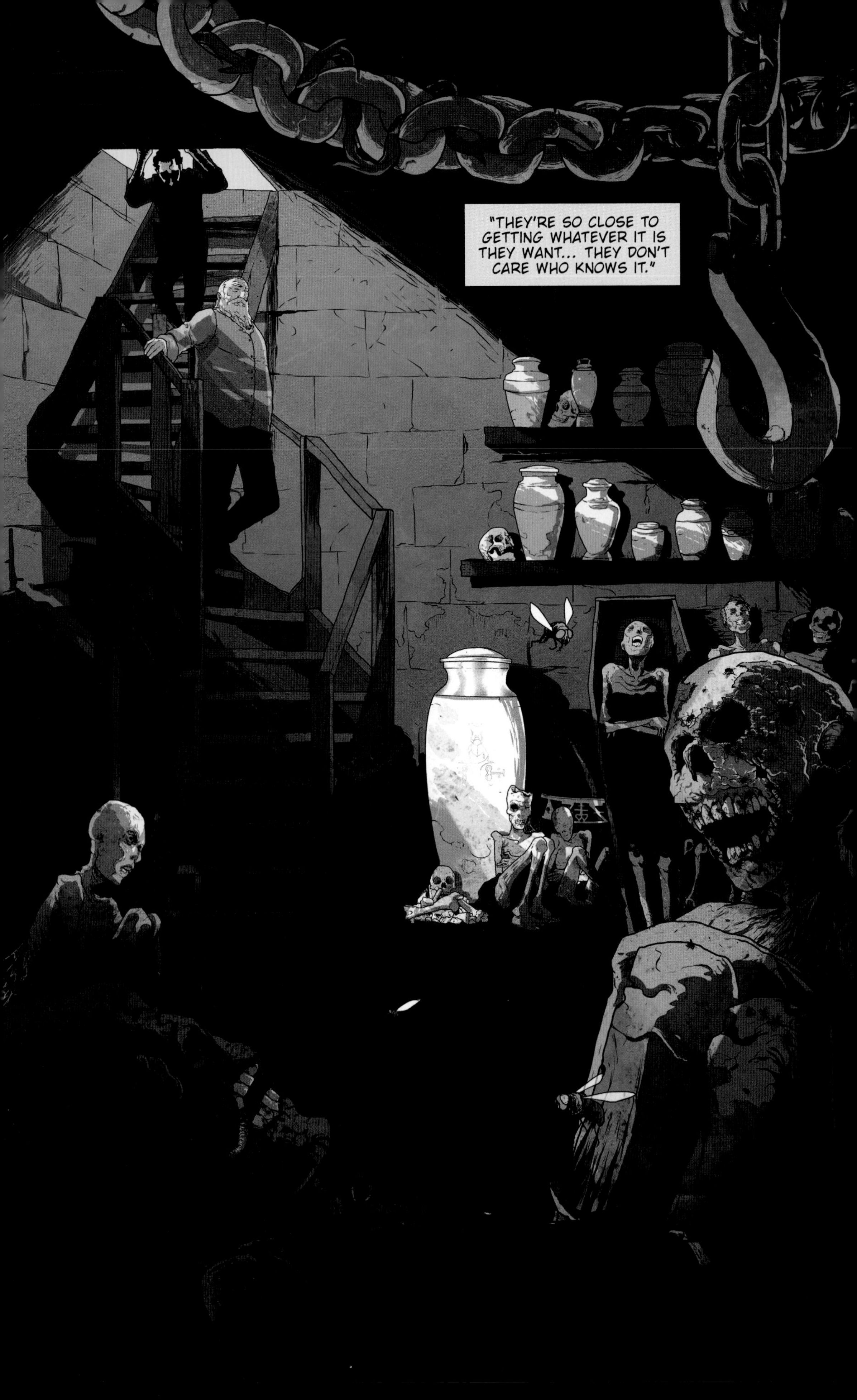
"THEY'RE SO CLOSE TO GETTING WHATEVER IT IS THEY WANT... THEY DON'T CARE WHO KNOWS IT."

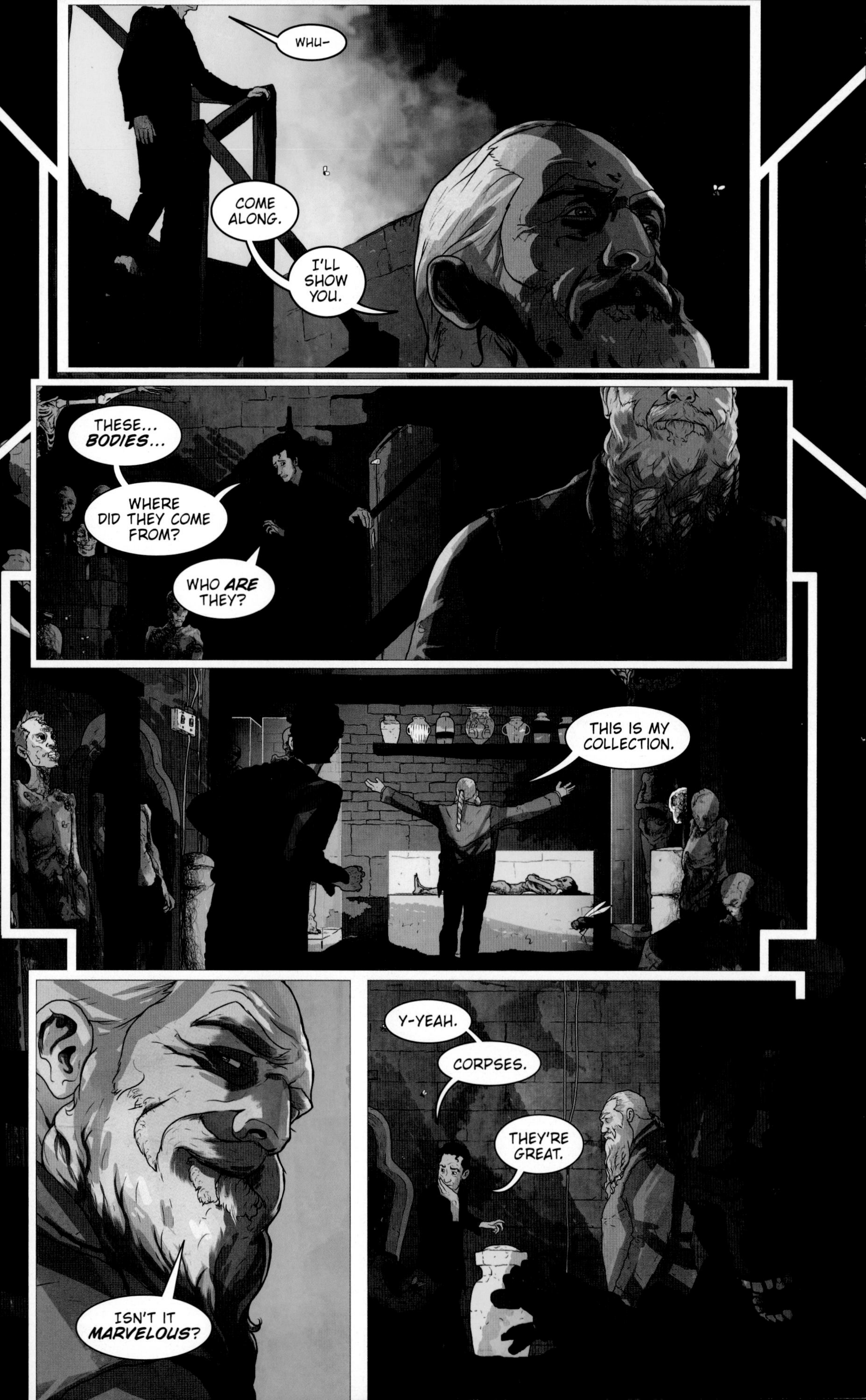
WHU-
COME ALONG.
I'LL SHOW YOU.
THESE... BODIES...
WHERE DID THEY COME FROM?
WHO ARE THEY?
THIS IS MY COLLECTION.
ISN'T IT MARVELOUS?
Y-YEAH.
CORPSES.
THEY'RE GREAT.

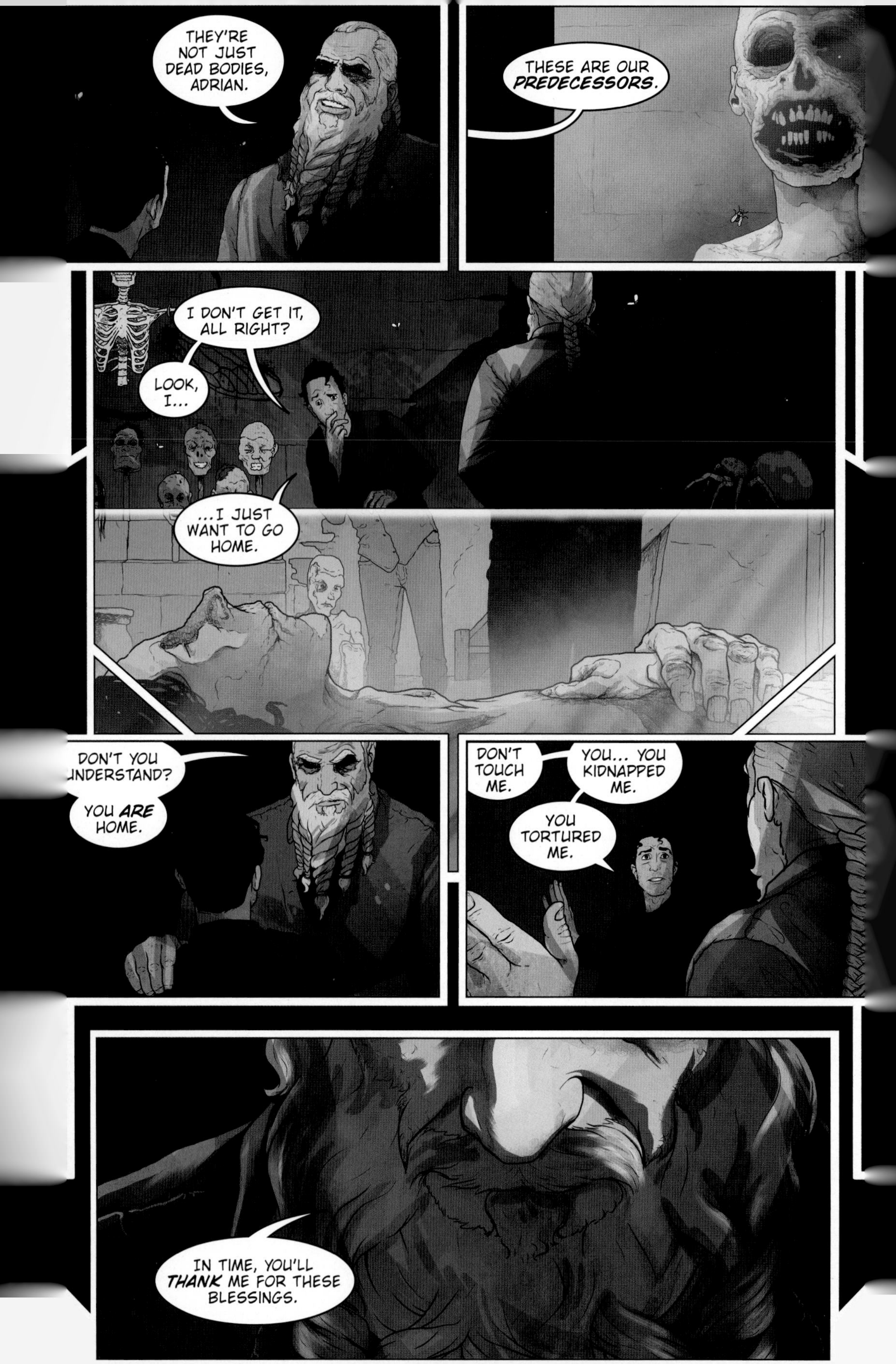
THEY'RE NOT JUST DEAD BODIES, ADRIAN.
THESE ARE OUR *PREDECESSORS*.
I DON'T GET IT, ALL RIGHT?
LOOK, I...
...I JUST WANT TO GO HOME.
DON'T YOU UNDERSTAND?
YOU *ARE* HOME.
DON'T TOUCH ME.
YOU... YOU KIDNAPPED ME.
YOU TORTURED ME.
IN TIME, YOU'LL *THANK* ME FOR THESE BLESSINGS.

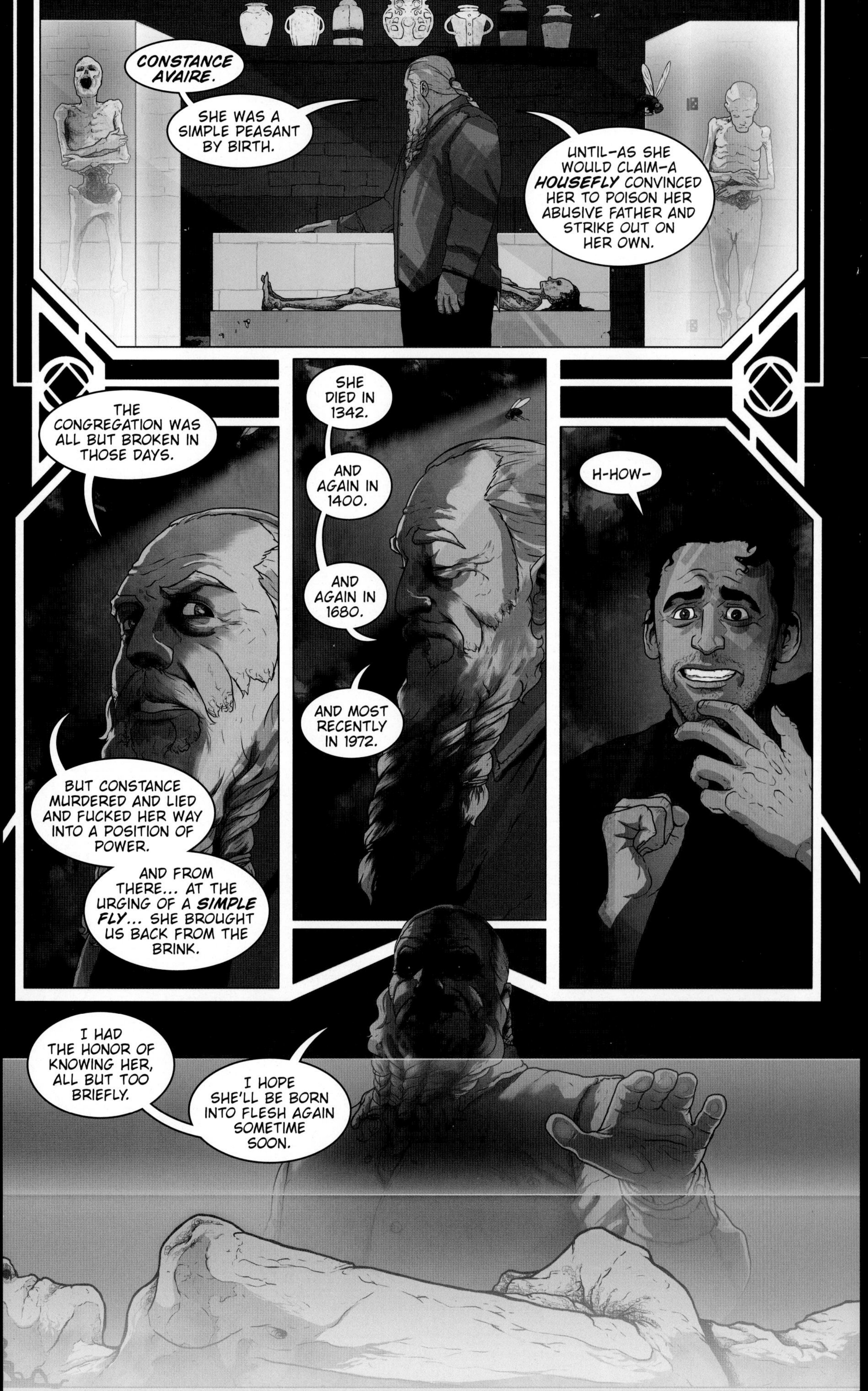

CONSTANCE AVAIRE.
SHE WAS A SIMPLE PEASANT BY BIRTH.
UNTIL-AS SHE WOULD CLAIM-A HOUSEFLY CONVINCED HER TO POISON HER ABUSIVE FATHER AND STRIKE OUT ON HER OWN.
THE CONGREGATION WAS ALL BUT BROKEN IN THOSE DAYS.
BUT CONSTANCE MURDERED AND LIED AND FUCKED HER WAY INTO A POSITION OF POWER.
AND FROM THERE... AT THE URGING OF A SIMPLE FLY... SHE BROUGHT US BACK FROM THE BRINK.
SHE DIED IN 1342.
AND AGAIN IN 1400.
AND AGAIN IN 1680.
AND MOST RECENTLY IN 1972.
H-HOW-
I HAD THE HONOR OF KNOWING HER, ALL BUT TOO BRIEFLY.
I HOPE SHE'LL BE BORN INTO FLESH AGAIN SOMETIME SOON.

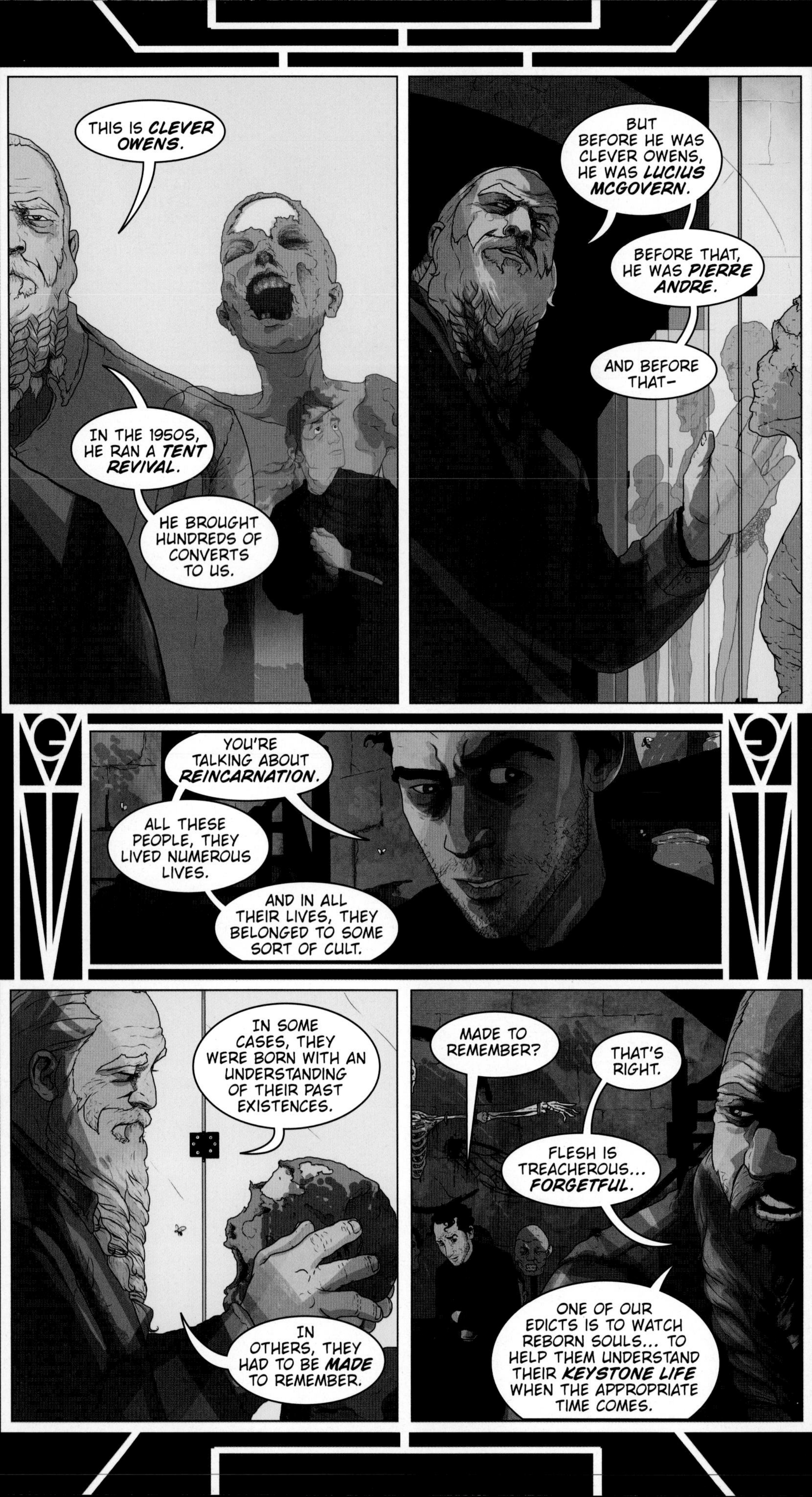
THIS IS CLEVER OWENS.
IN THE 1950S, HE RAN A TENT REVIVAL.
HE BROUGHT HUNDREDS OF CONVERTS TO US.
BUT BEFORE HE WAS CLEVER OWENS, HE WAS LUCIUS MCGOVERN.
BEFORE THAT, HE WAS PIERRE ANDRE.
AND BEFORE THAT–
YOU'RE TALKING ABOUT REINCARNATION.
ALL THESE PEOPLE, THEY LIVED NUMEROUS LIVES.
AND IN ALL THEIR LIVES, THEY BELONGED TO SOME SORT OF CULT.
IN SOME CASES, THEY WERE BORN WITH AN UNDERSTANDING OF THEIR PAST EXISTENCES.
IN OTHERS, THEY HAD TO BE MADE TO REMEMBER.
MADE TO REMEMBER?
THAT'S RIGHT.
FLESH IS TREACHEROUS... FORGETFUL.
ONE OF OUR EDICTS IS TO WATCH REBORN SOULS... TO HELP THEM UNDERSTAND THEIR KEYSTONE LIFE WHEN THE APPROPRIATE TIME COMES.

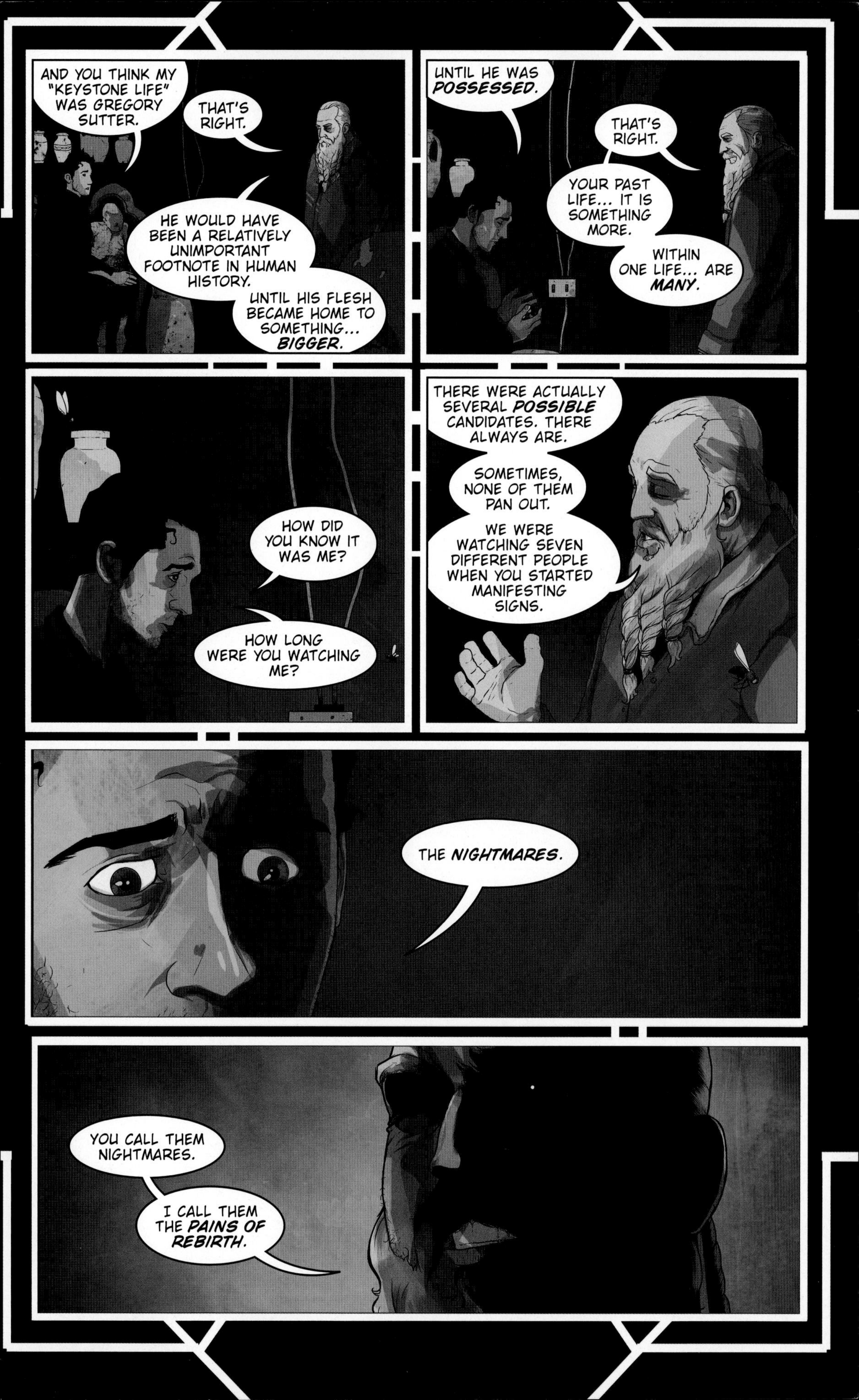
AND YOU THINK MY "KEYSTONE LIFE" WAS GREGORY SUTTER.
THAT'S RIGHT.
HE WOULD HAVE BEEN A RELATIVELY UNIMPORTANT FOOTNOTE IN HUMAN HISTORY.
UNTIL HIS FLESH BECAME HOME TO SOMETHING... BIGGER.
UNTIL HE WAS POSSESSED.
THAT'S RIGHT.
YOUR PAST LIFE... IT IS SOMETHING MORE.
WITHIN ONE LIFE... ARE MANY.
HOW DID YOU KNOW IT WAS ME?
HOW LONG WERE YOU WATCHING ME?
THERE WERE ACTUALLY SEVERAL POSSIBLE CANDIDATES. THERE ALWAYS ARE.
SOMETIMES, NONE OF THEM PAN OUT.
WE WERE WATCHING SEVEN DIFFERENT PEOPLE WHEN YOU STARTED MANIFESTING SIGNS.
THE NIGHTMARES.
YOU CALL THEM NIGHTMARES.
I CALL THEM THE PAINS OF REBIRTH.

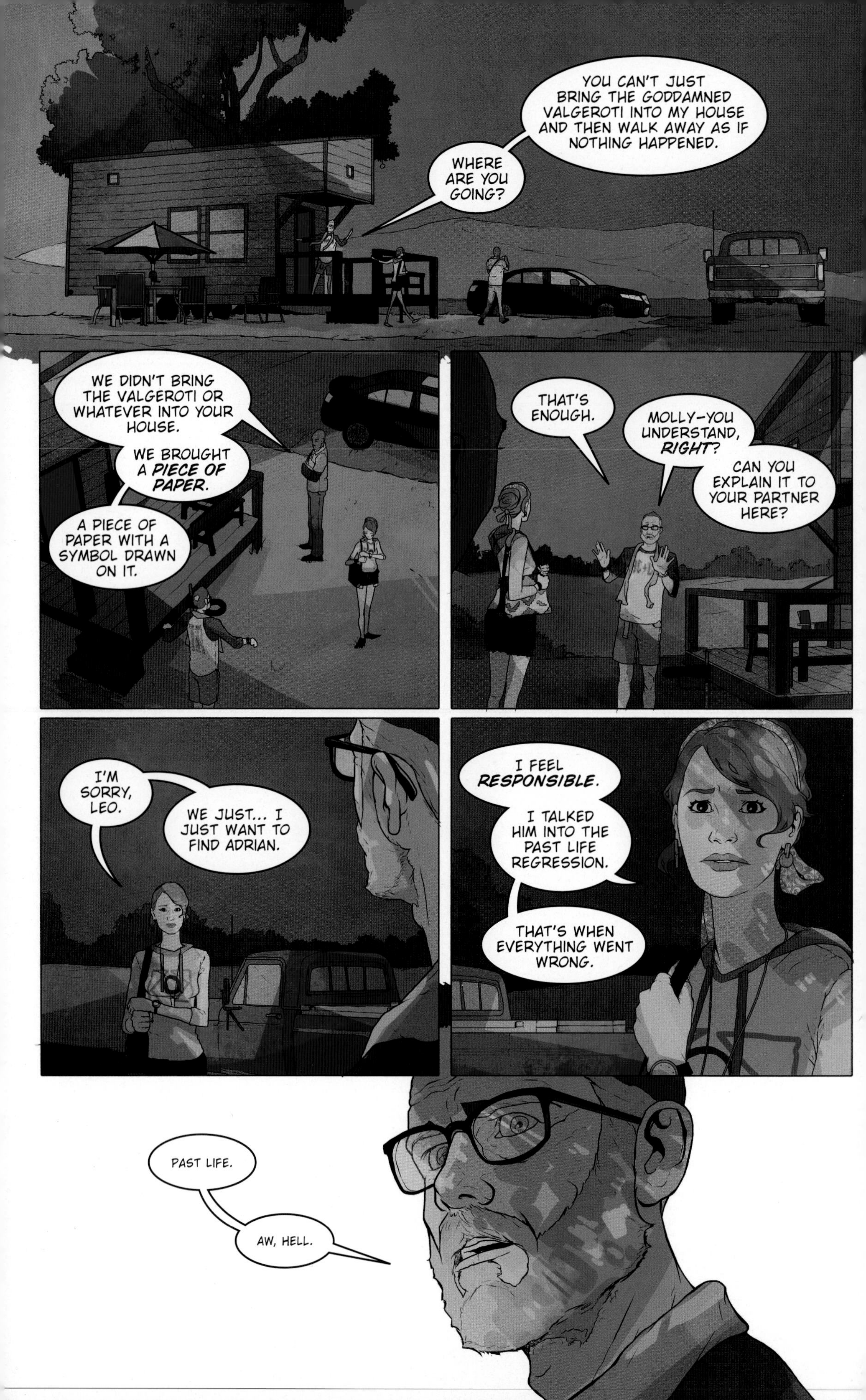
YOU CAN'T JUST BRING THE GODDAMNED VALGEROTI INTO MY HOUSE AND THEN WALK AWAY AS IF NOTHING HAPPENED.
WHERE ARE YOU GOING?
WE DIDN'T BRING THE VALGEROTI OR WHATEVER INTO YOUR HOUSE.
WE BROUGHT A *PIECE OF PAPER*.
A PIECE OF PAPER WITH A SYMBOL DRAWN ON IT.
THAT'S ENOUGH.
MOLLY—YOU UNDERSTAND, *RIGHT*?
CAN YOU EXPLAIN IT TO YOUR PARTNER HERE?
I'M SORRY, LEO.
WE JUST... I JUST WANT TO FIND ADRIAN.
I FEEL *RESPONSIBLE*.
I TALKED HIM INTO THE PAST LIFE REGRESSION.
THAT'S WHEN EVERYTHING WENT WRONG.
PAST LIFE.
AW, HELL.

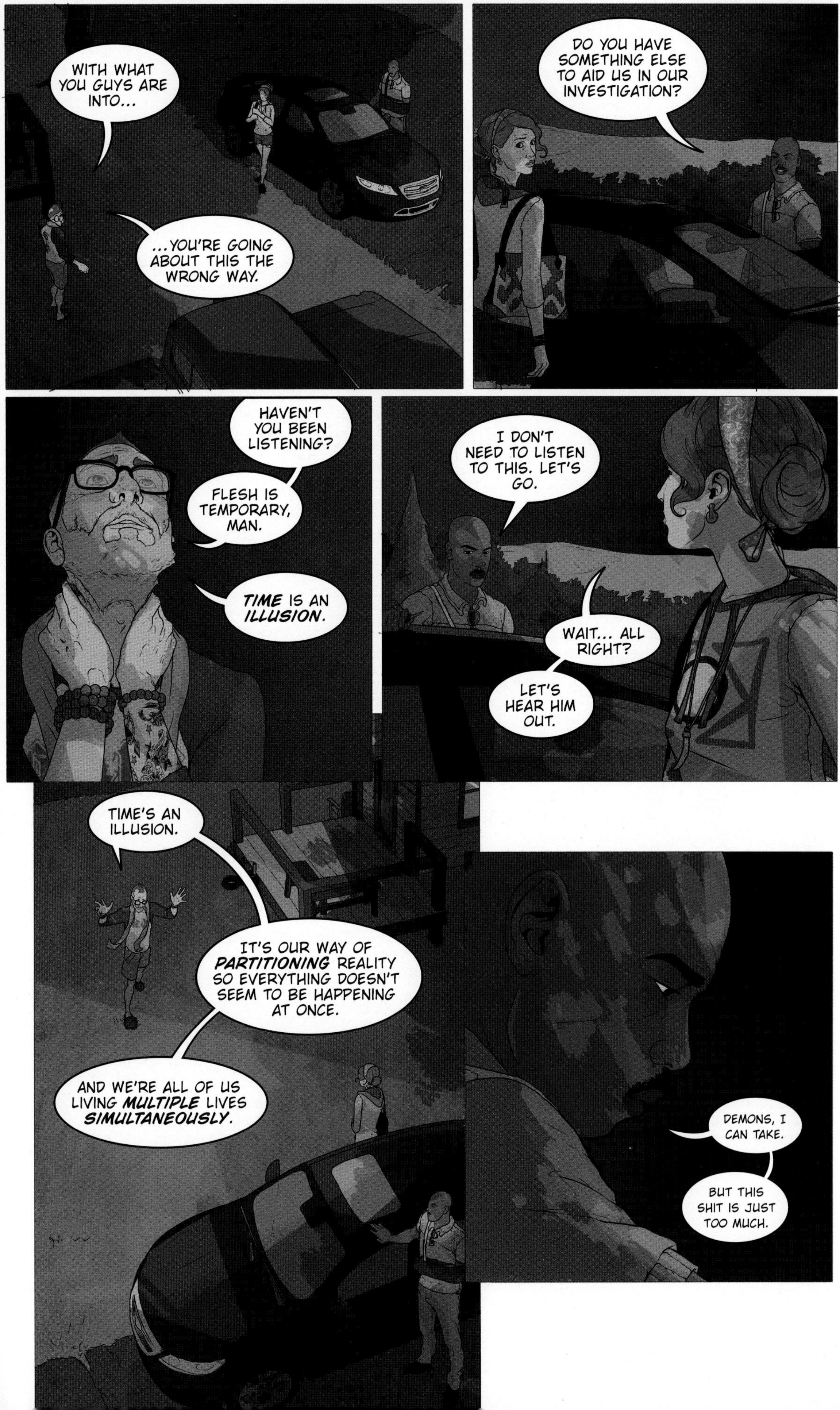
WITH WHAT YOU GUYS ARE INTO...
...YOU'RE GOING ABOUT THIS THE WRONG WAY.
DO YOU HAVE SOMETHING ELSE TO AID US IN OUR INVESTIGATION?
HAVEN'T YOU BEEN LISTENING?
FLESH IS TEMPORARY, MAN.
TIME IS AN *ILLUSION*.
I DON'T NEED TO LISTEN TO THIS. LET'S GO.
WAIT... ALL RIGHT?
LET'S HEAR HIM OUT.
TIME'S AN ILLUSION.
IT'S OUR WAY OF *PARTITIONING* REALITY SO EVERYTHING DOESN'T SEEM TO BE HAPPENING AT ONCE.
AND WE'RE ALL OF US LIVING *MULTIPLE* LIVES *SIMULTANEOUSLY*.
DEMONS, I CAN TAKE.
BUT THIS SHIT IS JUST TOO MUCH.

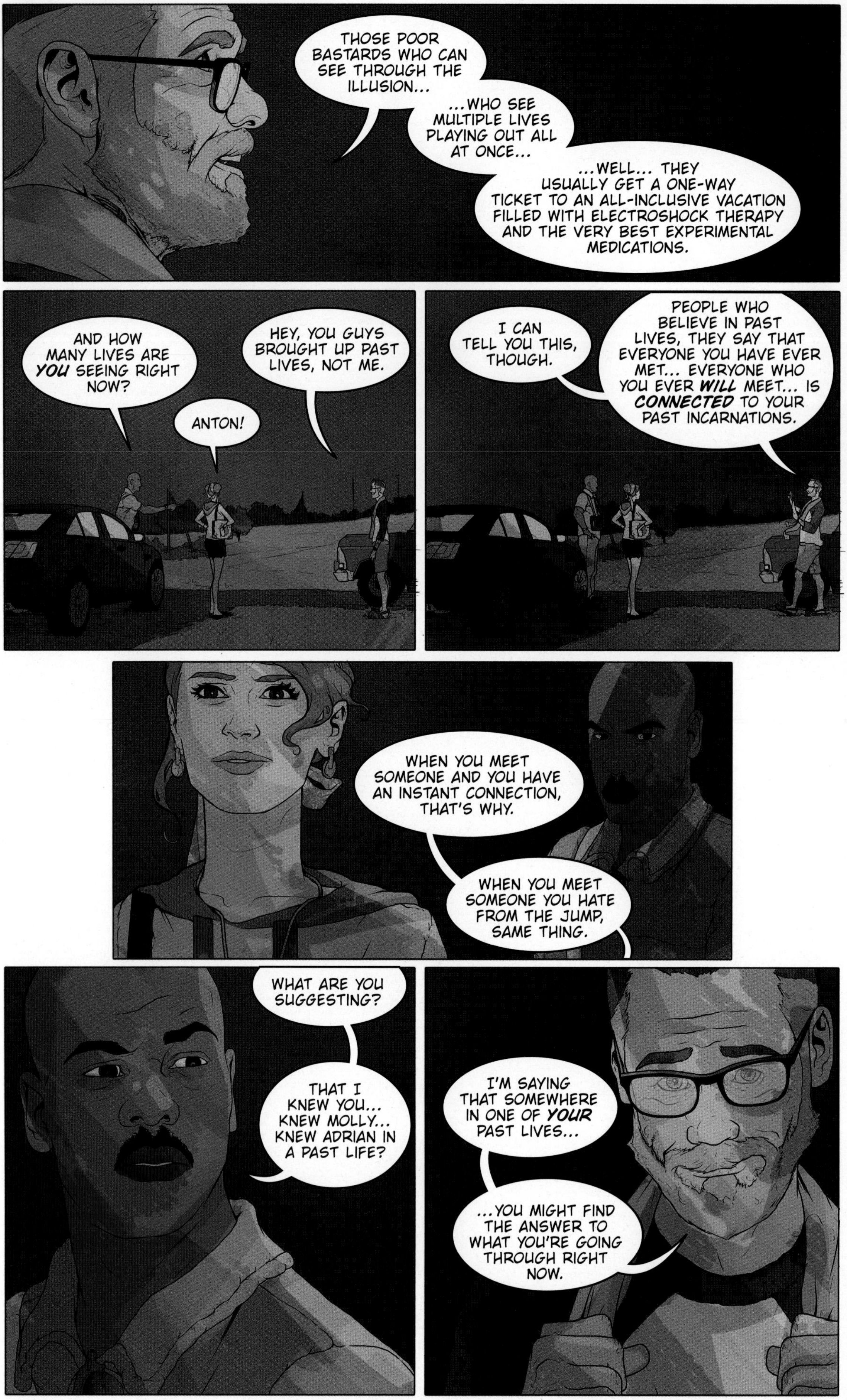
THOSE POOR BASTARDS WHO CAN SEE THROUGH THE ILLUSION...
...WHO SEE MULTIPLE LIVES PLAYING OUT ALL AT ONCE...
...WELL... THEY USUALLY GET A ONE-WAY TICKET TO AN ALL-INCLUSIVE VACATION FILLED WITH ELECTROSHOCK THERAPY AND THE VERY BEST EXPERIMENTAL MEDICATIONS.
AND HOW MANY LIVES ARE *YOU* SEEING RIGHT NOW?
ANTON!
HEY, YOU GUYS BROUGHT UP PAST LIVES, NOT ME.
I CAN TELL YOU THIS, THOUGH.
PEOPLE WHO BELIEVE IN PAST LIVES, THEY SAY THAT EVERYONE YOU HAVE EVER MET... EVERYONE WHO YOU EVER *WILL* MEET... IS *CONNECTED* TO YOUR PAST INCARNATIONS.
WHEN YOU MEET SOMEONE AND YOU HAVE AN INSTANT CONNECTION, THAT'S WHY.
WHEN YOU MEET SOMEONE YOU HATE FROM THE JUMP, SAME THING.
WHAT ARE YOU SUGGESTING?
THAT I KNEW YOU... KNEW MOLLY... KNEW ADRIAN IN A PAST LIFE?
I'M SAYING THAT SOMEWHERE IN ONE OF *YOUR* PAST LIVES...
...YOU MIGHT FIND THE ANSWER TO WHAT YOU'RE GOING THROUGH RIGHT NOW.

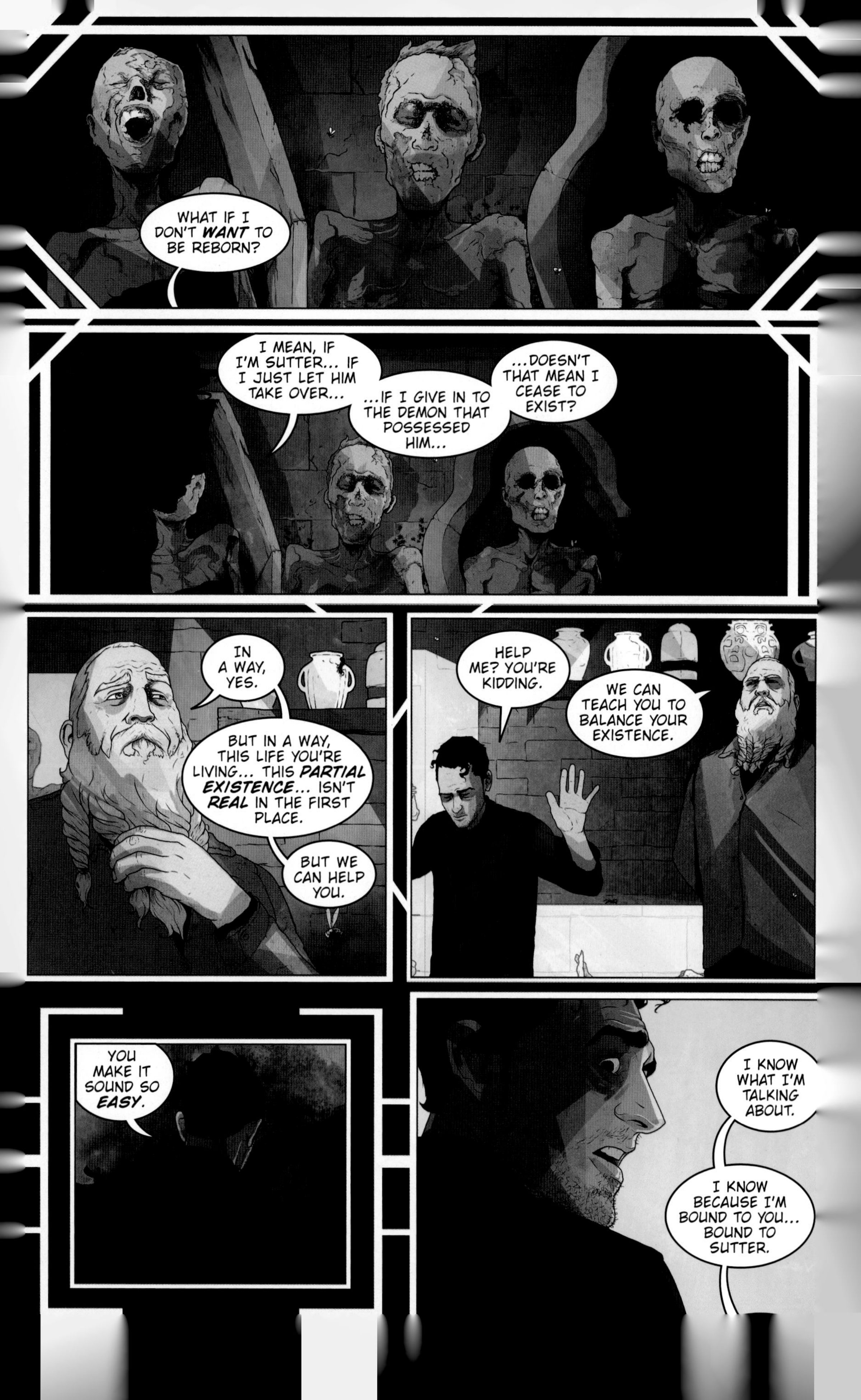
WHAT IF I DON'T **WANT** TO BE REBORN?
I MEAN, IF I'M SUTTER... IF I JUST LET HIM TAKE OVER...
...IF I GIVE IN TO THE DEMON THAT POSSESSED HIM...
...DOESN'T THAT MEAN I CEASE TO EXIST?
IN A WAY, YES.
BUT IN A WAY, THIS LIFE YOU'RE LIVING... THIS ***PARTIAL EXISTENCE***... ISN'T ***REAL*** IN THE FIRST PLACE.
BUT WE CAN HELP YOU.
HELP ME? YOU'RE KIDDING.
WE CAN TEACH YOU TO BALANCE YOUR EXISTENCE.
YOU MAKE IT SOUND SO ***EASY***.
I KNOW WHAT I'M TALKING ABOUT.
I KNOW BECAUSE I'M BOUND TO YOU... BOUND TO SUTTER.

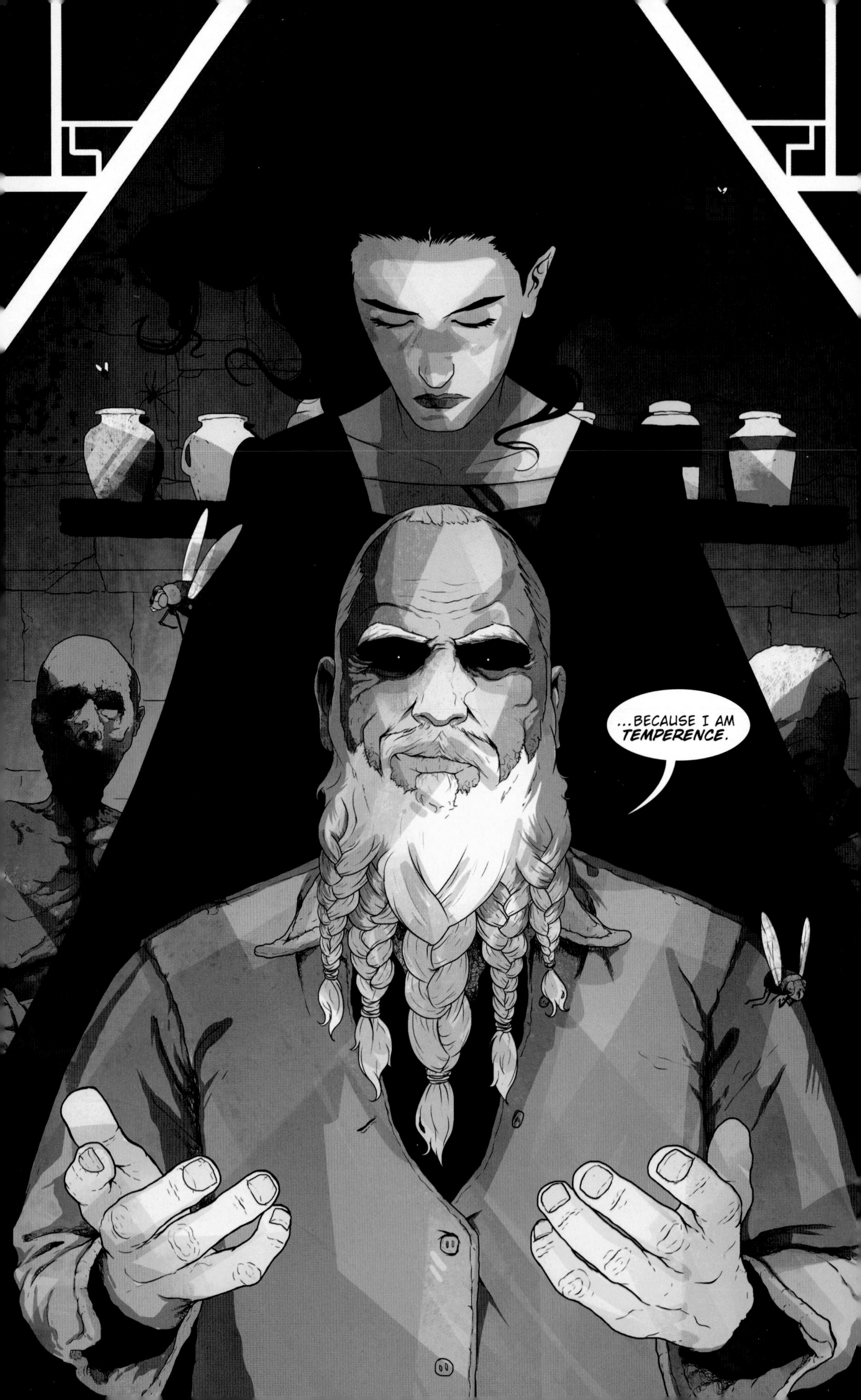
...BECAUSE I AM TEMPERENCE.

EIGHT

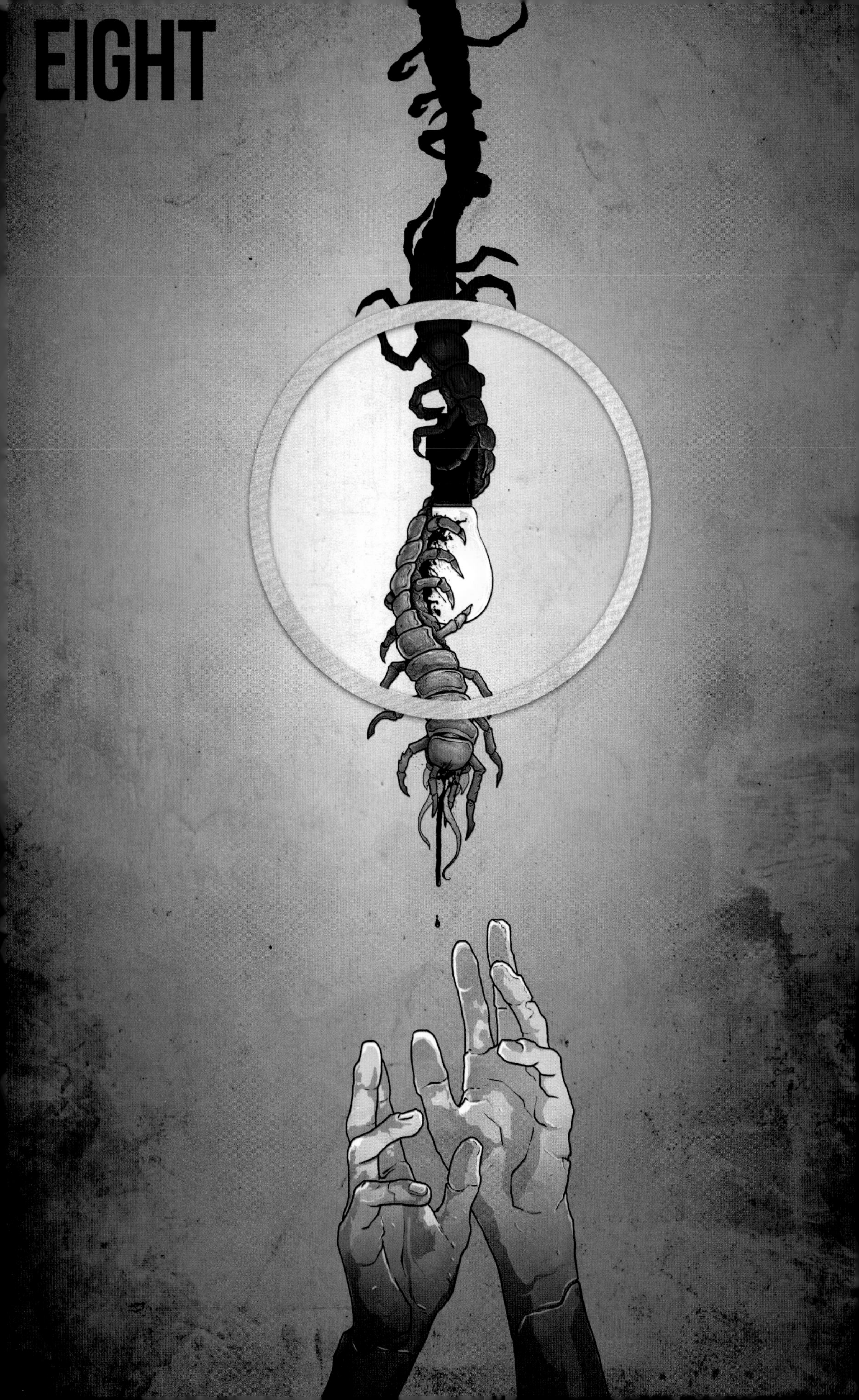

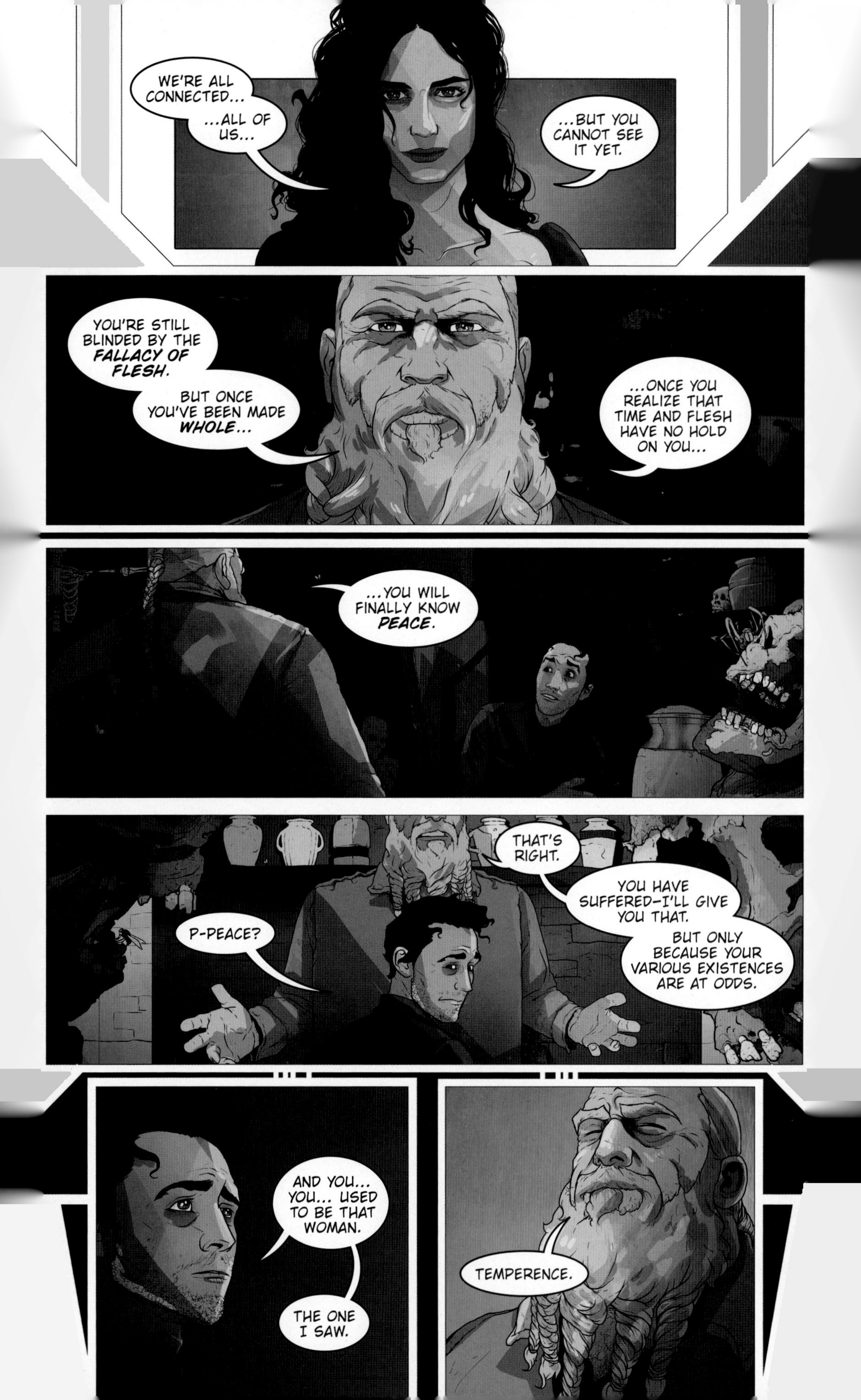
WE'RE ALL CONNECTED...
...ALL OF US...
...BUT YOU CANNOT SEE IT YET.
YOU'RE STILL BLINDED BY THE **FALLACY OF FLESH**.
BUT ONCE YOU'VE BEEN MADE **WHOLE**...
...ONCE YOU REALIZE THAT TIME AND FLESH HAVE NO HOLD ON YOU...
...YOU WILL FINALLY KNOW **PEACE**.
P-PEACE?
THAT'S RIGHT.
YOU HAVE SUFFERED–I'LL GIVE YOU THAT.
BUT ONLY BECAUSE YOUR VARIOUS EXISTENCES ARE AT ODDS.
AND YOU... YOU... USED TO BE THAT WOMAN.
THE ONE I SAW.
TEMPERENCE.

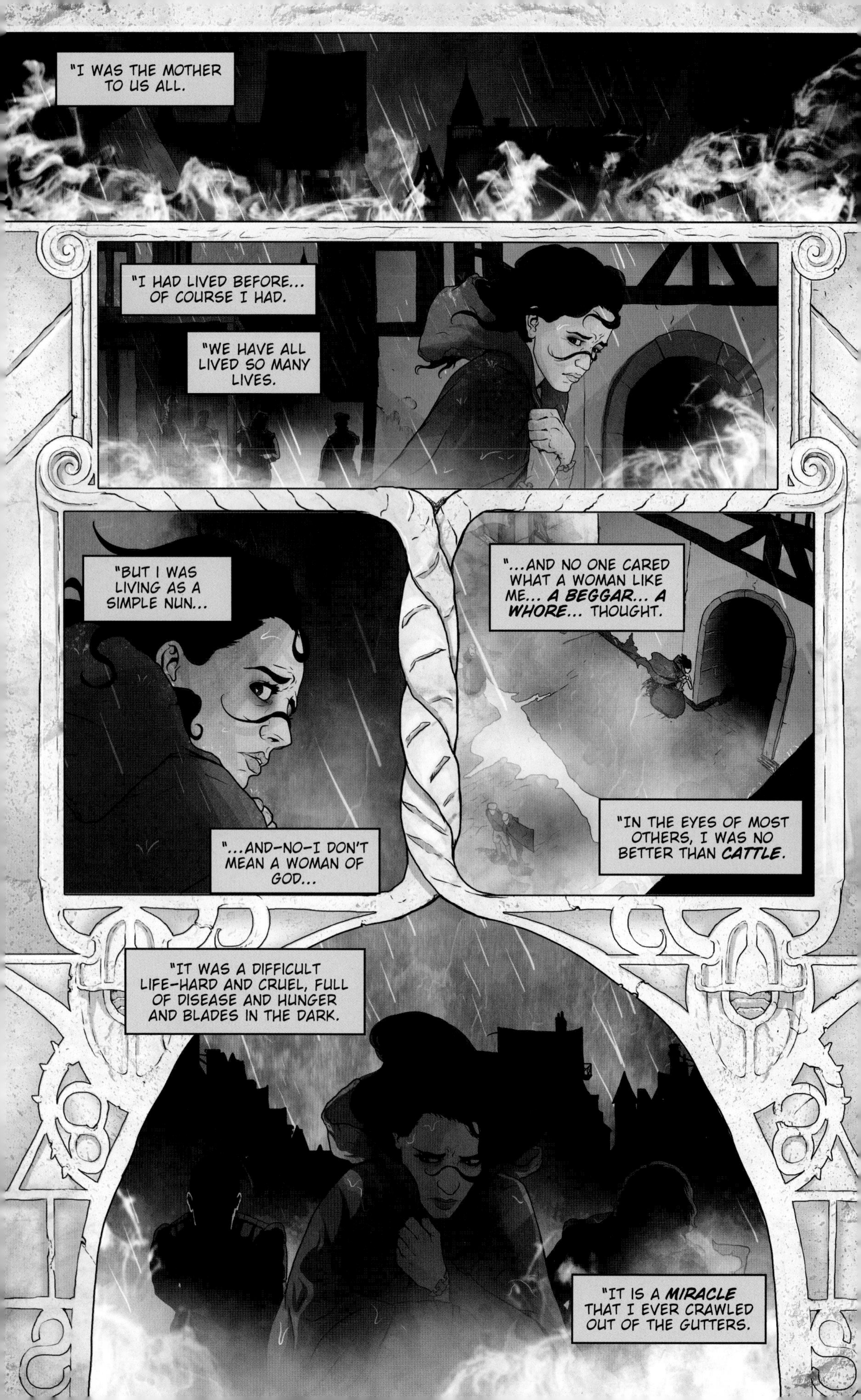
"I WAS THE MOTHER TO US ALL.
"I HAD LIVED BEFORE... OF COURSE I HAD.
"WE HAVE ALL LIVED SO MANY LIVES.
"BUT I WAS LIVING AS A SIMPLE NUN...
"...AND—NO—I DON'T MEAN A WOMAN OF GOD...
"...AND NO ONE CARED WHAT A WOMAN LIKE ME... A BEGGAR... A WHORE... THOUGHT.
"IN THE EYES OF MOST OTHERS, I WAS NO BETTER THAN CATTLE.
"IT WAS A DIFFICULT LIFE—HARD AND CRUEL, FULL OF DISEASE AND HUNGER AND BLADES IN THE DARK.
"IT IS A MIRACLE THAT I EVER CRAWLED OUT OF THE GUTTERS.

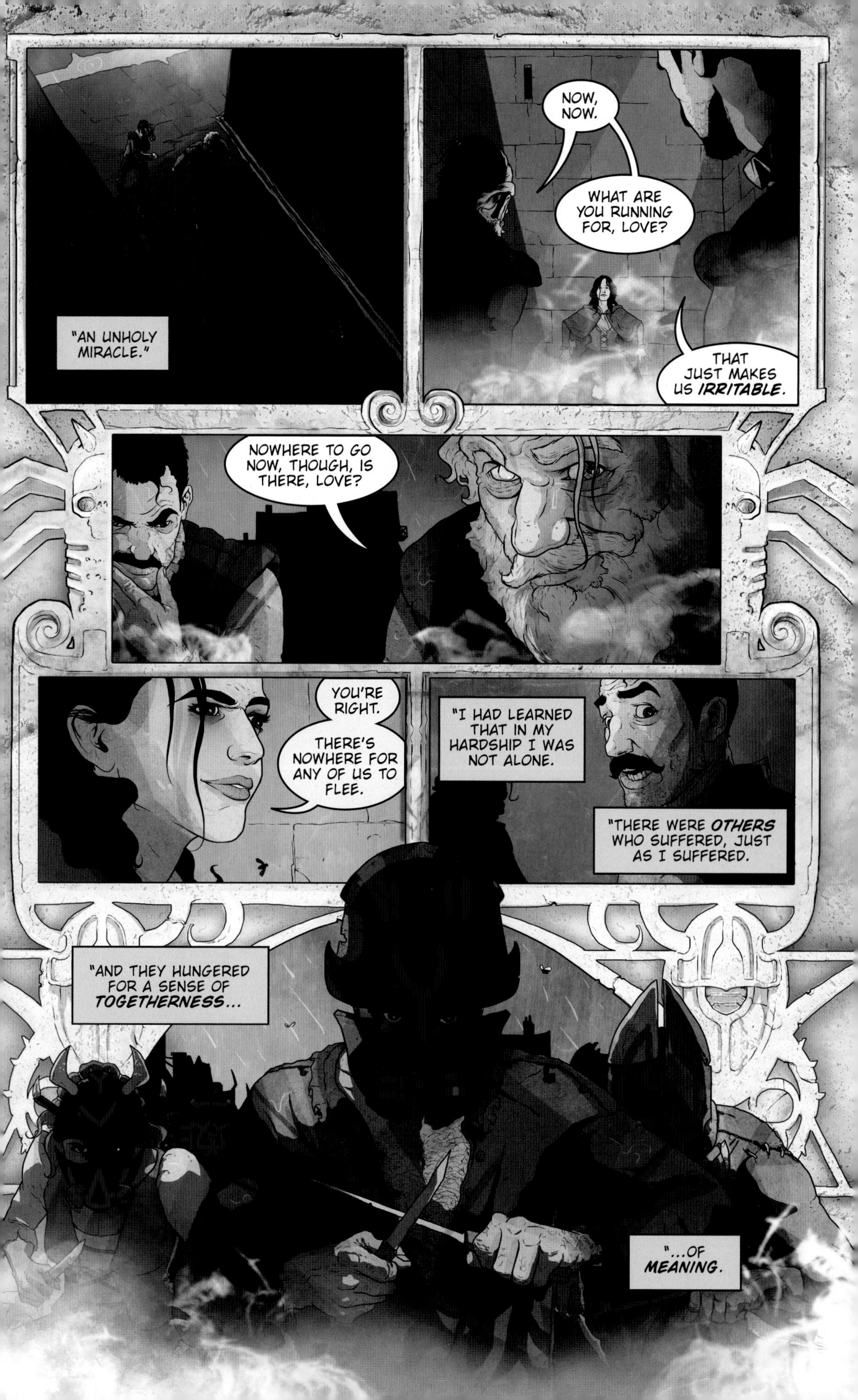
"AN UNHOLY MIRACLE."
NOW, NOW.
WHAT ARE YOU RUNNING FOR, LOVE?
THAT JUST MAKES US IRRITABLE.
NOWHERE TO GO NOW, THOUGH, IS THERE, LOVE?
YOU'RE RIGHT.
THERE'S NOWHERE FOR ANY OF US TO FLEE.
"I HAD LEARNED THAT IN MY HARDSHIP I WAS NOT ALONE.
"THERE WERE OTHERS WHO SUFFERED, JUST AS I SUFFERED.
"AND THEY HUNGERED FOR A SENSE OF TOGETHERNESS...
"...OF MEANING.

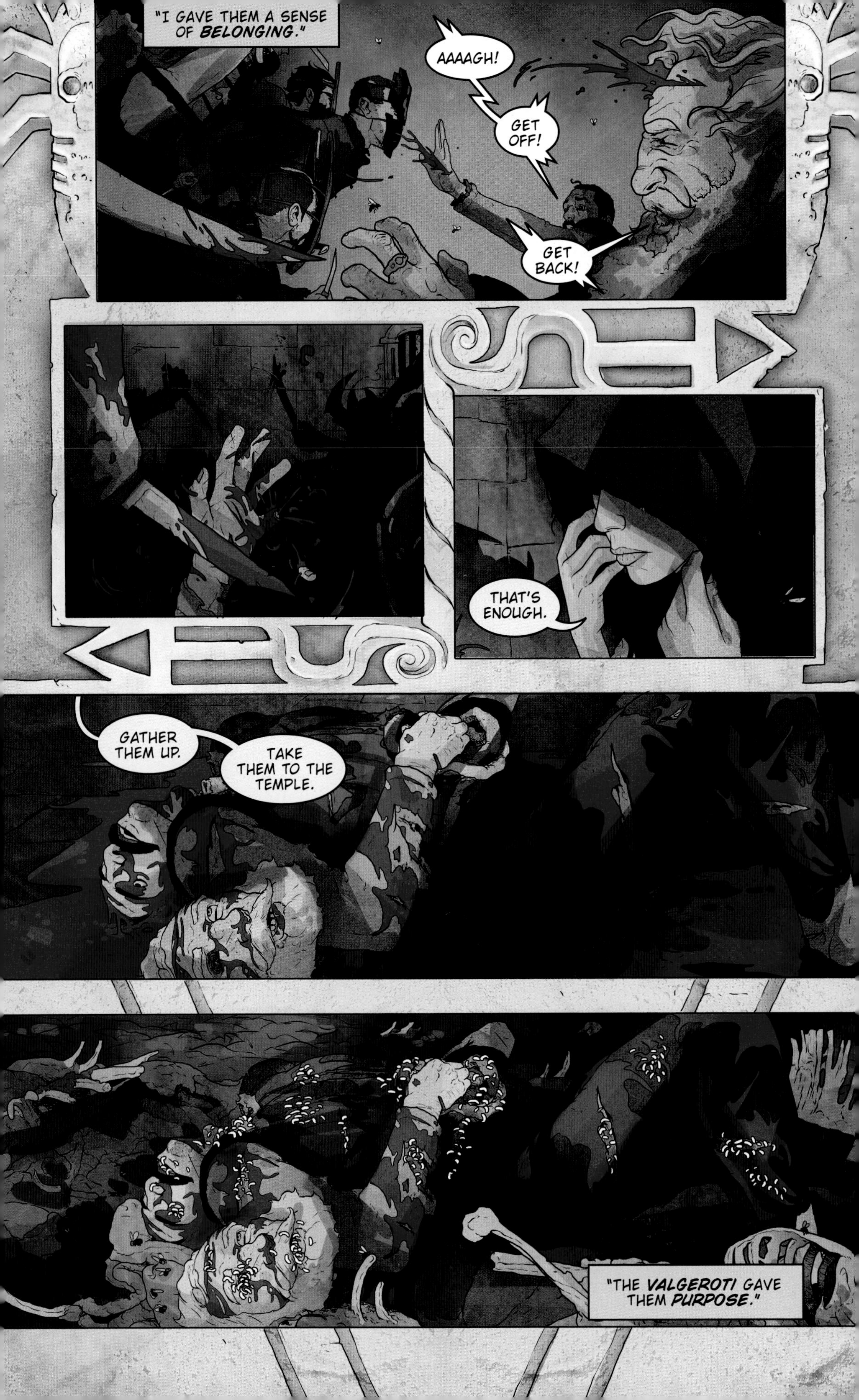
"I GAVE THEM A SENSE OF BELONGING."
AAAAGH!
GET OFF!
GET BACK!
THAT'S ENOUGH.
GATHER THEM UP.
TAKE THEM TO THE TEMPLE.
"THE VALGEROTI GAVE THEM PURPOSE."

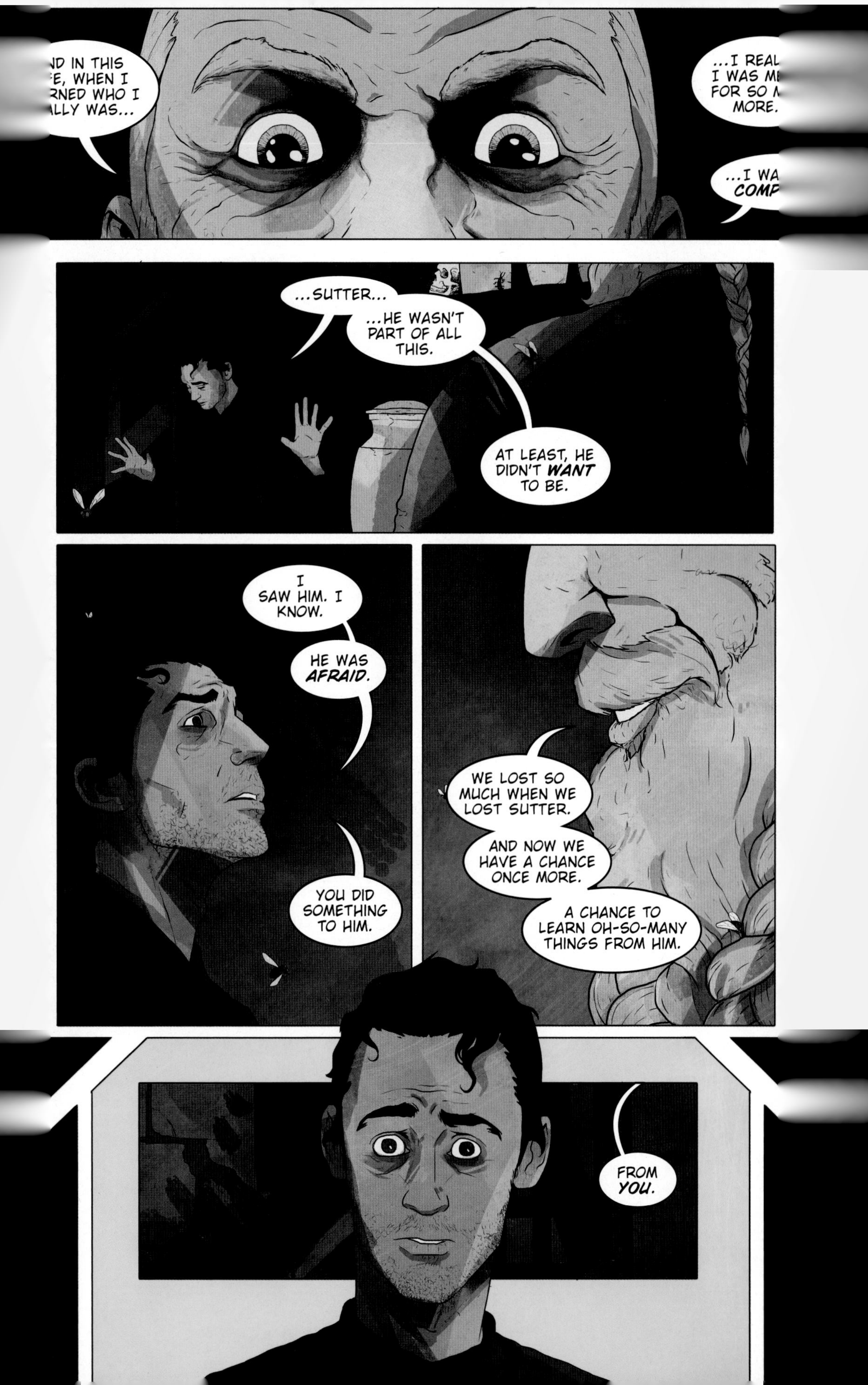
ND IN THIS FE, WHEN I RNED WHO I ALLY WAS...
...I REAL I WAS ME FOR SO M MORE.
...I WA COMP
...SUTTER...
...HE WASN'T PART OF ALL THIS.
AT LEAST, HE DIDN'T WANT TO BE.
I SAW HIM. I KNOW.
HE WAS AFRAID.
YOU DID SOMETHING TO HIM.
WE LOST SO MUCH WHEN WE LOST SUTTER.
AND NOW WE HAVE A CHANCE ONCE MORE.
A CHANCE TO LEARN OH-SO-MANY THINGS FROM HIM.
FROM YOU.

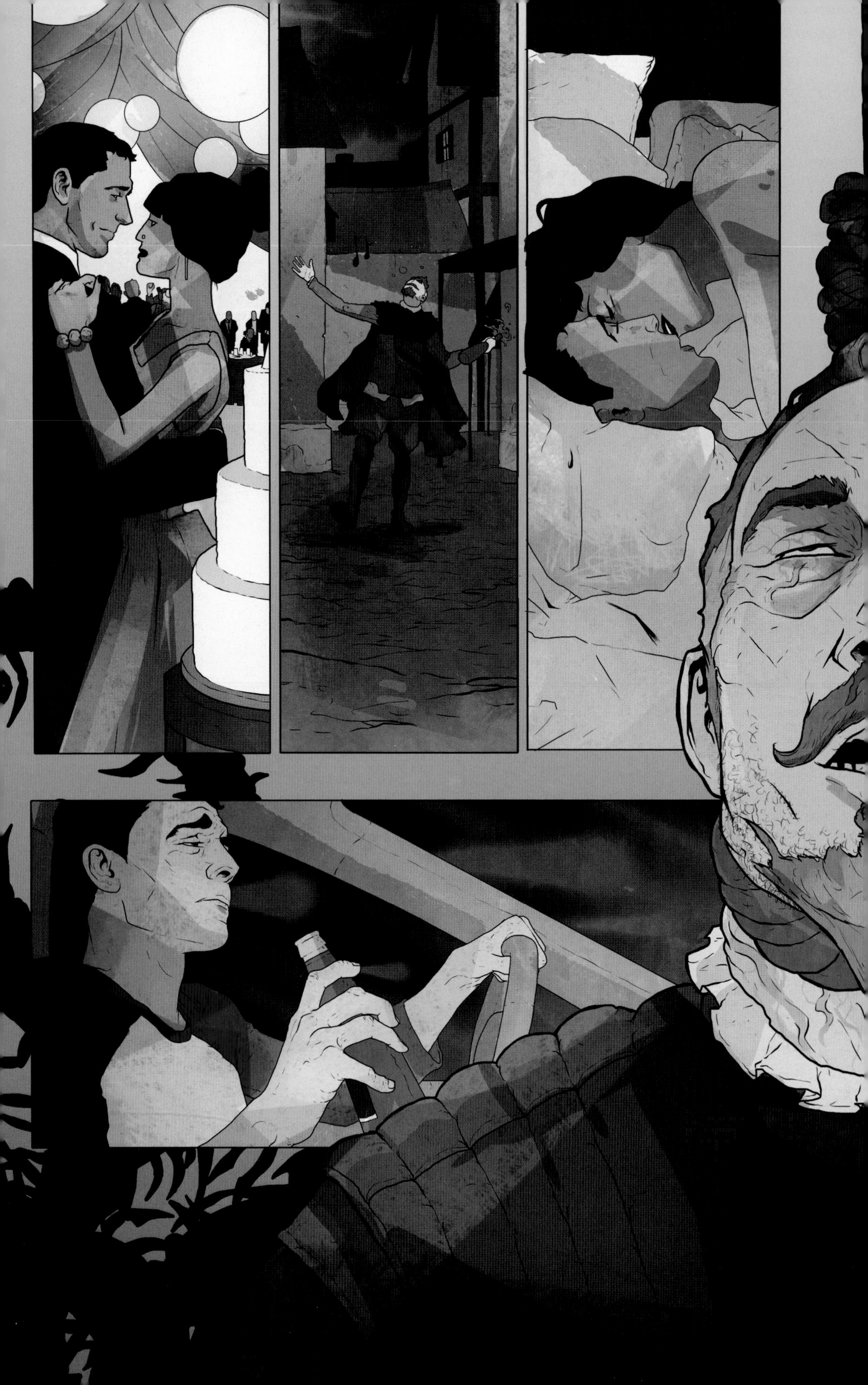

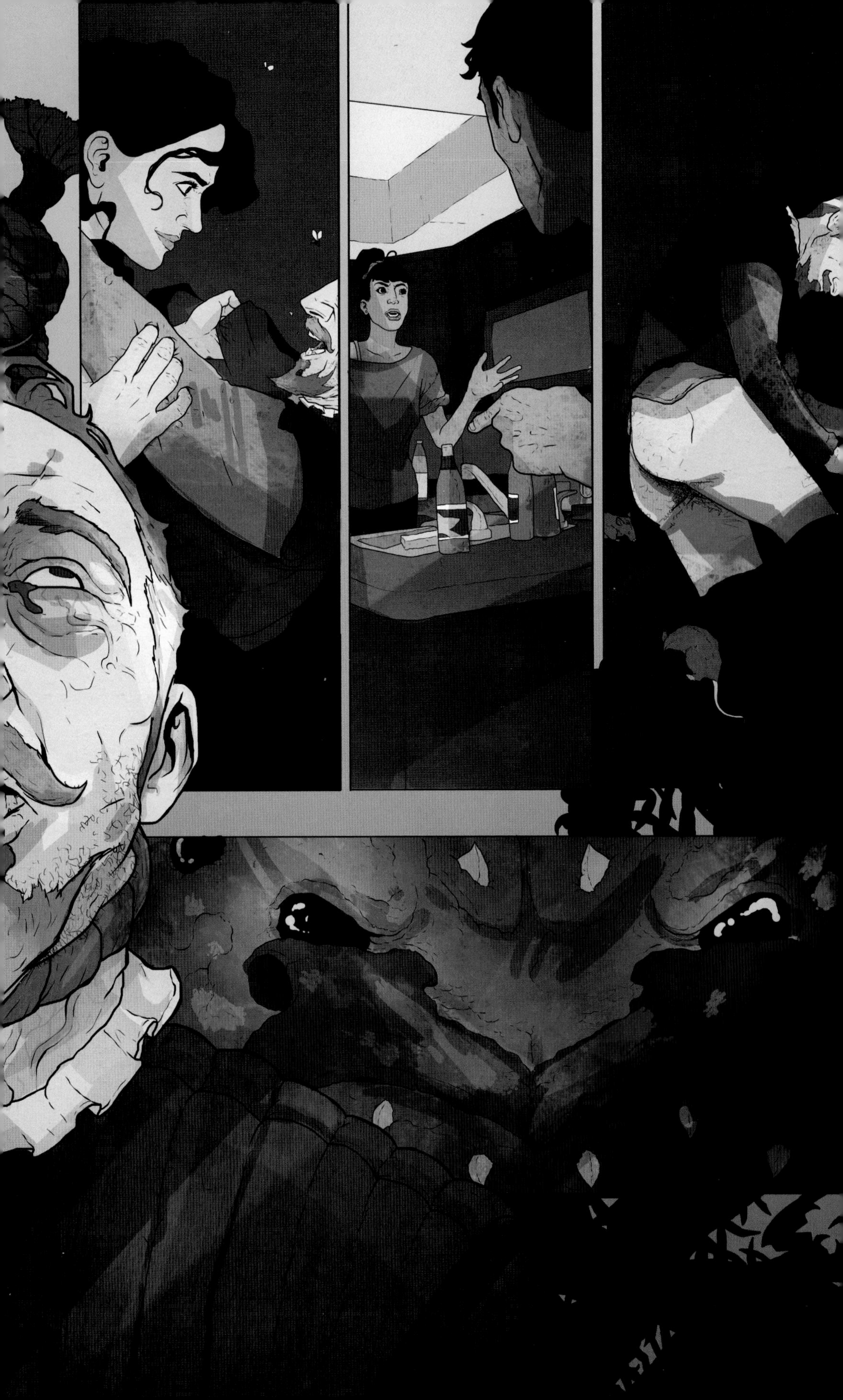

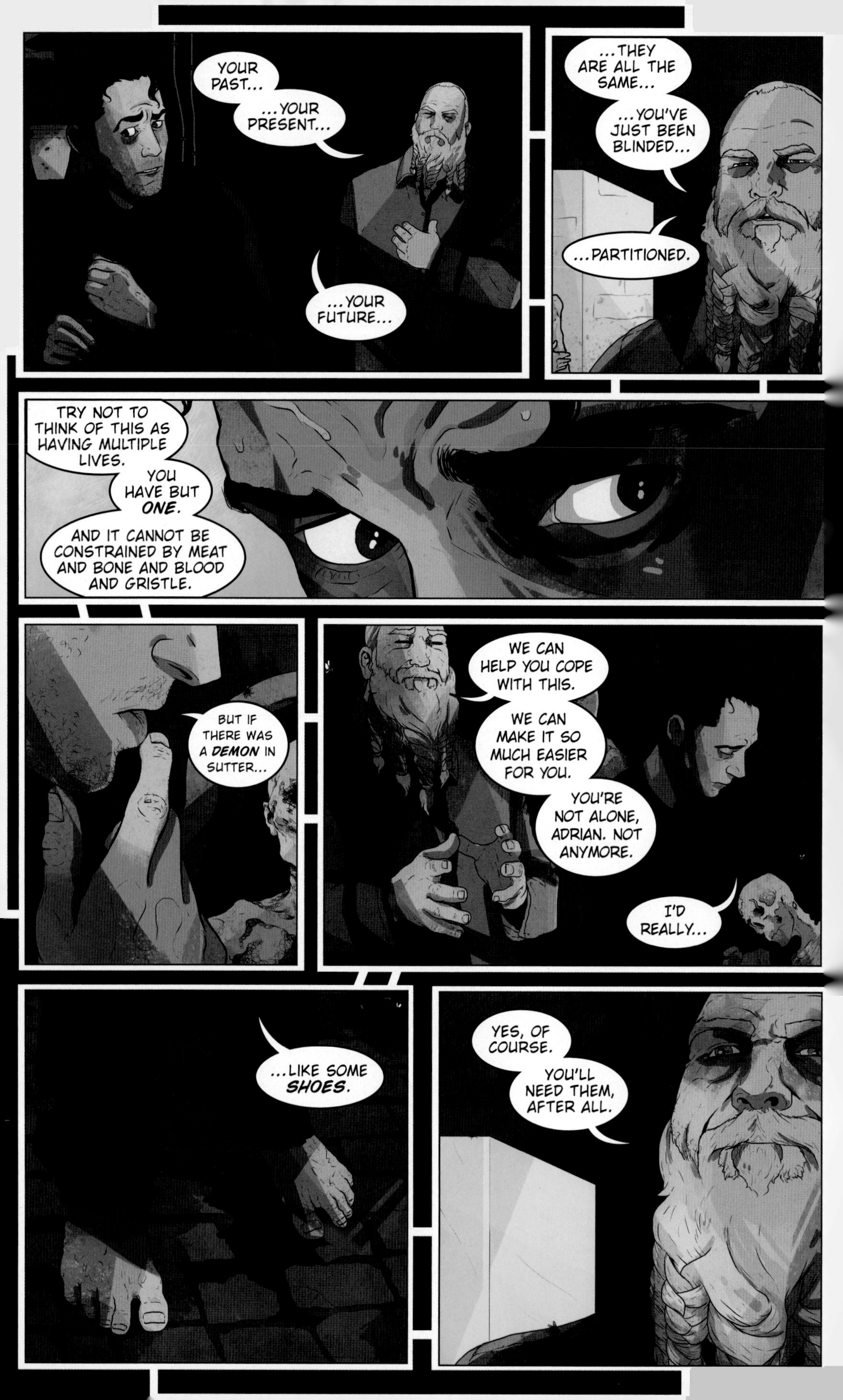
YOUR PAST...
...YOUR PRESENT...
...YOUR FUTURE...
...THEY ARE ALL THE SAME...
...YOU'VE JUST BEEN BLINDED...
...PARTITIONED.
TRY NOT TO THINK OF THIS AS HAVING MULTIPLE LIVES.
YOU HAVE BUT *ONE*.
AND IT CANNOT BE CONSTRAINED BY MEAT AND BONE AND BLOOD AND GRISTLE.
BUT IF THERE WAS A *DEMON* IN SUTTER...
WE CAN HELP YOU COPE WITH THIS.
WE CAN MAKE IT SO MUCH EASIER FOR YOU.
YOU'RE NOT ALONE, ADRIAN. NOT ANYMORE.
I'D REALLY...
...LIKE SOME *SHOES*.
YES, OF COURSE.
YOU'LL NEED THEM, AFTER ALL.

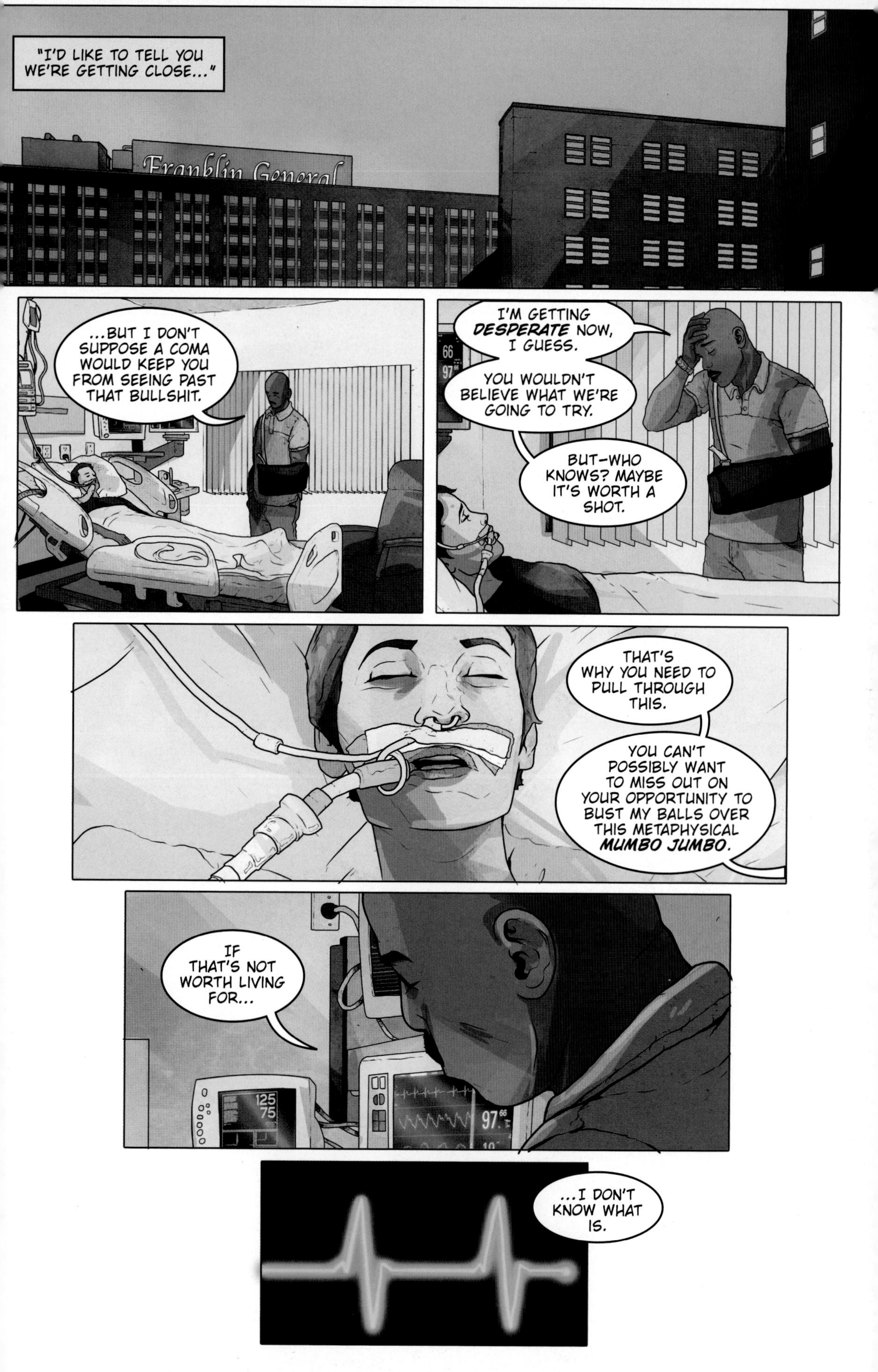
"I'D LIKE TO TELL YOU WE'RE GETTING CLOSE..."
Franklin General
...BUT I DON'T SUPPOSE A COMA WOULD KEEP YOU FROM SEEING PAST THAT BULLSHIT.
I'M GETTING DESPERATE NOW, I GUESS.
YOU WOULDN'T BELIEVE WHAT WE'RE GOING TO TRY.
BUT–WHO KNOWS? MAYBE IT'S WORTH A SHOT.
THAT'S WHY YOU NEED TO PULL THROUGH THIS.
YOU CAN'T POSSIBLY WANT TO MISS OUT ON YOUR OPPORTUNITY TO BUST MY BALLS OVER THIS METAPHYSICAL MUMBO JUMBO.
IF THAT'S NOT WORTH LIVING FOR...
...I DON'T KNOW WHAT IS.

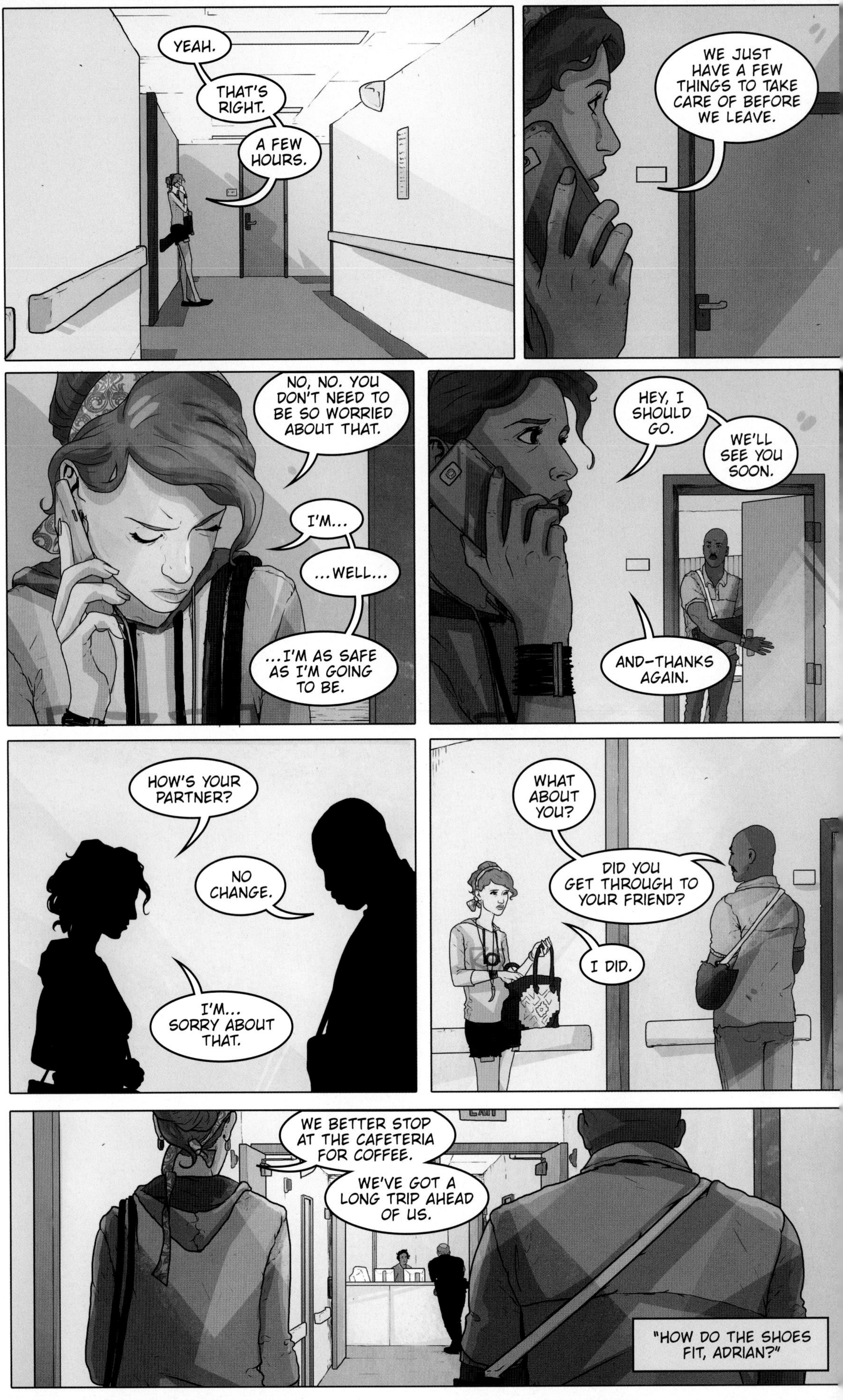
YEAH.
THAT'S RIGHT.
A FEW HOURS.
WE JUST HAVE A FEW THINGS TO TAKE CARE OF BEFORE WE LEAVE.
NO, NO. YOU DON'T NEED TO BE SO WORRIED ABOUT THAT.
I'M...
...WELL...
...I'M AS SAFE AS I'M GOING TO BE.
HEY, I SHOULD GO.
WE'LL SEE YOU SOON.
AND—THANKS AGAIN.
HOW'S YOUR PARTNER?
NO CHANGE.
I'M... SORRY ABOUT THAT.
WHAT ABOUT YOU?
DID YOU GET THROUGH TO YOUR FRIEND?
I DID.
WE BETTER STOP AT THE CAFETERIA FOR COFFEE.
WE'VE GOT A LONG TRIP AHEAD OF US.
"HOW DO THE SHOES FIT, ADRIAN?"

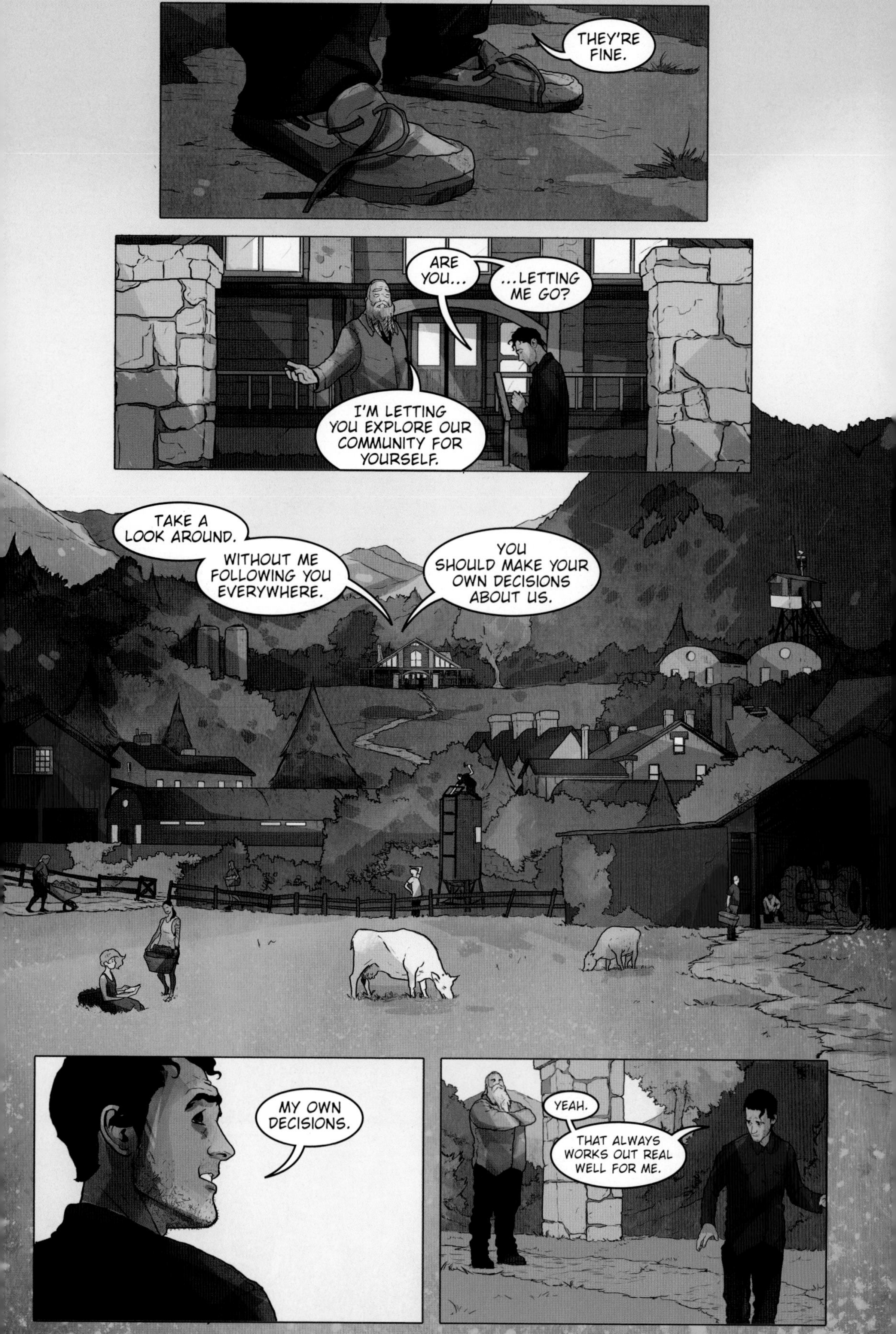
THEY'RE FINE.
ARE YOU...
...LETTING ME GO?
I'M LETTING YOU EXPLORE OUR COMMUNITY FOR YOURSELF.
TAKE A LOOK AROUND.
WITHOUT ME FOLLOWING YOU EVERYWHERE.
YOU SHOULD MAKE YOUR OWN DECISIONS ABOUT US.
MY OWN DECISIONS.
YEAH.
THAT ALWAYS WORKS OUT REAL WELL FOR ME.

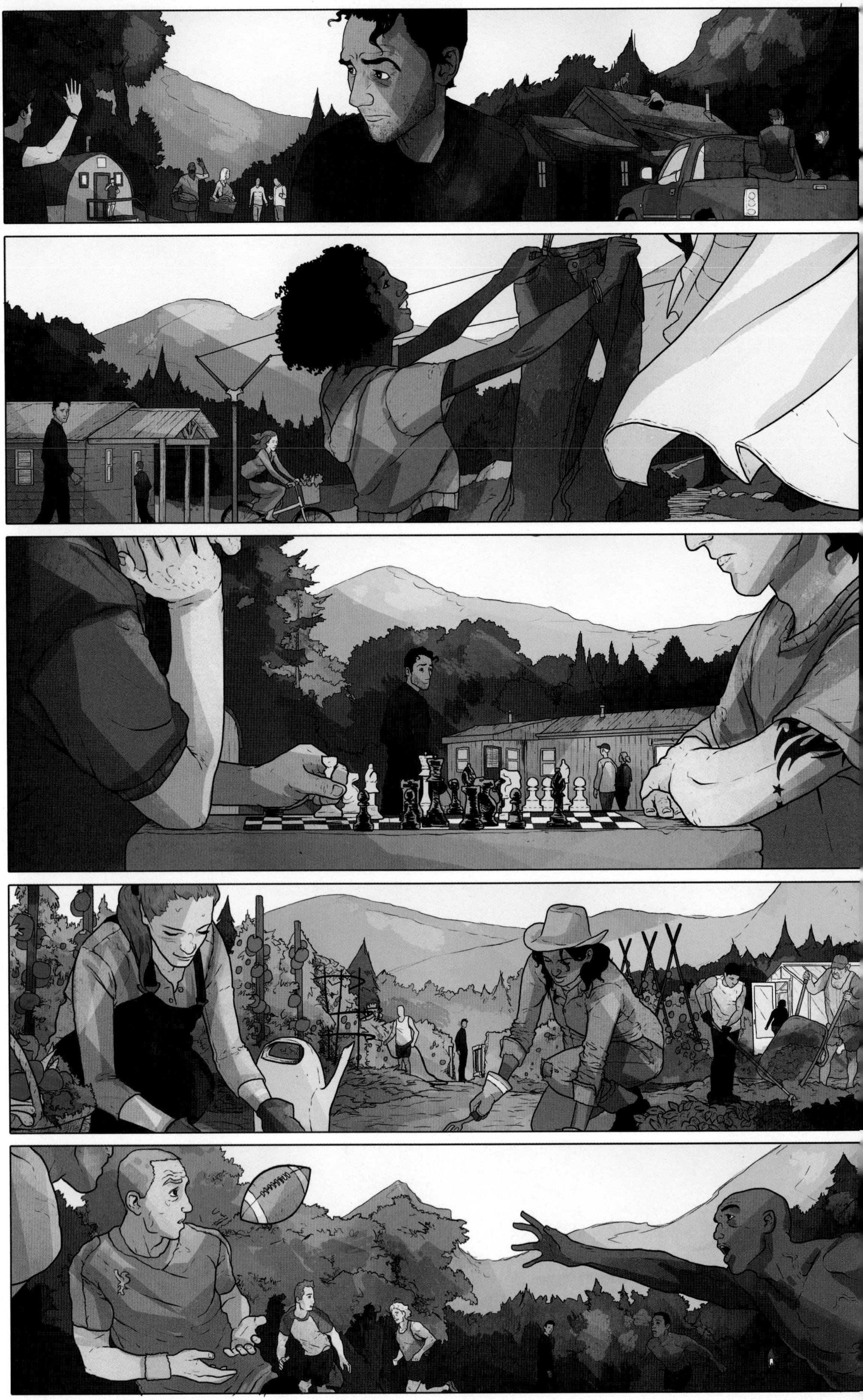

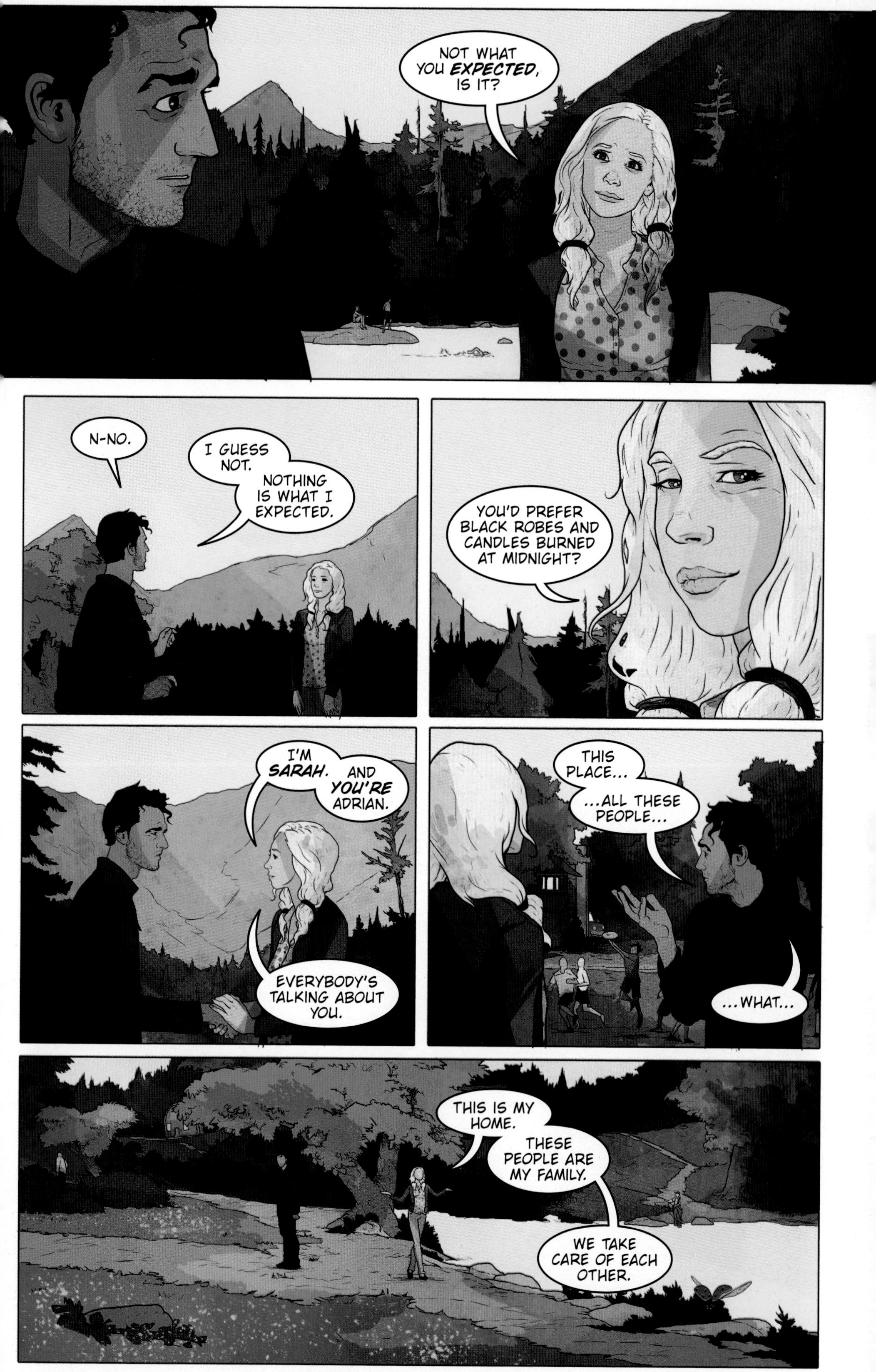
NOT WHAT YOU *EXPECTED*, IS IT?
N-NO.
I GUESS NOT.
NOTHING IS WHAT I EXPECTED.
YOU'D PREFER BLACK ROBES AND CANDLES BURNED AT MIDNIGHT?
I'M *SARAH*.
AND *YOU'RE* ADRIAN.
EVERYBODY'S TALKING ABOUT YOU.
THIS PLACE...
...ALL THESE PEOPLE...
...WHAT...
THIS IS MY HOME.
THESE PEOPLE ARE MY FAMILY.
WE TAKE CARE OF EACH OTHER.

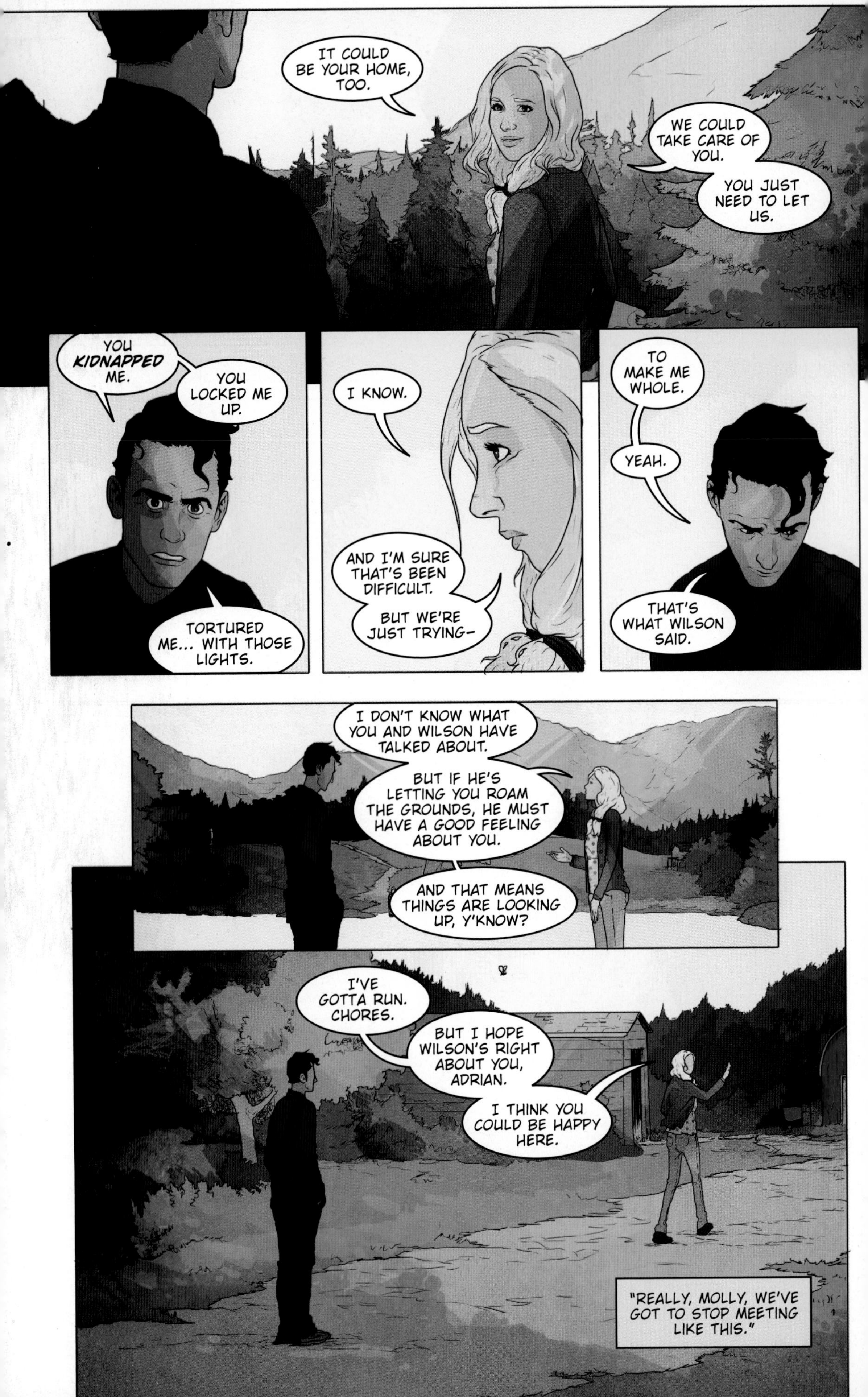
IT COULD BE YOUR HOME, TOO.
WE COULD TAKE CARE OF YOU.
YOU JUST NEED TO LET US.
YOU KIDNAPPED ME.
YOU LOCKED ME UP.
TORTURED ME... WITH THOSE LIGHTS.
I KNOW.
AND I'M SURE THAT'S BEEN DIFFICULT.
BUT WE'RE JUST TRYING–
TO MAKE ME WHOLE.
YEAH.
THAT'S WHAT WILSON SAID.
I DON'T KNOW WHAT YOU AND WILSON HAVE TALKED ABOUT.
BUT IF HE'S LETTING YOU ROAM THE GROUNDS, HE MUST HAVE A GOOD FEELING ABOUT YOU.
AND THAT MEANS THINGS ARE LOOKING UP, Y'KNOW?
I'VE GOTTA RUN. CHORES.
BUT I HOPE WILSON'S RIGHT ABOUT YOU, ADRIAN.
I THINK YOU COULD BE HAPPY HERE.
"REALLY, MOLLY, WE'VE GOT TO STOP MEETING LIKE THIS."

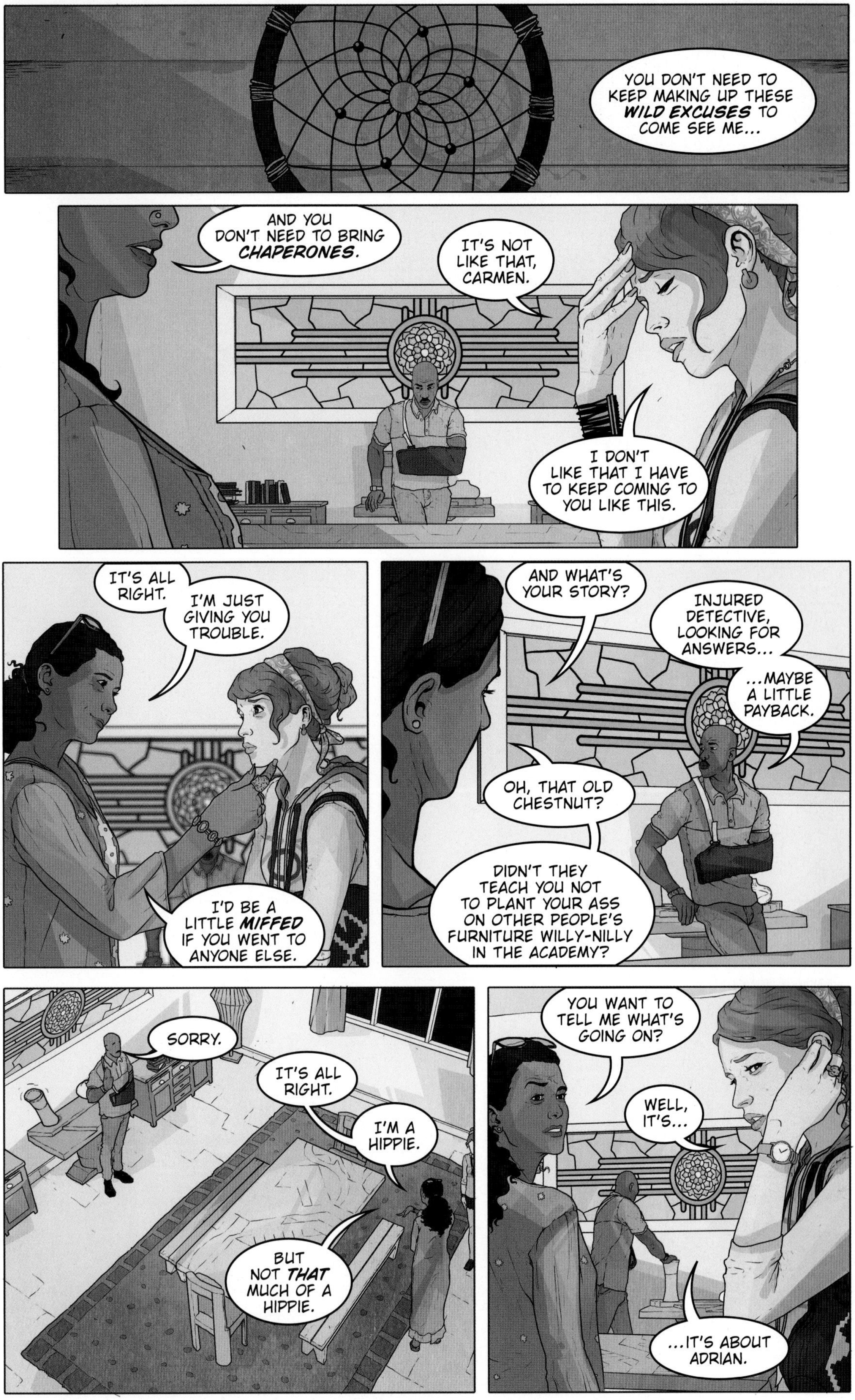
YOU DON'T NEED TO KEEP MAKING UP THESE WILD EXCUSES TO COME SEE ME...
AND YOU DON'T NEED TO BRING CHAPERONES.
IT'S NOT LIKE THAT, CARMEN.
I DON'T LIKE THAT I HAVE TO KEEP COMING TO YOU LIKE THIS.
IT'S ALL RIGHT.
I'M JUST GIVING YOU TROUBLE.
I'D BE A LITTLE MIFFED IF YOU WENT TO ANYONE ELSE.
AND WHAT'S YOUR STORY?
INJURED DETECTIVE, LOOKING FOR ANSWERS...
...MAYBE A LITTLE PAYBACK.
OH, THAT OLD CHESTNUT?
DIDN'T THEY TEACH YOU NOT TO PLANT YOUR ASS ON OTHER PEOPLE'S FURNITURE WILLY-NILLY IN THE ACADEMY?
SORRY.
IT'S ALL RIGHT.
I'M A HIPPIE.
BUT NOT THAT MUCH OF A HIPPIE.
YOU WANT TO TELL ME WHAT'S GOING ON?
WELL, IT'S...
...IT'S ABOUT ADRIAN.

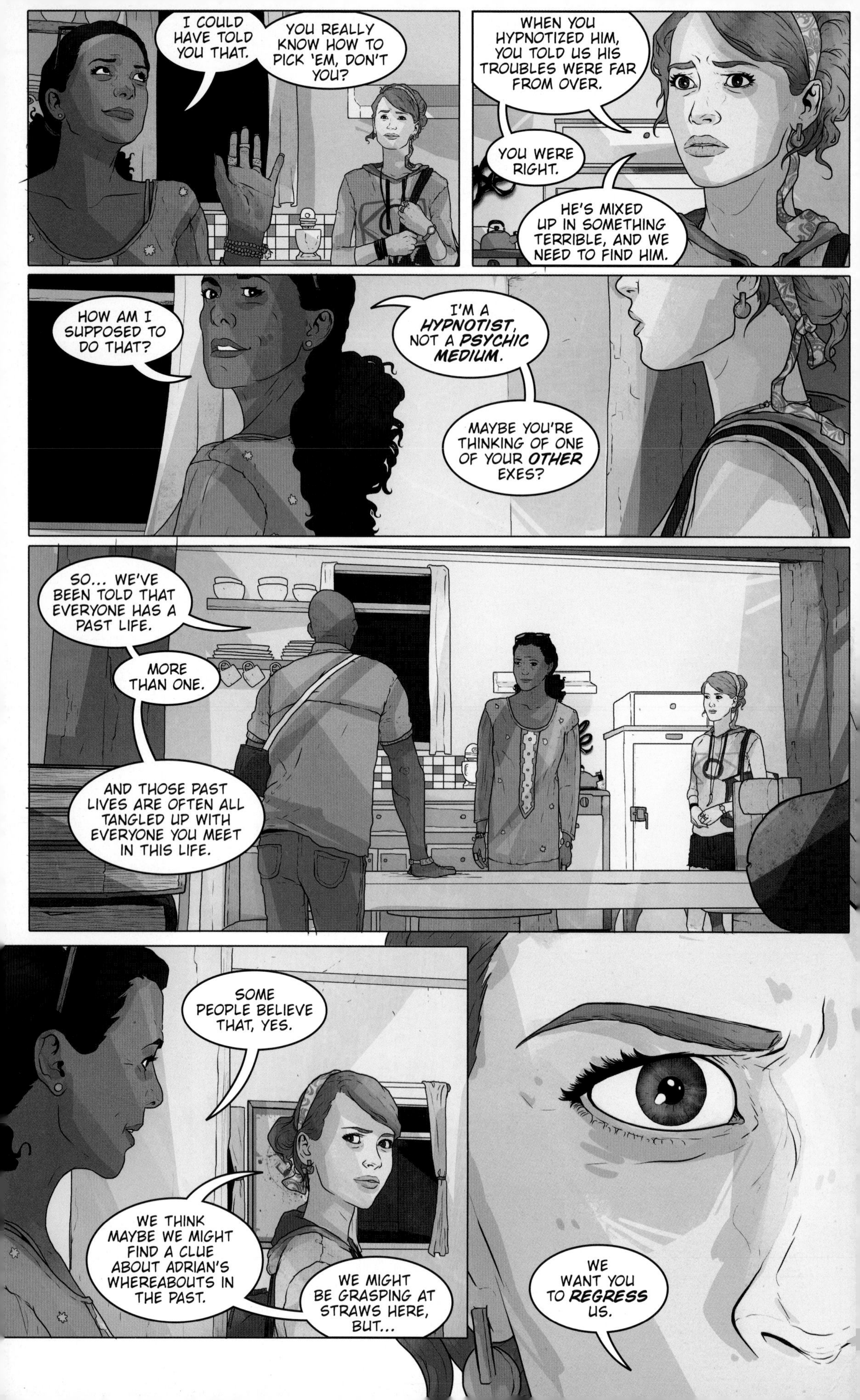
I COULD HAVE TOLD YOU THAT.
YOU REALLY KNOW HOW TO PICK 'EM, DON'T YOU?
WHEN YOU HYPNOTIZED HIM, YOU TOLD US HIS TROUBLES WERE FAR FROM OVER.
YOU WERE RIGHT.
HE'S MIXED UP IN SOMETHING TERRIBLE, AND WE NEED TO FIND HIM.
HOW AM I SUPPOSED TO DO THAT?
I'M A HYPNOTIST, NOT A PSYCHIC MEDIUM.
MAYBE YOU'RE THINKING OF ONE OF YOUR OTHER EXES?
SO... WE'VE BEEN TOLD THAT EVERYONE HAS A PAST LIFE.
MORE THAN ONE.
AND THOSE PAST LIVES ARE OFTEN ALL TANGLED UP WITH EVERYONE YOU MEET IN THIS LIFE.
SOME PEOPLE BELIEVE THAT, YES.
WE THINK MAYBE WE MIGHT FIND A CLUE ABOUT ADRIAN'S WHEREABOUTS IN THE PAST.
WE MIGHT BE GRASPING AT STRAWS HERE, BUT...
WE WANT YOU TO REGRESS US.

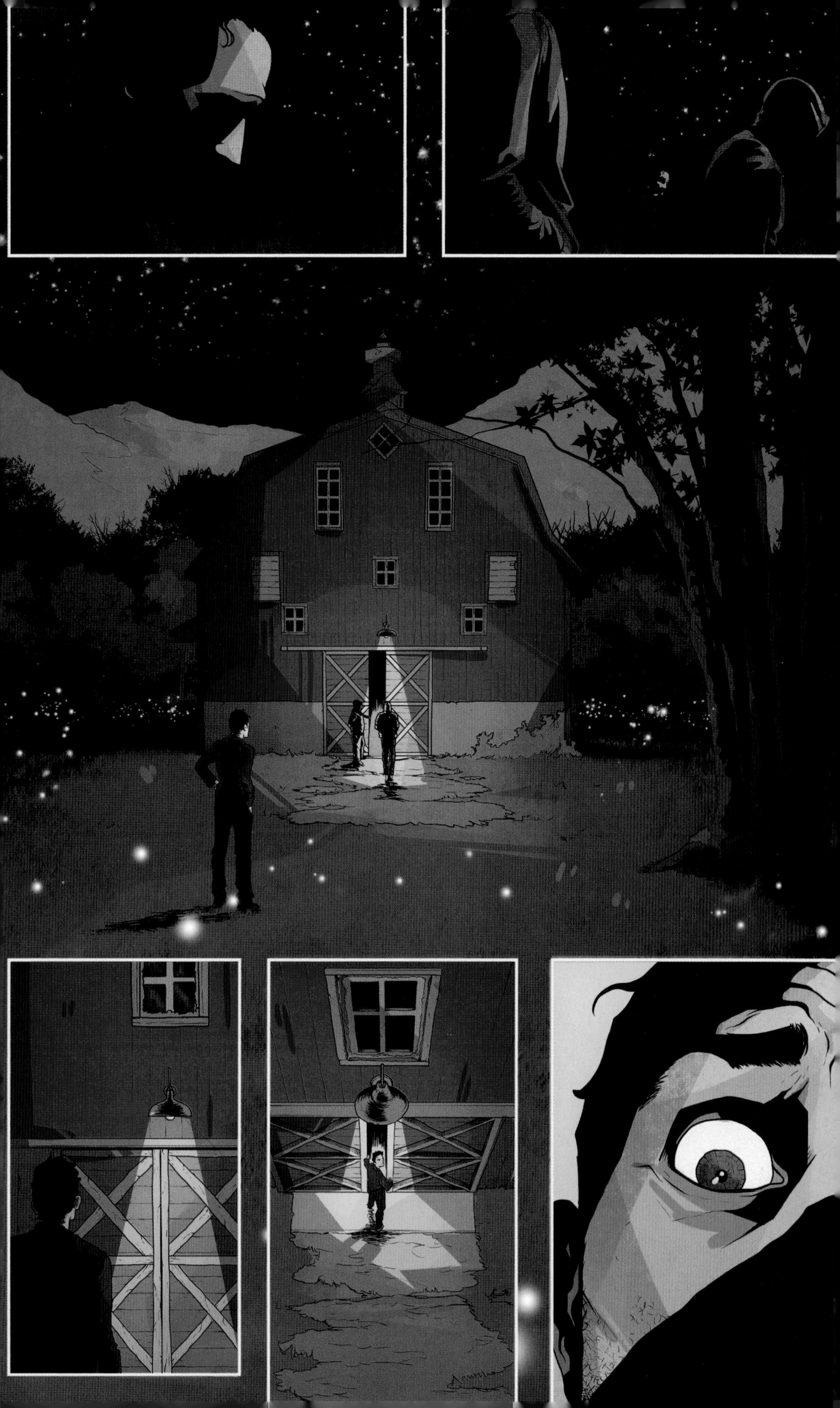

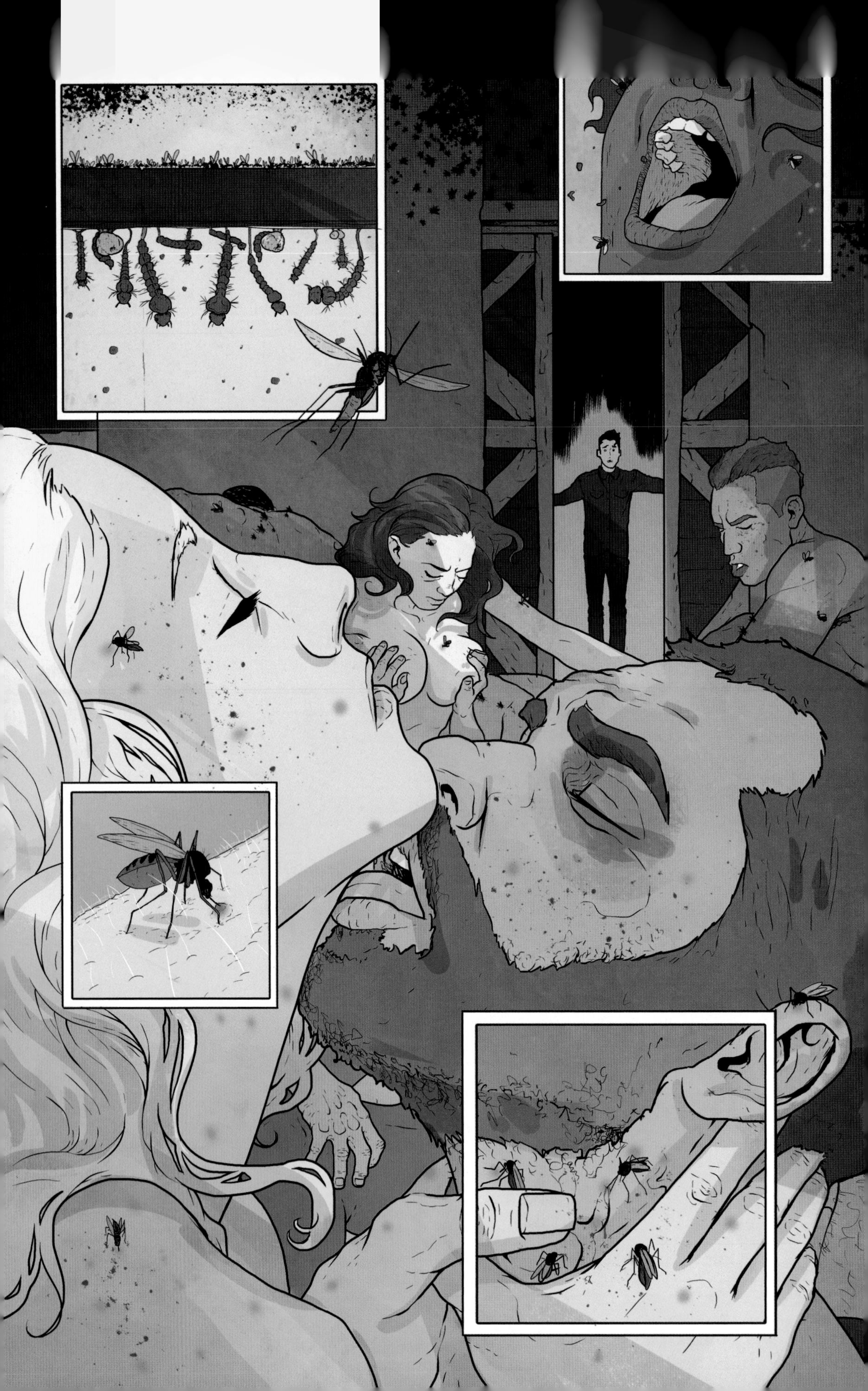

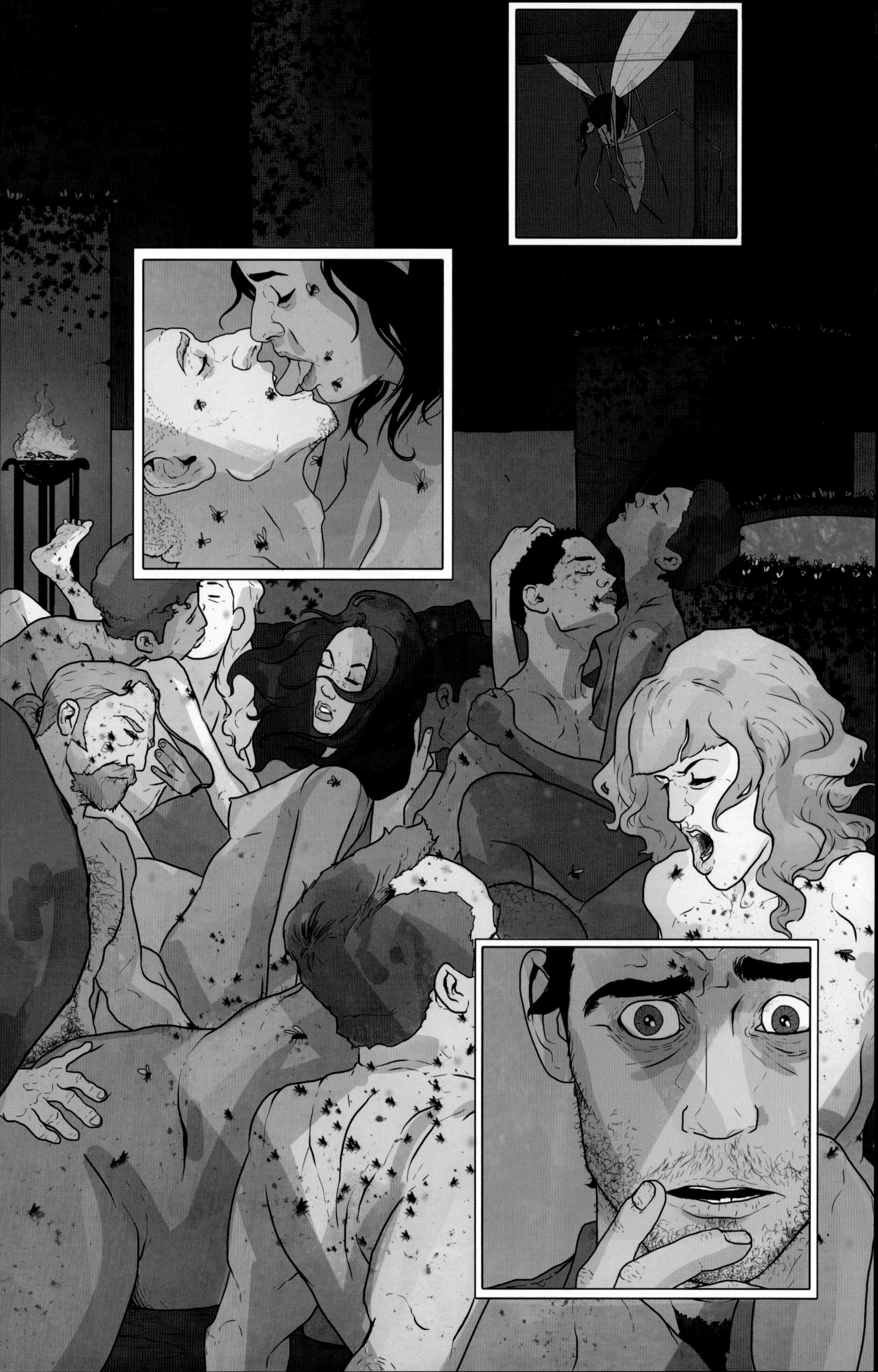

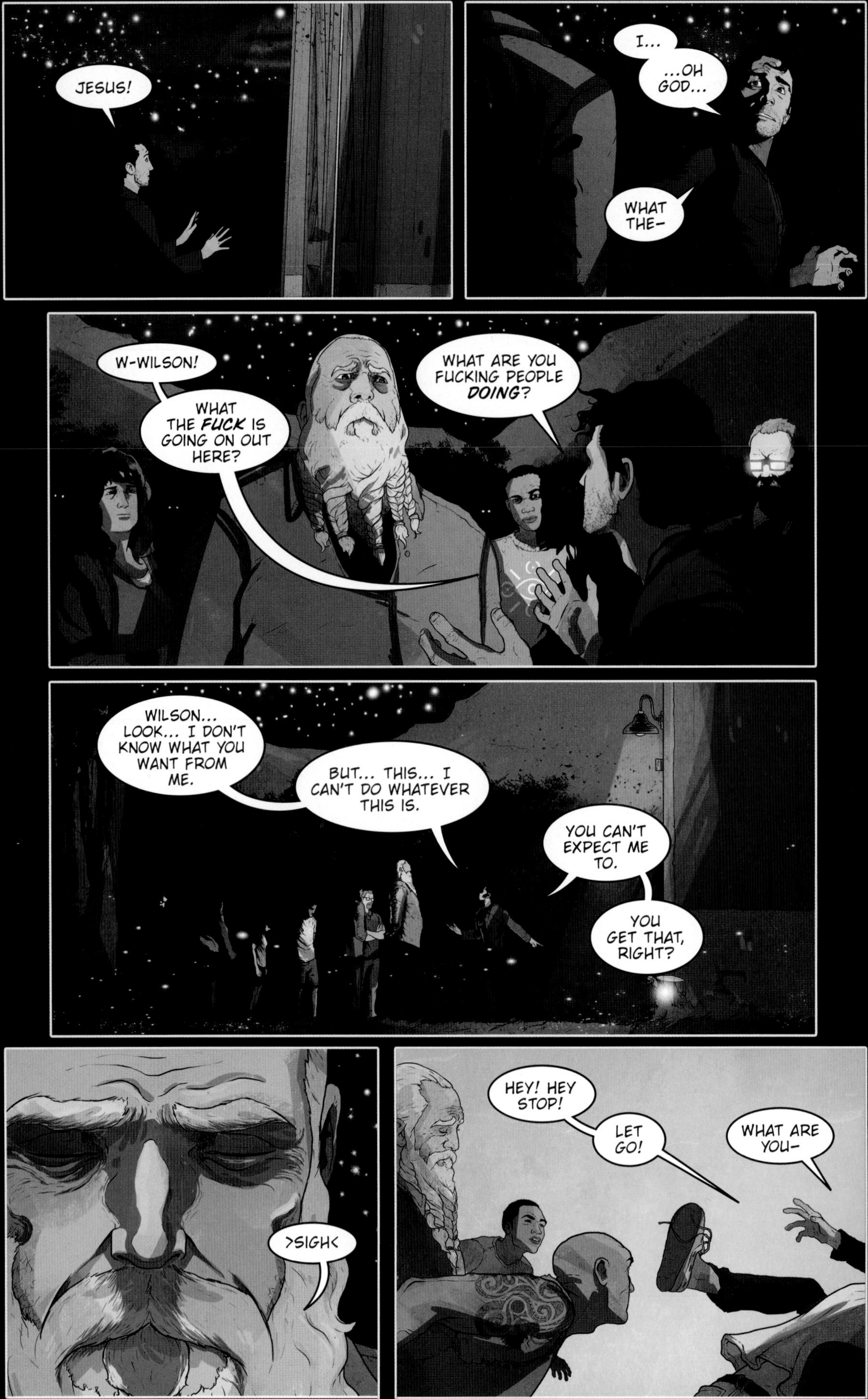
JESUS!
I...
...OH GOD...
WHAT THE-
W-WILSON!
WHAT THE FUCK IS GOING ON OUT HERE?
WHAT ARE YOU FUCKING PEOPLE DOING?
WILSON... LOOK... I DON'T KNOW WHAT YOU WANT FROM ME.
BUT... THIS... I CAN'T DO WHATEVER THIS IS.
YOU CAN'T EXPECT ME TO.
YOU GET THAT, RIGHT?
>SIGH<
HEY! HEY STOP!
LET GO!
WHAT ARE YOU-

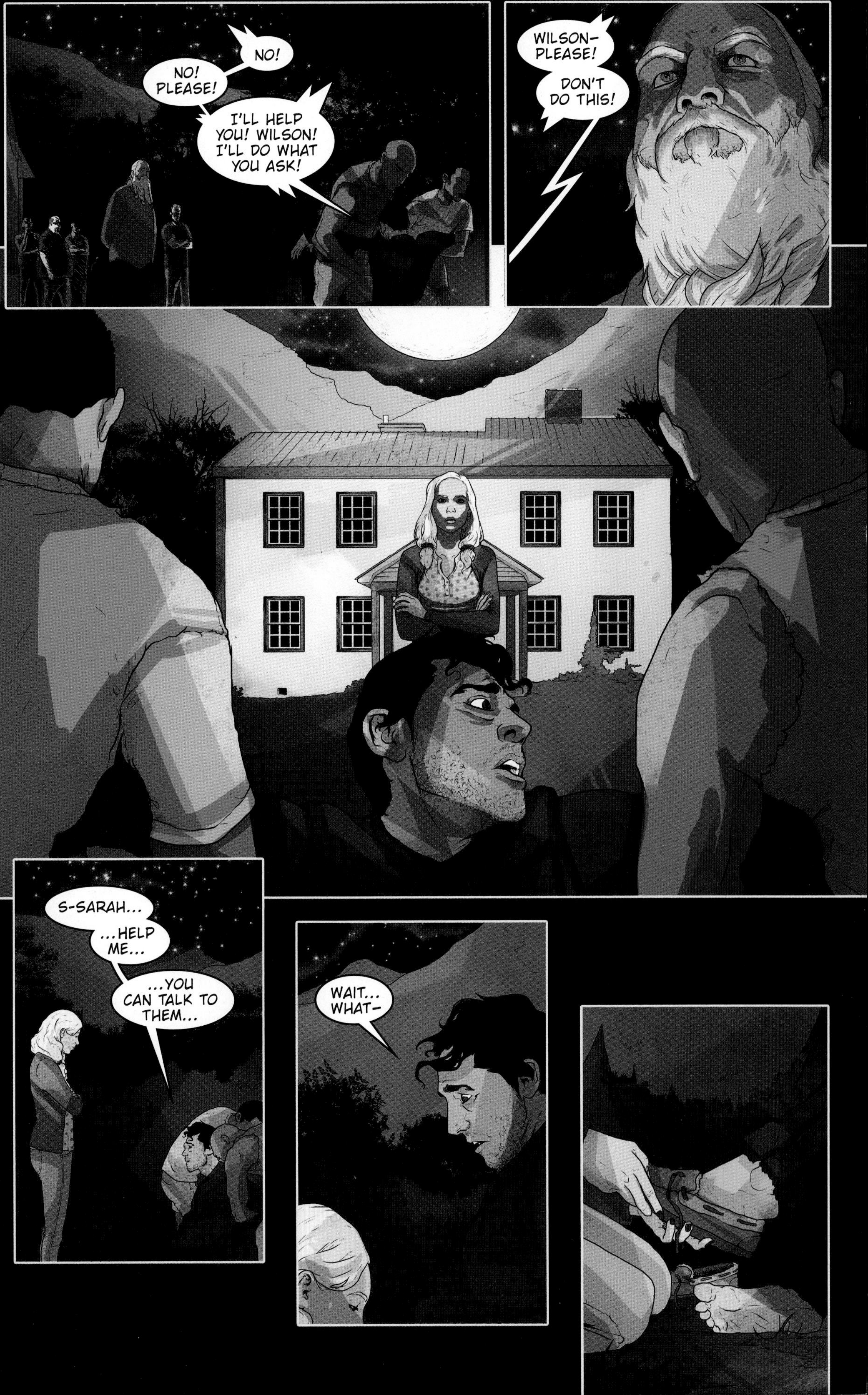
NO!
NO! PLEASE!
I'LL HELP YOU! WILSON! I'LL DO WHAT YOU ASK!
WILSON– PLEASE!
DON'T DO THIS!
S-SARAH...
...HELP ME...
...YOU CAN TALK TO THEM...
WAIT... WHAT–

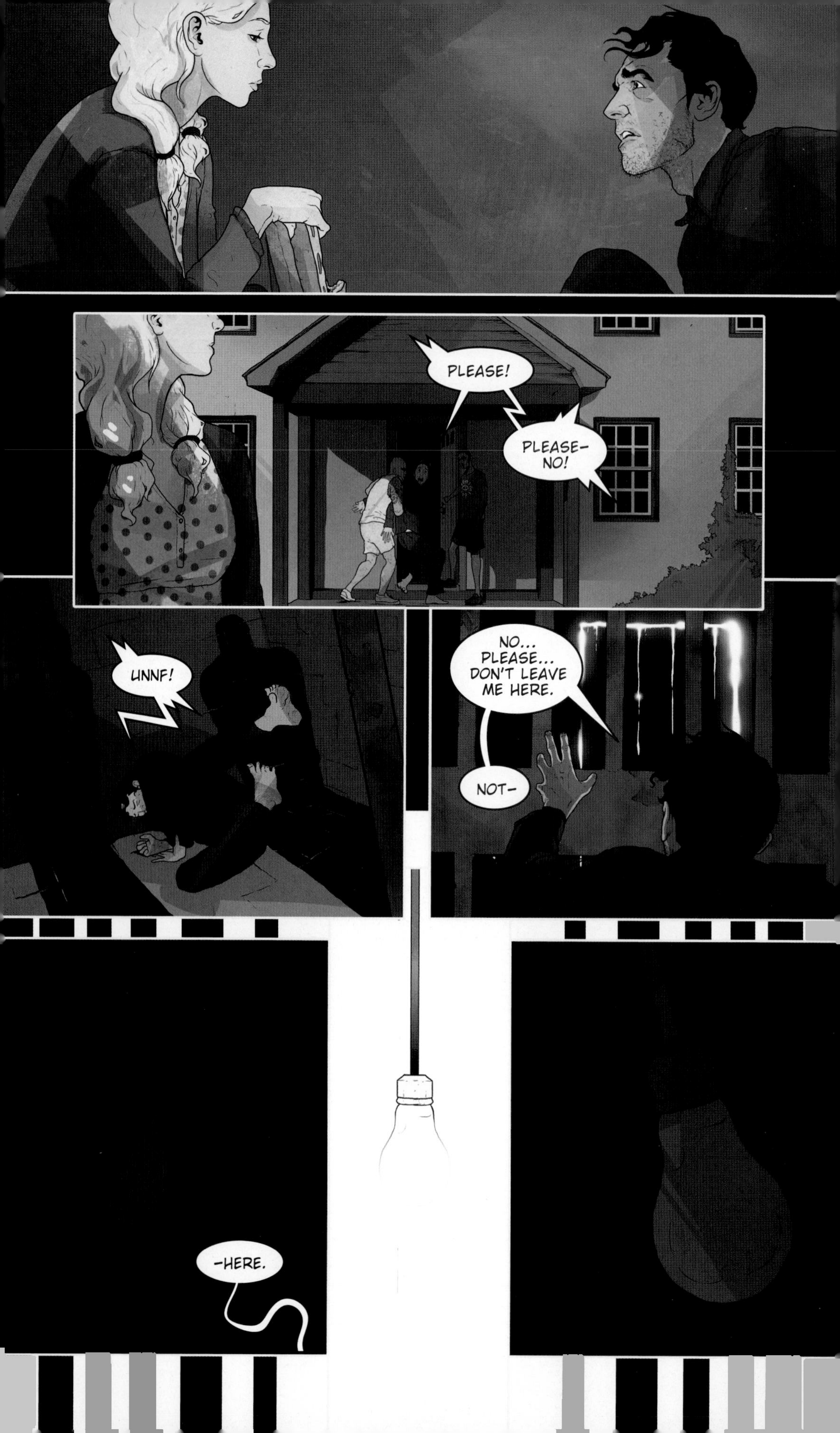
PLEASE!
PLEASE-NO!
UNNF!
NO... PLEASE... DON'T LEAVE ME HERE.
NOT-
-HERE.

NINE

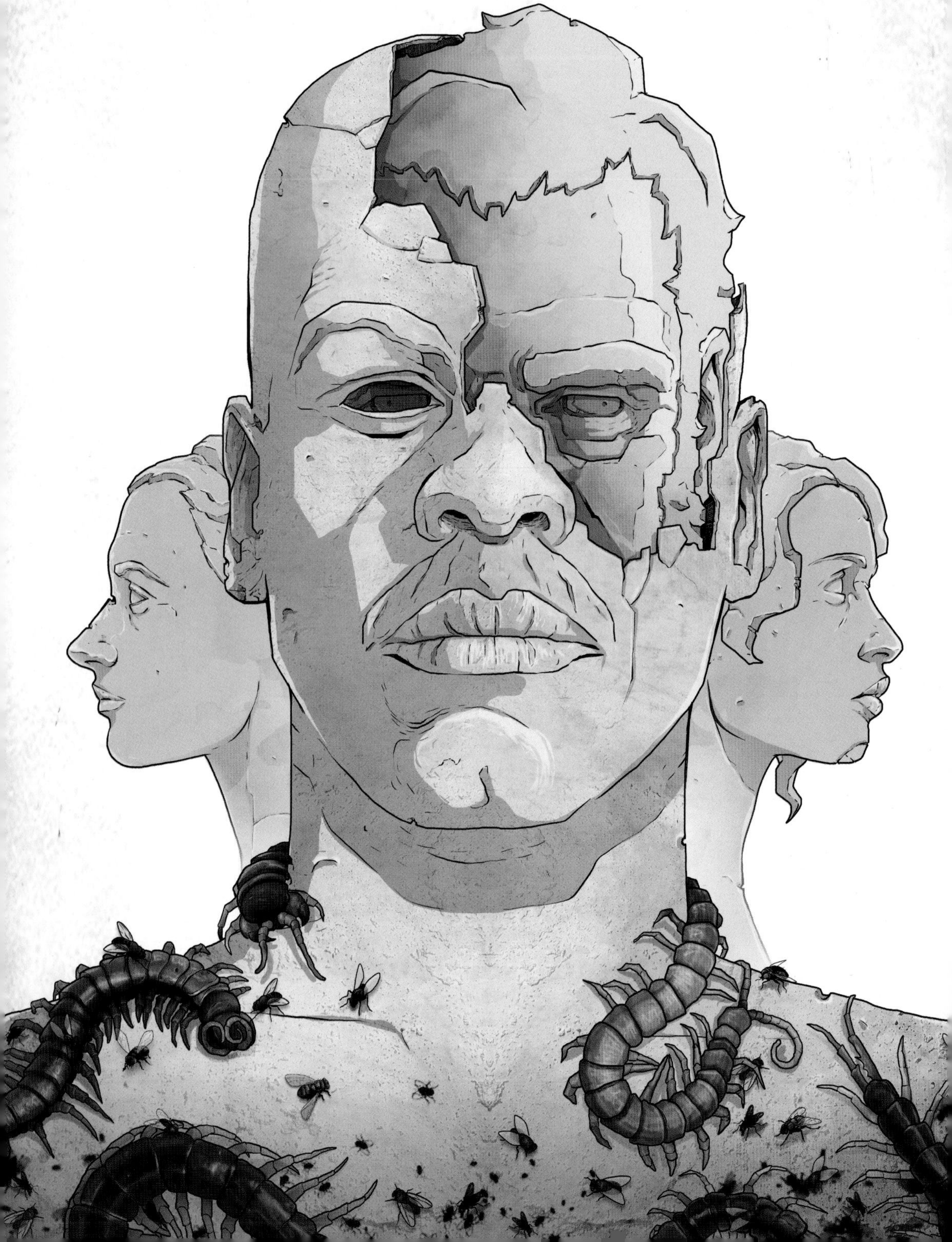

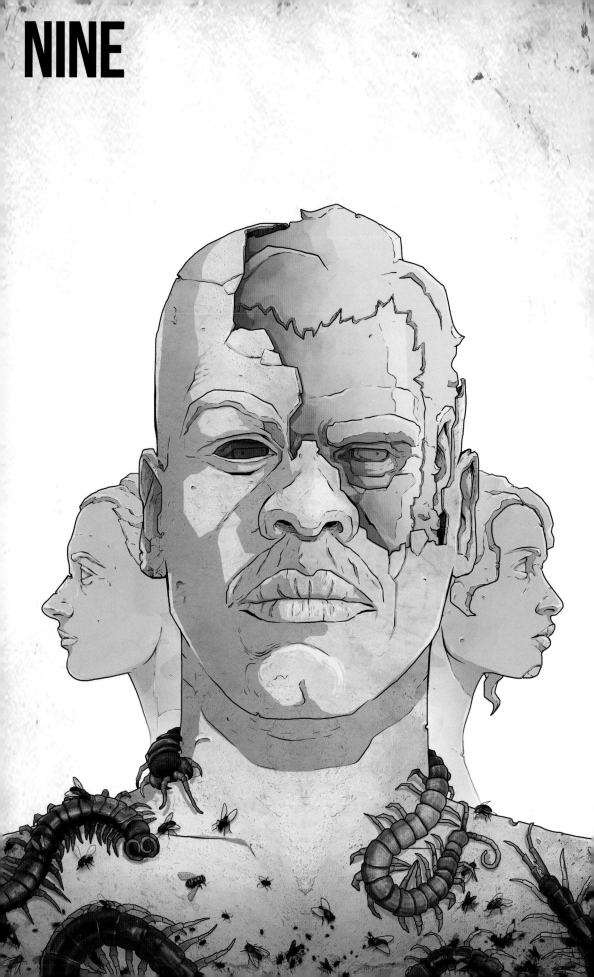

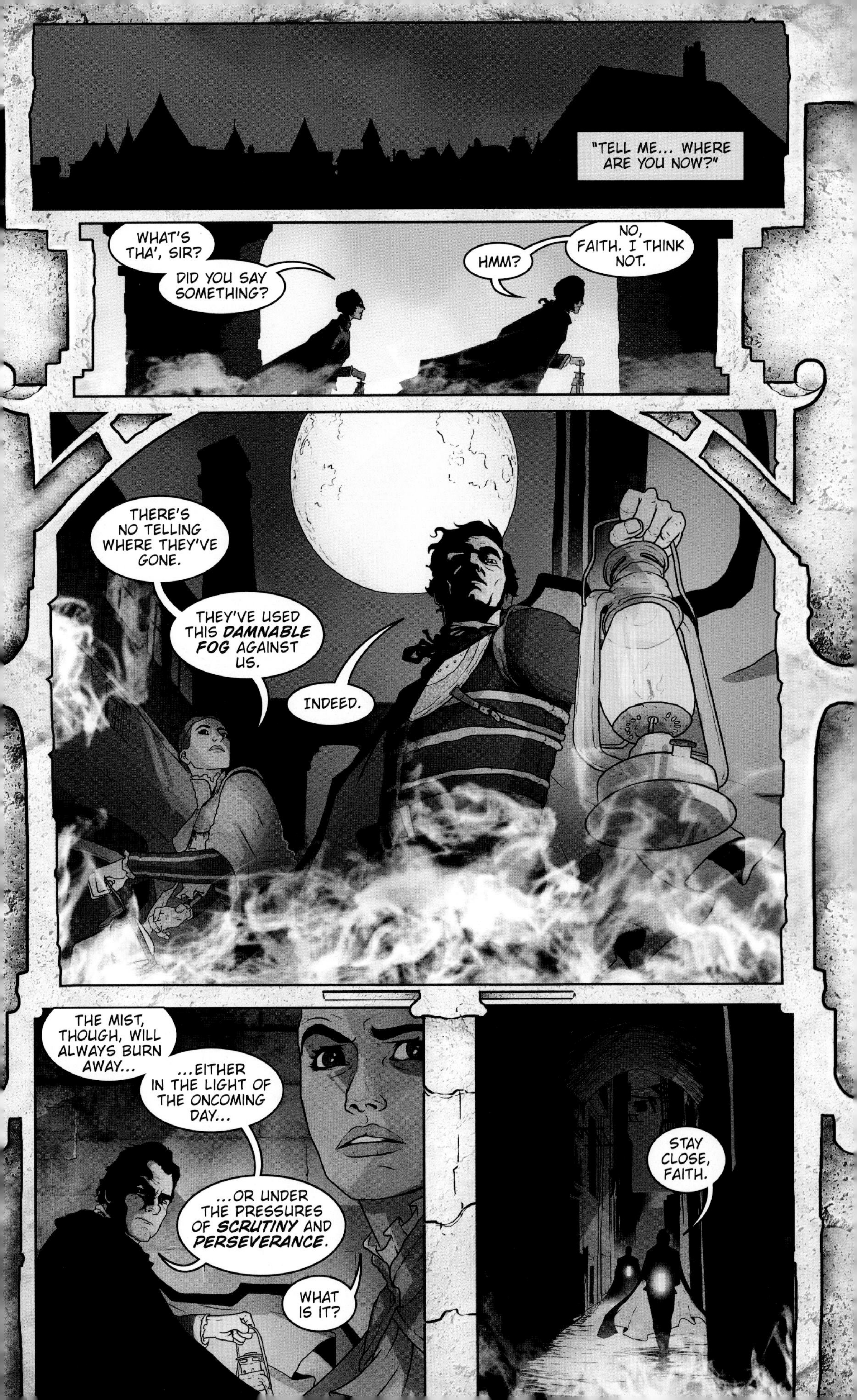
"TELL ME... WHERE ARE YOU NOW?"
WHAT'S THA', SIR?
DID YOU SAY SOMETHING?
HMM?
NO, FAITH. I THINK NOT.
THERE'S NO TELLING WHERE THEY'VE GONE.
THEY'VE USED THIS DAMNABLE FOG AGAINST US.
INDEED.
THE MIST, THOUGH, WILL ALWAYS BURN AWAY...
...EITHER IN THE LIGHT OF THE ONCOMING DAY...
...OR UNDER THE PRESSURES OF SCRUTINY AND PERSEVERANCE.
WHAT IS IT?
STAY CLOSE, FAITH.

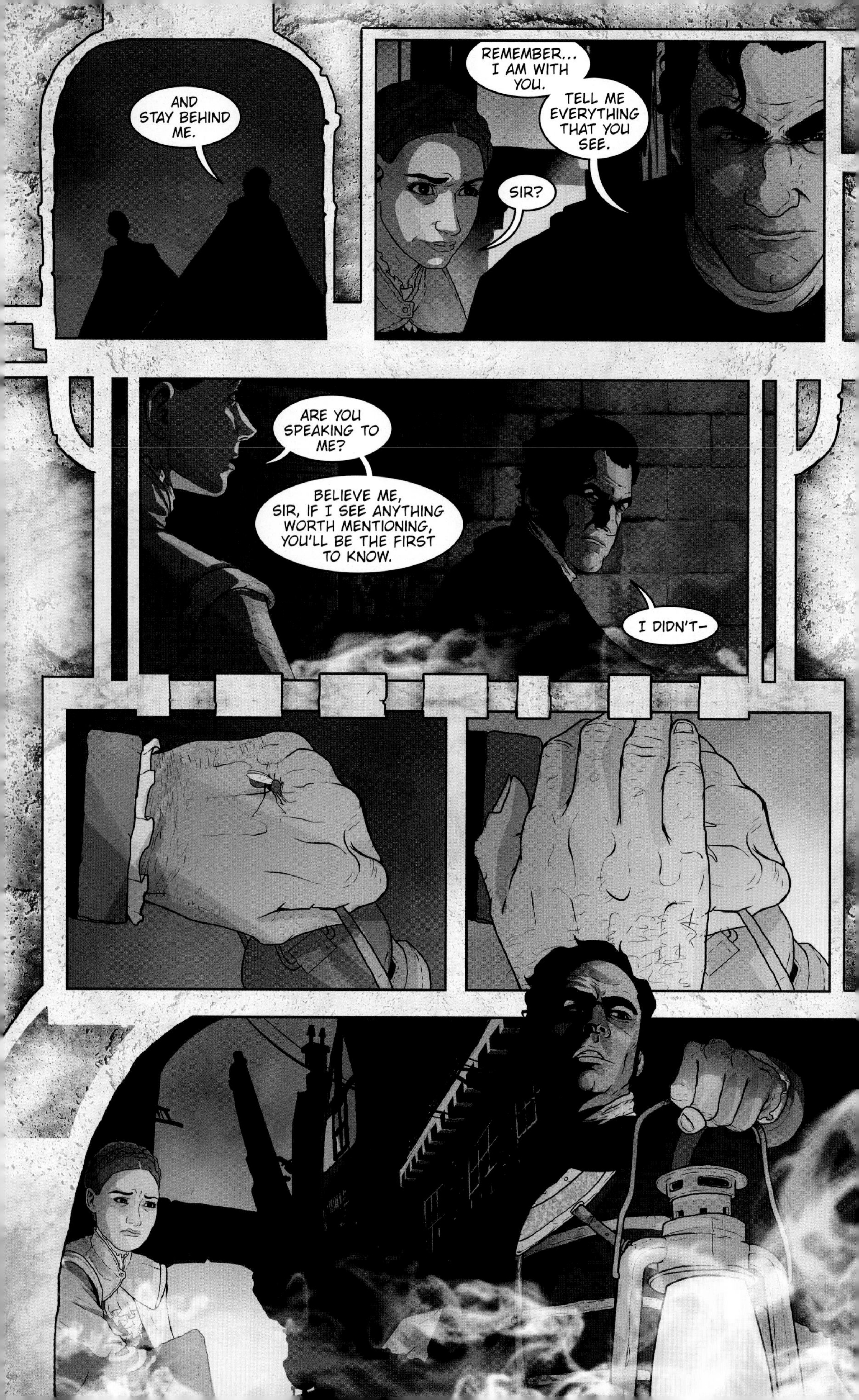
AND STAY BEHIND ME.
REMEMBER... I AM WITH YOU.
TELL ME EVERYTHING THAT YOU SEE.
SIR?
ARE YOU SPEAKING TO ME?
BELIEVE ME, SIR, IF I SEE ANYTHING WORTH MENTIONING, YOU'LL BE THE FIRST TO KNOW.
I DIDN'T-

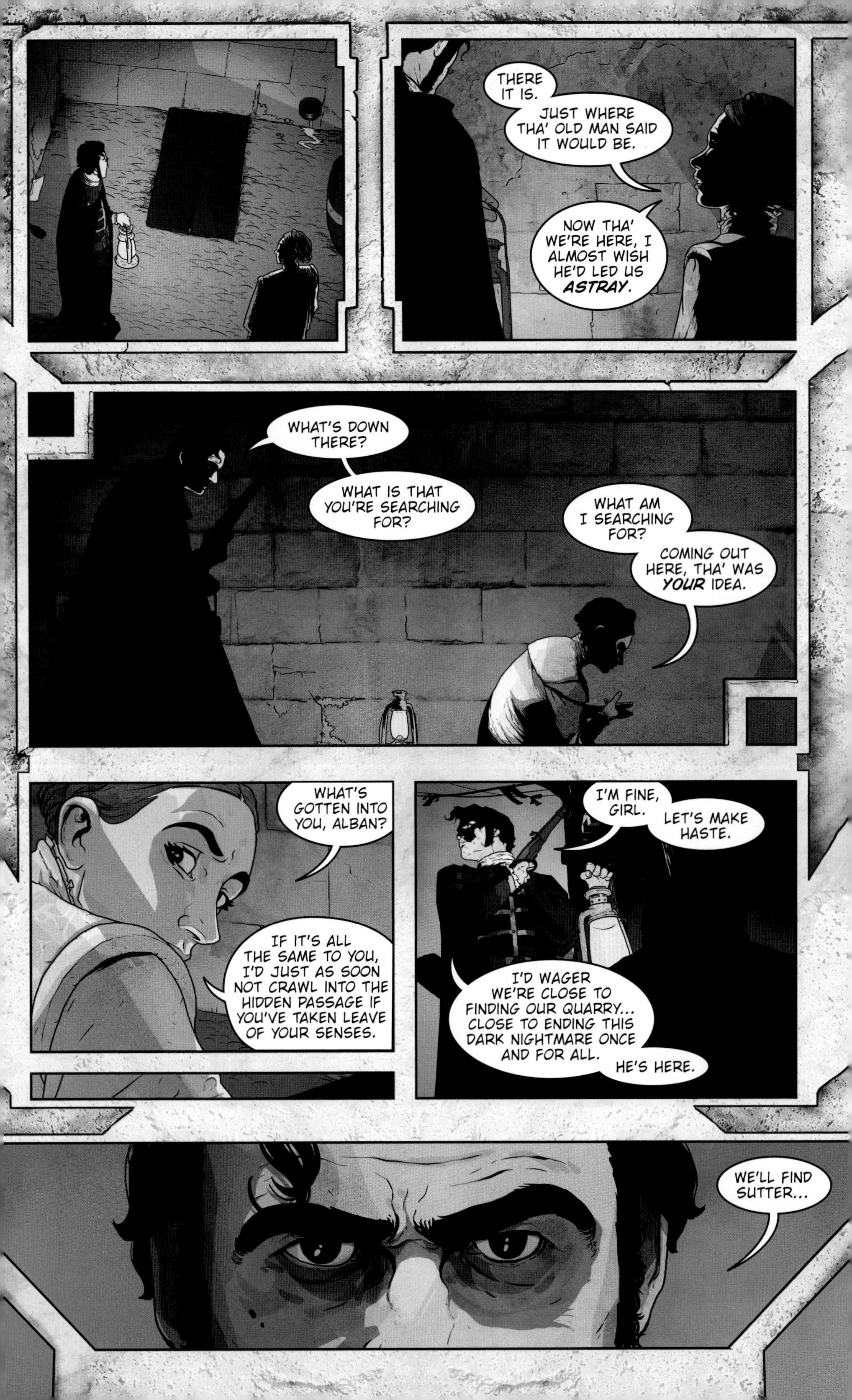
THERE IT IS.
JUST WHERE THA' OLD MAN SAID IT WOULD BE.
NOW THA' WE'RE HERE, I ALMOST WISH HE'D LED US ***ASTRAY***.
WHAT'S DOWN THERE?
WHAT IS THAT YOU'RE SEARCHING FOR?
WHAT AM I SEARCHING FOR?
COMING OUT HERE, THA' WAS ***YOUR*** IDEA.
WHAT'S GOTTEN INTO YOU, ALBAN?
IF IT'S ALL THE SAME TO YOU, I'D JUST AS SOON NOT CRAWL INTO THE HIDDEN PASSAGE IF YOU'VE TAKEN LEAVE OF YOUR SENSES.
I'M FINE, GIRL.
LET'S MAKE HASTE.
I'D WAGER WE'RE CLOSE TO FINDING OUR QUARRY... CLOSE TO ENDING THIS DARK NIGHTMARE ONCE AND FOR ALL.
HE'S HERE.
WE'LL FIND SUTTER...

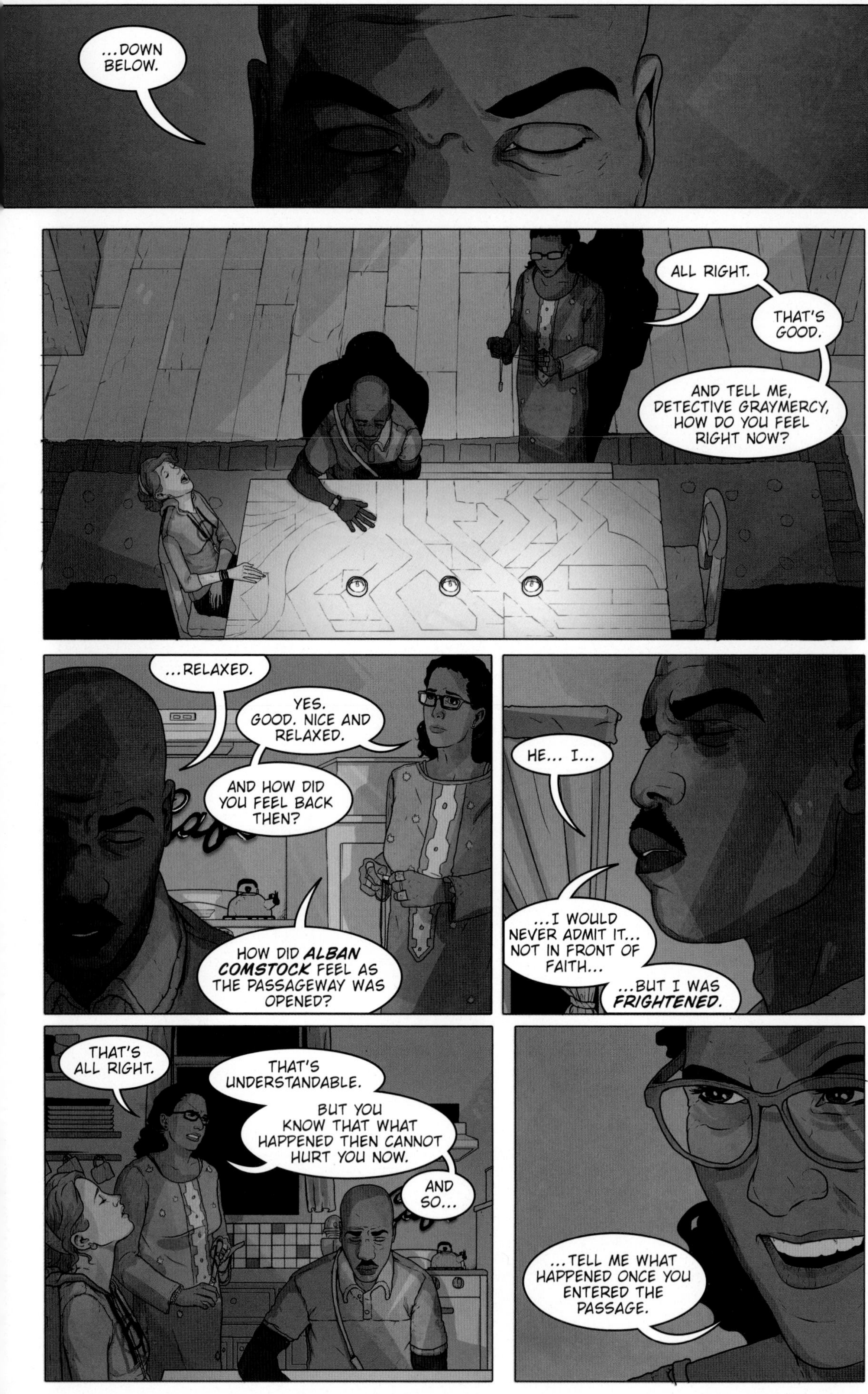
...DOWN BELOW.
ALL RIGHT.
THAT'S GOOD.
AND TELL ME, DETECTIVE GRAYMERCY, HOW DO YOU FEEL RIGHT NOW?
...RELAXED.
YES. GOOD. NICE AND RELAXED.
AND HOW DID YOU FEEL BACK THEN?
HOW DID ALBAN COMSTOCK FEEL AS THE PASSAGEWAY WAS OPENED?
HE... I...
...I WOULD NEVER ADMIT IT... NOT IN FRONT OF FAITH...
...BUT I WAS FRIGHTENED.
THAT'S ALL RIGHT.
THAT'S UNDERSTANDABLE.
BUT YOU KNOW THAT WHAT HAPPENED THEN CANNOT HURT YOU NOW.
AND SO...
...TELL ME WHAT HAPPENED ONCE YOU ENTERED THE PASSAGE.

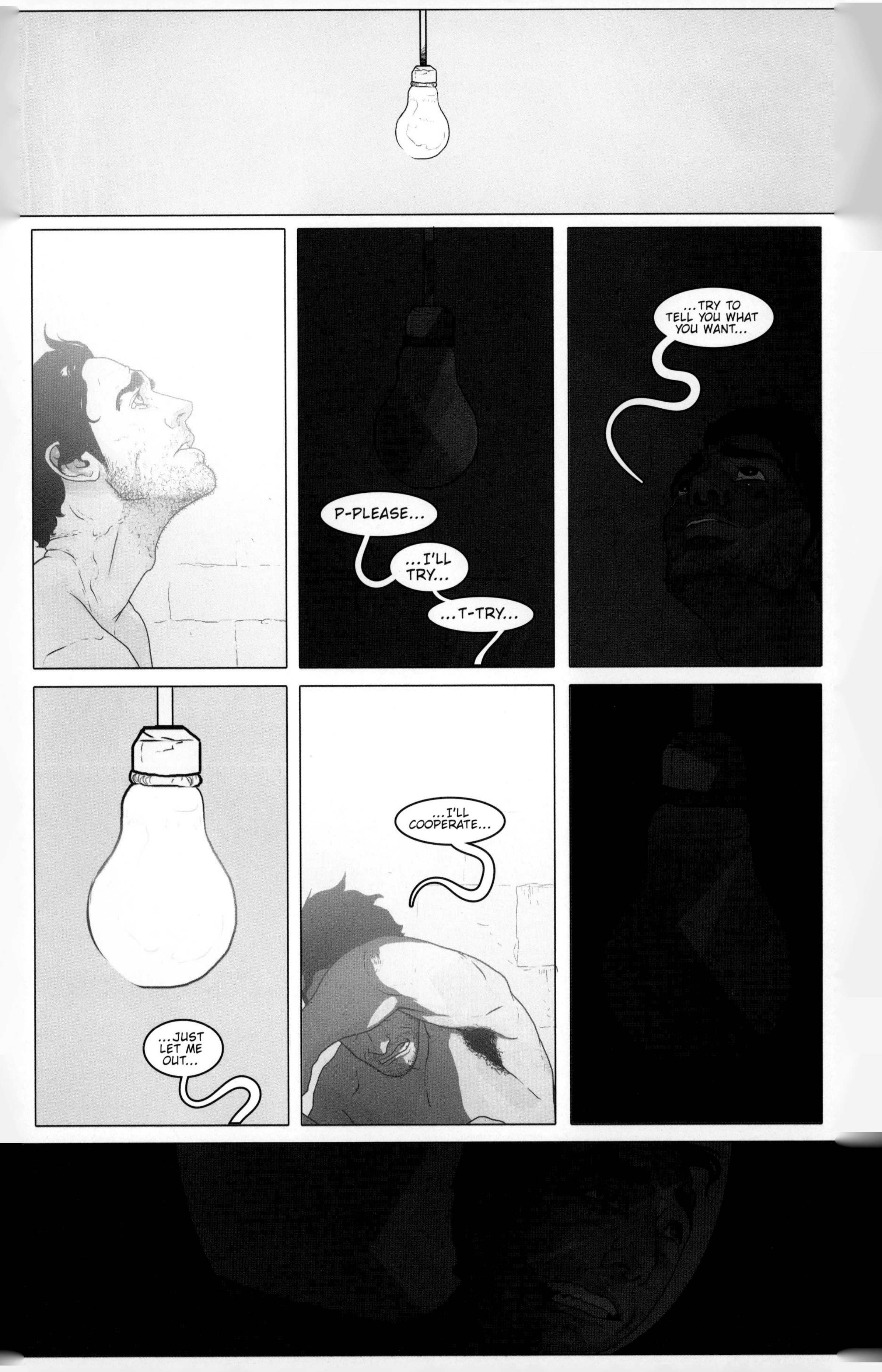
P-PLEASE...
...I'LL TRY...
...T-TRY...
...TRY TO TELL YOU WHAT YOU WANT...
...JUST LET ME OUT...
...I'LL COOPERATE...

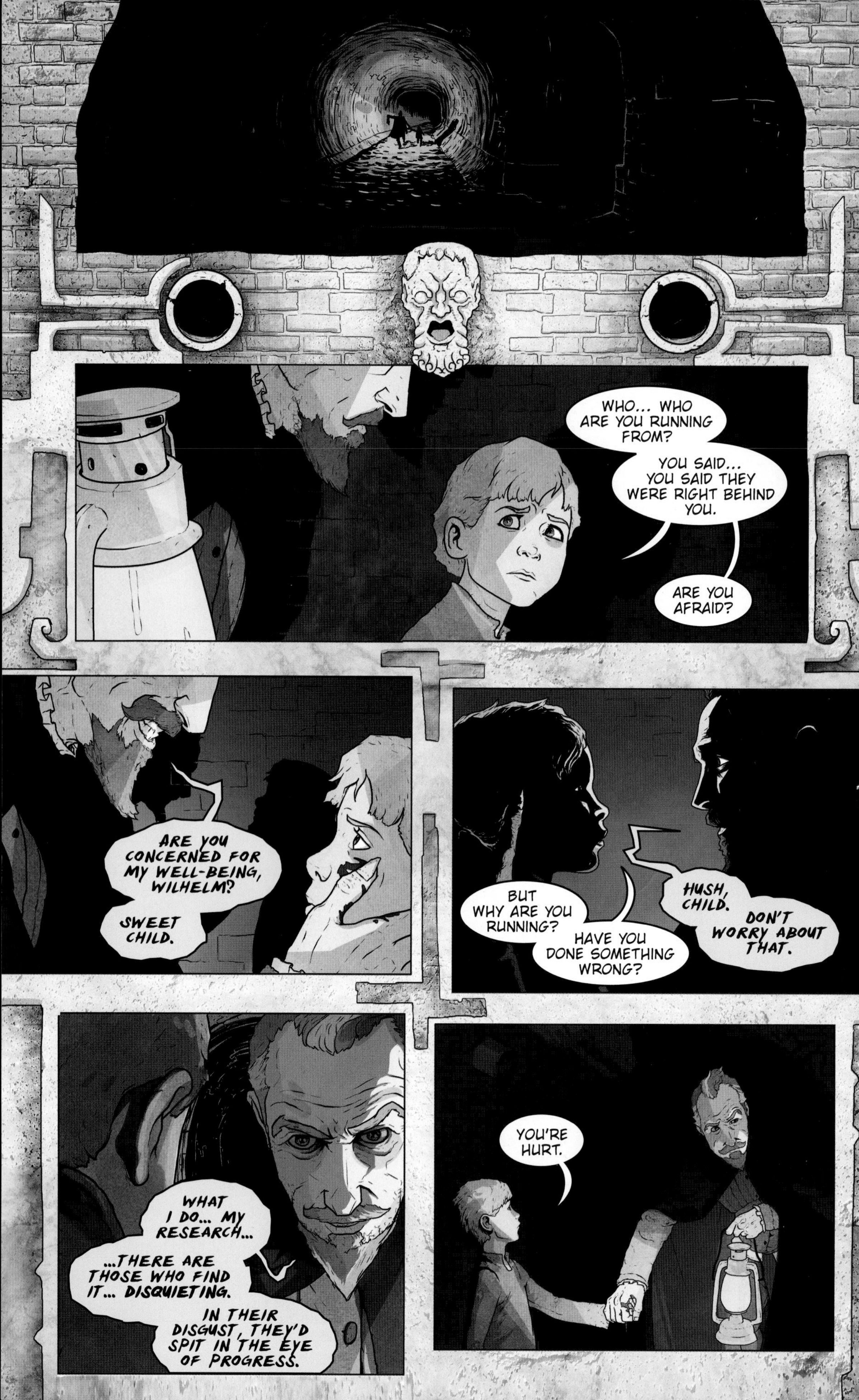
WHO... WHO ARE YOU RUNNING FROM?
YOU SAID... YOU SAID THEY WERE RIGHT BEHIND YOU.
ARE YOU AFRAID?
ARE YOU CONCERNED FOR MY WELL-BEING, WILHELM?
SWEET CHILD.
BUT WHY ARE YOU RUNNING?
HAVE YOU DONE SOMETHING WRONG?
HUSH, CHILD.
DON'T WORRY ABOUT THAT.
WHAT I DO... MY RESEARCH...
...THERE ARE THOSE WHO FIND IT... DISQUIETING.
IN THEIR DISGUST, THEY'D SPIT IN THE EYE OF PROGRESS.
YOU'RE HURT.

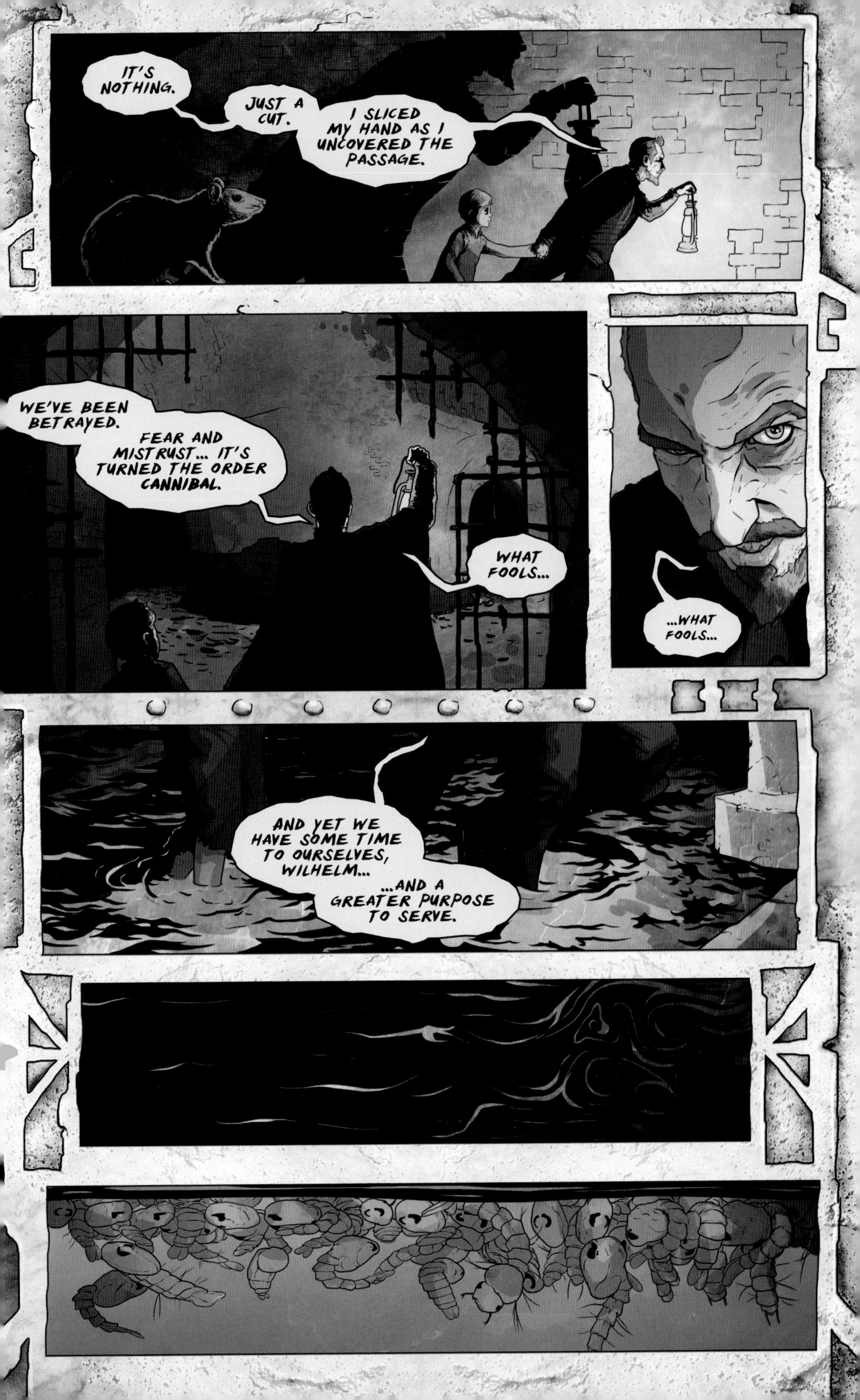
IT'S NOTHING.
JUST A CUT.
I SLICED MY HAND AS I UNCOVERED THE PASSAGE.
WE'VE BEEN BETRAYED.
FEAR AND MISTRUST... IT'S TURNED THE ORDER CANNIBAL.
WHAT FOOLS...
...WHAT FOOLS...
AND YET WE HAVE SOME TIME TO OURSELVES, WILHELM...
...AND A GREATER PURPOSE TO SERVE.

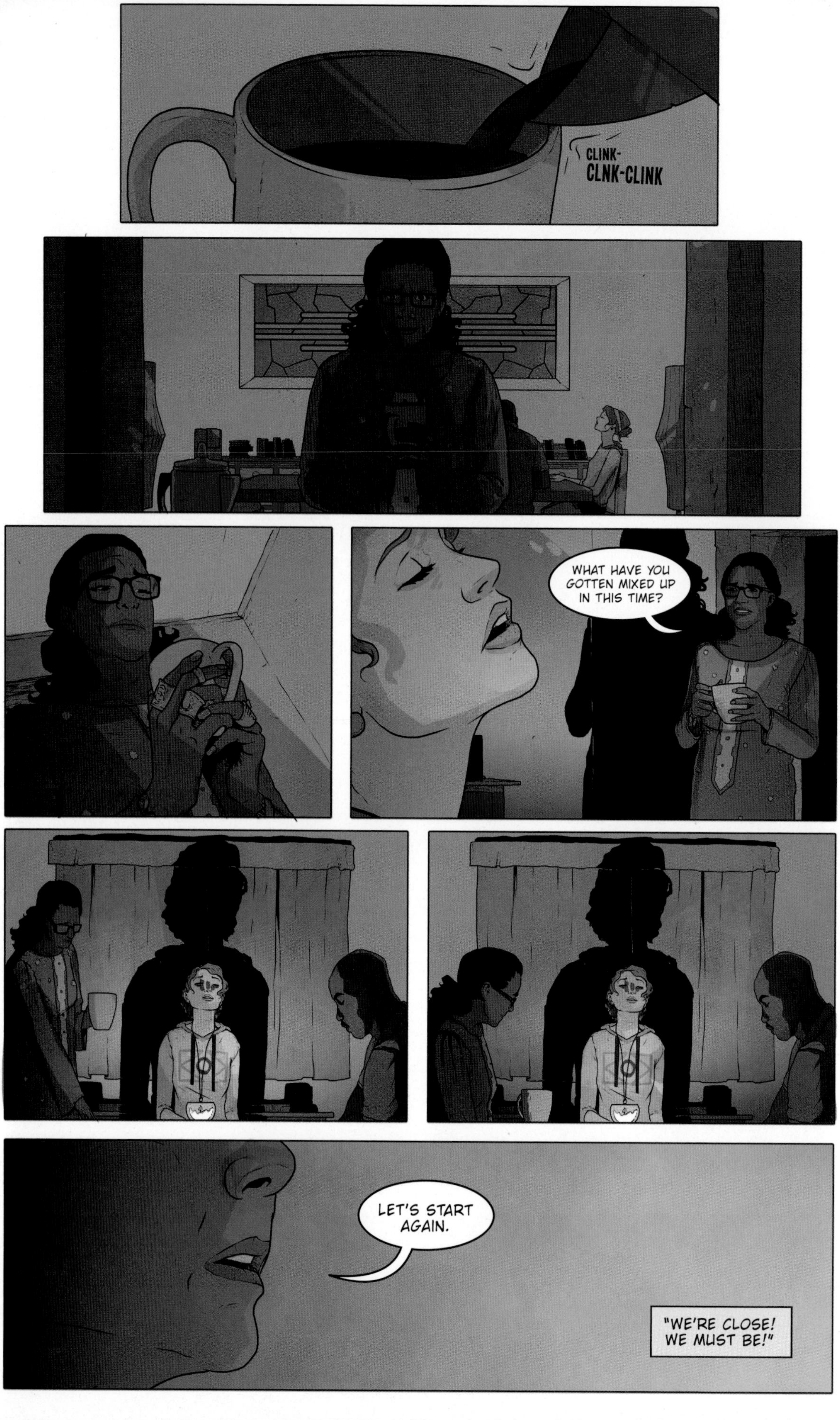
CLINK-
CLNK-CLINK
WHAT HAVE YOU GOTTEN MIXED UP IN THIS TIME?
LET'S START AGAIN.
"WE'RE CLOSE! WE MUST BE!"

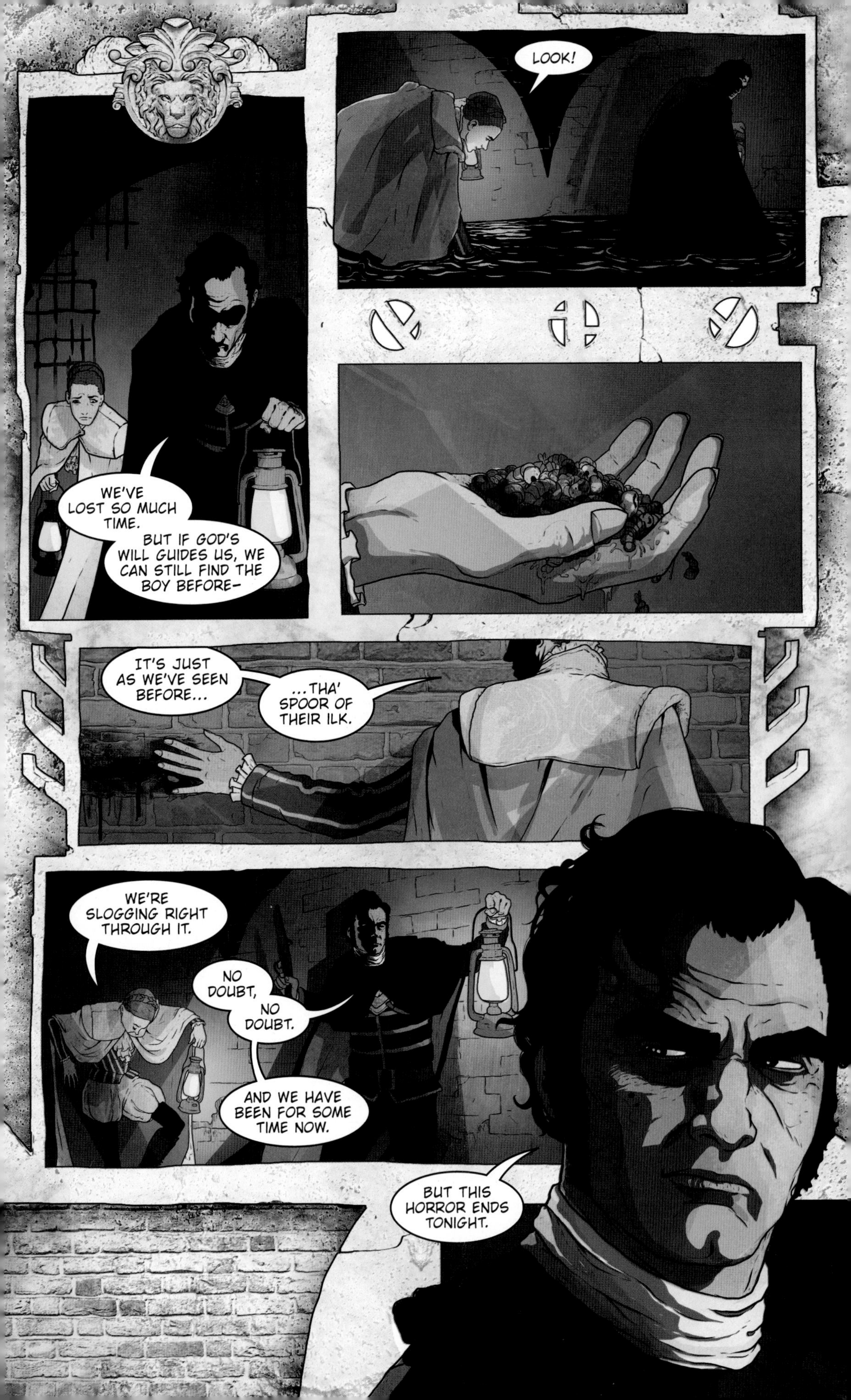
WE'VE LOST SO MUCH TIME.
BUT IF GOD'S WILL GUIDES US, WE CAN STILL FIND THE BOY BEFORE–
LOOK!
IT'S JUST AS WE'VE SEEN BEFORE...
...THA' SPOOR OF THEIR ILK.
WE'RE SLOGGING RIGHT THROUGH IT.
NO DOUBT,
NO DOUBT.
AND WE HAVE BEEN FOR SOME TIME NOW.
BUT THIS HORROR ENDS TONIGHT.

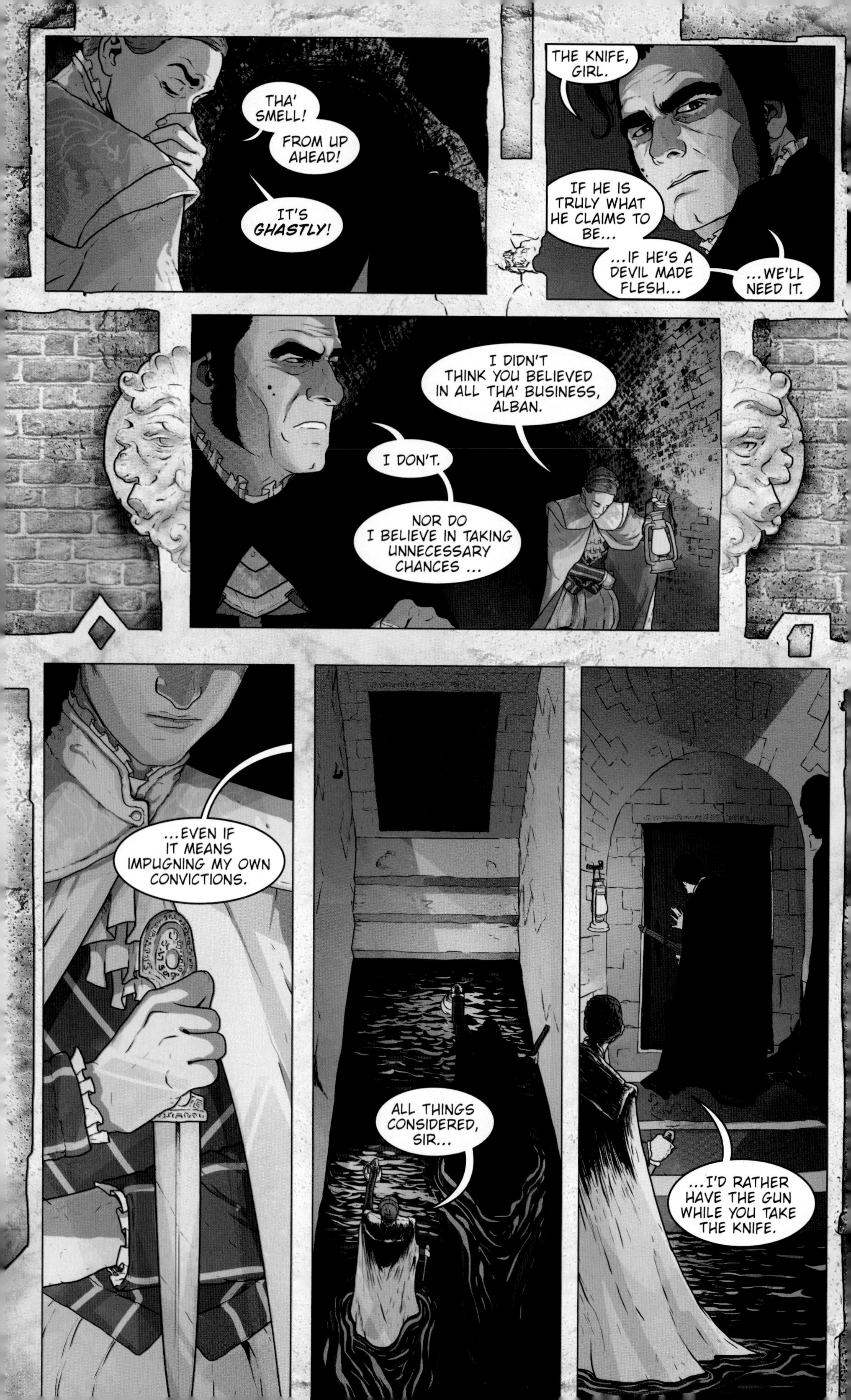
THA' SMELL!
FROM UP AHEAD!
IT'S *GHASTLY*!
THE KNIFE, GIRL.
IF HE IS TRULY WHAT HE CLAIMS TO BE...
...IF HE'S A DEVIL MADE FLESH...
...WE'LL NEED IT.
I DIDN'T THINK YOU BELIEVED IN ALL THA' BUSINESS, ALBAN.
I DON'T.
NOR DO I BELIEVE IN TAKING UNNECESSARY CHANCES ...
...EVEN IF IT MEANS IMPUGNING MY OWN CONVICTIONS.
ALL THINGS CONSIDERED, SIR...
...I'D RATHER HAVE THE GUN WHILE YOU TAKE THE KNIFE.

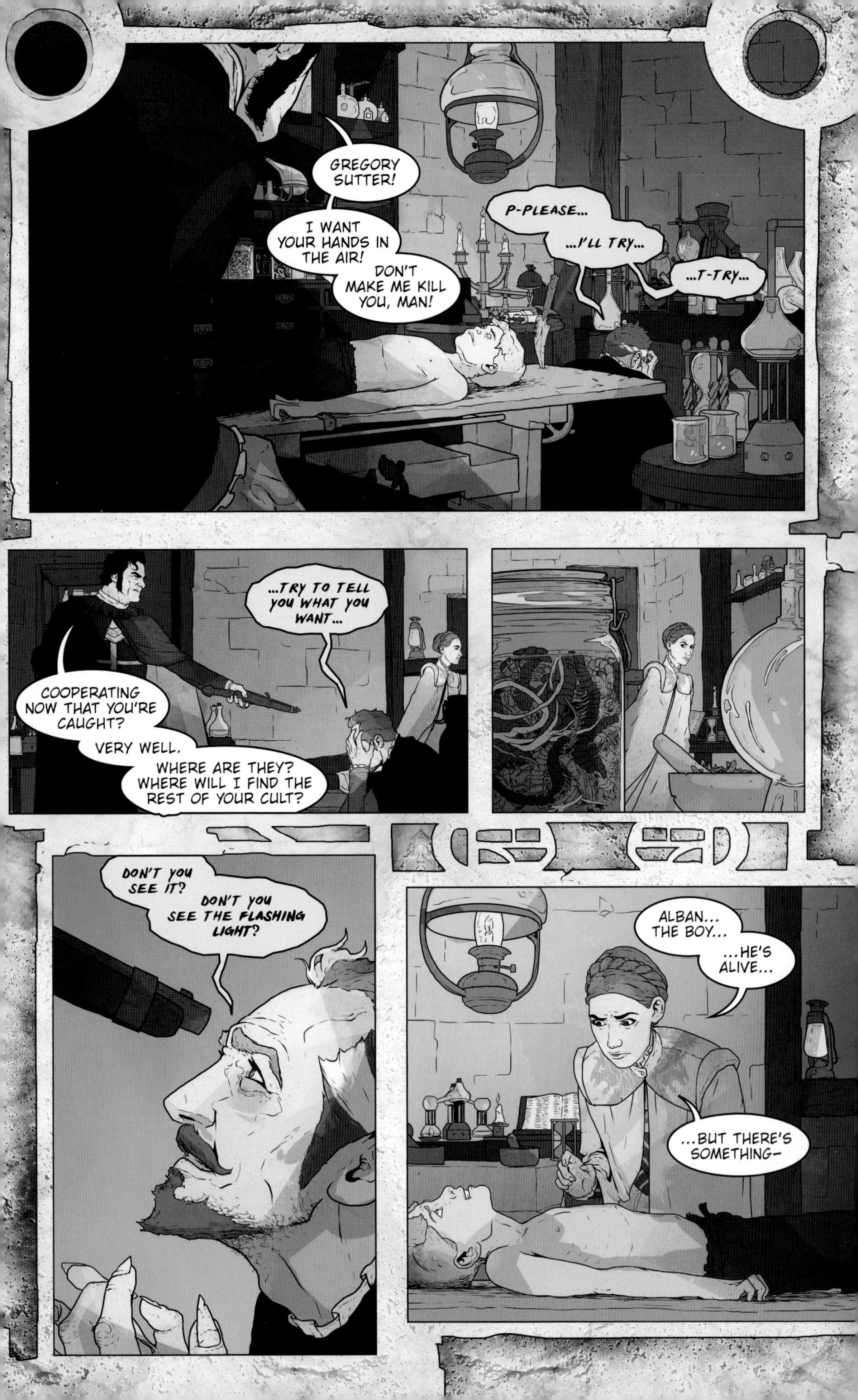
GREGORY SUTTER!
I WANT YOUR HANDS IN THE AIR!
DON'T MAKE ME KILL YOU, MAN!
P-PLEASE...
...I'LL TRY...
...T-TRY...
...TRY TO TELL YOU WHAT YOU WANT...
COOPERATING NOW THAT YOU'RE CAUGHT?
VERY WELL.
WHERE ARE THEY? WHERE WILL I FIND THE REST OF YOUR CULT?
DON'T YOU SEE IT?
DON'T YOU SEE THE FLASHING LIGHT?
ALBAN... THE BOY...
...HE'S ALIVE...
...BUT THERE'S SOMETHING—

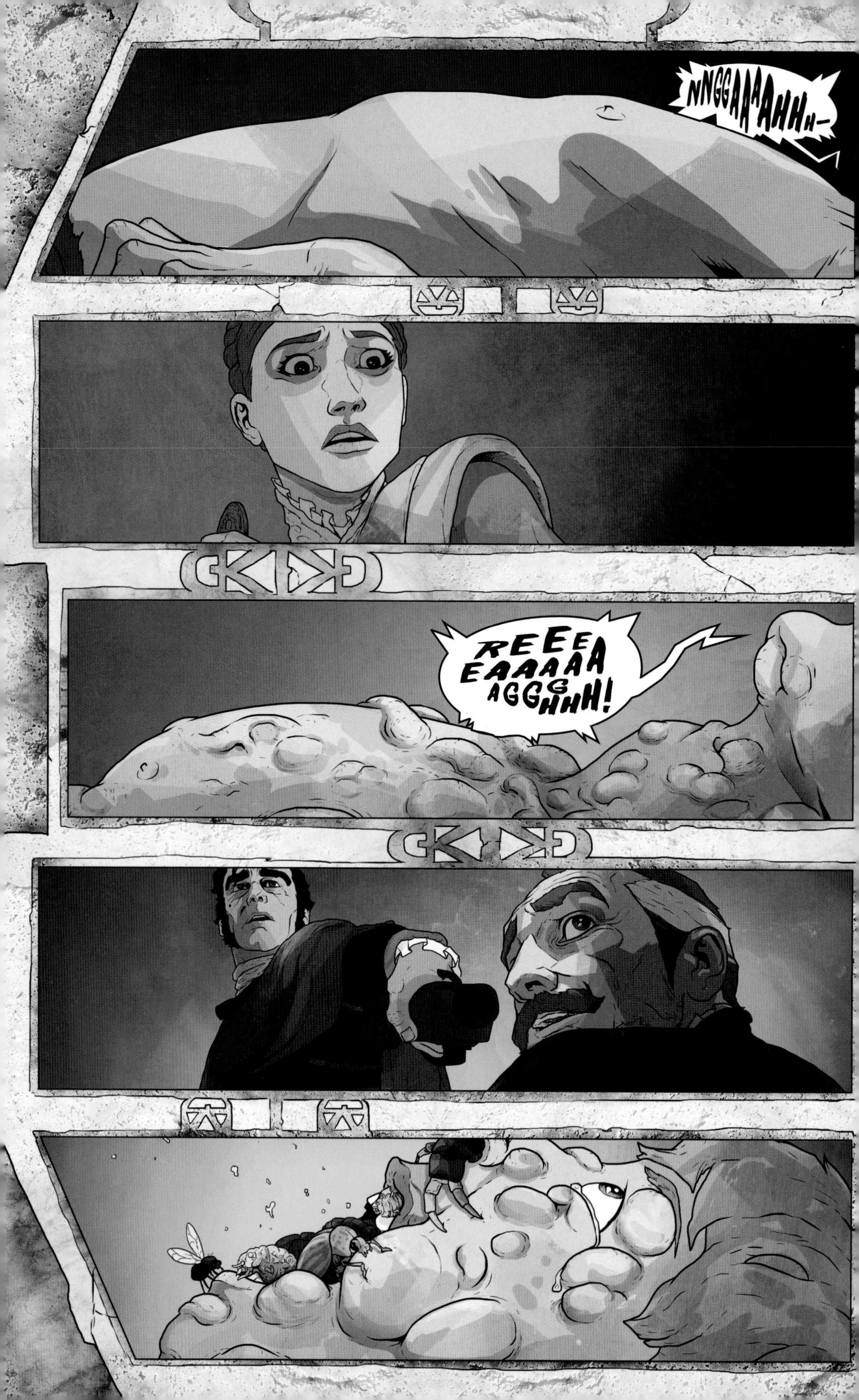
NNGGAAAAHHH-
REEEEAAAAAGGGHHH!

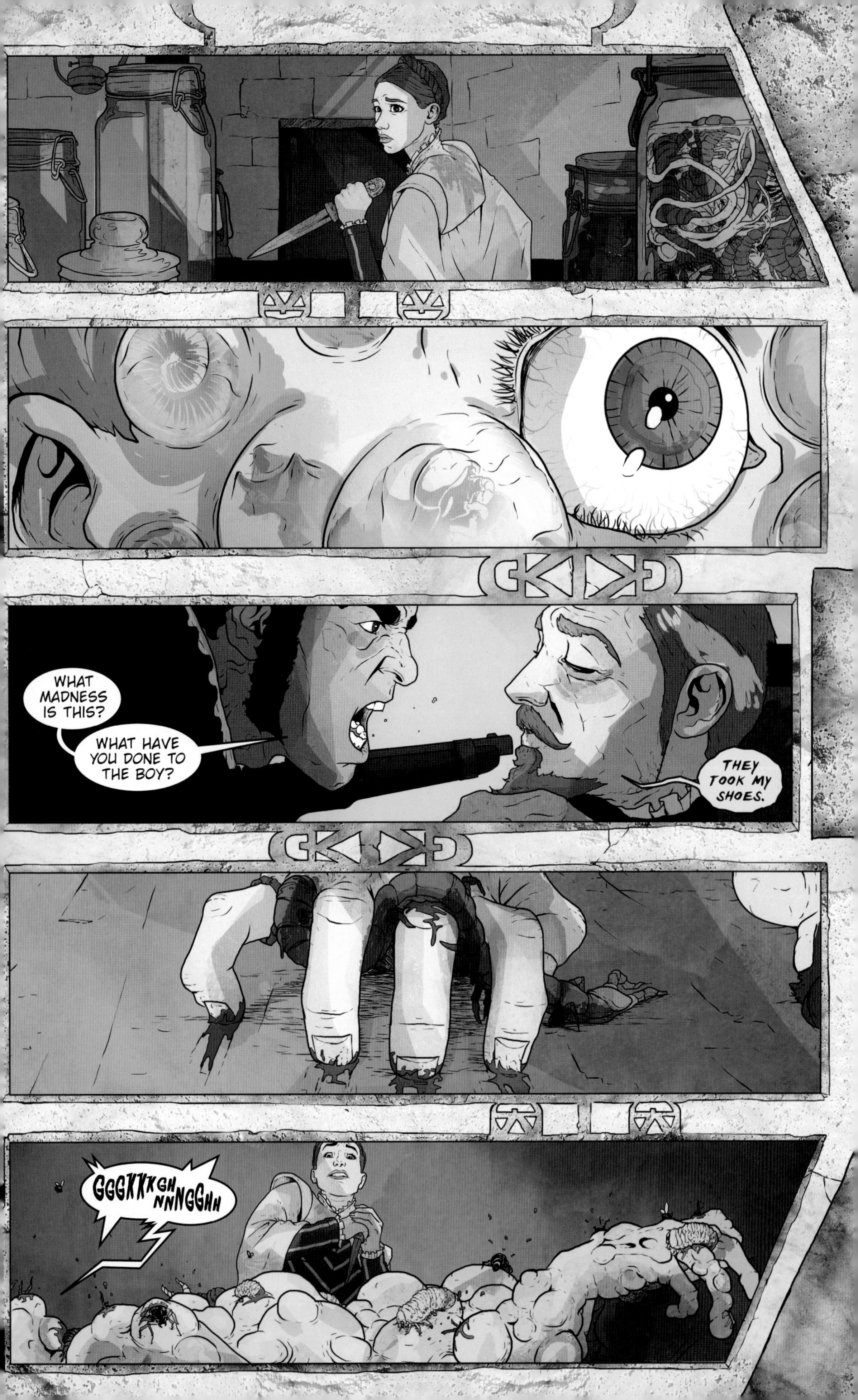
WHAT MADNESS IS THIS?
WHAT HAVE YOU DONE TO THE BOY?
THEY TOOK MY SHOES.
GGGKKKGH NNNGGHH

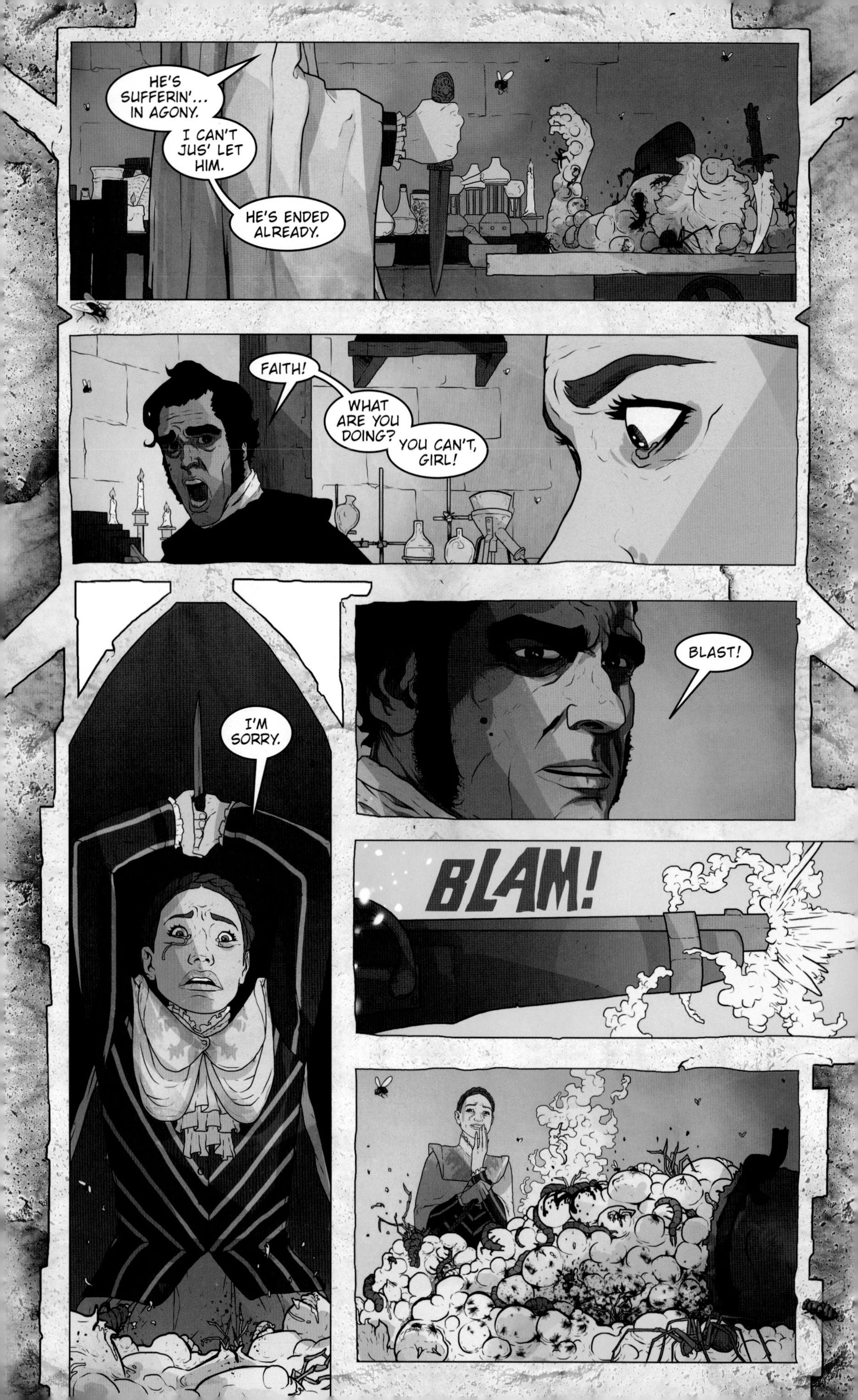
HE'S SUFFERIN'... IN AGONY.
I CAN'T JUS' LET HIM.
HE'S ENDED ALREADY.
FAITH!
WHAT ARE YOU DOING?
YOU CAN'T, GIRL!
I'M SORRY.
BLAST!
BLAM!

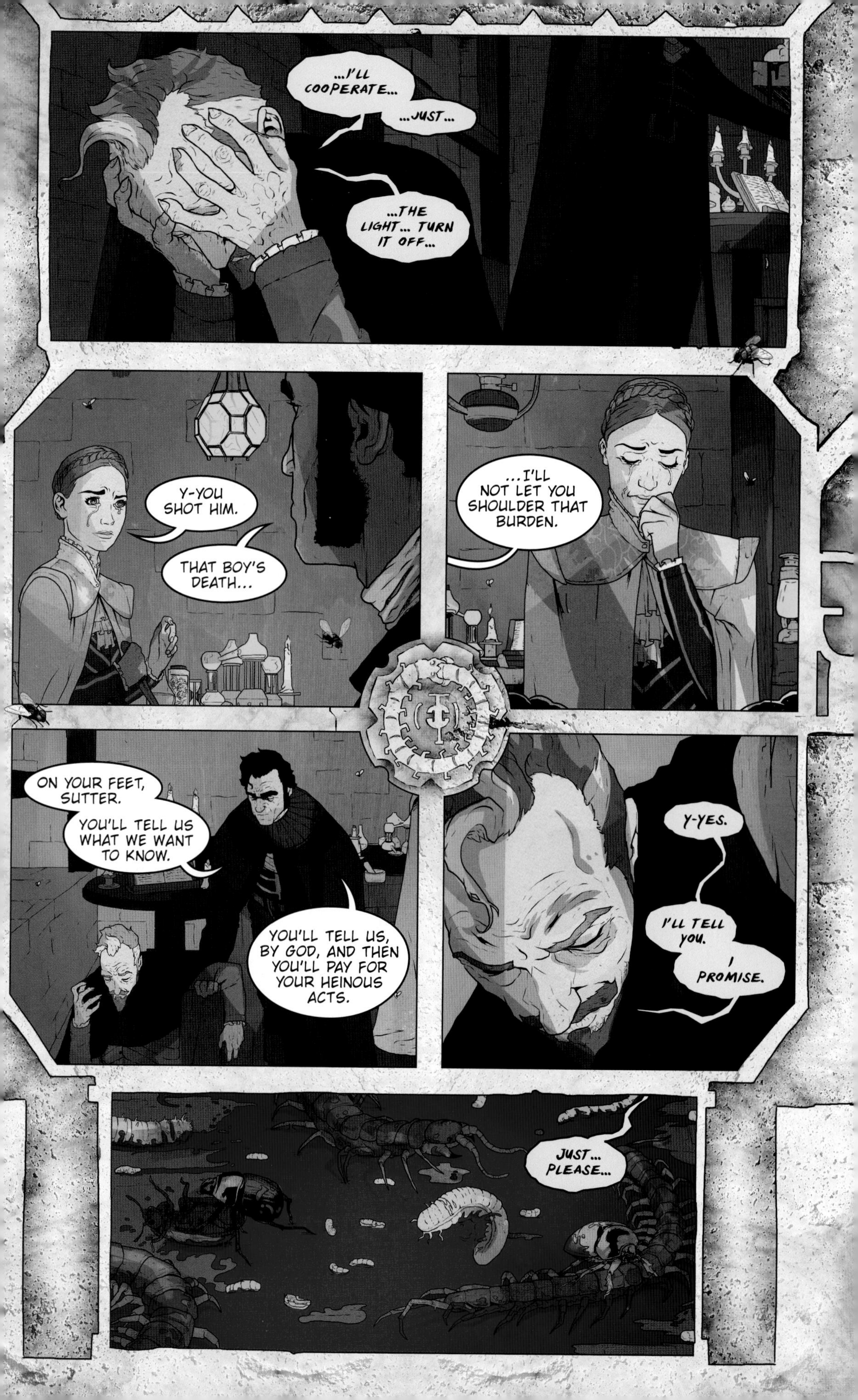
...I'LL COOPERATE...
...JUST...
...THE LIGHT... TURN IT OFF...
Y-YOU SHOT HIM.
THAT BOY'S DEATH...
...I'LL NOT LET YOU SHOULDER THAT BURDEN.
ON YOUR FEET, SUTTER.
YOU'LL TELL US WHAT WE WANT TO KNOW.
YOU'LL TELL US, BY GOD, AND THEN YOU'LL PAY FOR YOUR HEINOUS ACTS.
Y-YES.
I'LL TELL YOU.
I PROMISE.
JUST... PLEASE...

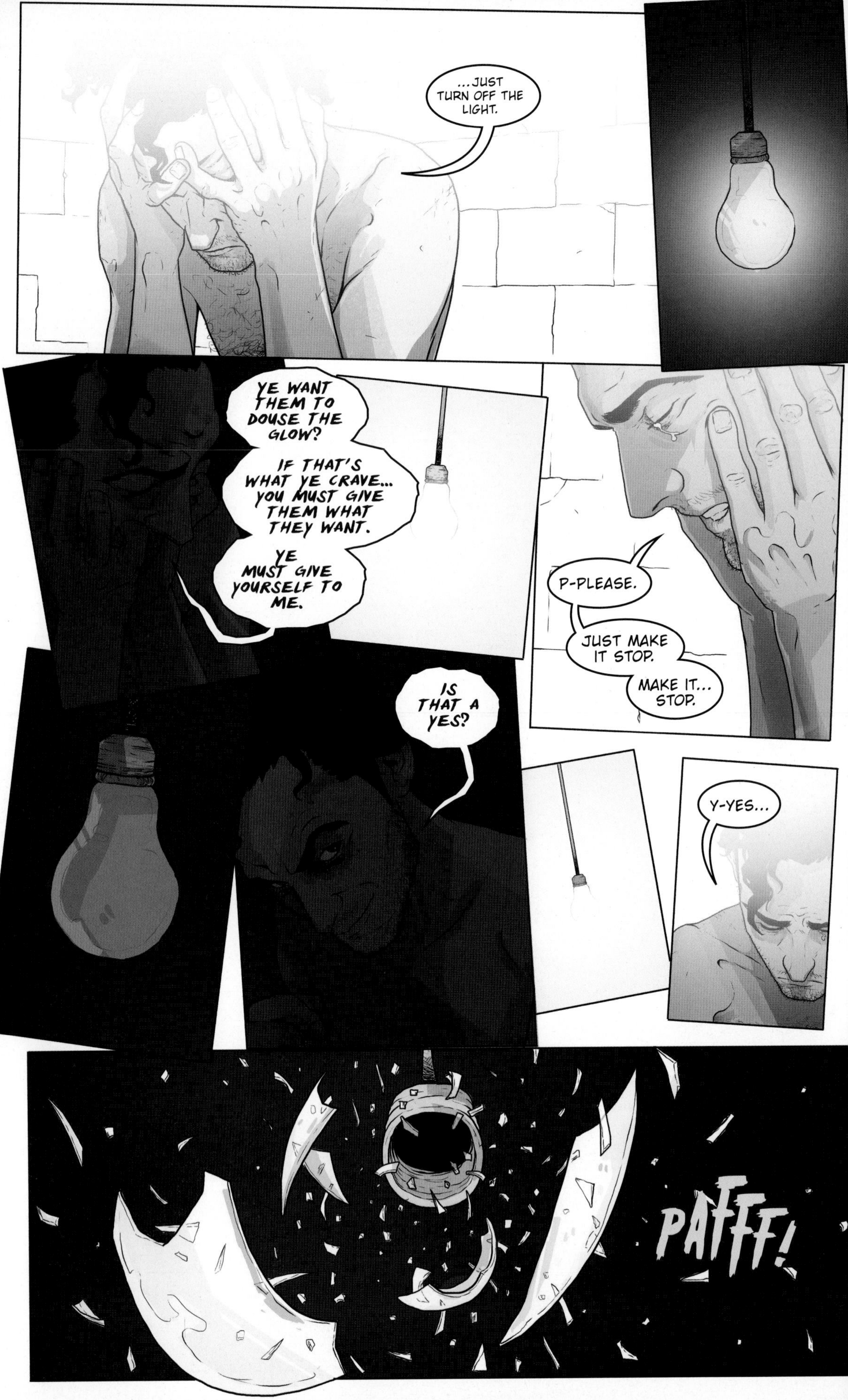
...JUST TURN OFF THE LIGHT.
YE WANT THEM TO DOUSE THE GLOW?
IF THAT'S WHAT YE CRAVE... YOU MUST GIVE THEM WHAT THEY WANT.
YE MUST GIVE YOURSELF TO ME.
P-PLEASE.
JUST MAKE IT STOP.
MAKE IT... STOP.
IS THAT A YES?
Y-YES...
PAFFF!

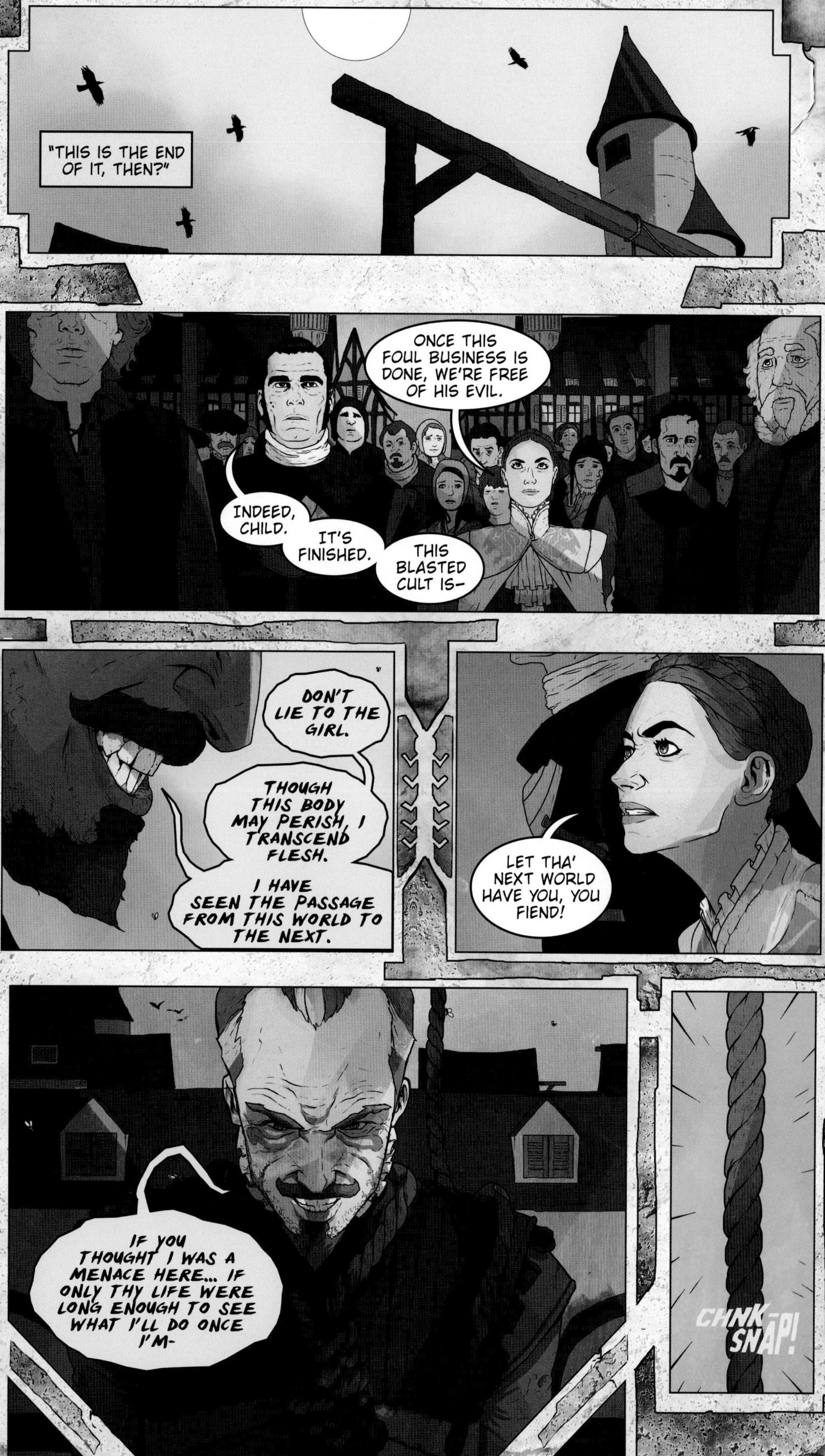
"THIS IS THE END OF IT, THEN?"
ONCE THIS FOUL BUSINESS IS DONE, WE'RE FREE OF HIS EVIL.
INDEED, CHILD.
IT'S FINISHED.
THIS BLASTED CULT IS-
DON'T LIE TO THE GIRL.
THOUGH THIS BODY MAY PERISH, I TRANSCEND FLESH.
I HAVE SEEN THE PASSAGE FROM THIS WORLD TO THE NEXT.
LET THA' NEXT WORLD HAVE YOU, YOU FIEND!
IF YOU THOUGHT I WAS A MENACE HERE... IF ONLY THY LIFE WERE LONG ENOUGH TO SEE WHAT I'LL DO ONCE I'M-
CHNK-SNAP!

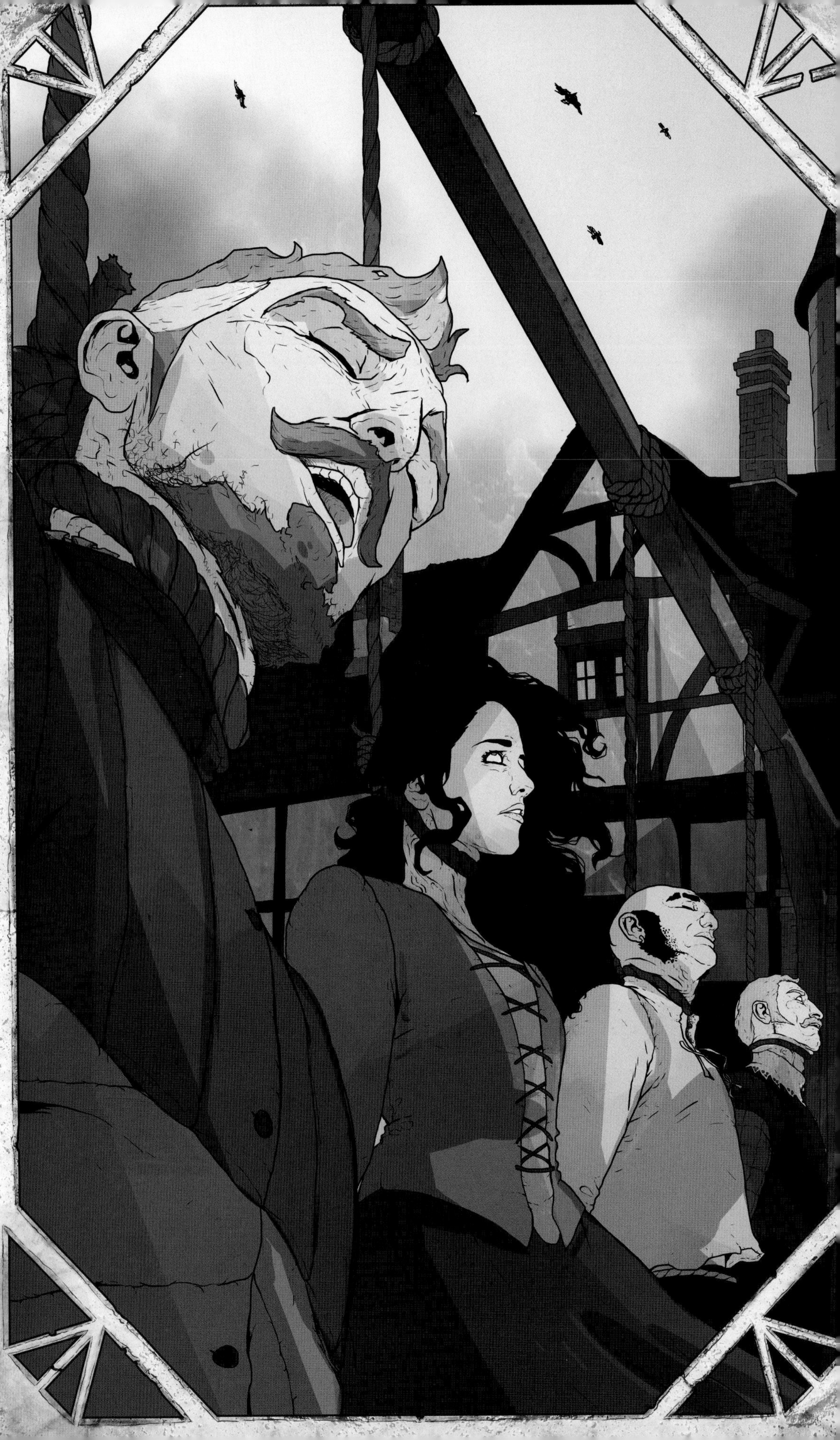

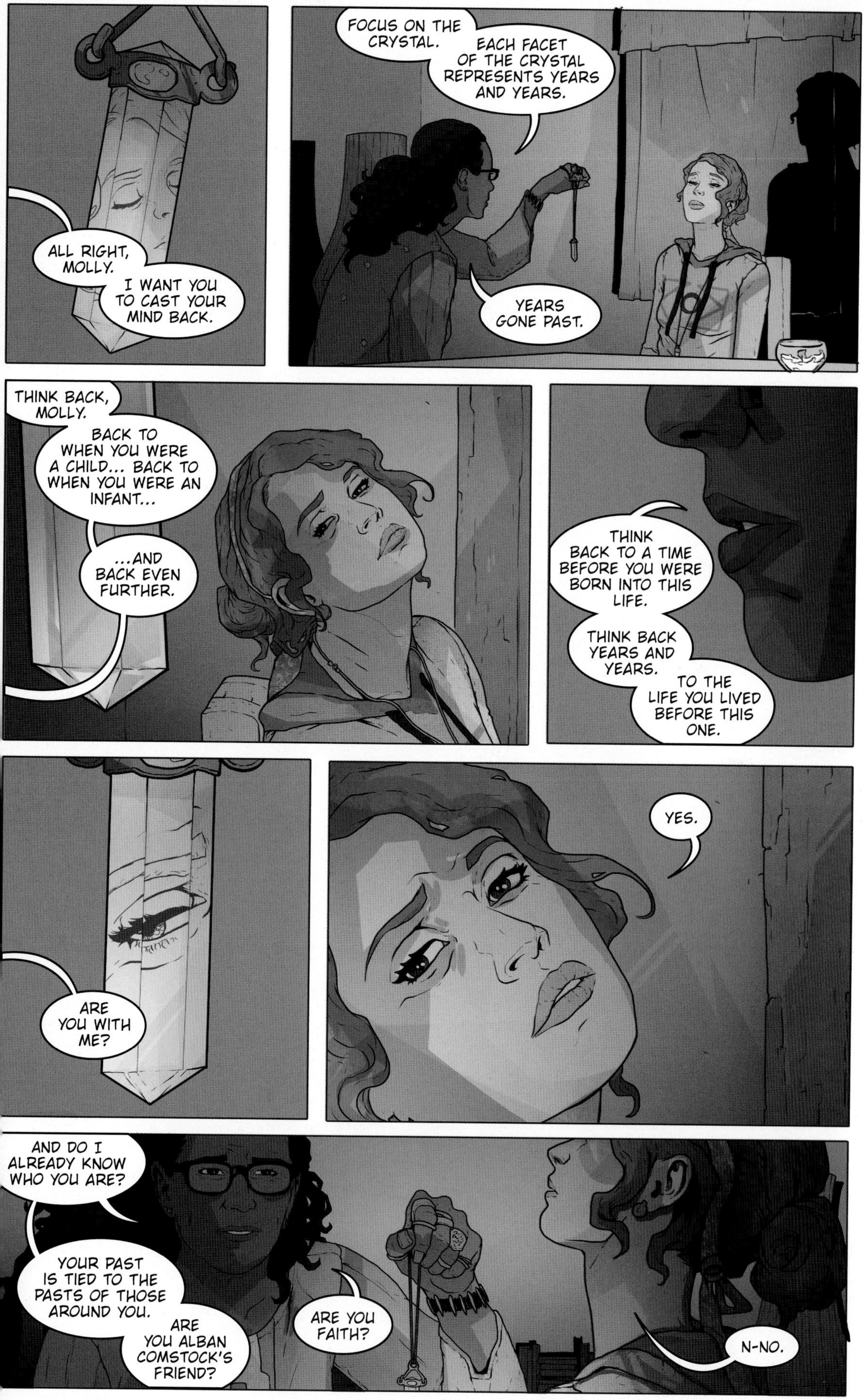
ALL RIGHT, MOLLY.
I WANT YOU TO CAST YOUR MIND BACK.
FOCUS ON THE CRYSTAL.
EACH FACET OF THE CRYSTAL REPRESENTS YEARS AND YEARS.
YEARS GONE PAST.
THINK BACK, MOLLY.
BACK TO WHEN YOU WERE A CHILD... BACK TO WHEN YOU WERE AN INFANT...
...AND BACK EVEN FURTHER.
THINK BACK TO A TIME BEFORE YOU WERE BORN INTO THIS LIFE.
THINK BACK YEARS AND YEARS.
TO THE LIFE YOU LIVED BEFORE THIS ONE.
ARE YOU WITH ME?
YES.
AND DO I ALREADY KNOW WHO YOU ARE?
YOUR PAST IS TIED TO THE PASTS OF THOSE AROUND YOU.
ARE YOU ALBAN COMSTOCK'S FRIEND?
ARE YOU FAITH?
N-NO.

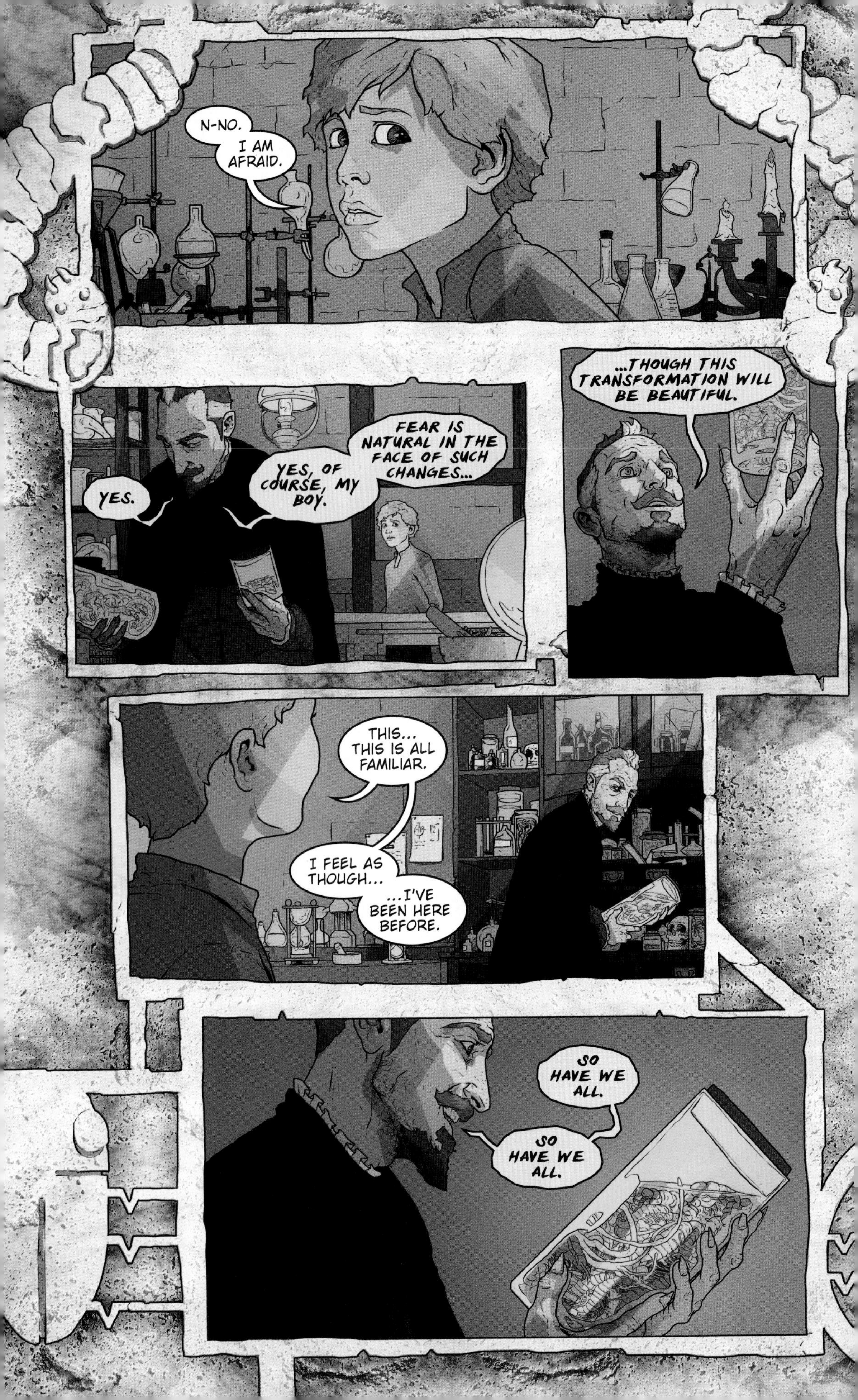
N-NO.
I AM AFRAID.
YES.
YES, OF COURSE, MY BOY.
FEAR IS NATURAL IN THE FACE OF SUCH CHANGES...
...THOUGH THIS TRANSFORMATION WILL BE BEAUTIFUL.
THIS... THIS IS ALL FAMILIAR.
I FEEL AS THOUGH...
...I'VE BEEN HERE BEFORE.
SO HAVE WE ALL.
SO HAVE WE ALL.

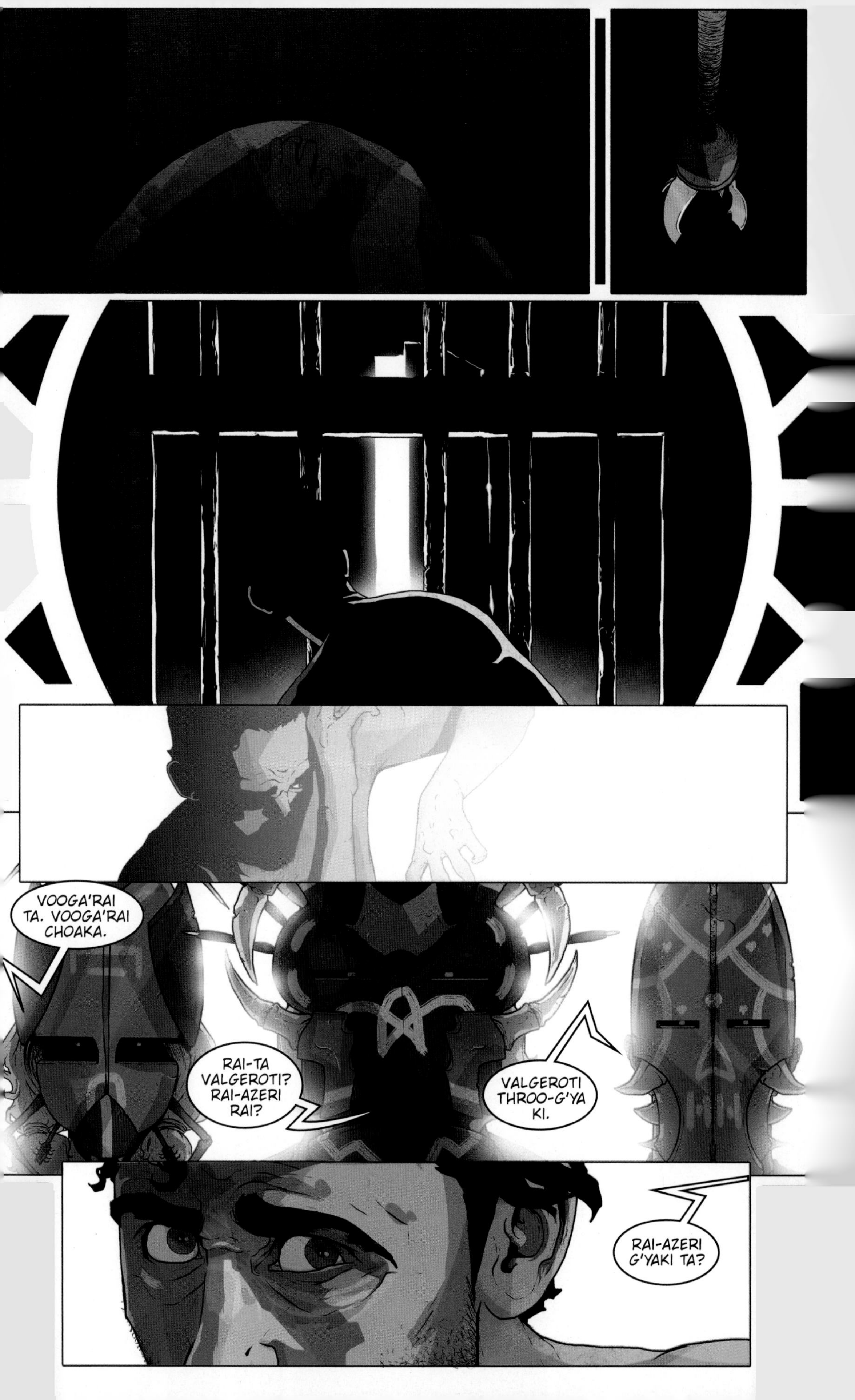
VOOGA'RAI TA. VOOGA'RAI CHOAKA.
RAI-TA VALGEROTI? RAI-AZERI RAI?
VALGEROTI THROO-G'YA KI.
RAI-AZERI G'YAKI TA?

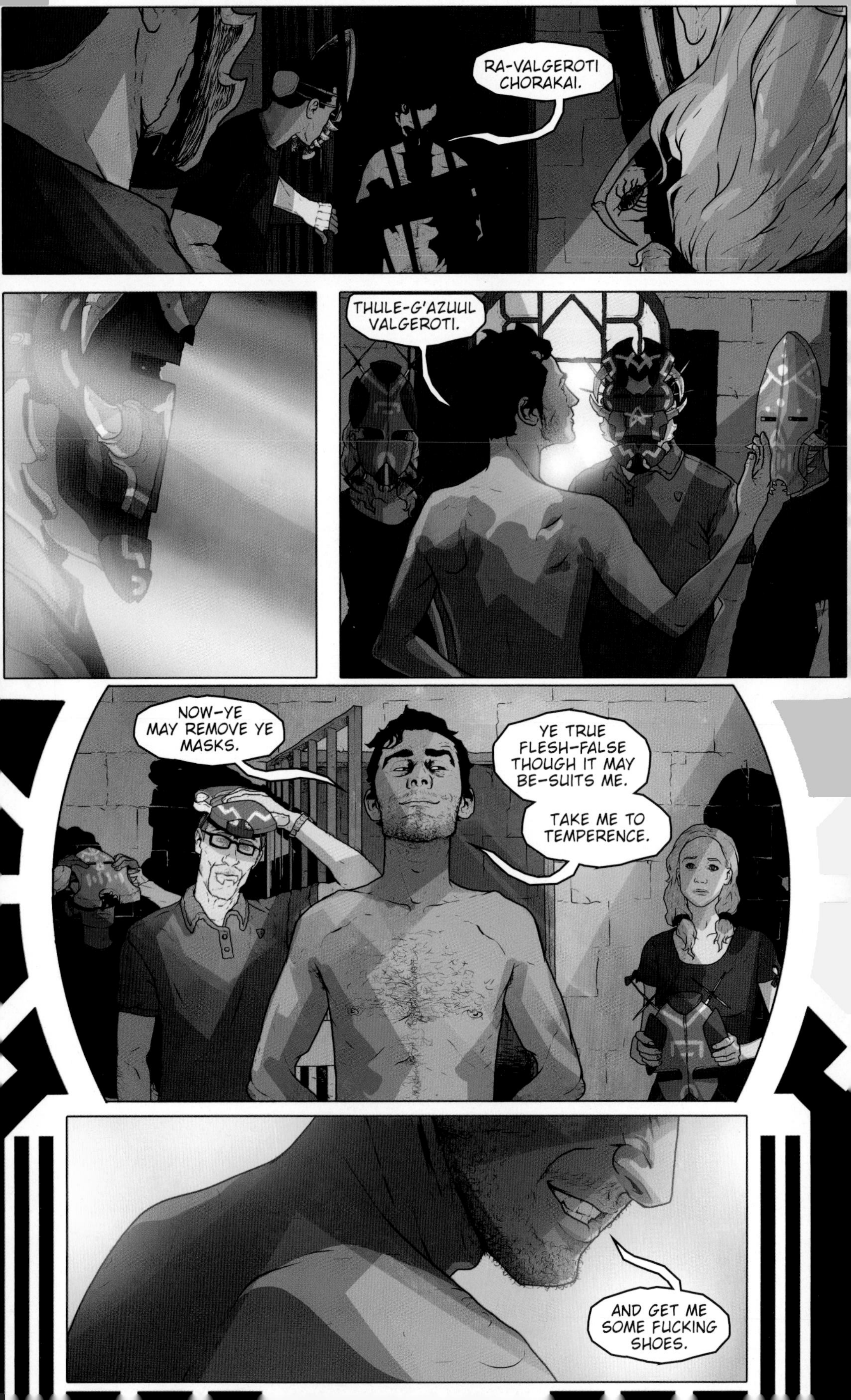
RA-VALGEROTI CHORAKAI.
THULE-G'AZUUL VALGEROTI.
NOW-YE MAY REMOVE YE MASKS.
YE TRUE FLESH-FALSE THOUGH IT MAY BE-SUITS ME.
TAKE ME TO TEMPERENCE.
AND GET ME SOME FUCKING SHOES.

TEN

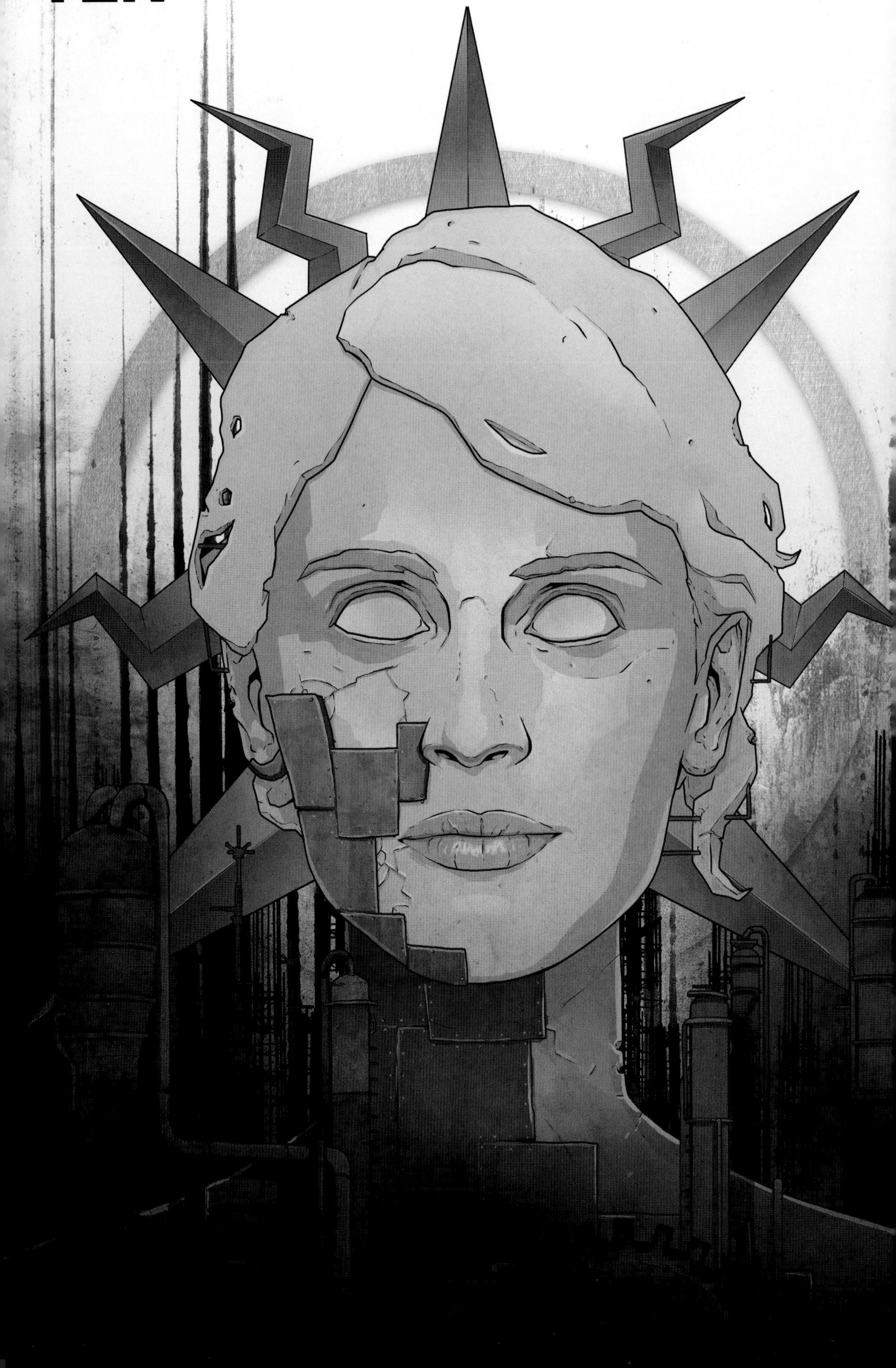

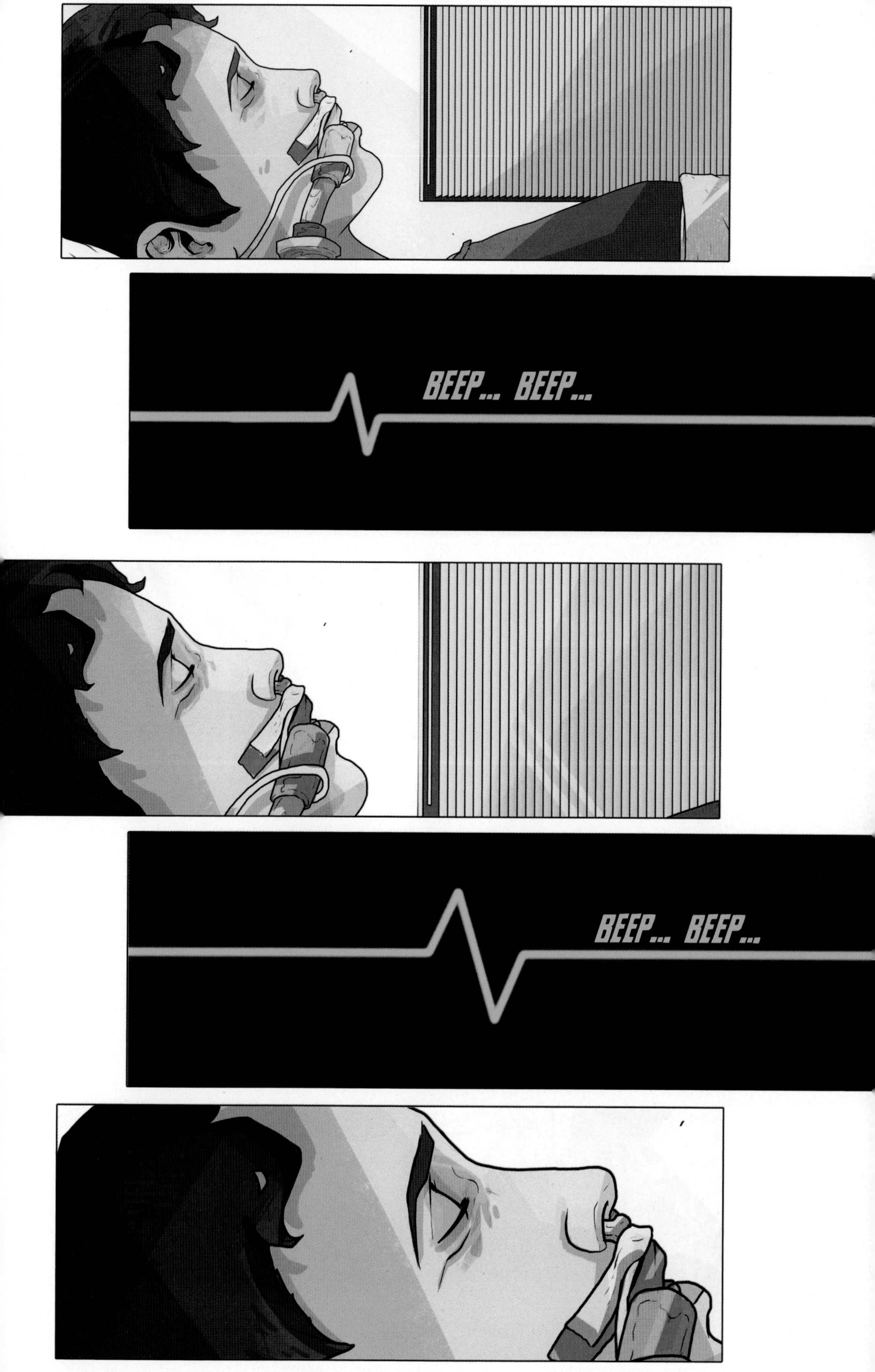
BEEP... BEEP...
BEEP... BEEP...

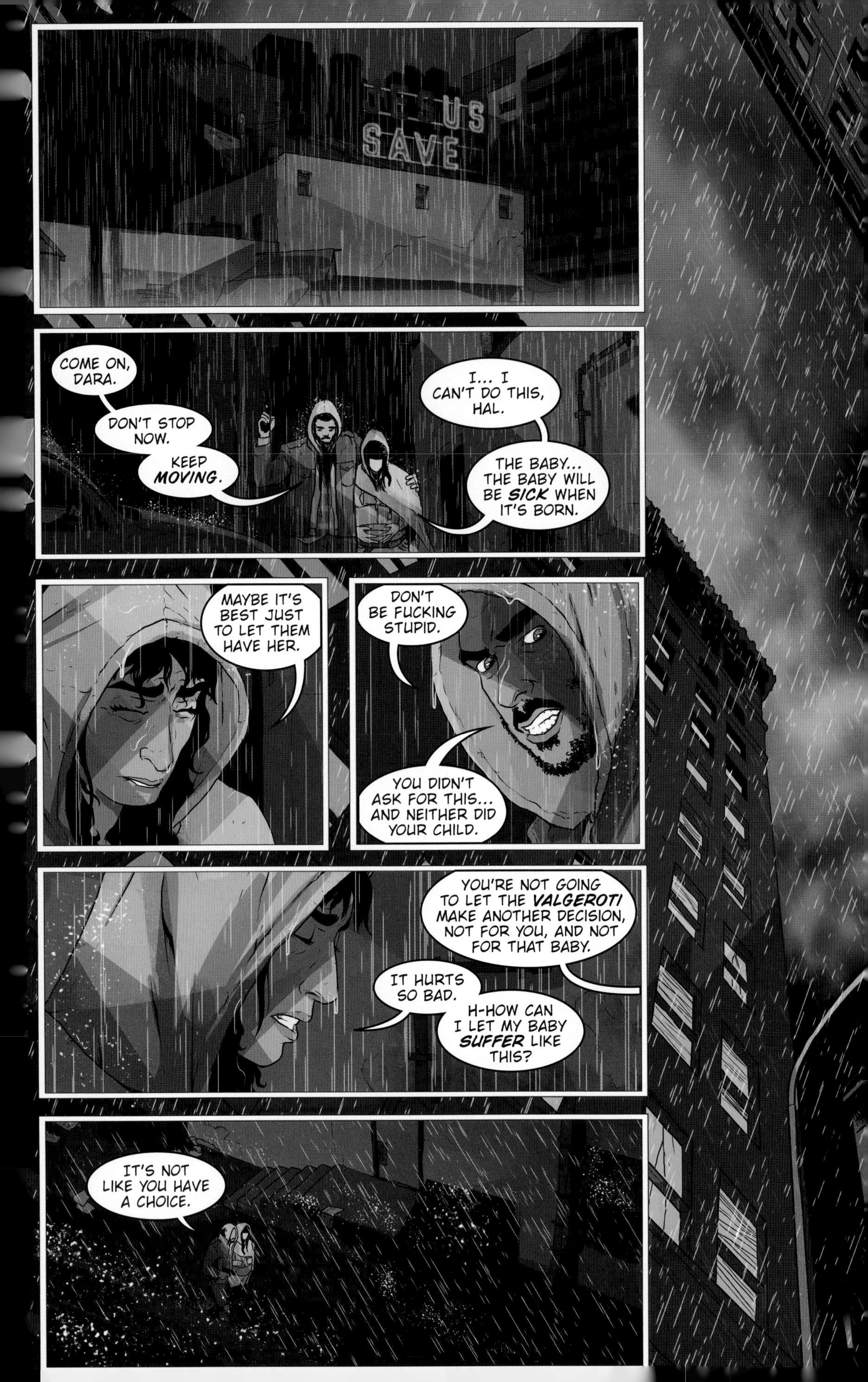

COME ON, DARA.
DON'T STOP NOW.
KEEP *MOVING*.
I... I CAN'T DO THIS, HAL.
THE BABY... THE BABY WILL BE *SICK* WHEN IT'S BORN.
MAYBE IT'S BEST JUST TO LET THEM HAVE HER.
DON'T BE FUCKING STUPID.
YOU DIDN'T ASK FOR THIS... AND NEITHER DID YOUR CHILD.
YOU'RE NOT GOING TO LET THE *VALGEROTI* MAKE ANOTHER DECISION, NOT FOR YOU, AND NOT FOR THAT BABY.
IT HURTS SO BAD.
H-HOW CAN I LET MY BABY *SUFFER* LIKE THIS?
IT'S NOT LIKE YOU HAVE A CHOICE.

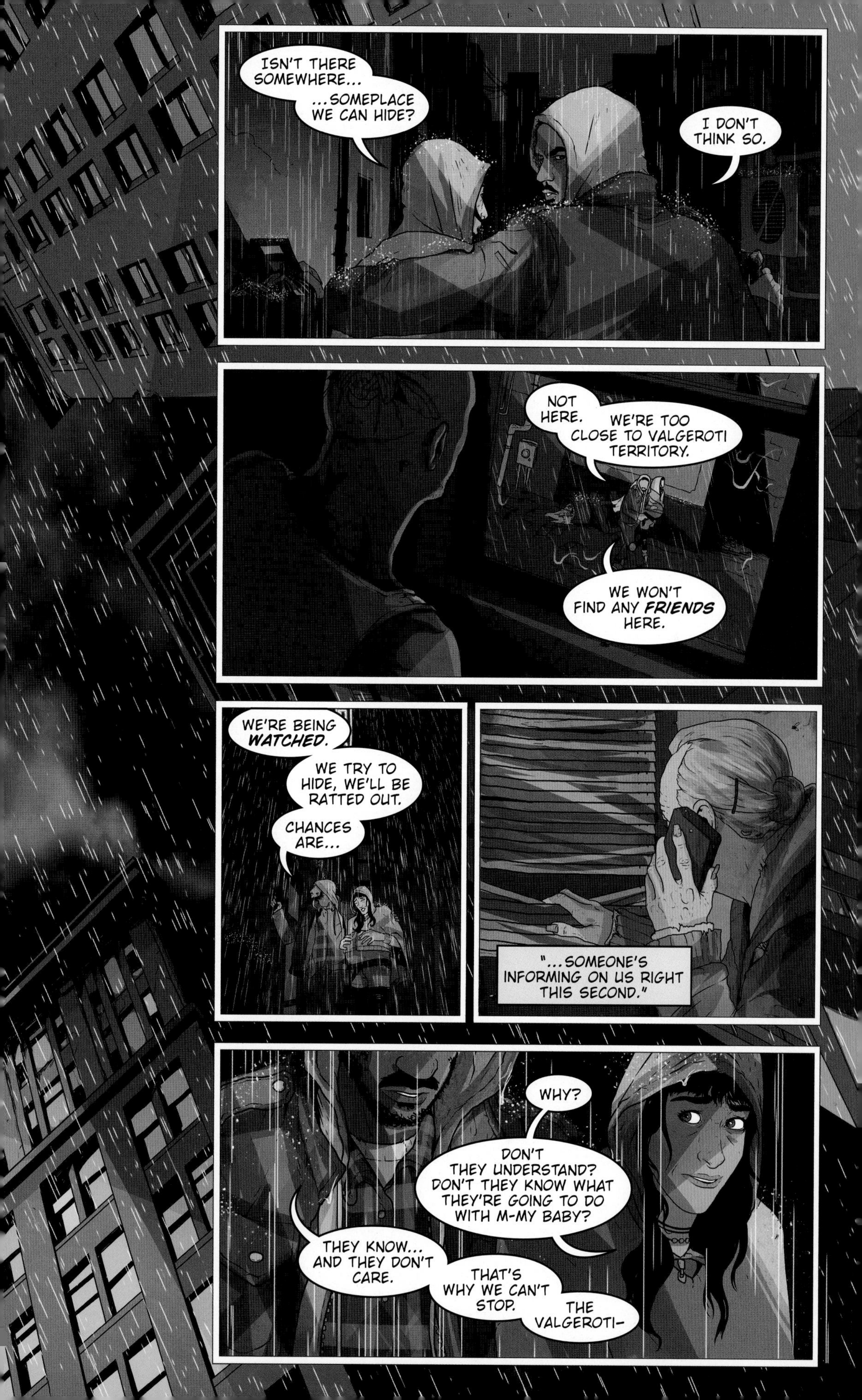
ISN'T THERE SOMEWHERE...
...SOMEPLACE WE CAN HIDE?
I DON'T THINK SO.
NOT HERE.
WE'RE TOO CLOSE TO VALGEROTI TERRITORY.
WE WON'T FIND ANY *FRIENDS* HERE.
WE'RE BEING *WATCHED*.
WE TRY TO HIDE, WE'LL BE RATTED OUT.
CHANCES ARE...
"...SOMEONE'S INFORMING ON US RIGHT THIS SECOND."
WHY?
DON'T THEY UNDERSTAND? DON'T THEY KNOW WHAT THEY'RE GOING TO DO WITH M-MY BABY?
THEY KNOW... AND THEY DON'T CARE.
THAT'S WHY WE CAN'T STOP.
THE VALGEROTI-

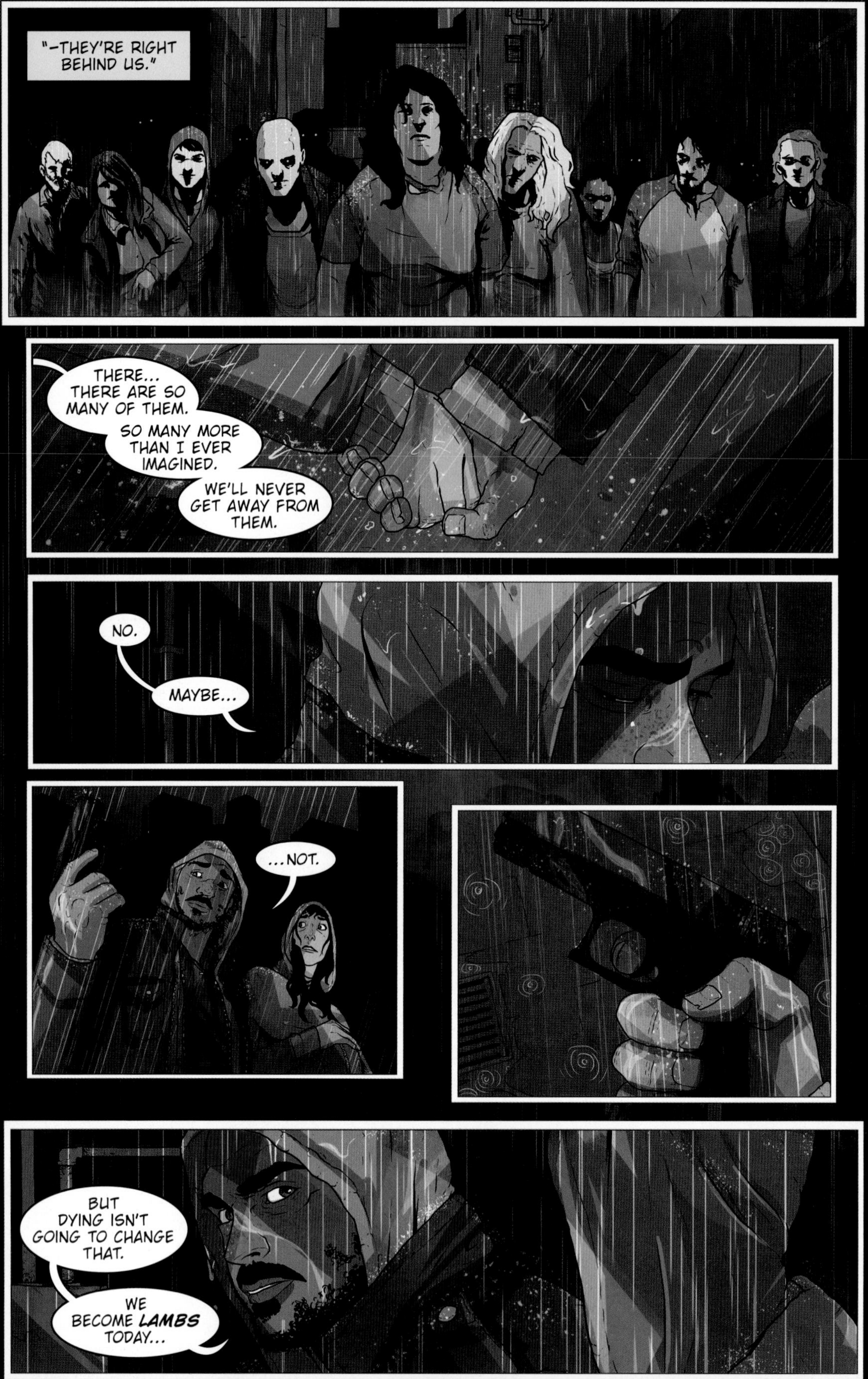
"–THEY'RE RIGHT BEHIND US."
THERE... THERE ARE SO MANY OF THEM.
SO MANY MORE THAN I EVER IMAGINED.
WE'LL NEVER GET AWAY FROM THEM.
NO.
MAYBE...
...NOT.
BUT DYING ISN'T GOING TO CHANGE THAT.
WE BECOME LAMBS TODAY...

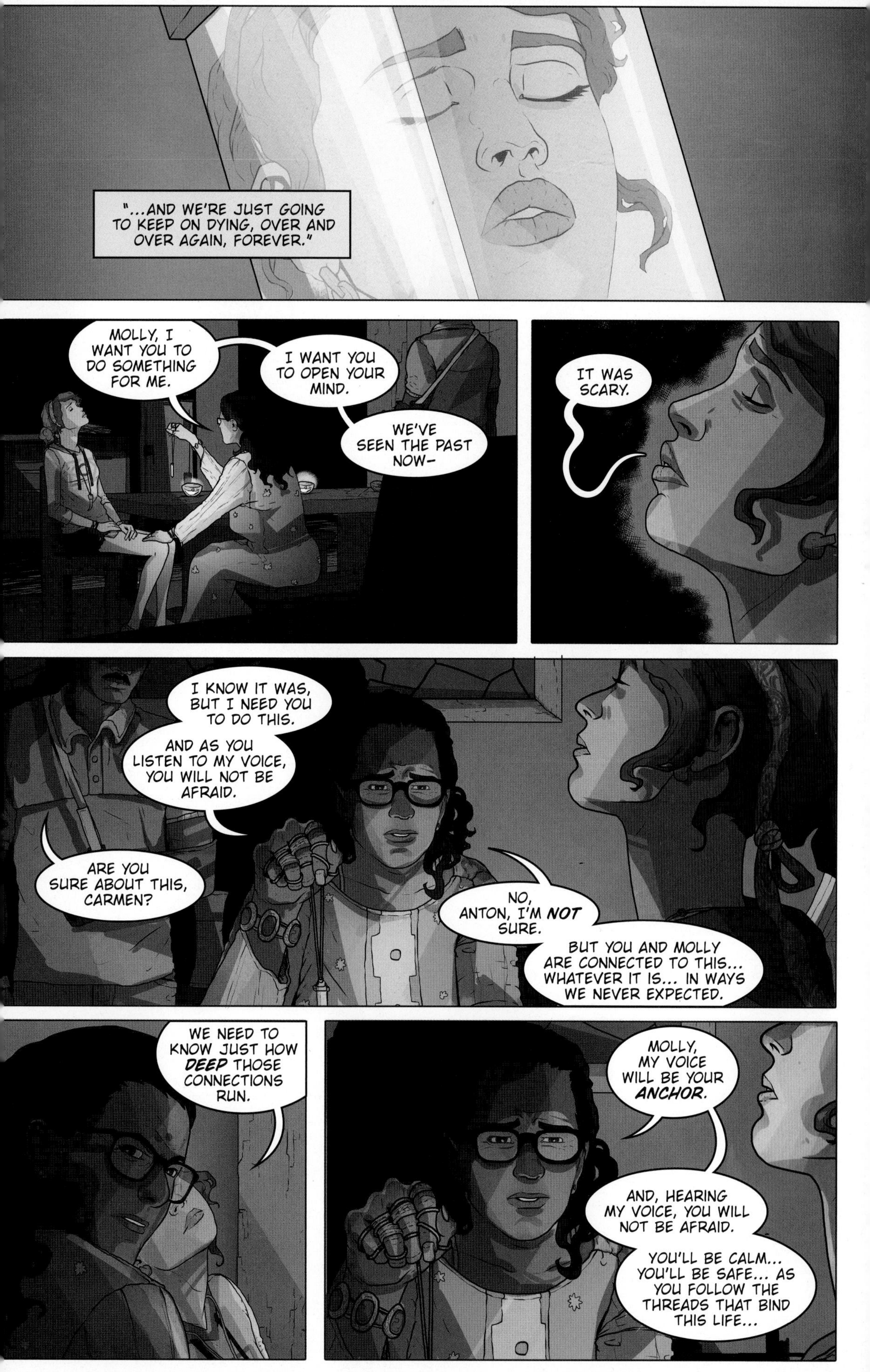
"...AND WE'RE JUST GOING TO KEEP ON DYING, OVER AND OVER AGAIN, FOREVER."
MOLLY, I WANT YOU TO DO SOMETHING FOR ME.
I WANT YOU TO OPEN YOUR MIND.
WE'VE SEEN THE PAST NOW–
IT WAS SCARY.
I KNOW IT WAS, BUT I NEED YOU TO DO THIS.
AND AS YOU LISTEN TO MY VOICE, YOU WILL NOT BE AFRAID.
ARE YOU SURE ABOUT THIS, CARMEN?
NO, ANTON, I'M NOT SURE.
BUT YOU AND MOLLY ARE CONNECTED TO THIS... WHATEVER IT IS... IN WAYS WE NEVER EXPECTED.
WE NEED TO KNOW JUST HOW DEEP THOSE CONNECTIONS RUN.
MOLLY, MY VOICE WILL BE YOUR ANCHOR.
AND, HEARING MY VOICE, YOU WILL NOT BE AFRAID.
YOU'LL BE CALM... YOU'LL BE SAFE... AS YOU FOLLOW THE THREADS THAT BIND THIS LIFE...

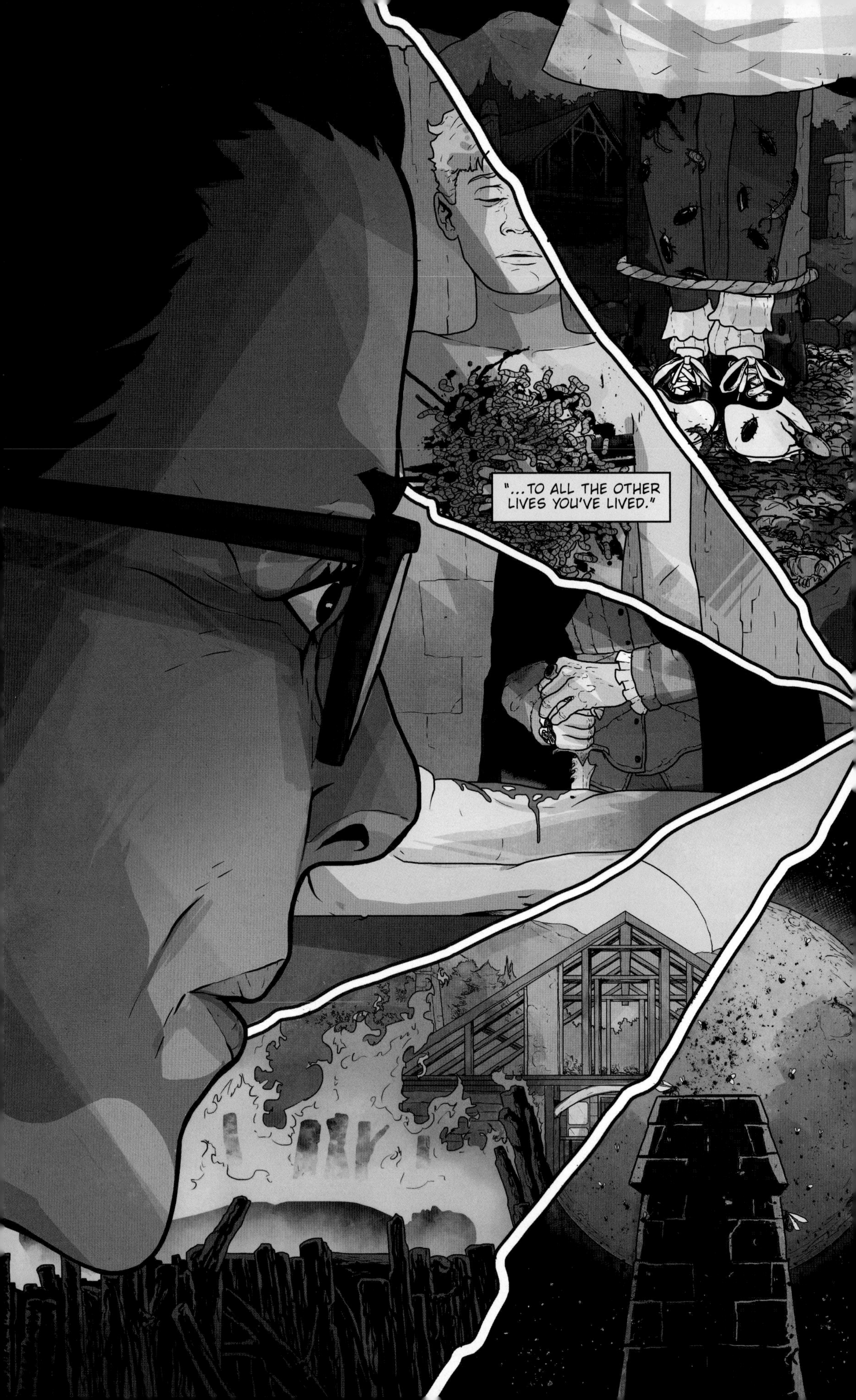
"...TO ALL THE OTHER LIVES YOU'VE LIVED."

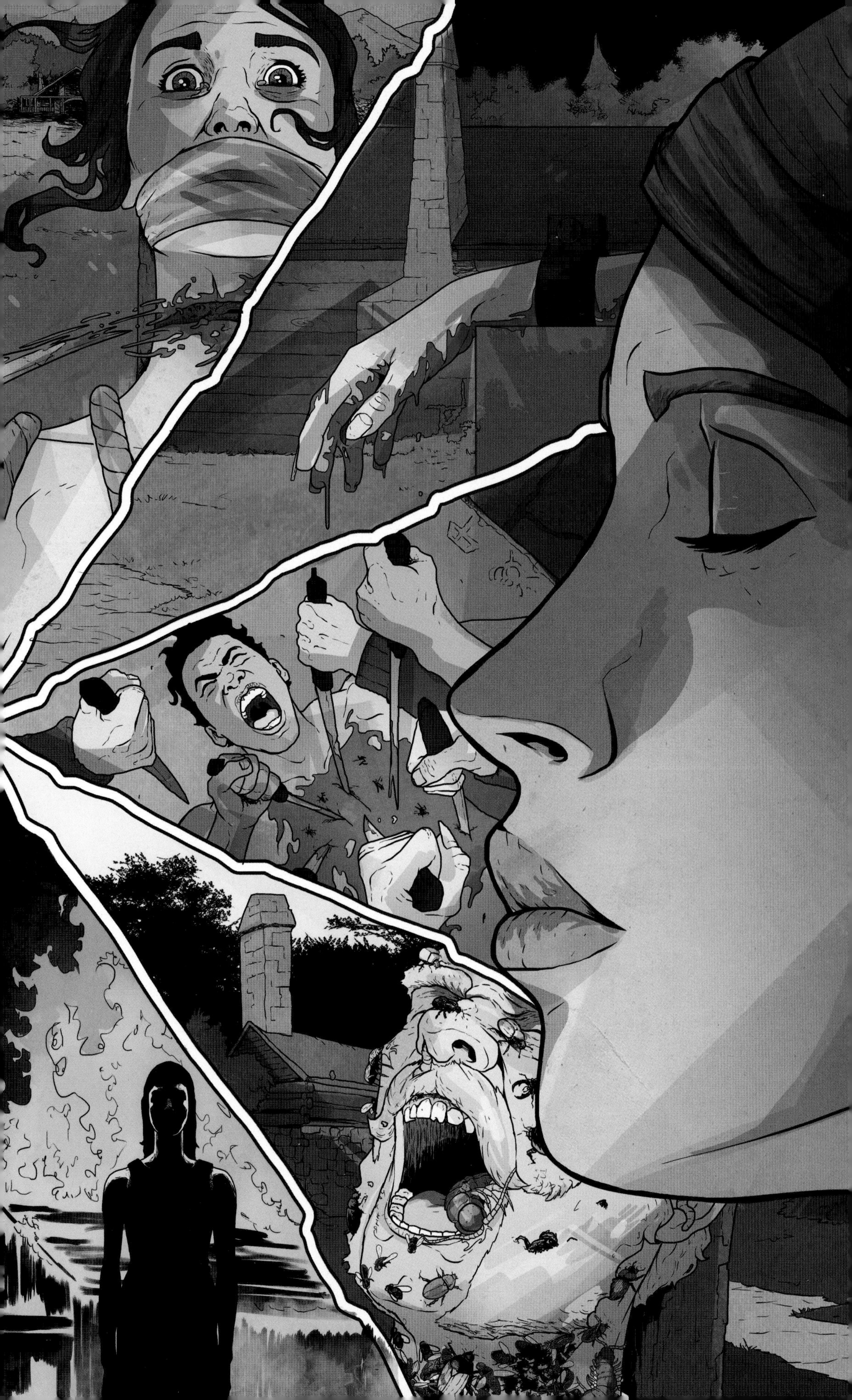

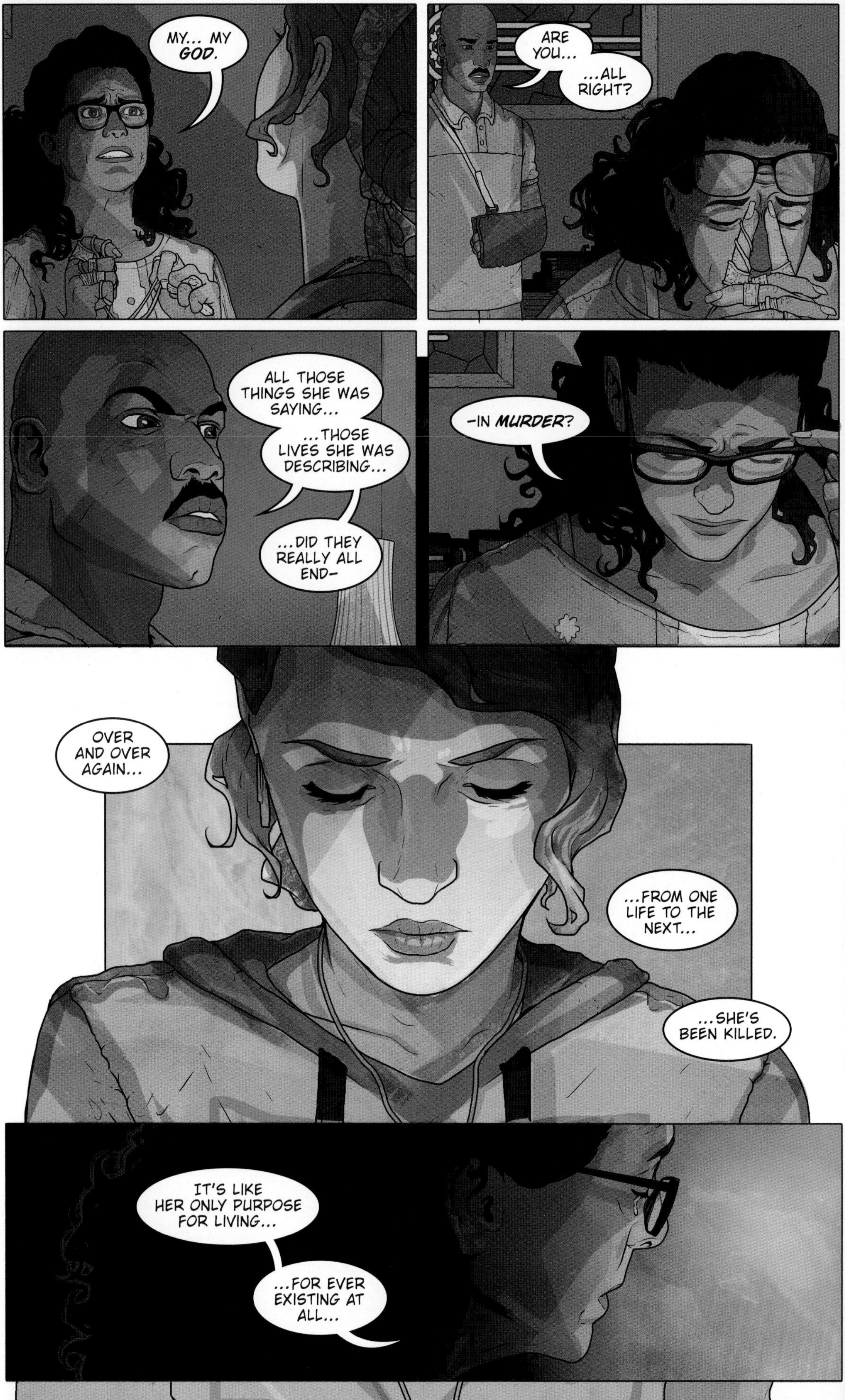
MY... MY GOD.
ARE YOU...
...ALL RIGHT?
ALL THOSE THINGS SHE WAS SAYING...
...THOSE LIVES SHE WAS DESCRIBING...
...DID THEY REALLY ALL END-
-IN MURDER?
OVER AND OVER AGAIN...
...FROM ONE LIFE TO THE NEXT...
...SHE'S BEEN KILLED.
IT'S LIKE HER ONLY PURPOSE FOR LIVING...
...FOR EVER EXISTING AT ALL...

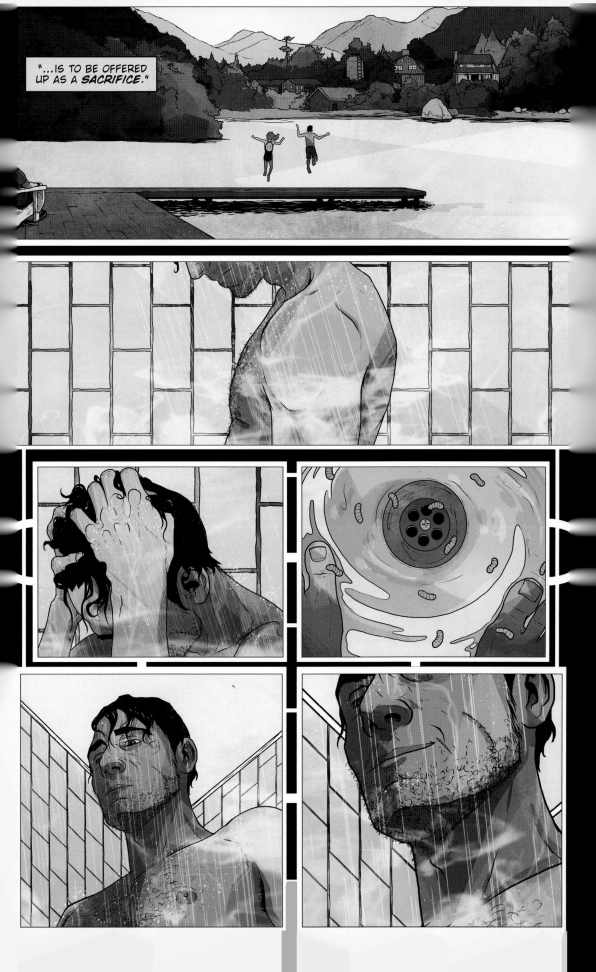

"...IS TO BE OFFERED UP AS A *SACRIFICE*."

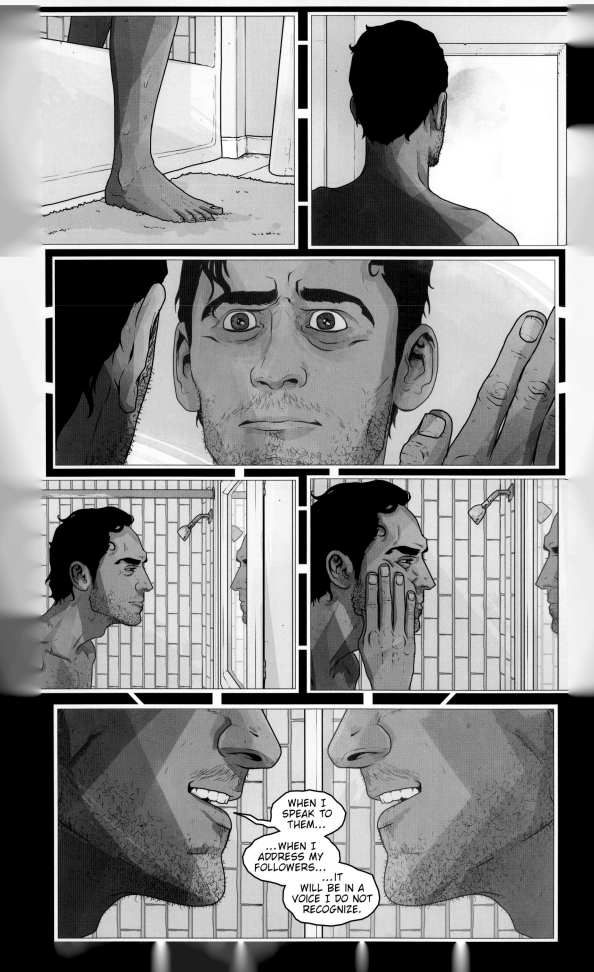

WHEN I SPEAK TO THEM...

...WHEN I ADDRESS MY FOLLOWERS...

...IT WILL BE IN A VOICE I DO NOT RECOGNIZE.

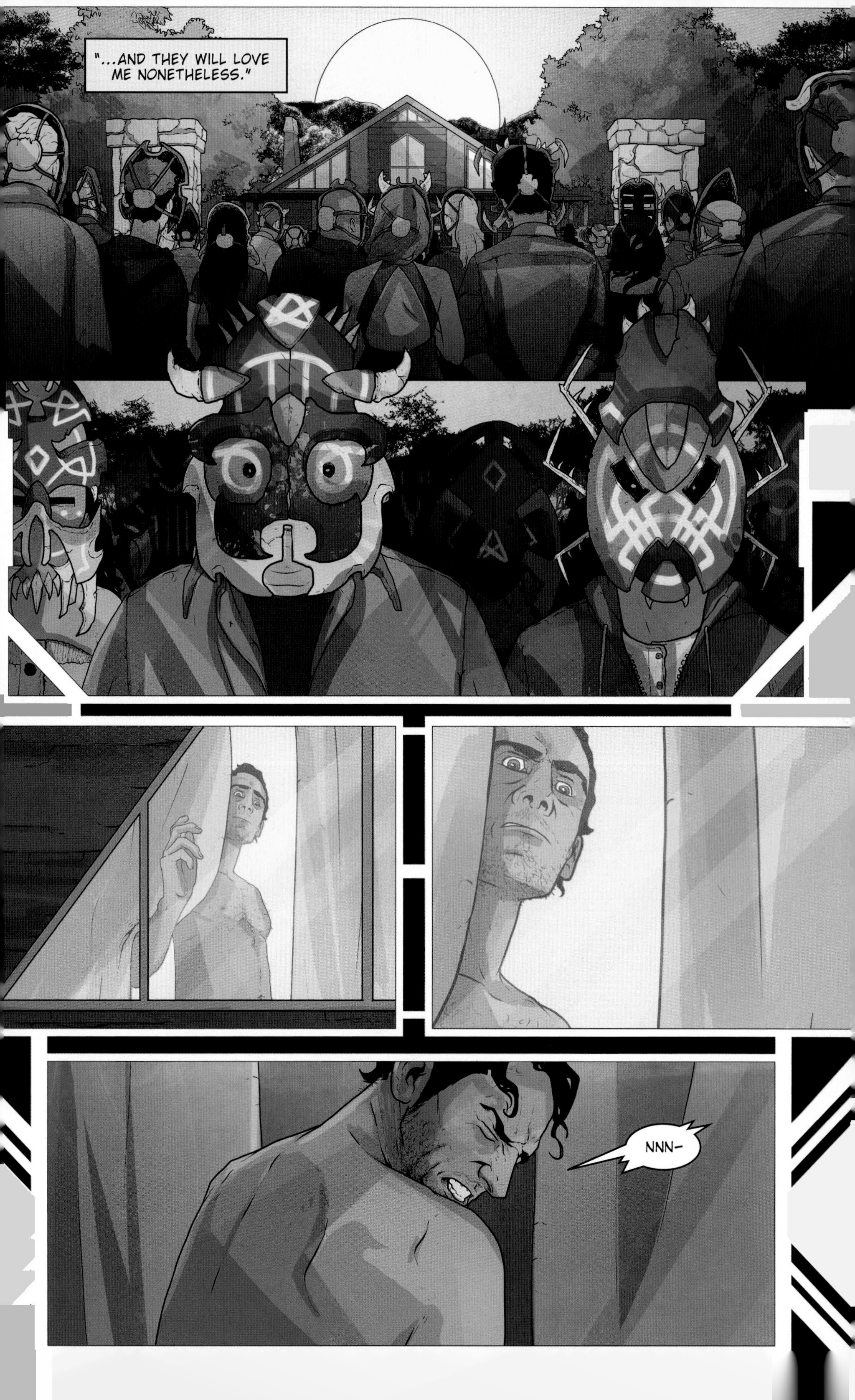
"...AND THEY WILL LOVE ME NONETHELESS."
NNN-

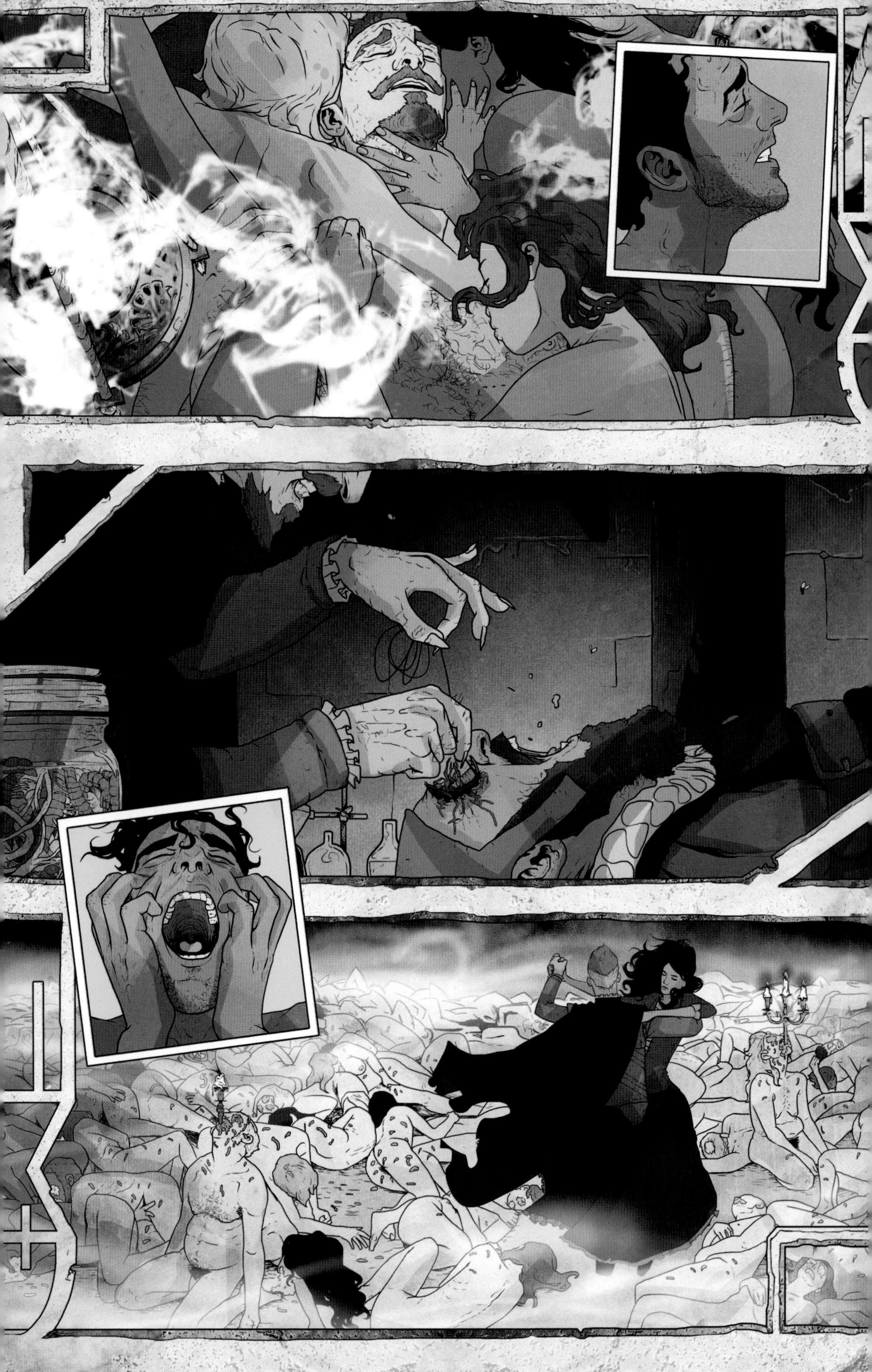

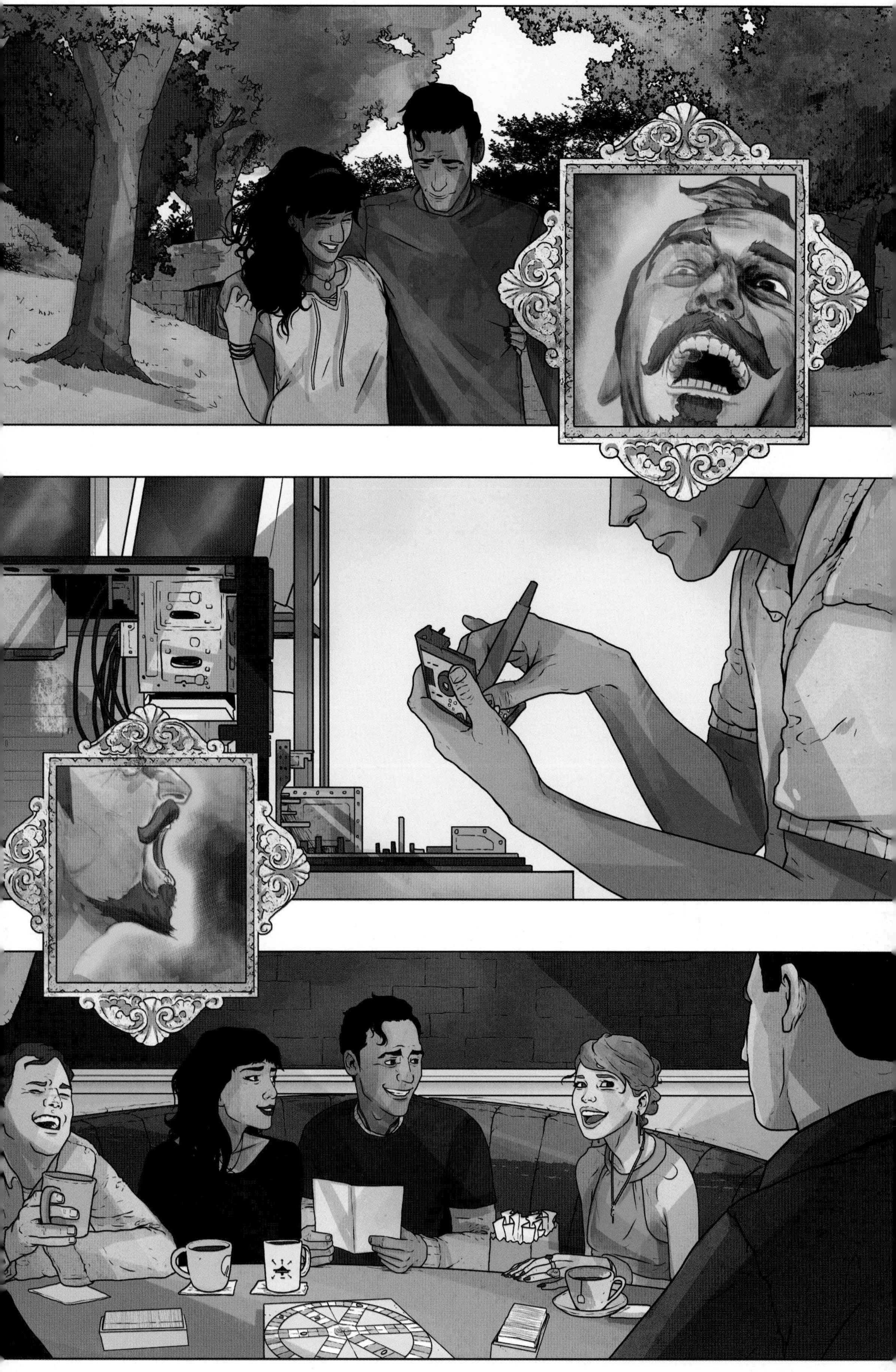

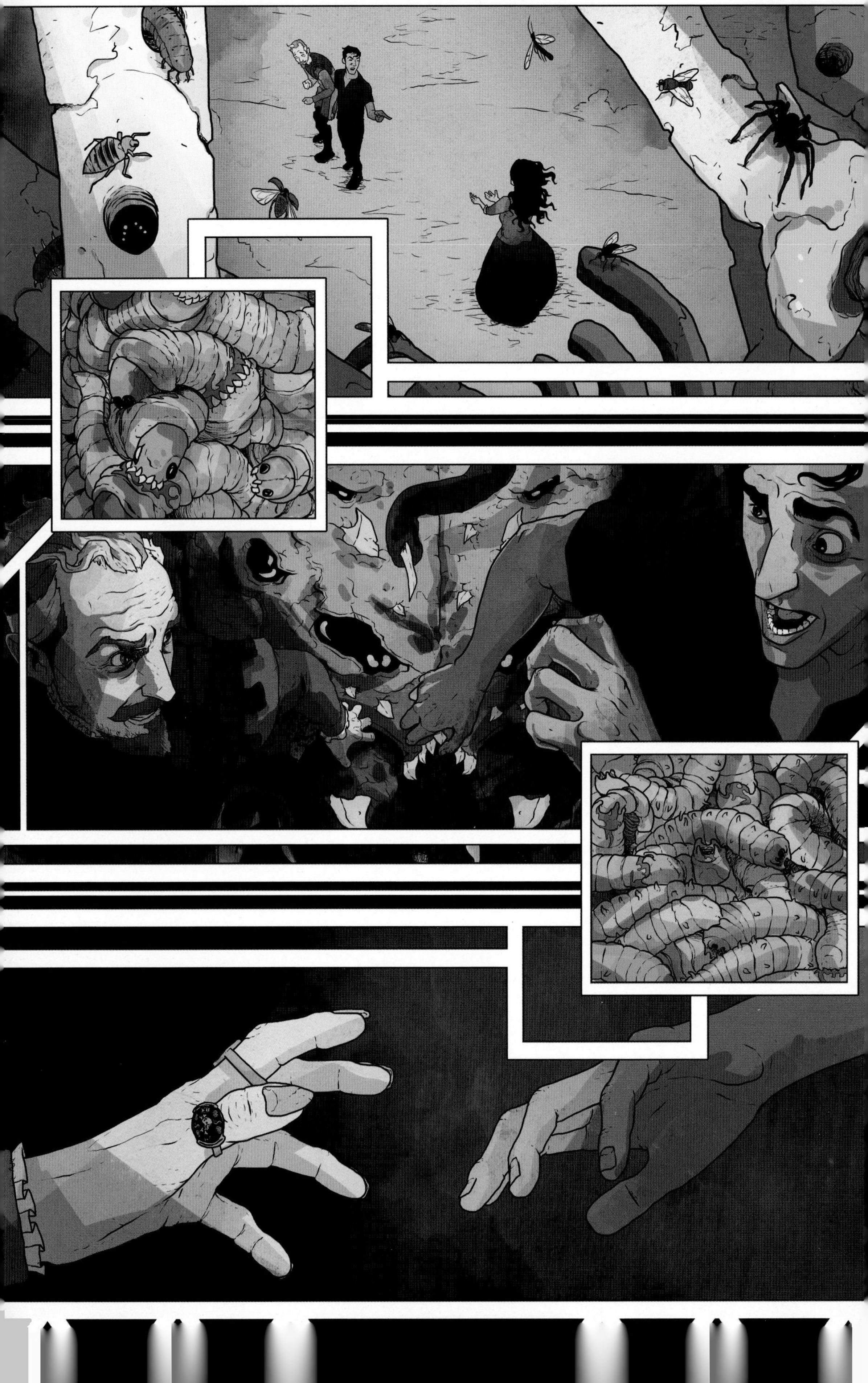

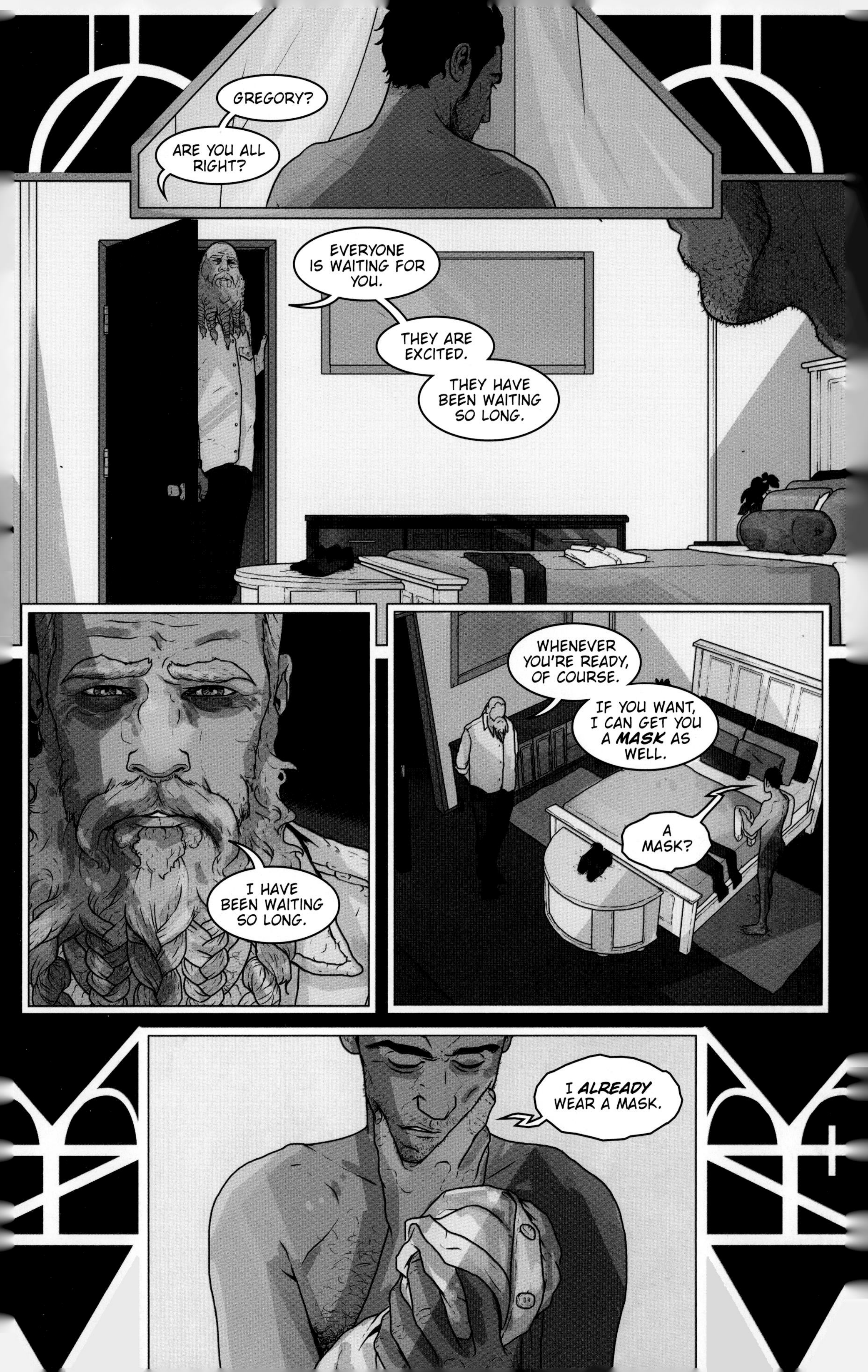
GREGORY?
ARE YOU ALL RIGHT?
EVERYONE IS WAITING FOR YOU.
THEY ARE EXCITED.
THEY HAVE BEEN WAITING SO LONG.
I HAVE BEEN WAITING SO LONG.
WHENEVER YOU'RE READY, OF COURSE.
IF YOU WANT, I CAN GET YOU A **MASK** AS WELL.
A MASK?
I ***ALREADY*** WEAR A MASK.

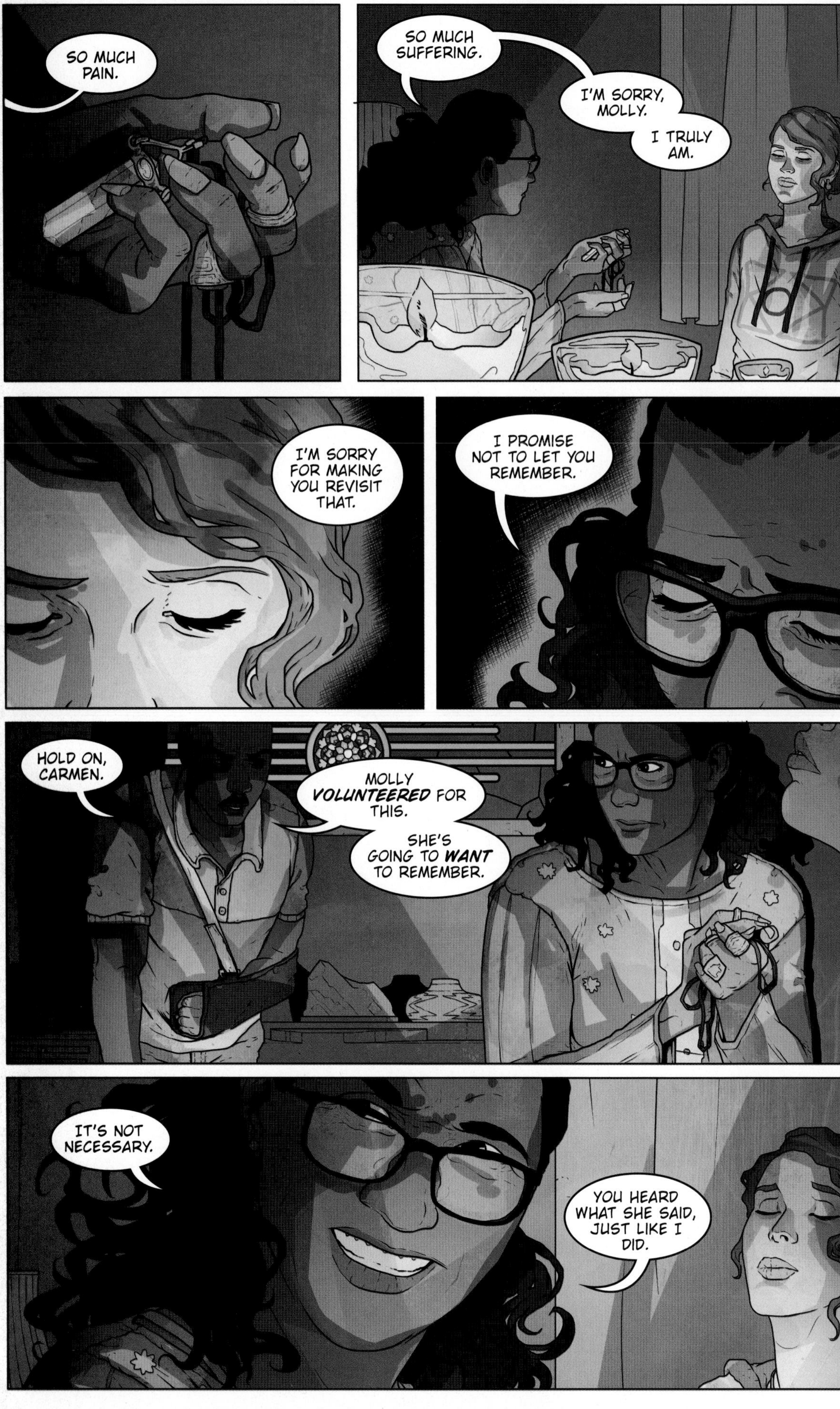
SO MUCH PAIN.
SO MUCH SUFFERING.
I'M SORRY, MOLLY.
I TRULY AM.
I'M SORRY FOR MAKING YOU REVISIT THAT.
I PROMISE NOT TO LET YOU REMEMBER.
HOLD ON, CARMEN.
MOLLY ***VOLUNTEERED*** FOR THIS.
SHE'S GOING TO ***WANT*** TO REMEMBER.
IT'S NOT NECESSARY.
YOU HEARD WHAT SHE SAID, JUST LIKE I DID.

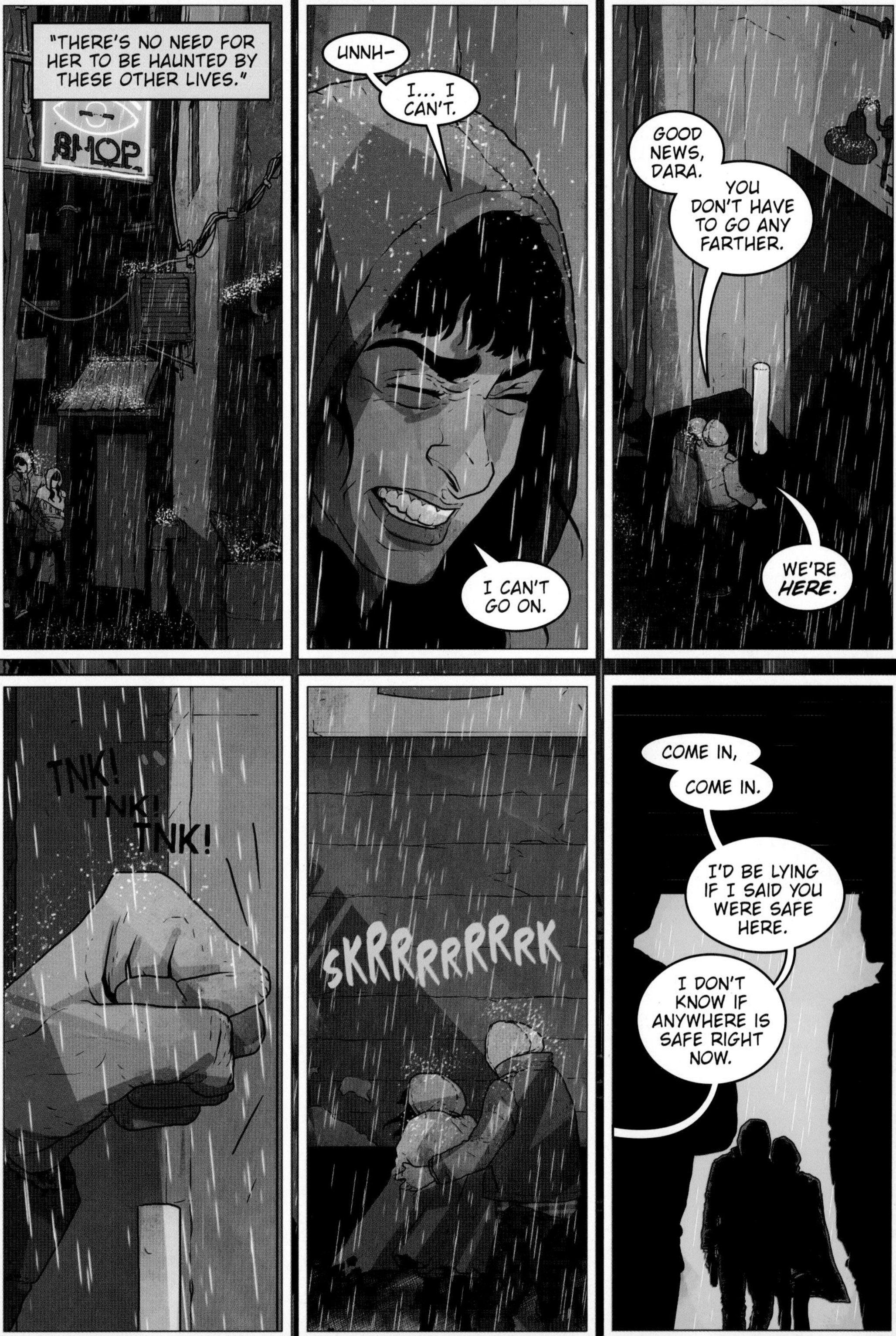
"THERE'S NO NEED FOR HER TO BE HAUNTED BY THESE OTHER LIVES."
SHOP
UNNH-
I... I CAN'T.
I CAN'T GO ON.
GOOD NEWS, DARA.
YOU DON'T HAVE TO GO ANY FARTHER.
WE'RE *HERE*.
TNK! TNK! TNK!
SKRRRRRRRK
COME IN,
COME IN.
I'D BE LYING IF I SAID YOU WERE SAFE HERE.
I DON'T KNOW IF ANYWHERE IS SAFE RIGHT NOW.

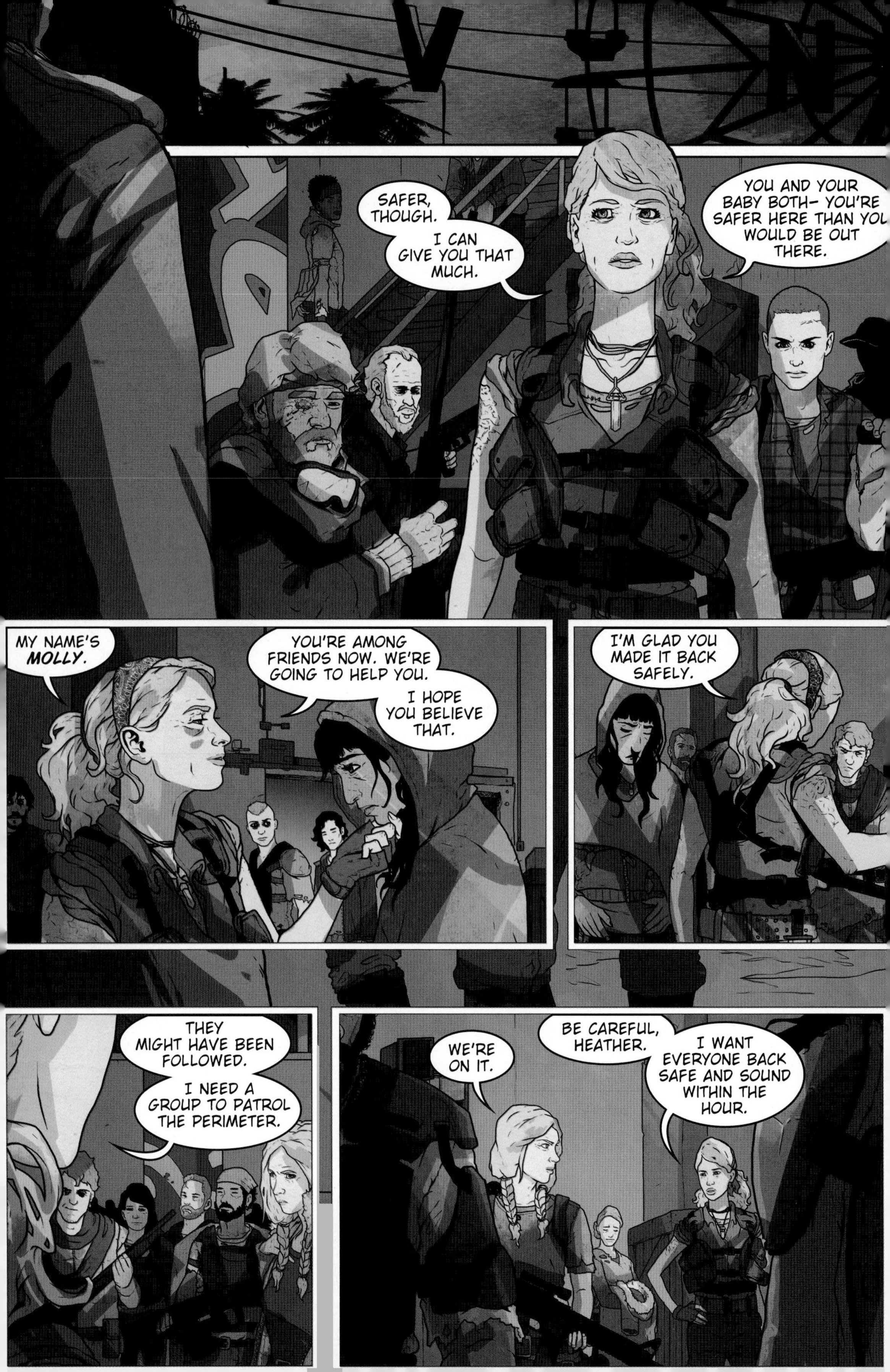
SAFER, THOUGH.
I CAN GIVE YOU THAT MUCH.
YOU AND YOUR BABY BOTH- YOU'RE SAFER HERE THAN YOU WOULD BE OUT THERE.
MY NAME'S **MOLLY**.
YOU'RE AMONG FRIENDS NOW. WE'RE GOING TO HELP YOU.
I HOPE YOU BELIEVE THAT.
I'M GLAD YOU MADE IT BACK SAFELY.
THEY MIGHT HAVE BEEN FOLLOWED.
I NEED A GROUP TO PATROL THE PERIMETER.
WE'RE ON IT.
BE CAREFUL, HEATHER.
I WANT EVERYONE BACK SAFE AND SOUND WITHIN THE HOUR.

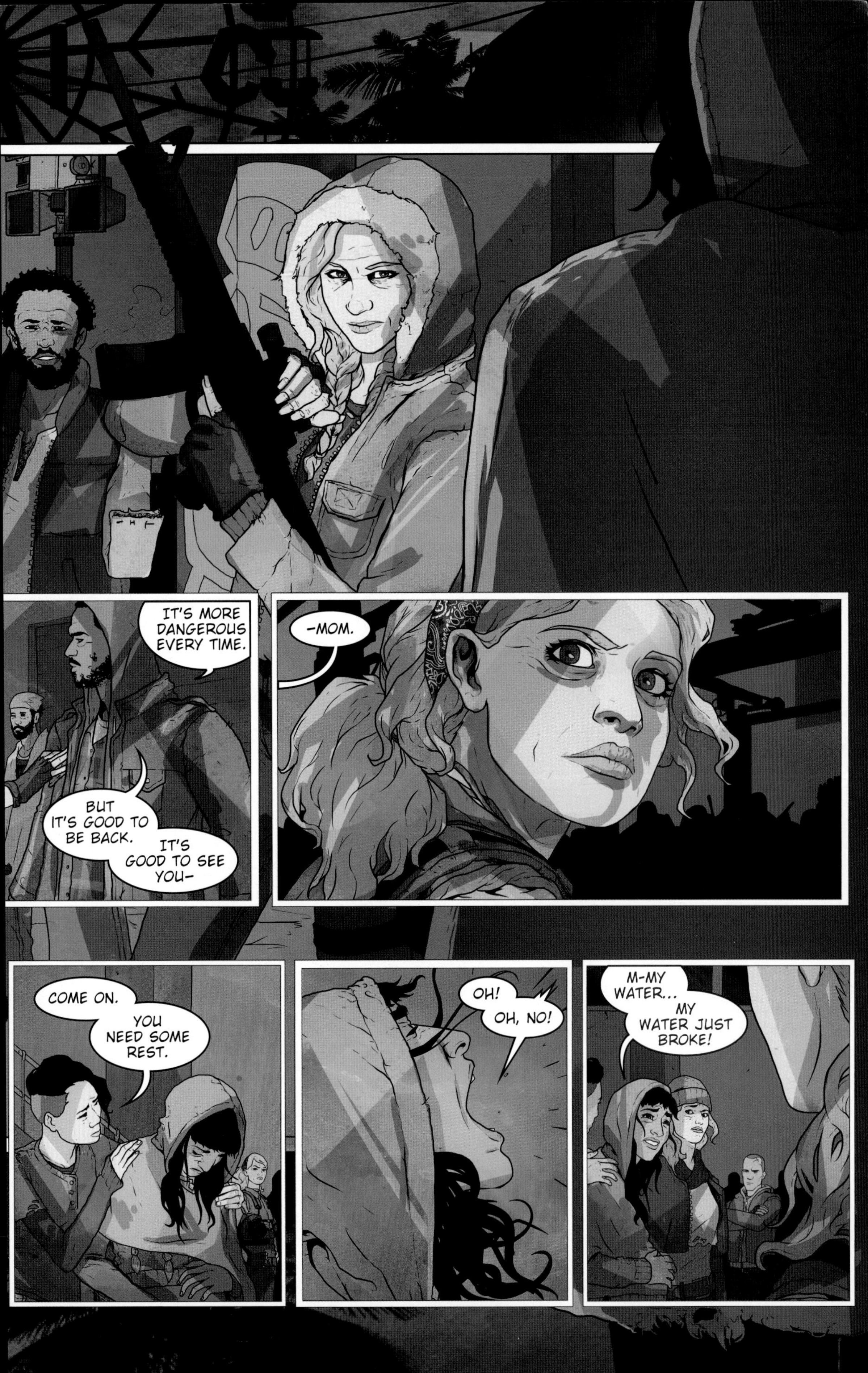
IT'S MORE DANGEROUS EVERY TIME.
BUT IT'S GOOD TO BE BACK.
IT'S GOOD TO SEE YOU—
—MOM.
COME ON.
YOU NEED SOME REST.
OH!
OH, NO!
M-MY WATER...
MY WATER JUST BROKE!

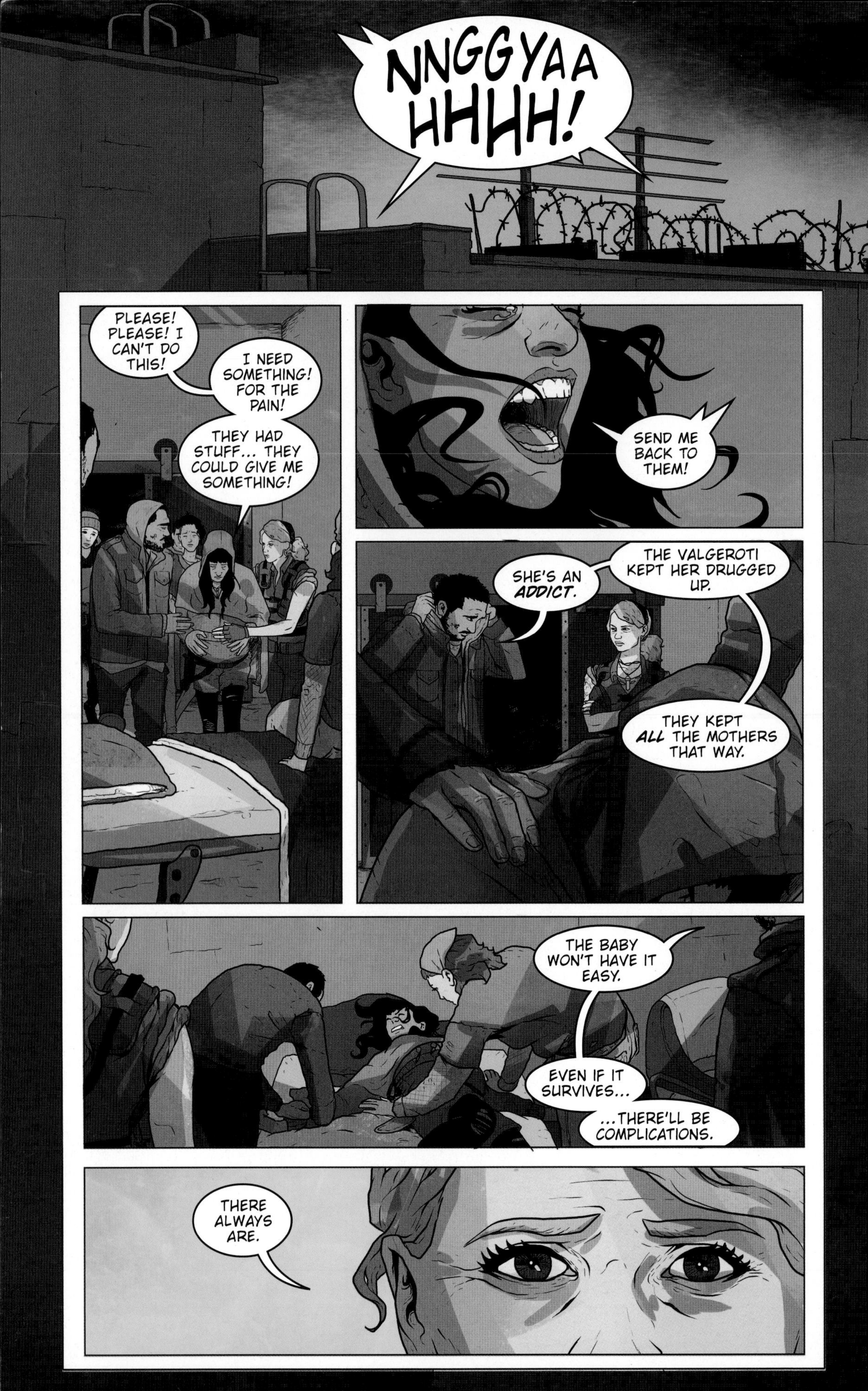
NNGGYAAHHHH!
PLEASE! PLEASE! I CAN'T DO THIS!
I NEED SOMETHING! FOR THE PAIN!
THEY HAD STUFF... THEY COULD GIVE ME SOMETHING!
SEND ME BACK TO THEM!
SHE'S AN ADDICT.
THE VALGEROTI KEPT HER DRUGGED UP.
THEY KEPT ALL THE MOTHERS THAT WAY.
THE BABY WON'T HAVE IT EASY.
EVEN IF IT SURVIVES...
...THERE'LL BE COMPLICATIONS.
THERE ALWAYS ARE.

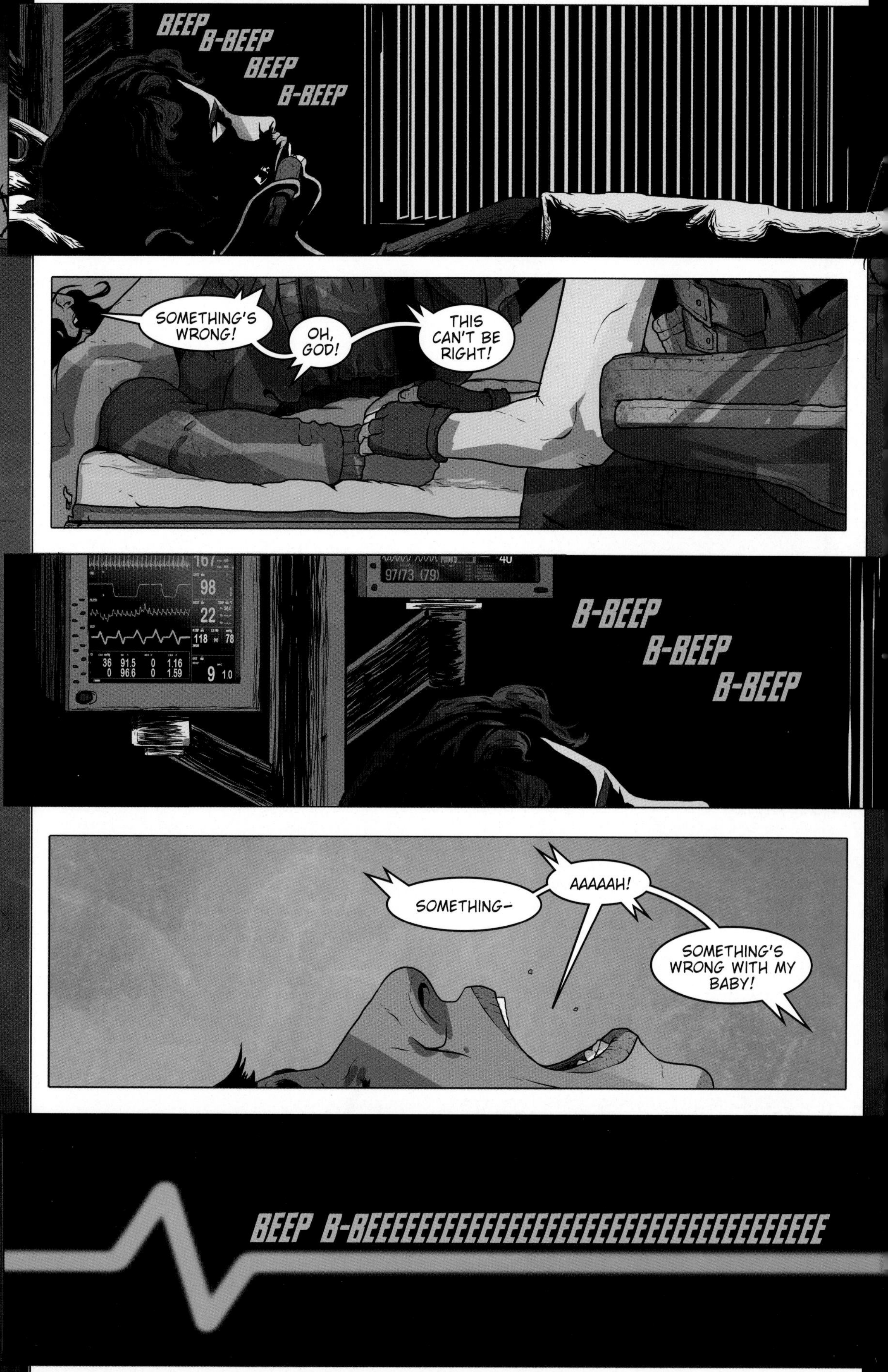
BEEP B-BEEP BEEP B-BEEP
SOMETHING'S WRONG!
OH, GOD!
THIS CAN'T BE RIGHT!
B-BEEP B-BEEP B-BEEP
SOMETHING–
AAAAAH!
SOMETHING'S WRONG WITH MY BABY!
BEEP B-BEEEEEEEEEEEEEEEEEEEEEEEEEEEEEEEEEEEE

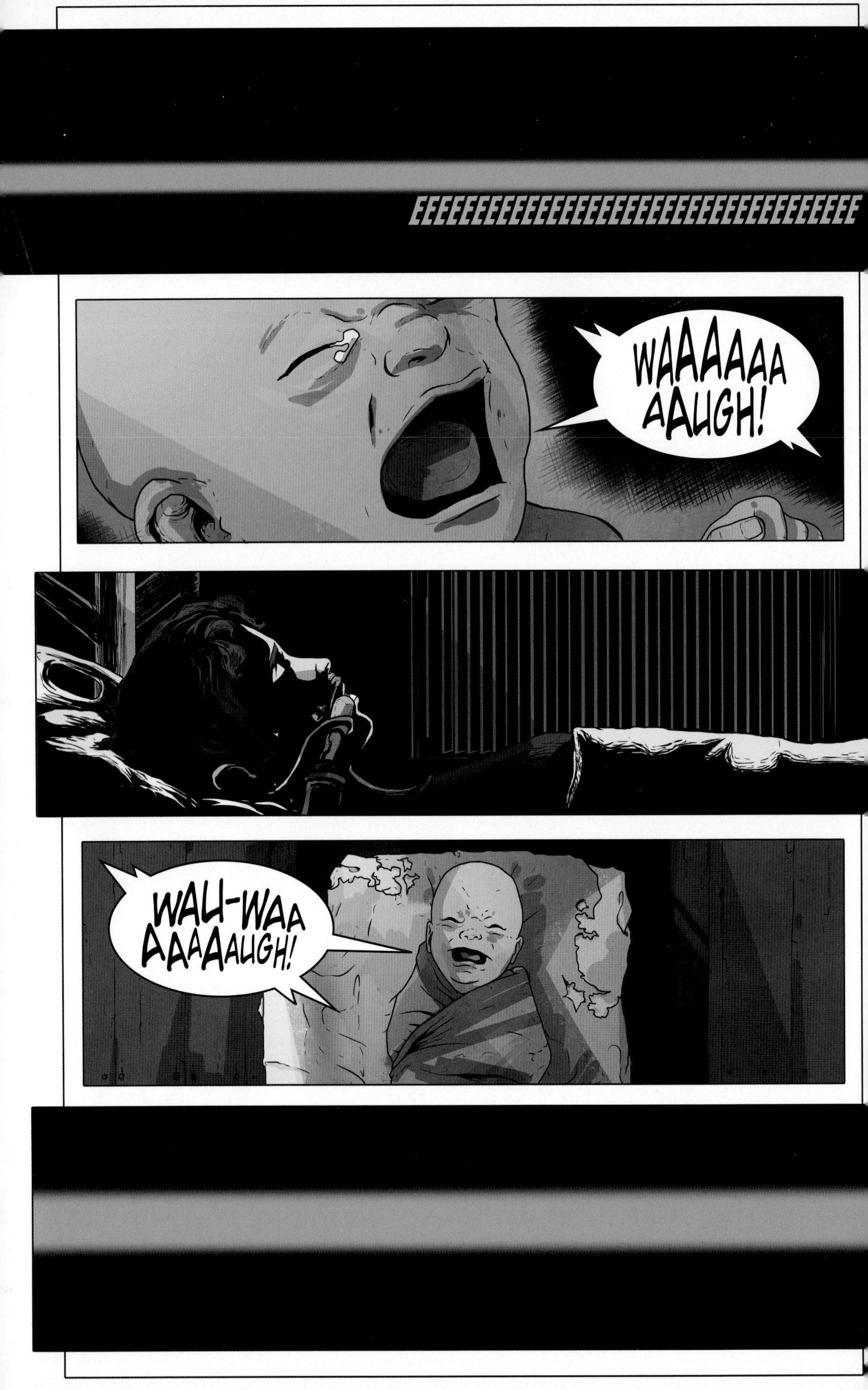
EEEEEEEEEEEEEEEEEEEEEEEEEEEEEEEEEEE
WAAAAAA AAUGH!
WAU-WAA AAAAAUGH!

WHAT THE HELL IS WRONG WITH US?

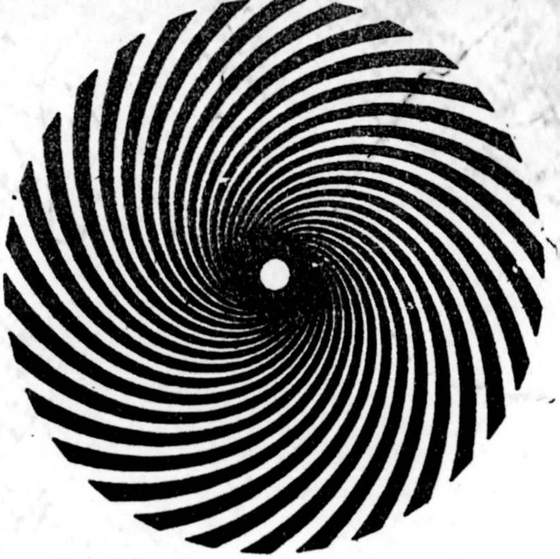

What's wrong with Marie? With Danny? With Joel for not offering a word of caution? What's wrong with me?

We could have left well enough alone. We could have let Molly, Graymercy, Coates, and Adrian ride off into the sunset. Well, in Adrian's case, he would have been thrown into the back of a van and dragged off into the night.

If we had left it alone, though, we might have speculated that Adrian escaped! That he turned the tables on the cult! That he lived happily ever after–under a fake name, sure, but alive at least. Hell, we might have just assumed he died and his nightmare ended. We might have comforted ourselves with any one of those possibilities--even death.

But we're just not that nice.

When we started telling a tale of past lives, we wanted to keep it small. We were dealing with Adrian and Sutter, two lives that were deeply and horrifically connected. But I always knew that we'd expand on the idea. I always knew the story would get more and more twisted. All because of one little idea I heard long ago while discussing reincarnation. It's an idea Leo shares in this collection.

Everyone you have ever met... everyone you ever will meet... you have encountered before.

With that concept in hand, we embarked on the next leg of our story, and we start to see how others are linked to Adrian... to Sutter... to Temperence... to Molly... to Graymercy... And we discover that they have been involved in this tale of horror for centuries. Some of them have used life after life to advance the agenda of the Valgeroti. Some have worked to stop the cult's machinations. And others (poor Molly!) have always been victims.

This second leg of the story gives us the chance to introduce a number of new characters that I absolutely love to write about. Sarah, Comstock, Faith, and Leo are all precious to me in one way or another. And they have important roles to play in the story going forward.

Leo, in particular, roots this story in the real world for me. He's fictional, but over the years I've known several people who inspired his portrayal in this book. Even his little shop out in the middle of nowhere is based on a real place.

When I was in high school, a friend of mine—Daryl—told me about an occult bookstore he had just stumbled onto. This bookstore was out in the middle of nowhere, a double-wide mobile home with no signage or other indication that a wealth of esoteric information awaited within. One after-noon, another friend and I visited the shop. The trailer sat by itself in a field. There were no other cars nearby. There were a few crystals hanging on the door outside, but that's it. We almost turned away, but we decided to check it out. And, even though it looked like someone's home, we just walked in the front door.

Sure enough, the trailer had been converted into a bookstore. Shelves and shelves of books awaited us. There were statues and star charts and "books of shadow" and crystals—Lord, the crystals! The place looked like a magic item shop out of a bad D&D campaign! A woman dressed all in black greeted us as we stepped inside. She might have been a witch, for all I know. And this was rural North Carolina!

Country witches are not to be trifled with! She was nice enough, though, talking to us about pretty mundane topics.

She did mention H.P. Lovecraft, though, and she said something to the effect of "Good ol' H.P. He knew the truth about what's going on."

At some point, though, with no preamble, the woman just looked up and asked, "Did Daryl send you?"

My friend and I freaked out! How did she know Daryl had sent us? Of course, here were plenty of possible answers. Daryl might have been at the shop earlier and told her we were coming. Or we might have been the only other high school students to visit her store, so it wasn't too big of a leap to assume we knew him. But those reasons weren't much fun so we shuffled them back into the shadowy recesses of our mind and instead considered the possibility that the spirits or demons or "Good Ol' H.P." himself guided her revelation.

We only ever went to the store once. For all I know, it vanished not long after that visit. We didn't buy a lot that I remember, so I don't think we were helping to keep the shopkeeper afloat.

But from that shopping trip sprang Leo's shop.

And, just as I preferred the supernatural reasons of the North Carolina witch's knowledge to the mundane possibilities, I prefer the nightmarish possibilities of Adrian's story over anything that comes within miles of leaving well enough alone.

I've always been that way.

That's what is wrong with me.

And I think that's what is wrong with Marie and Danny and Joel, too.

And maybe with you.

- CULLEN BUNN
2018

ALBAN AND FAITH

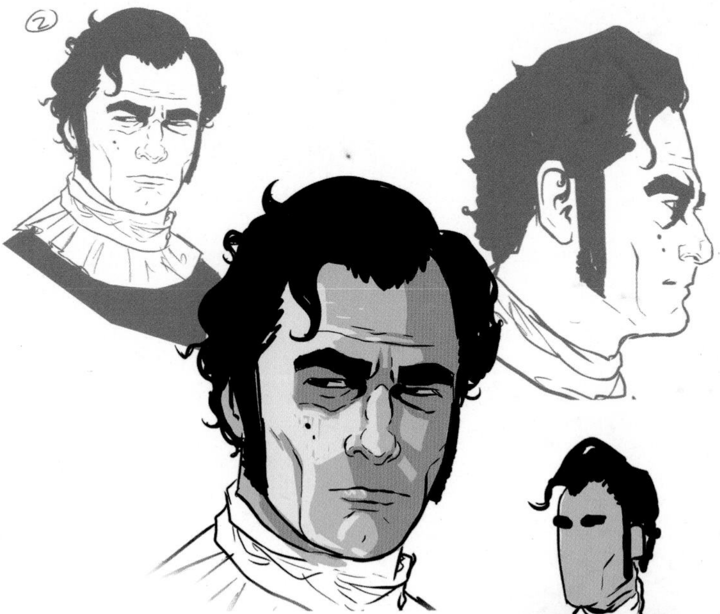

The grizzled mentor. The spunky upstart. The archetypes of Alban and Faith. I personally view them as the dynamic duo of Elizabethan England. With that thought rolling around in my head, it's no surprise that those traits really came through in the final design of these characters.

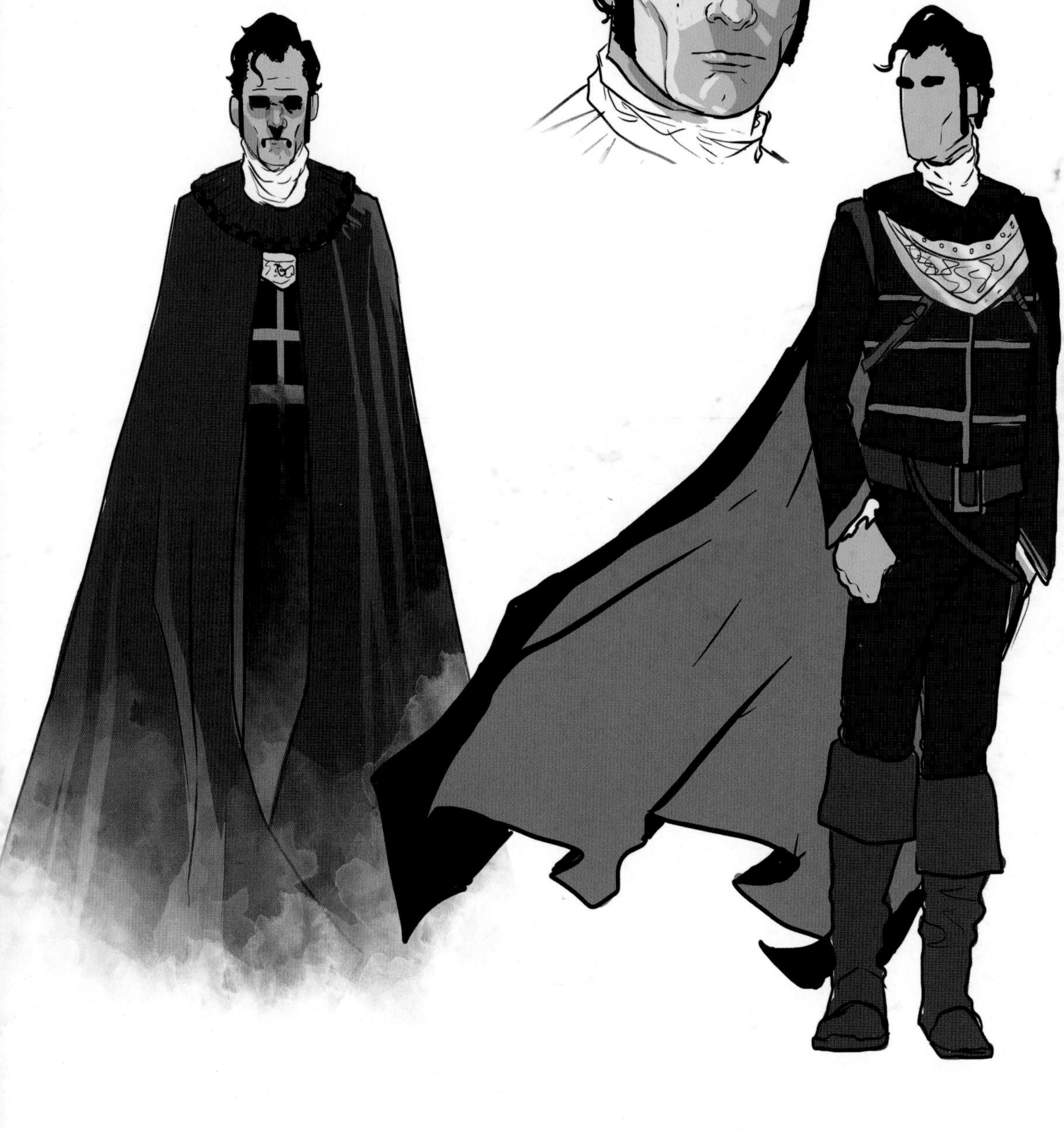

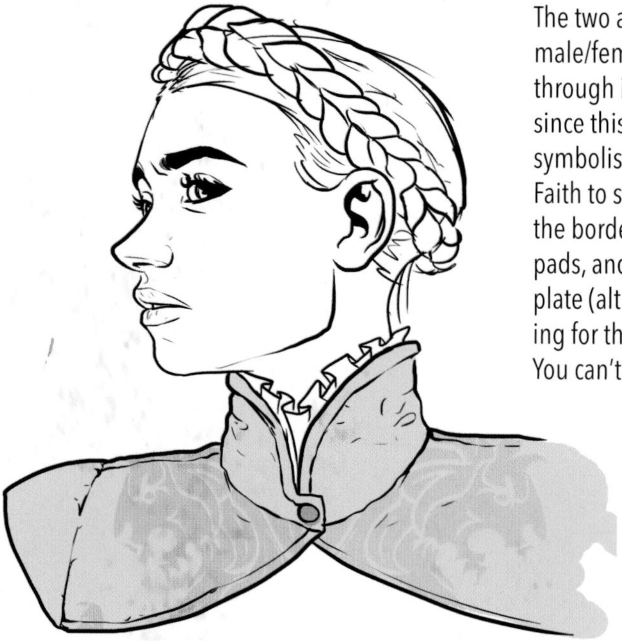

The two are by nature, opposites in a way: young/old, male/female, dark/light. And so I tried to bring that through in their appearances and color schemes. Also, since this book deals largely with symbols, sigils and symbolism, I wanted to craft a symbol for Alban and Faith to share. I came up with a Lion. You'll see it within the border of the pages, in Faith's pants and shoulder pads, and written into the design of Alban's steel chest plate (although there it is largely obscured). The reasoning for the lion as their sigil is still my secret, though. You can't give everything away!

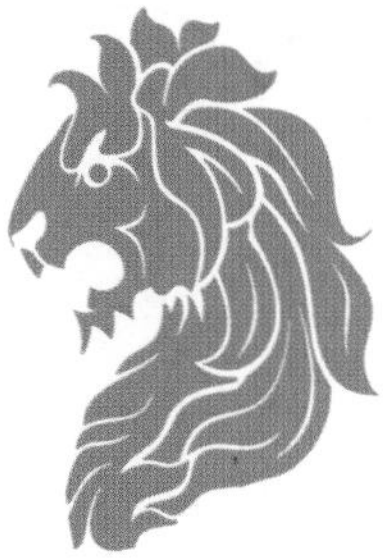

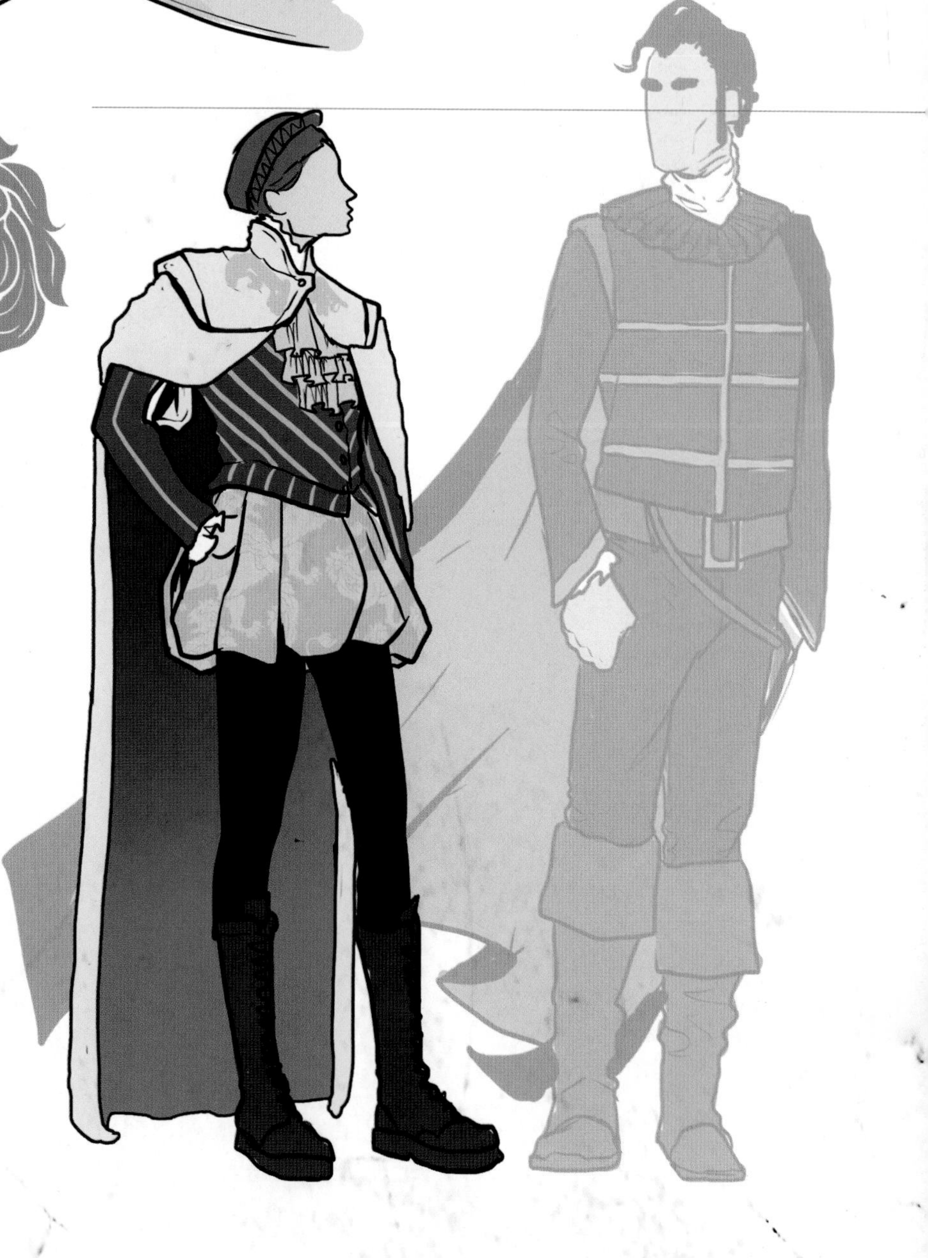

HAL AND DARA

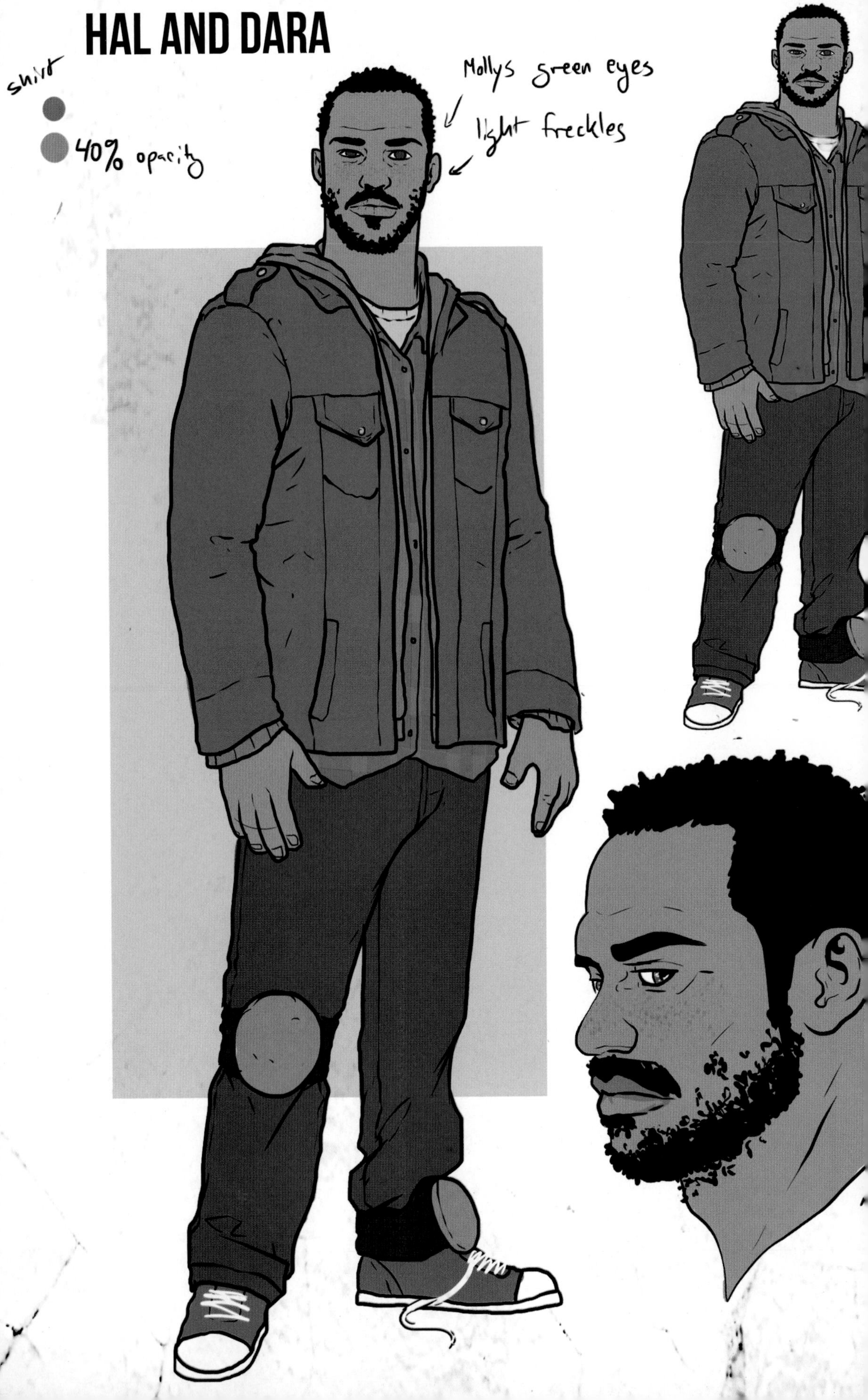
shirt
40% opacity
Mollys green eyes
light freckles

Just two lost souls dressed in whatever clothes they can find. A lot of inspiration for them, DARA in particular, came from the novel and movie *The Road*, by Cormac McCarthy.

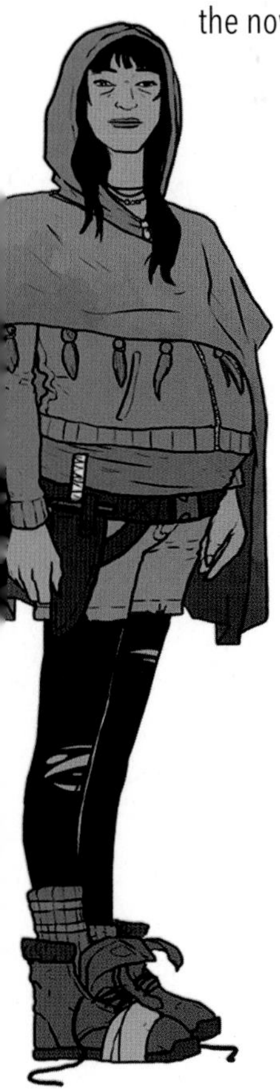

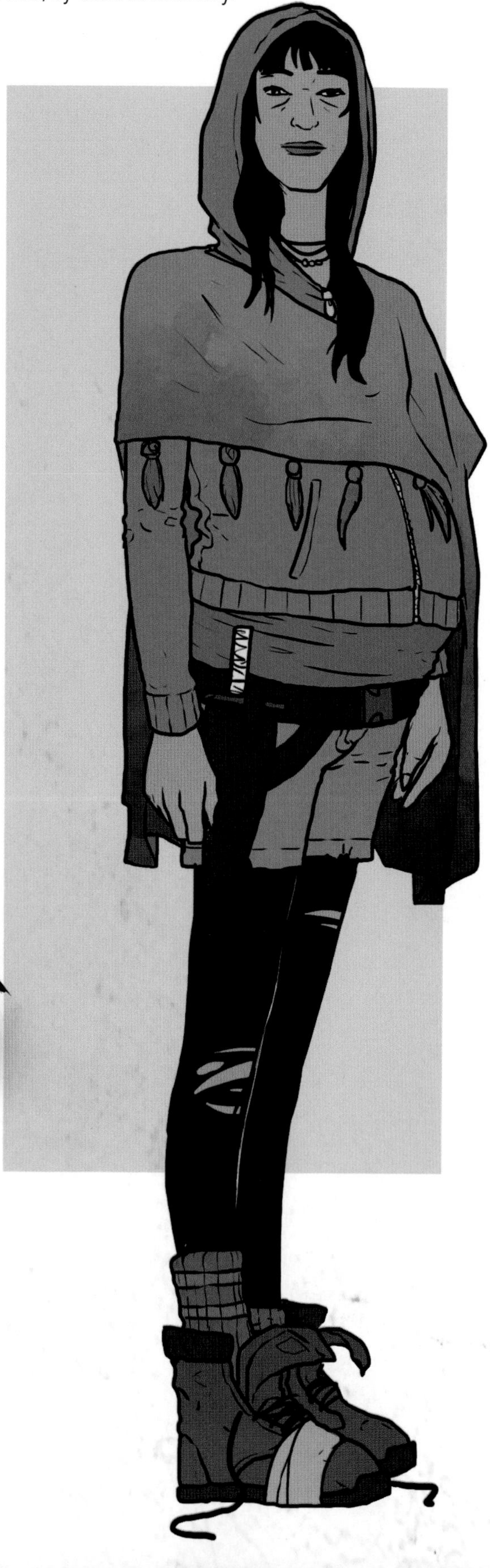

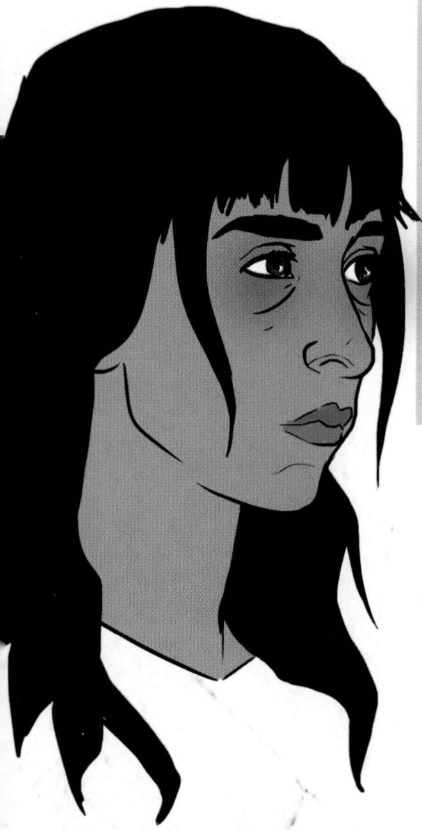

LEO

Leo is a character I just loved to design. If he was real, I would love to hang out with him. Just a real aging rocker, deadhead, hippie. Someone whose style and nature you think you have pinned down until he throws out a reference (or gold scarf) that's totally out of left field.

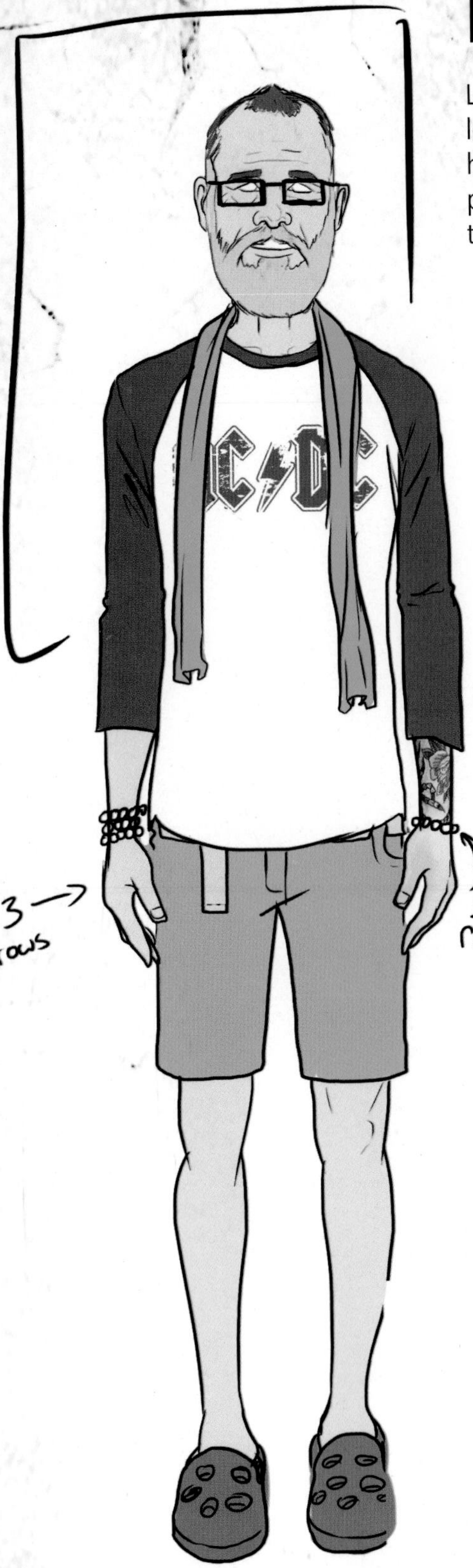

AC/DC
3 rows
1 row

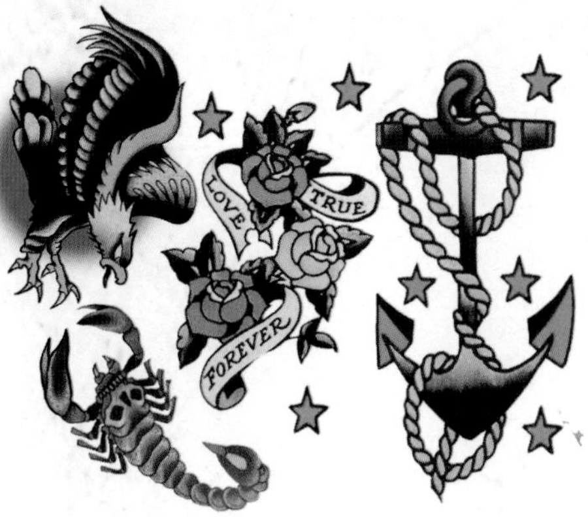

LOVE
TRUE
FOREVER

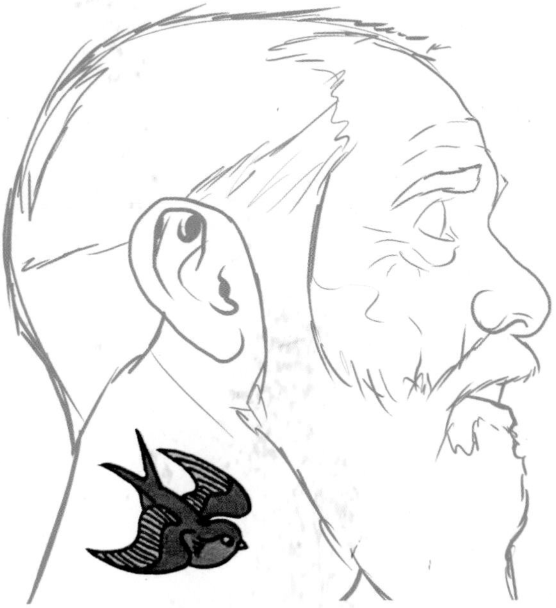

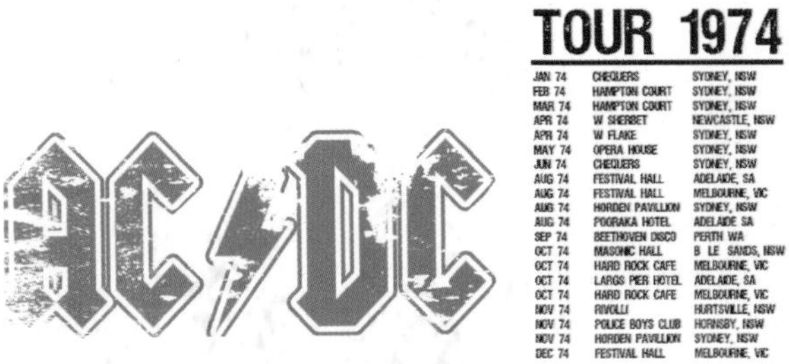

TOUR 1974
JAN 74 CHEQUERS SYDNEY, NSW
FEB 74 HAMPTON COURT SYDNEY, NSW
MAR 74 HAMPTON COURT SYDNEY, NSW
APR 74 W SHERBET NEWCASTLE, NSW
APR 74 W FLAKE SYDNEY, NSW
MAY 74 OPERA HOUSE SYDNEY, NSW
JUN 74 CHEQUERS SYDNEY, NSW
AUG 74 FESTIVAL HALL ADELAIDE, SA
AUG 74 FESTIVAL HALL MELBOURNE, VIC
AUG 74 HORDEN PAVILLION SYDNEY, NSW
AUG 74 POORAKA HOTEL ADELAIDE SA
SEP 74 BEETHOVEN DISCO PERTH WA
OCT 74 MASONIC HALL B LE SANDS, NSW
OCT 74 HARD ROCK CAFE MELBOURNE, VIC
OCT 74 LARGS PIER HOTEL ADELAIDE, SA
OCT 74 HARD ROCK CAFE MELBOURNE, VIC
NOV 74 RIVOLLI HURTSVILLE, NSW
NOV 74 POLICE BOYS CLUB HORNSBY, NSW
NOV 74 HORDEN PAVILLION SYDNEY, NSW
DEC 74 FESTIVAL HALL MELBOURNE, VIC
AC/DC